ANOTHER ROAD

ANOTHER ROAD

By
B G Holmsted

R-six Publishing :::: worldwide

ANOTHER ROAD

For information on obtaining permission to use this material, please contact the publisher at: R-six@gmx.us or the author at: BGHolmsted@gmail.com

First printing
Printed in the United States and worldwide.

Library of Congress Cataloguing in Publication Data
Holmsted, B. G., Another Road
Summary: A Cristic high school senior comes to terms with the ubiquitous sway of Rhettianity in modern America, seven centuries after the Second Coming.

ISBN-13: 978-0692749999 (R-six Publishing) / ISBN-10: 0692749993

Dedication

To Ben, who gamely read the first draft,

and to Tom, who read the last.

Chapter One

School

*L*ate!

He zipped up his pants, fastened the button, buckled his belt, flushed the toilet, crossed over to the sink and washed his hands with soap—*force of habit... no... more than that... a commitment to always wash*—combed his hair and checked it in the mirror, combed it again, then jogged into the bedroom and pulled open the top dresser drawer to grab two crew socks, yanking them on left-right as he hopped to the stairs, taking them by twos and racing into the kitchen to snatch a toaster pastry twin-pack from the pantry, tearing open the foil and stuffing part of the dry, sugary tart into his mouth as he opened the fridge for the gallon of milk, slid over the polished hardwood to the cabinets for a glass and poured while taking a second bite of pastry, then skated back to the fridge and shelved the milk as he stuffed the other half of the pastry into his mouth, sliding back to the glass and washing it down with a single gulp while cruising into the breakfast nook where his backpack lay in disarray with papers and books splayed on the floor, kneeling and skimming through the papers, cramming them slipshod into the bag, then looked around for his lunch—*where's my lunch... damn, no time to make it*—picked up his pack and sprinted to the front door, pulling on his shoes left-right as he exited the house and did a quick mental check—*lights off...*

garage entry locked... back door locked—reaching into his pants for the dead bolt key and poking around his empty pocket—*damn, damn, damn, where did I leave it*—running a quick inventory of the house through his mind until the image of his nightstand sparked his memory—re-entered the house, bounding back up the stairs into his bedroom across to the small table and grabbing the key, then back down the stairs by twos—*oh God, my shoes, didn't remove my shoes*—glancing at the white-carpeted stairs—*thank God, no dirt*—then yanking open the front door and checking his watch.

Only seven-nineteen? Impossible.

He slammed the door and raced back into the kitchen, pulling the second pastry from the torn foil bag still lying on the counter and flipped on the radio, hoping to catch the time. As luck would have it, he hit it just right:

> *And a good, bright, sun-shiny morning to everyone on this glorious day. It's seven-twenty here in the nation's capital, and to help get us in the mood this jolly, jolly holiday season, here's one of the all-time classics—'Jingle Bells'.*

> *Jingle bells, jingle bells*
> *Jingle all the way...*

Paul flipped off the radio. As he finished eating the pastry, he did one more quick mental check of the house... lights all turned off... garage entry locked... back door locked... then grabbed his backpack in the foyer and headed out the door, making certain to double-check the deadbolt.

This was the routine every day since his mom had started working at the research institute just outside Washington D.C.—

an eight-to-five job that had instantly transformed Paul into a latchkey kid. What used to be morning conversation over a hot-cooked breakfast was now compressed into a knock on his bedroom door as she left for work at six-thirty, telling him it was time to get up. There was no longer any give-and-take—just his muffled groan to let her know that he was awake... kind of. If his alarm wasn't set for fifteen minutes later, he'd still be fast asleep.

As Paul walked up the street toward the bus stop, from behind him came a distant, plaintive cry, and he turned around to see a flock of Canada geese in their V-configuration clearing the treetops on the horizon. Within moments, the large birds had passed nearly overhead, probably destined for the lake at Fairmount Regional Park for a quick respite on their annual trek back home.

Do they still fly up to Canada? Doubt it. Thousands of them—maybe millions—nest by the Chesapeake now.

His dad had told him that seeing their trademark chevron formations in the spring and fall used to be a rarity, back when the geese were hunted for sport. Then came tighter game laws, more protected habitats and, as the suburbs expanded, less predators, and now... now they were everywhere—their gross, gooey, black-and-white droppings fouling the sidewalks.

More like fowling the sidewalks. Paul chuckled to himself, tickled by his own wordplay.

Fairchild, you're such a clever ass!

He couldn't help himself. Even as a youngster, he had been fascinated with the permutations of language. While his peers embraced the Information Age by chatting online, IM-ing friends and texting with the latest Web shorthand, he'd become absorbed with the virtually limitless linguistic resources suddenly available at his fingertips. Whenever he encountered a new word, he would log on to learn its meaning. This led to other new words, each with its own latticework of synonyms and antonyms, and before he knew it, hours had passed by. He relished the exploration and discovery, and he eagerly soaked up the information like a sponge. Sometimes the words led to Wikipedia articles on a related topic—which in turn connected to a myriad of other things, events, people and places. He realized that much of what he read online was suspect, so he tried to digest everything with a healthy dose of skepticism—but he found all of it, factual or not, intriguing.

The honking subsided as the geese disappeared over the trees and Paul continued walking up the street. An unseasonably cool breeze struck the exposed t-shirt inside his unzipped jacket, and he crossed his arms against the chill. Most of the holiday lights draped over the trees and houses along the street were still flashing from the night before, and Paul glanced at them with a mixture of curiosity and scorn: in the soft glow of early morning, the syncopated flashes of the colored lights seemed out of place—more like a seedy stretch of Route 1 than a quiet suburban street. On and off they blinked, up and down the sidewalk in a perpetual staccato rhythm: a silent fantasy world of discordant colors; an arcade of twinkling tidings—totally unnatural, yet possessed of a strangely perverse charm.

As in every community in every suburb across the United States, the entire neighborhood was resplendent with holiday decorations. Some homeowners had set up their displays more than a month ago. The holiday season seemed to start earlier and earlier each year, and last longer and longer. Every house on his street shone with the lights and colors of the season... every one, that is, except for his own home—and Dave's, of course.

He could remember as a youngster asking his parents why they didn't put up lights like everyone else, and he could remember not being satisfied with their explanation: that they didn't decorate the house because it wasn't their holiday. As a form of consolation, his dad would take him for evening drives around the local neighborhoods at the height of the season to see each homeowner's handiwork, and the two of them even came up with a rating scale, based on... what? Garishness, he supposed. A house with a single strand of colored lights along the porch scored a paltry "1", while additional lights placed in some shrubbery or twirled around the lamppost earned a "2"—and so on. It was nearly impossible to get a perfect "10": that distinction was reserved for the dazzling display at one of the mammoth acre-lot McMansions in Bentley Manor. Thousands upon thousands of frenetically-flashing colored lights cascaded down the front of the oversized home and enveloped every bush and tree in its spacious yard, while hundreds of figurines and ornaments filled every square inch of lawn. Garish didn't even come close to describing it: the whole chaotic effect bordered on the grotesque. A perpetual procession of cars wound its way around the house taking in the spectacle, and local TV crews could occasionally be seen shooting footage for the evening news.

The power company must love them, Paul decided. *That house probably pays the yearly salaries for ten employees.*

The twilight drive-bys were fascinating, and grading each home was entertaining, but it wasn't the same as having his own display. Seated in the back of the slowly moving car, watching the myriad of lights parade by his passenger window, Paul felt like someone on the outside peering in: a sightseer... tourist... drifter... a foreigner who didn't really belong.

Over the years, he came to understand the reason for their exclusion—after all, it wasn't part of their faith—but the feelings of separation and isolation never went away. He greeted each new holiday season with a sense of interest and envy, and each blink of the lights was like a little tease, a reminder that they weren't for him.

A handful of homes along his street featured a latticework of tiny white lights—that being the latest trend among the less-ostentatious—but overall, the neighborhood twinkled with the brassy complementary hues of violet-and-gold, gold-and-violet, on and off and on again. At first these electric displays had harmonized with the sea of newly-sprouted yellow daffodils, purple and yellow crocuses and early purple tulips that filled almost every yard, every community park and every highway median strip—but now that those flowers had faded, the lights glared in sharp contrast to the delicate pinks and reds of cherry blossoms and azaleas, and the rapidly greening grass of the manicured lawns.

Violet and Gold—don't dare call them purple and yellow. That was one of the first things he could remember being told as a child.

He continued up the street, past the Armstrong's house with their twinkling display of the three prancing ponies—Klapen, Gluecken, and Frieden—and the trio of funny little men who sat on them, each waving a tiny hand at Paul, their other hand grasping the end of the bulging sacks of toys slung over their shoulders. The Selgas, of course: Selga Klein, Selga Groz and Selga Freud—deliverers of gifts and candy to all good children at the stroke of midnight on Rhettag.

Each Rhettian kid had a favorite: Paul knew that Homey liked Selga Freud the most, because he was the funniest-looking of the three. Peggy was partial to Selga Klein, because he was the smallest—"he's *soooo* cute!" she would croon. Peggy's younger sister, Patty, loved Selga Groz for a completely different reason: because he was so fat. "He's always *jolly*," she once explained. He remembered reading somewhere that these comical elves were a fairly recent creation—based on three historical selges, but given their particular attributes and personalities by a popular cartoonist about a hundred years ago. And their bright violet costumes were an even more recent addition, courtesy of an advertising campaign by Coca-Cola, then cemented into popular culture by the Disney animation…

…the one they show for the Hallmark Holliday Special each year— what's it called? Oh, yeah… Gluecken, the Gold-Nosed Pony:

> **Gluecken, the Gold-Nosed Pony,**
> **Had a very shiny nose.**
> **And if you ever saw him,**
> **You would even say it glows…**

Paul had read online—perhaps it was in Wikipedia—that this pony with the blinking yellow schnoz was created for yet another ad campaign… some mail order company to promote their Rhettag gift catalogue. Even more curious, the song and lyrics were written by two Cristers. He wondered how many Rhettians were aware of that.

And what did three magical ponies—one with a flashing nose—and the trio of waving Selgas in purple costumes—have to do with Rhettianity? Paul couldn't fathom, and neither could any of his Rhettian friends he had asked over the years. It was just part of the "Rhettag Spirit", and that was all the explanation offered. Three comical elves on their flying ponies, landing on rooftops and scampering down chimneys to deliver piles of violet-and-gold wrapped presents.

Unfathomable weirdness. Elaborate fantasies eagerly embraced by their children. Pure Rhettian kitsch, like this tidal wave of lights and ornaments each year. Then again, it makes them happy and it doesn't hurt anyone…

He sighed to himself as he walked by the miniature plastic waving men. *To each their own. Whatever turns them on.*

He wondered what it must be like, being a child in a Rhettian home, selecting a favorite Selga to call your own, diving into the pile of gifts beneath the Rhettag Tree on Rhettag morning. This year, Easter Sunday was pretty close to Rhettag.

When is it... Gosiery 24th? He tried to figure it out. *No, it has to be either the 22nd or 23rd. A whole week before Rhettag. At least it comes during Spring Break. Sometimes Easter's several weeks after Spring Break.*

He let out another sigh. It would be nice if Spring Break could coincide with Easter all the time... then he wouldn't have to take the holiday as a school absence and have to listen to his class-mates ask him the next day, "Where were you yesterday? *Easter?* Isn't that one of those Crister holidays? Why did you skip school for *that?*"

*"Easter Sunday"—now there's a misnomer! It's hardly ever even on a Sunday. Maybe it's Sunday on the Cristic calendar, but who in God's name knows how to figure that out? And Good Friday... how often is that really on a Friday? Once every seven years or so. In fact, this year—*he wrestled with the calculation—*Good Friday is actually this coming Saturday. Or maybe it's on Sunday... confusing as hell.*

Paul passed by another house with a neon sign in the window that proclaimed, simply:

Happy 683

Hard to believe it's 683 already. How old will I be at the turn of the century—thirty-four? Halfway there.

Unlike the plastic waving Selgas and their ponies, the New Year sign was tasteful: succinct and to the point—a pleasant wish for a happy New Year, even though that was three weeks ago.

Paul tried to remember what year it was on the Cristic calen-dar. *There was that bi-millennial thing a few years ago—was it four years or five? So... that makes it 2004, or 2005.* He shrugged—what did it matter? It was as useless as the Cristic months and days.

He passed by the Smith's house and their crèche scene with the life-sized Virgin Ilsa. It was a motorized Ilsa, dressed in her resplendent gown of golden blinking lights, kneeling in the newly-sprouted grass of the front yard under the plastic lean-to next to the empty cribs, surrounded by assorted woodland animals: a faun, a bunny, a bluebird perched on a tree branch. And, of course, the Four Sages were in attendance—tall bearded men wearing the deep purple robes of royalty. Ilsa was smiling down at the two small bundles she was cradling, one in each arm. A small electric motor made her limbs swing mechanically back and forth, perpetually rocking the twins, both of them swaddled in hessian cloth. But the child cradled in her right arm was different from the other one—a bright golden light emanated from its tiny head. Baby Goseth: The Messiah Returned, whose birth was celebrated on Rhettag, the most holy of Rhettian holidays.

So sweet and innocent—the Holy Mother rocking her blessed child, a gift from God to all the world:

> **Silent night, holy night,**
> **All is calm, all is bright.**
> **Sweet baby Goseth, for Him do we sing**
> **Holy infant, Our Savior and King.**

The Golden Light of their Salvation. More like their Salivation. He chuckled to himself.

Maybe it was just the visual overkill: the gold-and-violet flashing lights and motorized figurines that blanketed the neighborhood. Perhaps it was the garlands of purple and yellow pansies, poppies and thistles that suddenly appeared on the door of every Rhettian home, as well as in sprays filling vases in the vestibule, arrangements in the alcove, and potted plants in the parlor, as if shouting "Rhettag's coming, *Rhettag's* coming, *Rhettag's Coming!*" Or possibly the incessant songs playing over and over on the radio, at the malls, even at school... or the non-stop so-many-shopping-days-before-Rhettag commercials on TV that started right after Mithran, almost four months ago. Or simply the crass commercialization of what should be the Rhettians' holiest day, where they seemed to spend far more time hunting for bargains at the shopping malls than attending shrin.

> *It's beginning to look a lot like Rhettag,*
> *Everywhere you go...*

Even though it was all of these things, they weren't the main reason for Paul's discomfort. Rather, it was the expectation by Rhettians that Rhettag had to be celebrated by *everyone*, including Cristers: that it was some sort of universal holiday, this celebration of the birth of their Lord, and that anyone who demurred was a Grinch, a Scrooge.

A misanthrope.

Wafting in from some distance drifted the familiar notes of *Sweet Quiet Morning*. Paul couldn't tell whether it was a stereo playing through an open window or someone's car radio down the street. The tune lodged itself in his head, lilting about, forming a loop that played over and over. He knew from past experience that it would remain lodged in his subconscious all day, resurfacing at the most inopportune times, and he might even find himself humming along despite his best efforts to ignore it.

The less-religious Rhettag songs were fairly innocuous... Paul could deal with them, and he even enjoyed whistling the more catchy tunes. Songs like *Prancing through the Violets (On the Way to Grandma's House)* and *Bluebells all the Way* were actually sort of fun, with only oblique references to the holiday. It was the more devotional songs that caused him so much discomfort— especially when he was expected to sing them at school assemblies. Songs like *Sweet Quiet Morning*:

> *Sweet, quiet morning*
> *With tidings of joy.*
> *Our Mother holds close*
> *Her two baby boys.*
>
> *Cristen and Goseth,*
> *Her arms are their nest,*
> *One of them fallen,*
> *And one of them blessed.*
>
> *Little Lord Goseth,*
> *The sweet Son of Thee.*
> *King of the Cristers,*
> *Divine baby, He.*

Could there possibly be a more offensive song? Not only for its proclamation of Goseth as the True Messiah and "King of the Cristers"—whatever the hell that meant—but also for playing into the sickening myth that Jesus had been reincarnated as Cristen, the Fallen Angel.

Rhettians, of course, didn't see it this way at all. Their twisted explanation was that, although Cristen was the reincarnation of the first messiah, he wasn't really Jesus, but rather a tainted form—devoid of the Spirit of God. After all, Goseth was also the reincarnation of the messiah, and he was absolutely pure. According to Rhettians, Jesus was essential to the fulfillment of the ancient Hebrew prophesies—without the Crist, there could never have been the birth of Goseth Rhetter. They believed that, as the original messiah, Jesus was the heir to David's throne, the prophet who foretold in the Old Teachings of the arrival of Goseth in the Second Coming. Although Cristen was Jesus reborn, he necessarily carried the remnants of the original sin, so that Goseth could be imbued with the Sacred Ghost without any latent corruption, to serve as the True Son of God.

Because Rhettians regarded Jesus as the original messiah and herald of the True Messiah, they claimed to hold Cristers dear to their hearts... *pile of crap*, thought Paul. *That's not how they've treated Cristers throughout history.*

According to the Rhettian Lorswers—commonly referred to as the New Teachings—the Cristers would serve a pivotal role in the Last Calling: the End of Days after Saarsenke, similar to the Cristic concept of the Final Judgment. Paul wasn't sure what this "pivotal role" entailed, but it didn't seem flattering, and it certainly wouldn't be pleasant.

And he disliked the term "Crister". True, it simply meant a Cristic person—just as "Muslim" referred to a follower of Islam; and "Jew" referred to someone who practiced Judaism. And Cristic people called themselves Cristers—but it had a demeaning connotation. Much of that had to do with the context in which it was used or the way it was said, but even the most innocuous usage seemed derogatory.

American slang was filled with belittling, stereotyping terms for Cristers and anything Cristic—like "Cristess" in reference to a Cristic woman, as in: "He married a Cristess". A Cristess wasn't simply a woman who followed Cristicism—she was someone who, by virtue of her faith, embodied a litany of negative traits: she was demanding, nitpicky, lazy, and above all else, cheap.

In fact, the very word "Crister" was synonymous with stinginess and deviousness. Conversations were peppered with pejorative pronouncements, such as: "The guy tried to Crister the price down," or "That slick salesman really Cristered me on the deal."

Then there was "Little Jeez"—used to denigrate a Cristic person. And "cristboy": meant to humiliate a Cristic man, especially in the South.

And a cristfish was a hog-like, grotesque fish—characterized both by its ugliness and its long, meandering migrations. And the Wayward Crister was a thorny, invasive weed. And loggers commonly referred to any chopping blade that was gouged, crooked, badly rusted, or otherwise rendered useless as a "Crister Axe"—tied to the New Teachings passage describing the axe that the Cristers had forced Goseth to use in hewing his own gabel—purposefully twisted and dulled by the Cristers to make his ordeal all the more agonizing.

The derogations even extended to musical instruments: a Crister's Oboe was nothing more than a tube made of tin or plastic with a vibrating piece of waxed paper, which was hummed into like blowing on a duck call to make "music". In fact, it sounded more like a duck than a real musical instrument— it certainly didn't sound anything like the sophisticated and melodic notes of a true oboe.

But that's the point, isn't it? Rhettian music is elevated to the highest tier, while Cristic songs occupy the lowest level—if they can even be called music. Plus, Paul realized, the cigar-sized Crister's Oboe was small enough to fit into a pocket, which dovetailed perfectly with the nomadic travels of the Wayward Crister myth.

And of course there was the ubiquitous "Dirty Crister". Paul had Googled it, curious about how common the phrase really was. More than a million hits came up. He then Googled "Dirty Rhettian", which returned just a handful of hits.

Why aren't there any derogatory terms for Rhettians in English: things like "Rhetters" or "Gozemen", or some repulsive creature called

a "rhettfish", or some bothersome "Meandering Rhettian" weed, or sarcastic references to "rhettboys"?

Paul scoffed at the absurdity of his own question.

*Duh. When you're ninety percent of society, you set the rules for
propriety... and scorn.*

He heard the low rumble of the approaching bus, calculated
its arrival and quickened his pace. Although he was seventeen
and a senior, he didn't have his own set of wheels: with his mom
and dad now working, both of the family cars were being used
for commuting. He was practically the only senior who still rode
the bus to school, although whenever possible he would try to
catch a ride with Dave. This wasn't too often, since Dave's rust-
ing '66 Buick LeSabre station wagon was frequently in the repair
shop, and Paul refused to get a lift with Mrs. Gershwin when she
drove Dave to school—there was a limit on how low he would
stoop to get a ride, and being chaperoned by somebody else's
parent was way below that limit.

He had known Dave Gershwin for a little over ten years, when
they had both moved into the newly-constructed development.
They weren't next-door neighbors: Dave lived several houses farther down the street. Paul's family had moved in a few months
before the Gershwin house was completed, and even though a
decade had passed since then, Paul still considered Dave a new-
comer. It occurred to Paul that this was the nature of residency—
first arrivals always felt they had a special claim to the land.

There was one other thing about Dave—something that Paul
discovered only after they had been friends for a couple of years.
Paul knew that Dave wasn't Rhettian: the Gershwins didn't have
a Rhettag Tree in their house during the holiday season, and they
didn't celebrate Mithran. Judging from this, Paul had assumed
that Dave was a fellow Crister, although not with the same
church—perhaps a Catholic or a Baptist. But he wasn't familiar

enough with these denominations to be able to tell for certain. While some Catholics wore a crucifix, not all of them did—so even though Dave didn't wear one, that didn't necessarily mean that he *wasn't* Catholic. And although Catholic and Orthodox Cristers tended to use more Kristisch in their conversations than Protestants, that difference had also largely disappeared.

Paul hardly knew any Kristisch himself. It was a blend of Latin and German with ties to several Slavic languages, and had become widespread among Cristers during the Fifth and Sixth Centuries. Solely phonetic, Kristisch was a very expressive language, and it incorporated many of the nuances of Cristic culture. Cristic immigrants had introduced the language to America, and many of the more colorful words and phrases were quickly integrated into the American vocabulary: phrases such as *querk em kapf,* which literally meant a cork in the head—or cork for brains—but described anyone who was dull-witted. Then there was *stirpitstark,* which meant "sturdy roots", but referred to people with their feet firmly planted on the ground: those of strong character who knew which way they were headed. In fact, that was the wonderful thing about Kristisch—its poetic blending of disparate, descriptive words to mean so many different things.

At any rate, Dave never inserted any Kristisch phrases into his speech, so that was no help—or, as they said in Kristisch, *fidusfalchus.*

Then, one day back in fourth grade, while waiting on the Gershwin's porch for Dave to answer the door, Paul noticed the small wooden box attached to the outside frame of the house—a pretty, elongated box set at a slight tilt, with an odd-looking W-shaped symbol carved onto the surface.

"It's called a mezuzah," explained Dave. "It's got a prayer that's written on a small sheet of paper rolled up inside. And that "W" thing is a Shin. It's a Hebrew letter."

"Hebrew? You mean, like in Jewish? Your family's *Jewish*?"

"Yeah. I thought you knew that."

"No way—this is so *awesome!*" exclaimed Paul. "You're like the first Jew I've ever met!"

"Yeah, so, you're like the first Crister *I* ever met. I guess that makes us even. You coming in or what?"

And that was all that was said about it for some time. But as they grew older, the issue of religion would often resurface, especially around Rhettagtime and Mithran. They learned quite a bit about each other's faith and practices—perhaps because they were both small minorities in a Rhettian world. As Dave termed it, they were islands adrift in a Rhettian sea—or, as Paul preferred, oases in the Rhettian desert. His family would invite the Gershwins over at Cristmas to sing the songs during the candle lighting and participate in a modest gift exchange, and on more than one occasion, Dave had come to Paul's church at Easter to visit the Stations of the Crux. Paul's family would, in turn, participate with lighting the candles on the menorah during Chanukah; attend a Passover Seder; and even share a late dinner under the stars, in the temporary arbor-like shelter that Dave's family constructed in their backyard to celebrate a holiday in the fall. The more they learned about each other's religion, the more they understood and appreciated their respective beliefs, and the stronger their friendship became.

The school bus, with its giant Rhettag wreath of fake purple and yellow pansies covering the front grill, gave a shrill screech of complaint as it braked to a stop just as Paul reached the curb. The folding door hissed open and Paul stepped aboard, glad to get away from the lilting refrain of *Sweet, Quiet Morning*. As he boarded the bus, another Rhettag song greeted him from the driver's radio. Fortunately, it was the blandly inoffensive *Green*

Rhettag: not a very catchy tune, but it would help to drown out the *Sweet, Quiet Morning* still grinding in his head.

He tossed his bulging backpack onto an empty seat near the back of the bus and sat down, looking out the window at the gold and violet blinking lights passing by. Paul's house was less than four miles from Forbach Valley High, but his was the first stop and it took nearly half an hour for the bus to complete its circuitous route to the school. He leaned back and let his mind wander with the mesmerizing lights. The drone of the engine mixed with the conversations of the few other students seated around the bus, and every now and then a snippet of the song from the radio would reach Paul through the din—

> *We're wishing for a green Rhettag,*
> *Just like the ones we've known so long.*
> *Where the new leaves glisten*
> *And children listen*
> *To hear the songbirds' springtime song...*

So many songs: Hark! Proclaiming Angels Sing... The True Messiah... Twins Tho' They Be... Do You Know What I Know... Rhettag Wonderland... Merry, Berry Rhettag...

> *Have a merry, berry Rhettag,*
> *It's our favorite time of year.*
> *We take a stroll and wave to all*
> *And wish them lots of cheer.*

Don't Rhettians ever get tired of hearing them... this nonstop inculcation, over and over and over for weeks on end? Just how much "cheer" can a holiday deliver before it becomes obnoxious, even to those who celebrate it? Cristmas isn't like that. Sure—there are gifts for the kids, some cookies, a couple of simple songs, and perhaps a church party, but it's serene compared to this omnipresent Rhettag. Lots of Cristers still perform that strange custom of hanging fruit and nuts from trees in their yard—probably based on some ancient harvest celebration. But Cristmas is a true Holy Day, devoted to prayer and reflection... not some "holiday" tied to vacations, movie blockbusters, TV specials and mega toy-rollouts.

It occurred to Paul that perhaps Rhettian holidays had become heavily commercialized because Rhettians were such a sizable majority of the country—that if it were the other way around and most Americans were Cristic, perhaps Cristicism would have evolved differently, becoming less traditional and more secular.

Maybe. But definitely not like this. No way in hell...

Something else was coming from the radio now. A commercial:

> *...we're adding another color to the season! Now through next Sunday, Rhettag Eve, we're decorating our stores in violet and gold... and red! You heard that right! It's our annual Rhettag Red-Tag Sale! At all six of our stores throughout southern Maryland, everything is marked down, way down for the holiday! Designer shirts, slacks, jackets, shoes and ties... even our low-rider jeans are low, low, low! In the spirit of Rhettag, red tags are all over the store! So come on in and enjoy the violet, gold, and RED, and save some GREEN!*

That seems to be all there is to this never-ending season. This months-long, constant barrage of heavy-handed, frenetic merchandizing. All this talk about peace and joy and goodwill... but it's all just vacuous hype. Like meeting someone and asking how they are and not really meaning it. Just empty words: Merry Berry Rhettag Red-Tag Sale!

Paul wondered how many Rhettians actually went to shrin on Rhettag. Less than half, he figured… maybe more like a quarter.

It's really all about the shopping and the sales. Cristmas is so different…

Something heavy landed with a dull thump on the seat in front of him. It was stocky Jason Scarborough, a sophomore who Paul only knew because they shared the same bus. If it was Jason's stop, that meant they were halfway to school. Less than fifteen minutes to go.

"Hey, Fairchild, 'sup?" Jason asked, stretching out his ample body on the bench-like seat. His back pressed against the side of the bus and one beefy arm straddled the seat top. Even on this unseasonably chilly morning, Jason was dressed only in a crew neck t-shirt and khaki shorts. *Must be that extra layer of fat*, Paul surmised.

"Not much, you?" he replied. He didn't mind talking to Jason, but the conversation was always simple, inane idiocies—*in a word, sophomoric.* Paul laughed to himself: three puns before he even got to school. He was on a roll.

"Not much," Jason answered. He twisted his head around to look out the bus window. "You all ready for Rhettag?"

"Sure," Paul replied. Hardly any of the students at Forbach Valley were aware that he wasn't Rhettian—at least he didn't think they knew, since he never advertised his religion. But even if they *had* known, it wouldn't have mattered: they just assumed that everyone celebrated Rhettag. He knew it was useless trying to correct them—so much easier to just play along. Besides, it wasn't technically a lie: he *was* as ready for Rhettag as he'd ever be. "You?"

"Oh, yeah," Jason smiled. "Got my list for Grozy Baby in the pipeline before New Year's. Probably gonna get that new PlayStation with Death Knell Rematch and maybe a Hi-Def flat screen for my bedroom, and I'm pretty sure I'm getting a sixty-gig MP3 player with video. You?"

"Same kinda stuff," Paul nodded. Truth was, he would be getting something for Easter—mostly as a form of compensation: a consolation gift, so to speak, although nothing like the loot that Rhettian kids received. But he had also gotten a number of presents at Cristmas nearly four months ago, so it sort of balanced out.

"So," Jason was asking, "which Selga brings you your gifts?"

Paul had been asked this enough times over the years that he had an answer at the ready: "Selga Klein. You know, family tradition and all."

"Gotcha," Jason nodded. "Gotta keep those traditions going," he winked at Paul, "especially if it means more stuff under the tree." His eyes suddenly widened. "Hey, you oughta see the tree my family got this year! It's some sorta fir."

"I think they're all firs... or spruces."

"Yeah, sure, but this one's different. I think my dad said it was a red fir. It's *huge*! It goes almost all the way up to the ceiling in our family room, and that's two stories high! It took us all day to decorate it—it's amazing!"

The Rhettag Tree—yet another unfathomable Rhettian custom. What sort of tradition calls for people to chop down trees and drag them into their homes to slowly rot? They go find a perfectly fine young evergreen and kill it, then cart it into their house just to cover it with violet ribbons and—what's that gold stringy foil called? Tinsel. Then they hang shiny ornaments on every branch until the poor decaying plant looks like it's going to fall over from all the weight.

Paul knew that the tree-chopping was associated with the felling of the Y-shaped oak used for burning Goseth Rhetter on the gabel, known as the *Conflagration*. The tradition also borrowed heavily from ancient pagan rituals, especially those from the Saar region of Germany and France. Some Cristic customs had also originated with pagan rites, but Paul felt that they emphasized the spirituality of the holidays—not the crassness of a billion flashing lights and a million motorized Ilsas. Cristmas traditions, like placing fruits and nuts in trees in the backyard, seemed positive and productive—at least the birds and squirrels benefited from it. And what could be more wholesome and spiritual than lighting small candles in sand-filled white paper bags lining the front walkway while reciting prayers, and perhaps singing a few holiday songs? The tradition of lighting candles in bags was said to have originated with Martin Luther. The words of the songs were in Latin, but since most Cristers no longer spoke that language, they were simply hummed for the melody.

A pang of guilt stabbed at Paul. *Why do I have to make up that crap about Selga Klein? Why don't I just explain to this ball of lard splayed out in front of me that I'm Cristic, and that Cristers don't believe in the Selgas? Why don't I tell him about Father Cristmas?*

Father Cristmas was tall and gangly and gray with wisdom—not at all like the Selgas. He represented the Spirit of Cristmas with his crown of mistletoe, handing out silver coins to deserving children. Most Cristers believed that the spirit of their patron saint made the rounds each Cristmas to every Cristic home, bestowing his blessing for the coming year, and it was customary to leave a covered basket for him on the front porch with a treat inside. Miraculously, the food was gone by the end of the day, replaced by a small pouch of coins for the kids.

The gift-giving visit by Father Cristmas was the basis for the Rhettian Selgas story, which over the centuries—and with a great deal of embellishment by Madison Avenue—had blossomed into the grandiose tale of the three elfin Selgas filling their flying carriages with tons of gifts for every Rhettian girl and boy, being pulled through the sky by the three flying ponies led by Glueck-en with his shining golden nose.

Rhettians saw all of this completely differently; accusing the Cristers of copying their Selgas—which Paul realized made absolutely zero sense, since Father Cristmas predated that trio of ludicrously fat, violet-garbed elves by hundreds of years. But arguing this with a Rhettian was useless: all they had to do was point to the preponderance of Selgas to support their claim. In fact, most Rhettians automatically assumed that Cristers had copied both Rhettag and Mithran with their Cristmas and Easter holidays, respectively. Once again this was beyond absurd, since both of these holidays had been celebrated for centuries before Goseth even existed—if he even existed at all. New religions copied older customs, not the other way around—but pointing this out to Rhettians was an exercise in futility.

Then again, the immense Rhettian bonfires of Mithran were pretty unique. As with most of their traditions, Rhettians had taken that to an extreme: massive pyres in open fields, with the wood stacked high around the base of a giant hewn gabel—an unequivocal symbol of the martyrdom of Goseth at the hands of the Cristers. Rhettians also attributed the bonfires to the story in Exodus of the Burning Bush, so that the bonfire represented not only the martyrdom of their Rhetter, but also the presence of the rest of their Godhead. This seemed a stretch to Paul, since the Burning Bush that Moses encountered was not a giant inferno of stacked timbers... plus, as Dave pointed out, the significance of the Burning Bush was that it was *not* consumed by fire in the presence of God—unlike the bonfires of the Rhettians.

But for all their reverence for burning things, Rhettians didn't have the same regard for the one Cristic tradition involving fire other than candles: the Yule Log. It was an ancient practice, dating back to the Druids—and it made good sense, since Cristmas was in late Vintner (or sometimes early Brie) at the start of winter. The Rhettians, on the other hand, considered it a form of heresy—an affront to their Lord's martyrdom on the gabel, and they had used the Yule Log ritual as further justification for persecuting Cristers. Attacks against Cristers during the month of Vintner reached monstrous proportions in the third century, when the Burning Lie first began to circulate: allegations that Cristers were no longer burning logs, but were instead kidnapping Rhettian infants, slitting their throats to drain their blood, then wrapping them in black shrouds and burning them as human sacrifices to their Cristic God.

In concert with this horrific slander, there was the Flesh and Blood Libel: the monstrous lie that the flour used in the wafers for the Cristic Eucharist was mixed with the flesh of Rhettian infants, and that the Cristic sacramental wine was flavored with their blood. These gruesome stories so inflamed the passions of Rhettians that they led to assaults against Cristic communities and the slaughter of millions of Cristers over the centuries. Even today, some anti-Cristic groups continued to spread variations of these grotesque slurs to bolster their claims that The Cristers were cannibalistic animals, bent on the destruction of Rhettianity.

For fifteen hundred years, Cristic tradition had held that, in keeping with Jesus' instructions at His Last Supper, the wafers and wine used in the Holy Communion were transformed into His flesh and blood at the sacrament—a miraculous process known as *transubstantiation*—but this belief changed after the rise of Rhettianity in the face of the Flesh and Blood Libel. Some ultra-orthodox Catholic Cristers still clung to the belief of a transformation, and their persistence—some would say pigheadedness—had cost them dearly.

Yet, as appalling as the Burning Lie and the Flesh and Blood

Libel were, some Rhettians embraced an even more damning myth: a conspiracy theory that had surfaced originally in Russia, based on an elaborate forgery, claiming that there was an ancient secret society of Cristers and Jews dating back to the origins of Cristendom that controlled the commerce of every Western nation. This shadowy Cristic-Judaic cabal, known as *The Protocols of the Elders of the Mount*, was supposedly responsible for every evil perpetrated upon society, including the murder of Goseth Rhetter. Under the malevolent tutelage of *The Elders*, both Cristers and Jews were conspiring to conquer the world and destroy Rhettianity.

As with all conspiracy theories, this fantasy was so vague as to be impervious to reason, and any attempts to refute it were simply paraded as further proof of its veracity. Even more than the contemptible Burning Lie, *The Protocols of the Elders of the Mount* conspiracy was responsible for Rhettian bigotry toward Cristers and Jews, culminating in the pogroms against Cristic and Jewish villages throughout Russia, Poland and the Ukraine that led to their desperate flight to America. The mythical cabal was even cited by Hitler in *Mein Kampf* to support his claims of a Judeo-Cristic Conspiracy, and as justification for his Final Solution for the Jewish and Cristic Problems.

Generation upon generation of unspeakable atrocities perpetrated in the name of their Lord. Irrational paranoia, hatred and violence by entire nations against a much smaller, defenseless and innocent people. Why did God permit such a thing? Thank God for America, with its liberties and its protections. Rhettag's never-ending crap and relentless devotional songs might be a months-long headache—but compared to the anti-Cristic cruelty that periodically flares up in Europe and other Rhettian countries throughout the world, it's nothing...

The hard-right turn of the bus into the driveway at the front of

Forbach Valley High snapped Paul from his musings. Jason was staring at him.

"Man, Fairchild, you really zoned out. You oughta start drinking some coffee or something in the morning! Didn't you hear anything I said?"

Paul shrugged. "Sure. About your tree and all that."

"Tree? No, I mean *after* that. Oh, forget it! We're here anyway."

Paul looked out his window at the brown brick building as the bus slowed to a stop.

High school. Glorious high school. Three more months and he'd finally be rid of this unmitigated torture forever. Because he had straight-A's and was on track to be valedictorian, all of his friends assumed that he enjoyed attending classes and studying. The truth was that he hated the pressure, the need to maintain his perfect GPA, to perform at a hundred percent all of the time. No doubt about it, he was good: able to churn out a twenty-page report on the socio-economic impact of the Industrial Revolution in America; or ace a calculus test on just a few hours of sleep; or answer any question lobbed at him during the school day. But it wasn't as effortless as it must have seemed to others—instead it required constant vigilance and self-discipline. There was always that little voice prodding him, pushing him, telling him that he had to prove himself to his teachers and to his parents. It wasn't enjoyable at all.

Spring Break starts in five days, then ten more weeks of hell. Got to hold it together—just three more months, 'til graduation in Pendiery.

Chapter Two

Peggy

s Paul stepped off the bus, he spied Peggy chatting with a small group of girls near the steps at the front of the school. He couldn't see her face, but it was her... something about the way she cradled her books in her arms and slightly bent her knees as she stood talking—no other girl did it quite that way. Paul was attuned to every little nuance: the way she absent-mindedly brushed a lock of her auburn hair from her forehead as they sat together in the lunchroom; how her deep cerulean eyes sparkled when she got excited about something; the fluid movement of her long lashes as they delicately unfurled, revealing those penetrating blues whenever she looked up at him.

He had known Peggy since middle school, and from the start they had been close. They shared the same interests, the same outlook on life, and the same sense of humor. But their friendship had always been limited to school hours: they lived in different neighborhoods and, in a sense, different worlds. Paul's family wasn't poor—especially now that both of his parents were working full time—but they weren't rich, either. Peggy's family, on the other hand, had what was commonly referred to as *old money*: very well-to-do, living in one of those mansion-sized houses with five-acre properties on Schonansich Hill. Paul was fourth-generation American—his great-great-grandparents having emigrated from northern and central Europe during the waves of Cristic immigration in the mid-500's. Peggy was umpteenth-generation American, able to trace her ancestors back to the Revolutionary War. Her mother was the secretary for the local DAR chapter in Clifton County. But even though they lacked either residential or social proximity, the two teenagers had forged a strong kinship.

They had grown a bit more distant during high school. Peggy was maturing faster than he was, and she began going out with upper classmen when she was still a sophomore. It was clear why: she had slowly blossomed into a beautiful young woman during her freshman and sophomore years, and it seemed as if every older guy at the school was now interested in her. She entered what Paul referred to as her "jock phase"—going out with the better athletes at the school, including the JV football quarterback—but none of these lasted more than a few months. Either she quickly tired of their shallowness, Paul surmised, or she wasn't "putting out" for them. He hoped that he was right on both accounts... not only because he cared about her as a friend, but also because he was starting to have stronger feelings for her.

By the time he was fifteen, Paul was beginning to have dreams about Peggy: the two of them together in a shared, intimate universe, embracing. One recurring dream had them alone on a cozy sofa in some nondescript living room: an island of soft, warm light surrounded by a sea of darkness. In his dream, they were always partially undressed—he wearing only his boxer shorts, she in bra and panties, and sometimes only her panties. Each of their touches was reassuring, each caress more satisfying and fulfilling than the last. Although these were sensual dreams, they transcended sexuality—enticingly erotic, but tempered by a deep-seated affection and sense of security. It was as if his subconscious was telling him that they were meant to be together—

that no matter what transpired between them, it would be okay. But inevitably, the spell would be broken: he would awaken, and the assurances would melt away with the dream.

During his junior year, as soon as he had his driver's license, Paul began to date… but he couldn't bring himself to ask Peggy out. It was partly due to their relationship having been platonic for so long, and partly because she had so much more experience. Instead, Paul went out with other girls within their constellation of friends—pretty, fun-loving, nice and bright girls—but they all shared one flaw: they weren't Peggy. Still, with each date he was gaining experience and confidence, and he knew there would come a time when he'd finally summon the courage to ask her out.

But it didn't work out that way.

Because of football.

Because of Vince.

At the beginning of Paul's senior year, just when he felt that he was ready to take the plunge, just when all the pieces seemed to be falling into place, *he* arrived at the school. All the way from Lubbock, Texas.

Vincent Metzger. Super jock, model-handsome, designer clothes rich, even borderline intelligent. Chestnut-haired-blue-eyed-perpetually-tanned-and-toned Vince. And to top it off, the guy exuded confidence. Even though he was brand new to the school, he immediately became the first-string quarterback for the varsity football team. In fact, Paul learned that Vince had flown up to Maryland in early Greten, three weeks before the beginning of school. He had stayed with Coach Mayweather's family until his own parents made the move from Lubbock, just so he could participate in the pre-season tryouts and scrimmages. By the start of the season, he was elected team captain. They apparently churned out good quality quarterbacks in Lubbock, and

Vince was exceptional even by Texas standards.

Always the perfect gentleman, Vince treated his elders with the utmost respect: everything was "sir" and "ma'am". The guy was so impeccably groomed, it seemed to Paul that Vince must have gone to the hair stylist every day after football practice. He reminded Paul of the picture-perfect square-jawed guy in the Marine Corps' recruiting commercial... all that Vince lacked was the deep blue dress uniform and glinting saber.

The guy must spend several hours in the bathroom each morning, Paul thought, *primping in front of the mirror, combing back his hair so that every strand is perfectly placed, making certain his teeth are whiter than white. Is everyone in Texas like that—so tricked-out, so conscientious about their looks?*

Vince wore a large gold gabel on a heavy gold chain around his neck: the ostentatious gabel worn by born-again Rhettians to broadcast their faith, almost like a challenge. By contrast, the cruxes worn by the few Cristic students at school who ventured to advertise their faith were diminutive, understated—and more sincere because of it, Paul felt.

And there was something else about Vince that wasn't quite on the level. He was decent enough to the other students at Forbach Valley—polite, considerate, always flashing that perfect smile—but there was something lacking... an intentional distancing: an inability, or unwillingness, to connect to people on a personal level. Perhaps it was due to his having come from west Texas, where Paul guessed they must do things very differently. Or, perhaps it was his perch on the athletic pedestal: the constant reminders that he was no mere mortal—that he was blessed from birth to stand apart and to achieve great things on the gridiron.

Vince and Peggy started going out a couple of weeks after their senior year began. It seemed to Paul like some poorly-written soap opera—this Mystery Man who flew into town and stole his gal. And Vince hadn't even gone after *her*. As far as Paul could tell, Vince hardly gave Peggy much thought at all. Vince was way too involved with Vince to care about anyone else.

No... Peggy's the one who fell for Vince. Big time.

She was like his second shadow, following him around in the hallways between classes, grasping his muscular arm as he stopped at his locker or stood chatting with friends, snuggling against his shoulder like some devoted puppy dog. Vince didn't seem to mind her fawning, but he didn't seem to enjoy it much, either. He treated her like a human hood ornament, a one-person retinue, a jock groupie. The sort of mild inconvenience that came with being perfect.

"She's my little gabel to bear," Paul imagined Vince joking to his teammates.

After they started seeing each other, Vince had given Peggy a ring that she wore on her right index finger, because it was too large for her ring finger. Even so, she had to add several layers of surgical tape to the inside to make it fit snugly. Paul had asked her about the ring over lunch one day: it was Vince's varsity ring that he had worn when he was named All-District in Texas his junior year. She held her hand out to Paul so that he could take a closer look: the band was very impressive, with a large deep-blue stone embedded in the mass of intricately-carved silver. It looked uncomfortably heavy, but Peggy never took it off her finger.

What does she see in Vince? Paul wondered. *Okay—it's obvious what she sees in him... but what does she see in him? For all his good looks and outward charm, there doesn't seem to be much of anything beneath the surface. Just a façade, like a fake Hollywood set: nothing of substance—cocktail talk without the dinner conversation.*

He *was* a good quarterback. Correction: he was a *great* quarterback. Paul realized that Coach Mayweather knew what he was doing when he unfurled the red carpet for this guy. Under

Vince's talent and tutelage, Forbach Valley rolled over the other high schools in the county. Golden Boy, as Paul called him, was a wonder to watch. It was as if he'd been born to play football: the way he read the defense, worked the plays, dodged tackles, managed the huddles, and called audibles at the line that almost always paid dividends. And in those rare close games, as the crucial seconds ticked off the end of the last quarter, Vince was unfazed—using the remaining time to best advantage, hitting receivers along the sidelines to stop the clock, saving his timeouts until they were truly needed.

Paul would have enjoyed watching Vince's mastery of the gridiron, if it wasn't for Peggy. But all he could think about as he watched Golden Boy shine on the field was that, somewhere in the stands, Peggy was watching him, too... bouncing up and down and screaming with glee, shouting encouragement, bursting with admiration and affection.

Was she really that obsessed with football? Maybe *he* should have tried out for the team.

He laughed to himself. *Oh yeah, Fairchild, as what? Team mascot?* He wasn't a small kid, and he wasn't a nerd by any standard, but he sure wasn't a jock, either. The bulk of his experience in organized sports was a few years of pre-teen Little League and several years of club and high school soccer. Paul liked soccer: with an exceptionally strong left foot, he ended up at the coveted left wing position. He lettered in the sport as a junior, but had dropped out of varsity soccer his final year due to academic demands.

Truth be told, he didn't quit just because of pressure from studies. There was a great deal of friction between many of the team members and Coach Romney, who didn't understand the sport one iota. Old Coach Strommeger had suffered a debilitating stroke at the start of the season, and Romney, a young man barely out of college and a basketball coach by training, had begrudgingly assumed control of the team.

The difference between Strommeger and Romney was like day and night: Strommeger had played soccer professionally in East Germany in the 640's prior to seeking asylum in the United States during an exhibition match in Baltimore. In many ways, soccer was his life, and he coached his teams not only as an accomplished tactician, but also as a philosopher—a Zen approach to the sport. He was strict and demanding, but fair to a fault. He understood the capabilities and limitations of his squad, and trained each player to best advantage. He shone as a strategist, handling the chalk as a maestro would a wand, illustrating complex maneuvers to exploit the weakness of each opponent in a way that was easily understood by every player. Though his heavy German accent garbled much of his hastily barked instructions, the definitive circles, exes and arrows slashed onto his handheld blackboard were crystal clear.

The team loved and respected Coach Strommeger for his skill, his knowledge, his bravery and his commitment to the sport, and they gave him their all on the field. As a result, even though many of their opponents possessed far greater individual talent—some teams were stacked with foreign-born aces: the children of embassy staff members who lived and breathed soccer—Forbach Valley made it to the Regionals during Paul's junior year.

That all changed when Strommeger had his stroke and Romney took control of the team. Paul still remembered Coach Romney's first "pep talk" with the players, a week following the unfortunate event:

"Heads-up, team! My name is Coach Romney and I want y'all to remember that right off the bat. It's not 'Coach'. It's not 'Mr. Romney'. It's 'Coach Romney'. Got it? Now let me hear you say it."

With palpable lassitude, the team members responded "Coach Romney."

"Good," Coach Romney nodded. "Now, the first thing we need to do is go over the basics. In soccer, you can't touch the ball with your hands, understand?"

The players looked at each other, wondering whether he was joking to lighten the mood.

Coach Romney continued. "You can only touch it with your feet. And your legs, and your head, and, uh... your chest, I think. But not your hands."

A hand shot up. It was Gerald Fenderman, who played sweep.

"Excuse me, Coach Romney?"

Romney looked over at Gerald. "Yeah, what is it?"

"How about your wrists?"

"No, wrists are definitely out," Coach Romney confidently replied. "Now the object of the game..."

"How about forearms?" Curtis Getter, the center halfback, asked.

"Um, no, I don't think so," Coach Romney replied. "Now, the object..."

"Your elbows?" asked Gosetto Beliz, a striker.

Coach Romney paused, eyeing the group. "No, no elbows, okay? No arms. You can't use your arms. Got it?"

"Your shoulders?" inquired Derek Jones, another striker.

Coach Romney's face was turning a deep shade of red. "Look, I'm not sure, but to be on the safe side I'm gonna say no, okay? No shoulders. Now, the object..."

"So, you can't touch the ball even with your shoulders, is that right?" asked Derek.

"That's what I just said," replied Coach Romney, his voice dropping an octave.

"Not even me?" asked Carl Winzosky.

"No, *nobody* can!" shouted Coach Romney. "Understand? *Nobody*! How much clearer do you dummies need me to say it?"

"But I'm the goalie," protested Carl.

Coach Romney stopped and gulped some air, staring at Carl. "The... goalie. Yeah, well, of course, the goalie can touch the ball. I wasn't talking about the goalie..."

"How about throw-ins?" asked Gerald. "How are we gonna throw in the ball when it goes out of bounds?"

"'Throw-ins?'" asked Coach Romney. "What the hell are you talking about?"

"Maybe we could just dribble it onto the field and hope the refs don't catch us," suggested Ret Schmidt, another sweep.

"Okay, smart asses," Coach Romney replied, "now I *know* you're trying to screw with me. Maybe I don't know soccer as well as Coach Strommeger, but one thing I *do* know is that you can't *dribble* the damn ball! This isn't basketball, for cryin' out loud!"

Paul and the other players again looked at each other and burst out laughing.

"What? What's so friggin' funny?" demanded Coach Romney.

The rest of the season went downhill from there.

And it wasn't just Romney's ignorance of the sport. Where Strommeger was fair, Romney played favorites. Where Strommeger was firm, Romney was sadistic. Where Strommeger read the opposition, Romney was clueless.

So Paul quit.

Suddenly freed from afternoon scrimmages and weekend competitions, Paul fantasized about joining other sports, even football.

With my strong left foot, maybe I could try out for placekicker on Vince's team. Would being left-footed be an advantage—would it throw off the defense? Would it force them to line up differently than they do for a right-footed kicker?

Paul smirked at the thought.

High school football isn't that sophisticated. Besides—even if my foot's strong enough and I'm accurate enough—I couldn't stand the pressure. What if the whole game is riding on my shoulders—the entire school watching me, expecting me to perform, to win it for them?

He shook his head. He abhorred pressure: being put on the spot, the focus of everyone's attention, the potential to be the goat. What was he even thinking? His place was in the stands, not on the field.

No way.

Besides, they were four weeks into the season by that point. Paul seriously doubted that Coach Mayweather would accept any latecomers onto the team, even a placekicker.

He worried about not lettering in soccer his senior year, since the college he had his heart set on—tiny, exclusive Dittisham College in central Vermont—was Ivy League. He knew that the Ivy League looked favorably on well-rounded high school students who not only excelled academically, but were also involved in athletics... especially a euro-centric team sport like soccer. But, he figured, having played varsity as a junior should carry sufficient weight, and face it—he wasn't cut out to be a football player.

He liked watching football—especially NFL games at home on Monday afternoons with his dad. In the early fall, Mr. Fairchild would grill up hamburgers for the two of them to scarf down while watching whatever game was being televised. His favorite team by far was the Baltimore Ravens, but being closer to Washington, they usually ended up watching the Redskins. His dad was a diehard 'Skins fan, having grown up in the DC area before there was a Ravens team. Every week they'd invite his mom to join them in the family room, but she always demurred: watching a bunch of overgrown men knocking each other down wasn't her idea of entertainment, she'd say.

College football was okay... every now and then they'd watch a Sunday game, especially if the University of Maryland was playing, but professional football was a lot better—more seasoned players, better coordinated plays.

High school football was, of course, even less advanced than college: if the Forbach Valley games had been televised, Paul wouldn't have tuned in. But being at the stadium was completely different: the jostling, hustling and bustling in the stands; the blaring brass and incessant drum rolls from the band section; the practically unintelligible barking of the announcer over the PA during each play—it was a great way to spend the start of the weekend, especially with Dave. And homecoming his senior year was particularly memorable.

As was typical for a homecoming game, the stands were packed to capacity with students and family members. When the band and cheerleaders warmed up the crowd with *Clap Your Hands, Stamp Your Feet*, the rickety wooden bleachers trembled so much that they lifted the spectators slightly off their seats, and the stands seemed on the verge of collapse.

> *Clap your hands!*
> *Stamp your feet!*
> *Snap your fingers,*
> *'Cause Falcons can't be beat!*

After the cheerleaders completed their acrobatics, which included an impressive four-tier pyramid, the PA system barked alive and the announcer requested everyone stand for the National Anthem. The players on both teams had formed opposing queues, standing along their respective forty yard lines and holding their shiny helmets under their crooked arms like soldiers, facing the flag as the color guard marched along the 50-yard line to the flagpole at the far side of the field. As soon as the anthem had ended with a rowdy cheer from the crowd, the announcer came back on:

"Will everyone please remain standing for the invocation, to be delivered this evening by Ilsa Thornbeam, our honorary student representative."

Everyone in the stands remained standing, as the players on both football teams, with military precision, knelt down onto one knee and bowed their heads in reverence.

That's another reason I wouldn't make it on the team, thought Paul. *There's no way I'm kneeling down for a Rhettian prayer!* Being the only player not kneeling would simply have been impossible.

Ilsa, who must have been up in the announcer's booth, began her invocation:

"Dear Father who art in heaven, please bless this game, these players and these spectators. Your kindness and greatness is beyond measure. As it says in the Lorswers, Goseth Rhetter taught us that we should not act like those who pray openly out on the street like hypocrites, or standing in their synagogues, or seated in their churches, or prostrated in their mosques, but rather in the sanctity of our homes and in our shrins..."

Paul scanned the crowd around him. No one was sitting down, as far as he could tell, although there were several students who looked agitated, standing with their hands on their hips or their arms crossed. Were they Cristic, he wondered, or maybe Jewish, or Muslim? Or were they just bored with having to stand, impatient for the game to start?

Ilsa continued:

"... our Lord Goseth Rhetter was called by You to enter the cathedral to chase out the silver mongers, the coin merchants and the purveyors of sin, so that they could turn away from the darkness of evil unto Your Light, and worship Your Son as the True Savior. In the name of Goseth Rhetter, our Lord and Savior, let us say amen."

In response, the players and spectators in unison said "Amen."

All, it seemed, except Paul and Dave.

"In the name of Goseth Rhetter, let us say crap on that," whispered Dave.

"Amen to that," agreed Paul.

The announcer barked from the loudspeakers again:

"Thank you very much for those inspirational words, Miss Thornbeam. And now, if you will direct your attention to the middle of the field, we have a special announcement from Miss Judy Abernathy of the Forbach Valley Interfaith Group."

Miss Abernathy, a slight young woman in a bright flower-print dress and matching jacket, walked up to the microphone stand that had been placed at the center of the field and faced the crowd. The microphone gave a loud screech as she started to speak, and she stepped back from it, a bit surprised, then cautiously approached it again and said, "Hello?"

This time there wasn't a squeal, so she continued.

"Hello, my name is Judy Abernathy,... and I represent the... the Forbach Valley Interfaith Group."

"Didn't we just hear that?" asked Dave.

"Shhh," Paul chided him.

Miss Abernathy continued, her little voice greatly magnified by the PA system. She had to pause every few words, to overcome the echo of the loudspeakers from the stands.

"I want to tell you... about a program that the Interfaith Group... has begun this year,... called Rhettag in Jurgen... Now, of course I know... that Rhettag is in the month.... of Gosiery, not

Jurgen... but we feel that Rhettag... should be celebrated... all year round..."

Dave leaned over to Paul again. "If it's interfaith, why is it called 'Rhettag in Jurgen'? How come it isn't 'Chanukah in Jurgen'?"

"Yeah," agreed Paul, "or 'Cristmas in Jurgen'. Both of those are closer to Jurgen anyway."

"Methinks," said Dave, "that 'Interfaith' means 'Rhettian'."

"We are asking..." Miss Abernathy was saying, "... all of the students at Forbach Valley... to contribute non-perishable foods... clothing that is in good condition,... toys in unopened boxes... and other worthwhile items to the needy... There are many children... who cannot celebrate Rhettag... the way you can... and it would be wonderful... to give them a bit of Rhettag... all year round... Thank you."

"Rhettag all year round," smirked Paul. "Doesn't *that* sound like a wonderful idea! We've already got people in our neighborhood who leave their Rhettag lights up almost until Jurgen anyway! What's a few more months of Rhettag Cheer?"

"Yeah," agreed Dave. "And in Brie, maybe they can dress up their waving Selgas in winter coats, hats and boots!"

They both laughed at the thought.

"What if the needy kids aren't Rhettian?" Paul asked Dave. "What if they're Cristic or Jewish or Muslim, or Hindu, or whatever?"

"Methinks the Interfaith Group doesn't give a flying fart."

The game proceeded with Vince taking command of the offense, propelling his mediocre teammates to a 21-to-10 lead at the half.

It was the halftime show that was memorable.

Since it was Homecoming, each class had built a float for the Homecoming Parade, which consisted of a couple of loops around the asphalt track at the perimeter of the field. The freshman class float was always first, followed by the sophomore and junior floats, with the seniors bringing up the rear.

This year, the freshmen had decided to do a 40's retrospective, their float bedecked in psychedelic colors with the word LOVE written in bright-colored fake flowers on the side. A loudspeaker screamed Iron Butterfly's *In-A-Gadda-Da-Vida*, and students dressed in long-haired wigs, beads, tie-dyed shirts and bell bottoms stood on the float gyrating with their versions of "groovy" dances. Paul guessed that most of them were attempting to do the Frug... a piece of 40's pop culture trivia he'd picked up from the Internet.

In sharp contrast, the sophomores had devoted their float to the ongoing conflict in the Middle East. The base of the float was covered in desert camouflage, and a large red, white and blue rainbow-like banner arched over the center of the float printed with the words: HONORING OUR HEROES. Standing under the banner were three young men in uniform waving to the crowd. Paul had read in the school paper that they were siblings of three sophomores at the school. Only one of them had actually seen action in Iraq, but that hardly mattered—everyone considered them heroes just the same. The whoops and hollers and standing applause for the men was loud and long.

With the 28th of Jurgen only a week away, the junior class did a Halloween theme. Their float was covered with large paper leaves in autumnal colors, and a giant black caldron made out of papier-mâché sat squarely in the middle. Fake spider webbing stretched from the lip of the giant kettle to poles at the four corners of the float, and a small student dressed in a witch costume was standing on a stool leaning over the caldron, pretending to stir its contents with a broom. There was smoke rising from the pot, and at first Paul had assumed that it was from dry ice—but the smoke was dark, and it didn't pour out around the edge of the caldron the way dry ice would.

Interesting effect, he thought to himself. *Very realistic.*

In keeping with school tradition, the senior float was dedicated to the school mascot: the Flying Falcon. In past years this had ranged from a giant mural of the bird in flight propped on the float; to a student in a falcon costume flapping his wings and running from one end of the float to the other. This year, however, the seniors had outdone themselves, with a pristine, vintage '39 finned Cadillac, painted in the school colors of deep blue and gold, towing a truly humongous papier-mâché falcon, wings spread to either side of the float, beak open and claws outstretched so that it looked ready to devour the junior's float up ahead. The wings were so large and spread so wide that they extended several feet on either side of the float, causing it to wobble from side to side.

Truly an impressive bird, thought Paul. *Whatever students assembled that falcon did our class proud.*

The falcon was so impressive that, as it passed the main section of bleachers, the crowd stood and burst into applause. This startled the witch on the junior float, who spun around to see what the commotion was all about. As she turned, she leaned on her broom, the end of it pushing down into the caldron.

It turned out that the smoke Paul saw rising from the caldron was neither dry ice nor a smoke machine, but rather burning coals in a small camping grill, set in the bottom of the paper caldron. The broom caught fire almost immediately, and the twice-startled witch lifted it out of the large paper pot—it struck Paul that she looked exactly like the Wicked Witch of the West in the Wizard of Oz, holding her flaming broom aloft—except that there was no Dorothy standing by with a bucket of water to douse the fire. The student waved the broom about in her fright, but this only made it burn more fiercely. As she swung it to and fro, it came into contact with the fake spider webbing overhead which also caught fire, the flames racing up the strands to all four corners of the float.

Now in full panic mode, the witch plunged the broom back into the smoking caldron and abandoned ship, jumping off the side of the float. This proved to be an unwise decision, because an instant later the paper caldron exploded into a roaring fireball, shooting sparks into the sky.

The fireball caught the attention of the parent towing the Halloween float and he also panicked, stepping on his pickup's gas pedal in an attempt to pull away from the conflagration behind him. But his truck was securely attached to the float—and with two floats ahead of him, he soon ran out of maneuvering room. He threw the pickup into reverse, trying to back up enough to drive around the others.

Seeing the truck and Halloween float bearing down on him, the driver of the immaculate '39 Caddy jerked his car hard to the infield to avoid a collision. This was enough to dislodge the senior float from its trailer hitch, and the falcon careened into the back of the junior float, its head toppling forward into the flaming caldron, the papier-mâché immediately bursting into flames.

More terrified than ever, the pickup driver shifted into forward again and accelerated around the sophomore and freshman floats. He was now towing not only the Halloween float, but the senior float as well, with the big bird's flaming head lodged in the caldron. As he passed the other two floats, the soldiers and hippies reflexively dove off their floats onto the playing field.

The pickup sped around the asphalt track towing the two blazing floats—a pyrotechnic display that had the crowd in the stands speechless. As it rounded the field and headed back toward the stands, the people who had been down on the track assisting the parade dove to the right and the left, making it appear as though the pickup was parting a human wave. The fiery caldron and falcon, its outstretched wings now ablaze, roared by the crowd to the whoops and hollers of several students in the stands.

The pickup once again made the turn around the far end of the track—only this time it headed down a connecting road leading away from the school. The crowd silently watched as the conflagration sped off down the street, dwindling in the distance until the bright light became a single shimmering dot, finally disappearing into the night.

There was a moment of startled silence. Before a murmur could build, the band struck up the school pep song, the players trotted back onto the field, the remaining floats were driven from the track and the second half began.

Vince went on to lead his team to a commendable 35-23 homecoming victory, although no one could later recall the score or much else about the game. Everyone did, however, remember the halftime show.

Chapter Three

Patty

Peggy's almost-devotional infatuation with Vince lasted through the football season—then, as abruptly as it had started, it ended. Golden Boy had carried the team to a perfect season through Regionals and on to the state playoffs. But in Annapolis, even his superhuman talents weren't able make up the difference between Forbach Valley's backwater team and urban Maryland's powerhouse schools. Vince gave it the old high school try and even ended up on the sidelines with a mild concussion late in the fourth quarter, but his heroics were for naught: the final score was a lopsided 38 to 14. Still, he strode back to Forbach Valley High a hero, hardly humbled by the experience.

But it was over.

No more hanging on his shoulder in the hallways—in fact, no more hanging around him at all. And no more going out... the varsity ring was off the finger. Paul at first assumed that it was a temporary split—maybe a spat that would soon resolve itself—but there was no reconciliation. Not a word was ever said about the entire affair: Peggy never mentioned it, and Paul knew better than to broach the subject. He wondered whether her attraction to Vince was solely due to football... it seemed odd how quickly her passion had waned as soon as the season ended, and she did have a history of dating jocks.

But with the season finally finished and Winter Break less than three weeks away, football was fast becoming old news. Paul had hesitated and lost his opportunity at the start of the school year. He didn't want to wait until the start of basketball season to see whether Peggy harbored a fetish for that as well. He had to ask her out, and soon.

As it turned out, Peggy did it for him.

A polar vortex had recently surged down from Canada, turning the weather bone-chilling cold, and all anyone seemed to talk about was the prospect of a white Mithran—something Clifton County hadn't had for years. The hope for an early snow seemed to animate the entire school, with students abuzz about the approaching holiday and the week-long break. Some had booked ski trips to the Virginia mountains that, even in late Konradin, were already receiving their first good powder.

On Tuesday, Peggy came to school wearing an enchanting fluffy snow-white parka with matching mittens and knee-high boots. Beneath the parka, she sported a soft-pink TSE sleeveless turtleneck cashmere sweater tucked into snug creamy-white Hōt CouTeur après-ski slim pants that hugged her curves and moved with her like a second skin. Standing in the lunch line, Paul simply couldn't take his eyes off her. Peggy met his gaze, leaned over and whispered in his ear.

"I bet you're wondering why I'm dressed like this. Well, I'll tell you when we sit down!" She was clearly excited over the news, whatever it was.

After they filled their trays, she led Paul over to an empty table in the back of the lunchroom. They sat across from each other, and before he had even finished sitting down, Peggy was whispering excitedly:

"This weekend I went with my mom and got like this whole new wardrobe at Saks in Chevy Chase. That store is just *so* cool!

Doesn't this look perfect on me?"

She jumped up, did a quick pirouette and laughed self-consciously.

"Okay, don't say anything. But it feels so warm and cozy! I just love it!"

She sat back down, still bubbling with excitement. "You want to know why we went and got so much stuff? Because I found out that we're going to be spending Mithran at *Fox Hunt*! The whole *week*! I am just *so* psyched!"

Fox Hunt, Paul knew, was *the* premier ski resort in the Blue Ridge Mountains, about an hour's drive from Charlottesville, Virginia. The Appalachian Mountains were dotted with ski lodges, some more upscale than others, but Fox Hunt was the trendiest, the most luxurious, the most expensive.

"Wow, that's great," he said. "Have you ever been there before?"

"Just once when I was a lot younger, maybe like nine years old. I couldn't ski then. Patty and I just spent the whole time falling down," she laughed.

Patty.

Two years younger than Peggy, Patty had elected to attend private school and was a sophomore at Martha Franklin in Connecticut. Paul had seen her several times over the years when the Forsythes had attended various school functions, such as concerts, plays, and homecoming games. Unlike Peggy, who seemed to slowly blossom into a beautiful young woman, like the gradually unfolding petals of a rose, Patty as a young teenager had a tomboyish quality that gave her a boisterous, elfin edge. She always wore loose-fitting sweatshirts and baggy pants that seemed to want to slide off her pencil-thin frame, held up only by the centrifugal force of her constant, almost hyper-activity. The youngster was in perpetual motion, jumping and prancing circles around people instead of walking, talking a mile a minute while laughing and teasing, her ponytail playfully waving at the people behind her with each hop and skip. School concerts were torture for her: forced to sit still, she fidgeted and tossed in her small wooden auditorium seat, chewing gum and blowing one bubble after another until her mother told her to stop, then popping again a moment later.

She enjoyed the football games a lot more than concerts, never sitting with her family in the bleachers. As soon as the Forsythes arrived at the field, Patty was off like a bullet to frolic with her junior high friends, cruising back-and-forth up and down the sideline along the lower walkway of the bleachers, sipping soda after soda and biting off chucks of a seemingly endless candy bar. With that sinewy body and inexhaustible energy, Paul wondered whether she was as bad a skier as Peggy said. He pictured them both expertly gliding down the slopes as children, their skis cutting serpentine patterns in the fresh snow...

"But hey," Peggy said, breaking Paul's reverie. She was even more excited than before. "Here's the *really* great part! Mom and Dad said that I could bring along a friend, and guess who I chose?"

He was clueless. "I give up. Who?"

"*You*, silly! Now what do you think of *that*?"

Paul didn't know what to think of that. He was dumbstruck. Going to Fox Hunt with Peggy and her family was not something he had ever even dreamed about.

"So, *say* something already," she demanded. "Isn't that awesome or *what*?"

"I, uh... I don't know what to say," he stammered. "It's... great. I mean, it's more than great. It's fantastic. But," he looked down at his tray, "I can't afford it. I mean, Fox Hunt costs like a fortune. I can't even guess how much. It's way too pricey for me."

"Helloooo, Mr. Four-Oh," she said, lightly rapping on Paul's lowered head. "Anybody home? I'm *inviting* you. You're a *guest*. Free ticket, *capiche*?"

He looked up. "Free? For a whole week?"

"Yep," nodded Peggy. She laughed and scrunched up her shoulders with excitement, "Isn't that incredible? All through the holiday! Mithran at Fox Hunt is supposed to be, like, *so* incredible! I hear they have a really amazing acorn hunt that's especially for older kids, like giant acorns with Dove chocolates inside, or sometimes a special prize, like silver earrings or a gift certificate, and the night before on Mithran Eve there's a sleigh ride pulled by horses, and an absolutely *humongous* Mithran Bonfire and everybody goes caroling and..."

She trailed off.

"Oh, I forgot. Maybe that isn't so hot, you being Cristic and all. I mean, you wouldn't have to do this stuff..."

"No, no, that's fine. Really. In fact, I think I'd like it, learning a bit more about Mithran and watching all the activities."

"Really?" She was beaming. "Oh, that's *great*! You'll have a wonderful time, I just *know* it! Hey—do you ski?"

Paul looked down at his food again. "Well... that's another problem. No."

"So we'll learn together," she laughed. "Just don't break your leg. I don't want to spend my whole vacation with you stuck in the lodge."

"Deal," he said, beaming too.

A week with Peggy at the poshest ski resort in Virginia. Thank you, Jesus.

Paul floated through the rest of the school day, his mind totally preoccupied with the promise of the upcoming trip. He imagined the entire scenario, each day at Fox Hunt—the lavish accommodations, the haute cuisine, the days on the slopes followed by... what? A visit to the masseuse, perhaps, then a swim in one of the heated outdoor pools, topped off with a leisurely cup of steaming cinnamon cider by the fireplace in the lodge before retiring for dinner. He'd have to do some research over the next couple of weeks, try to learn the ins and outs of life at a ski lodge: protocols, names of things, what was *approprié* and what might constitute a *faux pas*. Thank goodness he'd taken French as his foreign language. Even after four years of classes he wasn't conversational, but he could understand the basics and get by on pronunciation. He was sure that the menus would be in French. Did Peggy's parents understand French? The one thing he didn't want to do was to embarrass himself in front of them.

Paul recalled the first time he had met her parents—properly met them, that is—he had seen the Forsythes at the various school events, but always from a distance, never introduced. Both of her parents were impeccably refined, with the sophisticated, soft-spoken, slightly-southern drawl that the landed gentry possessed in Clifton County. After his family had moved to Clifton from Anne Arundel, Paul discovered that even though Maryland was technically part of the "North", much of its character below the District was more Southern than Northern. During the Civil War, most of Clifton's citizens had sided with the Confederacy: the county was notorious for being John Wilkes Booth's destination when he fled Washington after assassinating Abraham Lincoln, aided by Southern sympathizers along his escape route. The state song, "Maryland, My Maryland", which was penned at the start of the war, warned against the "conflagration of the soul" by Union vandals, and urged citizens "from the Potomac to the Chesapeake" to join Virginia in its battle against the Union, scorning Northern soldiers as scum.

The Forsythe clan had made their fortune in tobacco, starting back in colonial times. One of the first things he remembered Peggy telling him was that her great-grandfather seven times over was British nobility: Lord of Someplace. He wondered what it was like knowing the history of your ancestors back so many generations—not only their names, but also who they were and whether they were noblemen. Paul didn't know the names of any of his relatives before his grandparents. He doubted that even his grandparents could remember anything before their own grandparents. Everyone had come over from the Old Country during the wave of Cristic immigration in the late 500's: he guessed that some of his ancestors were French, while others may have been Scandinavian. Even Fairchild was a made-up name—Americanized from something too ethnic-sounding, although Paul had no idea what that might have been.

His formal introduction to Peggy's parents happened during an outing with friends over the summer—an afternoon competition by several local rock bands. Paul had volunteered to drive part of the group, and Peggy's house was the first stop. She asked him to arrive a half-hour early, so that he would have time to meet her parents—and although he had gone through the same drill with other parents, this felt completely different. Perhaps his jitteriness was due to their conspicuous wealth and the ostentatious environs of Schonansich Hill: he felt like a peasant calling on a princess. Most likely though, it was because they were Peggy's parents.

A queen among the commoners. Paul had once asked Peggy why her parents were sending her to Forbach Valley, since it was clear that, like her younger sister, she could have attended any private school she pleased. Peggy confided that her parents had practically pleaded with her to attend a prep school, but that she had insisted on staying in public school because she didn't want to leave her friends from middle school. When she refused to even consider private schooling, her parents went to work on her younger sister, Patty. There they succeeded, sending Patty to one of the most prestigious boarding schools in the country.

It was Patty who answered Paul's knock at their door, wearing her trademark sweatshirt and ponytail.

Almost a year had passed since he last saw her. Now fifteen, she was different.

Stunningly different.

Gone was the tomboy, the youthful lankiness, the gum-popping childishness.

In its place was a young woman: her golden-toned skin framing dazzling blue eyes, her hair blonder than before, her perfect teeth displaying an alluring smile.

Gone too were the baggy pants, replaced by short cutoff jeans from which extended the most perfectly tanned pair of legs he had ever seen.

Patty's flower hadn't slowly unfolded like her sister's—it seemed to Paul to have blossomed overnight.

Dumbstruck, Paul stared at her shamelessly, unable to gather his thoughts enough to speak.

"Hey, you're Paul, right?" Patty asked, flashing her impossibly bright smile at him again. She turned back into the house, shouting "Peggy, your boyfriend's here!"

"I'm not..." Paul trailed off, tongue-tied.

"You're not what? You're not Paul?" asked Patty, her sleek eyebrows making the cutest little furrow.

"No, no, I'm Paul," he struggled, "what I meant is, we're not... uh, that is, we aren't really..."

"Oh, I know *that*," Patty said, wrinkling up her pert little nose in a way that made Paul's knees weak. "I was just teasing you."

How can she look like this all at once? Paul wondered. *How can anyone go from scamp to goddess in the space of a blink?*

Her parents approached the door: Mrs. Forsythe displayed her own gracious smile, somewhere between courteous and charming. Patty turned and skipped away, her lovely long legs teasing him until they disappeared around the corner.

"Hello, Paul," said Peggy's dad, removing the brier pipe from his mouth and extending his hand in greeting, "Nice to meet you. My name is Jim, and this is Peggy's mother, Amanda."

"Hello, Mr. and Mrs. Forsythe," Paul said, shaking his hand and trying to match their refined smiles. "I'm so glad to meet you."

"Hello, Paul," said Mrs. Forsythe in her soft southern lilt, "it's so very nice to meet you, too. Peggy has told us so much about you. Come in and have a seat. I see you've met her sister, Patty. Would you like something to drink?" She turned to Peggy, who was coming down the stairs. "Peggy, be a dear and see if there's some lemonade in the fridge for us."

Peggy's parents and Paul crossed through the foyer—an impressive entranceway with a ceiling that rose three stories. The ornate winding staircase Peggy had descended was decorated with carved wooden railings and fluted posts that reminded Paul of a picture he had seen in art class of the Baldaquin at the Selge Ergen Kathedrale in Luxembourg. Their house spoke of money— lots of it... *old money*, not the kind sequestered in banks or vaults, but residing in land and possessions. In this house, thought Paul, you could be sure that the antiques *were* antique—not some artificially stressed and stained reproduction. And they were original heirlooms, handed down through the generations—not purchased at some Annapolis boutique.

Off the foyer was a library, larger than the living room in Paul's house. On entering, Peggy's parents sat together on a tastefully upholstered love seat, and they offered a matching armchair to Paul. He sat down and looked around the room, taking in the deep red mahogany paneling, the intricate patterns in the Persian carpet under his feet, the dark cherry wood bookcases rising two stories, neatly filled with leather-bound books.

"So, Paul," said Mr. Forsythe, leaning forward and tapping his pipe into an ashtray on a small, delicately carved three-legged side table, then reaching into his jacket pocket for his tobacco pouch, "Peggy tells us that you're on track to be the valedictorian at commencement. Congratulations! That's quite an accomplishment. How many students are there in your senior class?"

"Um, about four hundred, I think," Paul answered, wishing he knew the exact number to better impress them.

"Four hundred," repeated Mr. Forsythe, dipping his pipe into the bag, then firmly pressing the tobacco into the bowl with his thumb. "Very good. Quite an achievement. You should be proud." He placed the pipe in his mouth and reached around in his pockets for a lighter. "Where did I put that thing? Oh, yes. Excuse me just for a moment, Paul." He got up and exited from the room.

There was a momentary silence that Mrs. Forsythe quickly filled before it became awkward.

"Peggy tells us that you're a Crister, Paul," she said in her soothing cadence. "Excuse me, I mean a Cristic person. Peggy told us that you prefer to be called that. We have some close friends who are Cristers... I mean, who are Cristic persons. They're all very nice people. In fact, we had the Lewis' over for dinner a few weeks ago. They're Cristic. Do you know them?"

"No, ma'am," Paul apologized, "I'm sorry, I don't. Are they Methodists?"

"Oh, dear, I really don't know. Does that matter?"

"Oh, no, not really. It's just that if they are, they might belong to our congregation, and my parents might know them."

"You said the Medidists, is that right? Is that the name of your shrin?"

"Yes. Well, actually, we don't call them shrins, Mrs. Forsythe. They're known as churches."

"Yes, forgive me. I knew that, I had just forgotten. Shurshes, is that right?"

"More like church, actually. With a 'c-h' sound, like, um… like 'chick'."

"Churck, like 'chick'," repeated Peggy's mother. "So, your parents belong to the Medidist shrin… excuse me, churck?"

"What now?" interrupted Mr. Forsythe, returning with his lighter. "Are we grilling Paul about his religion?"

"Of course not, dear. I was simply mentioning to Paul that John and Louise are Cristic persons like him. I thought he might like to know that we have friends who are Cristers… I mean, Cristic persons."

"Yes, they're extremely nice people," said Mr. Forsythe, sitting back down next to his wife. "Frankly, I think it's great that the Cristic people have been able to do so well in our society." He turned to his wife. "Just look at Paul, here—he's a perfect example, class valedictorian! You always hear about the value that Cristers place on education."

He turned back to Paul. "You're a fine example of that, Paul. The Cristic people have contributed a great deal to this country. It's the whole Cristo-Rhettian ethic." He lit his pipe. "Western civilization owes a great deal to the Cristers. We should remember that."

Peggy appeared with a tray holding a pitcher of lemonade and glasses. "I had to make a new batch. It might be kind of tart… I ran out of sugar. Mom, where do you keep the big bag?"

"It should be in the pantry, Peggy," said her mother, rising from the love seat. "Excuse me, Paul. I'll go fill the sugar bowl for us."

"Wait a minute, dear, I'll go with you," said Mr. Forsythe, quickly standing. "Peggy, why don't you sit here and talk with Paul while we're gone?"

Peggy sat down on the love seat. Watching her, Paul felt that she had never looked more beautiful. It was so strange seeing her somewhere other than at school. She was wearing a tube top and low-cuts—appropriate attire for going to see battling rock bands, but totally at odds with the plush décor of the library. Paul became self-conscious of his own outfit, and he looked down at his baggy shorts and t-shirt. Peggy read his mind.

"Hey, don't worry about it. You look fine! They know we're going out to the concert. What are you supposed to wear, a tuxedo?"

"Maybe I should have. I don't think I did a very good job impressing them."

"You're not supposed to impress *them*. You're supposed to impress *me*."

She rose and crossed over to him, extending her hand to help him up. He stood and found himself face-to-face with her.

"You did just fine, for a Cristic kid," she said, playfully tweaking his nose. "I overheard part of what they were saying. I'm sorry about that… they really aren't such jerks, usually."

"Hey, it was fine. No harm done. They seem very nice, really."

"They are. They just worry about me is all." She winked at him. "But I can tell they like you. They're in there talking about you right now."

"Where, in the kitchen, you mean?"

"Yes, silly," laughed Peggy. "It doesn't take both of them to get a bowl of sugar! Let's just leave. You can thank them for the lemonade on the way out."

"Lead and I'll follow," Paul smiled. He meant it in every way.

And now he was following her to Fox Hunt, on her invitation. Paul pinched himself, just to make sure it wasn't all a dream. Life was good.

On the way home from school, he caught himself whistling the popular Mithran song, *Here Comes Chipper Fluffytail*:

> *Here comes Chipper Fluffytail,*
> *Scurries down the Chipmunk Trail,*
> *Hiding acorns—Mithran's on its way!*

Normally, he would have tried to switch tunes, but this time he let it flow. In just over two weeks he'd be going native, he told himself, and he might as well get into the swing of things.

When his mom got home from work he broke the news to her, and she immediately started fretting about his clothes, worried that he didn't have anything appropriate to wear to Fox Hunt. They would have to do a major clothes shopping trip that weekend.

Over dinner, his dad pointed out that the trip meant Paul would miss Cristmas at home. It would be the first Cristmas that he wasn't home with the family. Paul hadn't realized this when he accepted Peggy's invitation—it was so hard to keep track of when, exactly, Cristmas was each year. One year it might fall on Friday, Vintner 27th, another year on Sunday the 29th, and yet another year on Monday, Brie 1st. He felt bad about being away during the holiday, but there was simply no way he'd miss this chance to be with Peggy.

With the trip to Fox Hunt looming, Winter Break now seemed years away. *Winter Break.* It used to be called the Mithran Holiday Season, but the school board had changed it for the same politically-correct reasons that the Rhettag holiday vacation was now called Spring Break. If there was one thing that got Paul's goat more than the pretentiousness of the Rhettian holidays, it was the hypocrisy that accompanied them. By changing the name to "Winter Break", it was supposed to make the suspension of school days universally applicable—but of course it wasn't applicable, since the break didn't correspond to Cristmas: on years when Cristmas landed on Friday or Saturday, Paul and the other Cristic students had to take an absence from school in order to attend church and observe the holiday with family. Paul's teachers couldn't grasp the importance of Cristmas, or why he had to miss class immediately after a week-long holiday break. They considered it just a convenient excuse to extend the vacation for another day or two. His being Cristic wasn't so much a curiosity as it was a nuisance.

It had apparently finally dawned on the Clifton County school board that Winter Break wasn't inclusive, because last year the board decided to move the start of the holiday period forward to the Friday before Mithran Weekend. This shift meant that it now included the weekend after Mithran, so that when Cristmas fell on Vinter 27th or 28th, Cristic students no longer had to miss school. That still didn't leave any time for travel when Cristmas fell on Brie 1st, but most Cristic families stayed at home to observe the holiday anyway… it wasn't like the big Rhettian celebrations, with their extended family get-togethers and cross-country travel.

However, among some Rhettians this shift in the Winter Break holiday schedule produced a firestorm of protest. They complained that, even with Friday and Saturday off, it didn't permit enough time for long-distance travelers to reach their destinations by Mithran Eve on Sunday night. Paul wondered what place they were traveling to that they couldn't reach it in two days—though it was true that the airports became gridlocked at that time of year. With the fickle winter weather, many northern destinations could experience major delays or get snowed-out altogether. Still, two days seemed to him a reasonable amount of time for travel, and it was two days longer than Cristic families were given to get back home after Cristmas.

As with Easter and the Cristic New Year, Paul's friends couldn't fathom why Cristmas didn't stay in one place on the calendar like the Rhettian holidays did. To his friends, Cristmas was a cheap imitation of Mithran: the handful of Cristmas songs sung while lighting the little candles in the paper bags seemed copied from the Mithran tradition of singing carols around the bonfires, and the exchange of gifts on Cristmas morning was obviously stolen from Rhettag's midnight surprise visit by the Selgas bearing gifts. Even Easter's jellied eggs were simply aping the Mithran Acorn Hunt.

Paul smirked... *the Mithran Acorn Hunt—where a giant rodent known as the Mithran Chipmunk buries gifts and treats in large colorful plastic acorns in the snow, and Rhettian children clutching their Mithran baskets gleefully bound through the white stuff trying to find them—what kind of religious ritual is that?* Paul realized it had something to do with the oak tree used for the gabel of the Conflagration, combined with the notion of rebirth through the resurrection of Goseth after the Conflagration—just as eggs had become a Cristic symbol of the resurrection of Jesus. In fact, Paul was certain that the Mithran acorn was taken from the Easter egg and not the other way around, in the same manner that their resurrection story was copied from the Gospels. Replacing eggs with acorns was okay by Paul, if it made the Rhettians feel less like they were plagiarizing. *But this thing with the chipmunk prancing about hiding acorns with treats in them is... well... nuts! Thank heaven Cristic traditions haven't sunk to such silliness.*

But Paul realized that there was a method to their madness: by entertaining the children with the acorn hunt and rewarding them with candy and with toys, Rhettian parents were making the holiday that much sweeter. Again, this was fine—every religion strove to indoctrinate its children in the faith. But the problem was that there were so many Rhettians, and the practice had become so immersed in the popular culture, so completely commercialized, that Cristic children invariably felt alienated during the Mithran season. True, they celebrated Cristmas at this time of year, singing obscure songs in Latin around backyard trees, and they received some presents and treats on Cristmas Day, but Paul secretly missed not being able to hunt for acorns in the snow. Southern Maryland didn't usually have snow on Vintner 23rd, so Rhettian parents would simply hide the nuts around bushes and shrubs. But in years when there actually was snow on the ground, some of the acorns would be missed during the hunt—as the snow melted, one or two of the neighbors' acorns would migrate into Paul's yard. When he found one, he would sneak it up to his bedroom and pry it open, curious to see what sort of treats the Rhettian children were getting. But he never, *ever* ate the candy that was inside the acorn: he considered it taboo, almost sinful—not intended for Cristic consumption.

Growing up, he had tried his best to enjoy Cristmas time, brushing off the Mithran games, decorations, music, movies, television specials, advertising blitz, shopping mall glitz, community events and school-sponsored activities. And he would try to ignore the teasing by his classmates that Cristmas was just a copy of Rhettag. How many times had he heard the demeaning suggestion that Cristers could decorate a "Cristmas Bush" in their homes in lieu of the Rhettag Tree? It was useless trying to explain to a Rhettian that Cristmas traditions pre-dated those of both Rhettag and Mithran, and that the Cristic people had no interest in adopting Rhettian rituals.

Jews endured just as much ridicule from Rhettians for celebrating Chanukah at around the same time of year as Mithran. Paul knew enough about Chanukah from his friendship with Dave to realize that it predated Mithran by more than a thousand years—it even predated Cristmas by hundreds of years. So, who was copying whom? Was the Cristic tradition of lighting candles borrowed from the Jewish Festival of Light, just as the Rhettian bonfires had their roots in both Cristic and pagan traditions? It struck Paul as strange that the primitive and violent practice of torching massive bonfires might have its origins in the almost-quaint Jewish tradition of lighting small colorful candles or oil lamps in a gilded candelabrum.

If religion is evolving, shouldn't religious ceremonies become more refined, not less so? Perhaps there isn't any correlation—perhaps the birth of a new religion isn't a process of maturation, but rather one of repudiation. Maybe religious movements aren't the result of evolution, but of revolution. And like many political revolutions, these changes aren't necessarily for the better.

Still, it was important to keep an open mind. There was always some value in learning more about other religions. As much as Paul disliked Rhettianity, he was willing to shelve his prejudices and participate—particularly at a Mithran festival at Fox Hunt with Peggy.

What will Dave think about this? Paul wondered. *He knows I have the hots for her—he ribs me enough whenever Peggy hitches up with a jock... although he is kind of sympathetic. This will blow his mind!* Paul made a mental note to find Dave at school the next day and tell him about the invitation: to get his reaction, and his advice.

Chapter Four

Dave

Dave had always been the bigger kid. Even at the tender age of seven, it was apparent that the boy would grow up large—with his adult-size winter gloves and size 6 shoes, just as a puppy with oversized paws invariably grows into them. Paul's mother used to dread when Dave came for a sleepover, because it meant having to serve him breakfast in the morning. By the time Dave was finished—after his seconds and thirds on eggs, waffles, toast, melon and cereal, the cupboard would be bare. Paul remembered Dave once asking for another helping and his mother tossing up her hands in surrender, proclaiming that there simply wasn't anything left to feed him.

As boys do, their play would sometimes end in scuffles: not really fights, although they often resulted in scraped arms or knees and the occasional bloodied nose. But even with his greater size, Dave always wrestled fair—in fact, in retrospect, Paul was convinced that Dave had deliberately restrained himself to better level the playing field.

By the time they were sixteen, they made an odd pair: a bit like George and Lenny in *Of Mice and Men*. It wasn't that Paul was so small—he was average height and build for his age—it was that Dave was so huge: a giant lumbering frame with the slight stoop in the shoulders that large people acquire. And unlike Steinbeck's Lenny, Dave was anything but slow-witted. His mind was razor keen—always in high gear, seeming to effortlessly dredge up facts and figures from a bottomless reservoir of knowledge: a human encyclopedia. In high school he earned the appellation The Professor, awarded after one particularly entertaining, if unappetizing, discourse during lunch on the dubitable history of the hotdog.

Dave was the first one to get his driver's license, and with it the Gershwin's station wagon: a '66 Buick LeSabre Estate that he named Matilda… deep blue, with faux wood paneling on the sides and an impressive 350 V8 engine. His parents had replaced it with a new Toyota Hybrid SUV, but they kept the mammoth gas-guzzling wagon as the perfect starter vehicle for their son.

It was a love-hate relationship from the start: love because it was Dave's first car as well as the same age as him; and hate because, at sixteen years old and approaching 200,000 miles, everything was in need of replacement for the second time around, and Dave had to pour most of his earnings from babysitting and odd jobs into the car just to keep it running. But the spacious front seat fit his immense body like a glove… Paul couldn't imagine Dave being comfortable in anything smaller.

On those rare instances when Matilda wasn't in the shop, Dave would provide Paul with a ride to and from school. The wagon would announce itself coming up the street from the Gershwin house, both by the deep rumble of its V8 engine and the occasional backfire from the exhaust. The old car would backfire at least once during the ride to and from school, and each time it happened Dave would mutter: "Gotta get that fixed," though he never did.

Dave had exceptionally piercing eyes—a crystalline quality that seemed to look inside a person, not at them. This, combined with his immense size, could at times be intimidating. But more often than not his mop of light brown hair and ready smile was more than enough to offset his imposing form, and he disarmed his opponents with the strength of his words, not his brawn.

Though there was no question that he had the brawn. By age seventeen, he had reached six feet eight inches and two hundred-sixty pounds. Rumors circulated around the school that Coach Mayweather had practically gotten down on his knees begging Dave to try out for defensive tackle, but Dave had no interest in playing football. Attending home games with Paul, he would spend most of the time ridiculing the sport and the antics of the players on the field. Beefed-up bozos, he called them: morons in jerseys with pigskin brains. Even so, he enjoyed watching the game—cheering wildly for the team whenever it put points on the board. He may have possessed the size, the power and the speed to make the varsity team, but, like Paul, Dave's love of football was in the stands, not on the field.

Dave's dad—himself a strapping fellow, albeit not as massive as his son—had set up a weightlifting station in their basement. When the urge hit them, Paul and Dave would head downstairs to do a few reps on the bench press, mostly for fun. There was no problem with Dave spotting Paul, whose limit for a single press was around 180 lbs. Dave also limited his presses to 180 lbs. simply because it was the most that Paul could reasonably spot. Dave didn't break a sweat at one-eighty; doing ten instead of the normal five reps without so much as a grunt, and Paul would simply stand there with nothing to do.

As they entered the weight room one day over the summer, Paul noticed that there were three fifty-pound weights and one ten-pound disc on each end of the barbell. Counting up the total in his head and adding twenty more for the bar, he let out a low whistle. "Man! That's three hundred and forty pounds! Is that what your dad presses? That's a load of weight on there."

Dave shook his head. "Nah, that's what I five-rep. Actually, four-twenty is my max on a single-lift."

"Four-twenty! C'mon, Professor, you're kidding me. That isn't humanly possible." Paul paused. "Okay, let me see you do the three-forty."

"Sure. When my old man gets home, I'll show you."

"No," Paul insisted. "Do it now."

"No way," laughed Dave. "You can't spot me. That's just stupid."

"Oh, c'mon," Paul pleaded. "We're talking about a single rep at three-forty. You just told me you do five reps with that!"

Dave lifted his arms over his head, clasped his beefy hands together and pulled them down behind his head in a stretch. "Yeah, normally five. But my dad said I shouldn't do anything close to my max without him here, and he's right."

"It's sitting there, all ready to go," protested Paul. "You know you can do it. Just one. C'mon."

"You can't spot me. What if my arms give out? What're you gonna do? Call 911?"

"Look, I know that I can get it off you if I have to," Paul assured his friend. "All I need to do is tilt one end. And besides, it's not like I'm handling all of the weight myself. I know we can do this. Trust me."

"Nope. Don't think so," Dave said, heading for the steps. "Let's do something else."

"Chicken," said Paul.

Dave stopped, slowly turning around. "What'd you say?"

"I said 'chicken', you chicken," Paul repeated. And he started doing a chicken dance around the weight room, hands tucked at his underarms, elbows flailing, his legs doing an exaggerated high-step. "You're a chicken. Bwawwwk!!! Bwawwwk!!! Chicken Dave. Can't do the bench press. Chicken Dave. Can't do the bench press."

Dave sauntered over to his friend and reached out, grabbing Paul by the back of the shirt and, with one hand, lifting him off the ground. Paul's legs spun furiously beneath him.

"Chicken, huh?"

"Okay, prove I'm wrong. Put me down, you asshole."

Dave slowly set him down and walked over to the bench. He turned back to Paul. "You think you can spot me, huh?"

"Positive," said Paul, shaking his shoulders to settle his ruffled shirt back into place. "Go ahead and get on the bench. We can do this. Piece of cake."

Dave slowly stretched his large frame on the bench and ducked under the bar. He shimmied slightly on his back, positioning himself under the weights with his knees extended beyond the end of the bench, his feet slightly apart and firmly planted on the floor. He looked up at Paul, who had moved to the back side of the bar, his legs almost straddling Dave's forehead.

"You sure you can spot me..." Dave asked again.

"Yeah, yeah. C'mon and do it already."

Dave grasped the barbell, making certain that his hands were positioned equidistant from the center and directly above his clavicles. He re-grasped the bar to get a firmer grip, then took a deep breath, exhaled, took another deep breath and pushed up on the bar, freeing it from its cradle.

Paul whistled. "Wow, that is *impressive*, man. So far so good. Just take it nice and easy."

Dave slowly swung the bar away from the cradle, then began to bring it down toward his chest. His face reddened from the exertion as he lowered it in a controlled movement, keeping it centered over the upper portion of his pectoral muscles. The bar, noticeably bending from the weights, came to within a couple inches of his chest and remained there, suspended. His face turned a deeper red.

"Okay, Dave" urged Paul, "Come on and do the press. Bring it up."

Dave was straining. This was a lot different from how he looked when he was just pressing 180 lbs. Something was wrong, seriously wrong.

"I... can't..." puffed Dave. "I can't... push it up. It's like... my arms... are stuck. Help me... lift it up."

Paul quickly reached over and grabbed the bar with both of his hands, then tried lifting it. His face drained as he suddenly realized just how heavy the bar was, how impossible this would be. Three hundred and forty pounds! What was he thinking?! He strained with all of his might, trying to lift. He might as well have been trying to lift Dave himself.

"Hurry!" groaned Dave. "My... arms hurt! Help me... lift it... please! Help... me!"

"I can't!" Paul exclaimed. "Dammit, Dave... I can't do this! Dammit! I'm trying!"

The bar slowly lowered until it was almost resting on Dave's chest.

"Please!" Dave gasped. "Can't... I can't... hold it! Get help! Get help! Hurry!!"

Paul let go of the bar and ran for the stairs, whimpering in panic, his mind racing. Call 911! Call 911! Phone, where's the phone? Where the hell was the phone in this house?!

"Paul!" shouted Dave.

Reaching the stairs, Paul spun around.

In one fluid motion, Dave was cleanly pressing the bar up and placing it back on the cradle. Then he slapped his hands together and sat up on the bench.

"Whew!" he said, rubbing his hands together. "That was

damn exciting!" He gave Paul a wink and started to laugh. "You should have seen the look on your face, Four-Oh. Man, that was priceless!"

"You... asshole," Paul stammered, his head still reeling. "That was *not* funny. I really thought you were in trouble."

"Yeah, but you were there to spot me. You had it all under control. Nothing to worry about. Piece of cake. I certainly felt confident, didn't you?"

"Okay, I was wrong. That is a *lot* of weight on there."

"Yes indeedy. A *lot* of weight. More than *you* can handle."

"Some friend," muttered Paul. "You played me for a real dweeb. I bet you loved every second. You *knew* I wouldn't be able to spot you."

Dave shrugged innocently. "So, you bit off more than you could chew and got snookered. Hey, maybe there's a lesson in that, you think?"

"Yeah, there sure is. Don't trust your friends."

"Yeah," said Dave. "Back at'cha."

And they punched each other and shared a laugh, as friends will.

Paul was an only child, as was Dave, and because of this they turned to each other for the emotional support that a brother or sister could have provided. Since they didn't live together, there was none of the sibling rivalry and envy that can bruise a family relationship for years, sometimes forever. They had become the other's sounding board on almost every matter that affects a child of the suburbs: problems with parents; difficulties at school; moral dilemmas; even affairs of the heart. Being guys, romantic entanglements were never deeply analyzed, but even the nuances of a shrug, a grin or a few choice words could speak volumes about the wisdom of pursuing a promising relationship or the need to bail out of a potential disaster.

So it was natural for Paul to seek Dave's advice on his upcoming trip to Fox Hunt. He found the gentle giant drawing doodles in second period study hall, the day after Peggy had extended her invitation.

"Hey, Professor, got a minute?" Paul asked in a low voice, sitting down across from Dave. The table was vacant save for the two of them—no one else was within earshot.

"I got more than a minute," said Dave, rapidly scribbling over his botched drawing and slamming his spiral binder shut. "I got the rest of friggin' study hall. Wassup?"

"You will not believe what happened to me yesterday."

"You finally got laid?"

"Shut up! I'm being serious."

"So was I," retorted Dave. "It's gotta happen sometime. Law of averages. Somebody's gonna take pity on you at some point."

"Okay, yeah, I got laid. It was great. Now, you want to hear what really happened or don't you?"

"I'm all ears," said Dave, using his index fingers to push his ears forward. "Shoot."

"I got invited to Fox Hunt over Winter Break."

"Fox Hunt... the resort? Wicked!" said Dave. "Who invited you?"

"A girl."

"A girl?? Double wicked!" exclaimed Dave in a loud whisper. "Must be a rich bitch." He thought for a moment, then his eyes widened. "Not our very own Pegmeister?"

"The one and only," Paul said with a snicker. "Can you beat that?"

"Not with a stick! You lucky S.O.B! How'd you finagle *that*?"

"No finagling. It just happened. Out of the blue. Yesterday in the cafeteria... she said her folks told her she could take someone along for the ride, and she chose me."

"Get out of here!" said Dave, pushing back in his chair. "Is this a joke? This *is* a joke, isn't it? This is pretty lame. First of all, you don't ski, or at least I've never seen you ski. Second, no offense, but you don't fit the Fox Hunt stereotype, as in 'I'm filthy rich'. Third, girls don't ask guys out on week-long dates, especially if they aren't even hooked up yet. And... what am I at, fourth? Fourth, we're talking about Miss Peggy here... Peggy-I-Only-Date-Jocks-And-Only-Jocks-Who-Win-Championship-Games-Peggy. Neither of which fits you."

"Yeah, well, regardless, it did happen. But I need your advice."

"What advice do you need from *me*? *You're* the one who should be giving *me* advice, like, how do I get Cindy to ask *me* to go skiing for a week at Fox Hunt? Or even WinterGlen. Or even a day trip to Clifton State Park?"

"They don't have any mountains at Clifton State Park."

"Cross-country skiing, then. I don't care. Look, you've been handed a rare gift here. My advice is take the ball and run with it."

"Okay, that's good," agreed Paul. "I've been handed the ball, and I'm ready to run with it. I really am. But I'm scared shitless I'm going to fumble it somehow. Big time."

Dave scooted his chair forward and leaned across the table, whispering "You worry too much, Four-Oh."

"Can't help it."

"Alright, here is Uncle Dave's advice, since you asked for it. My advice is: enjoy yourself. Do *not* outthink yourself on this. Do *not* second-guess your actions, words, thoughts. Do *not* plan ahead. Okay, scratch that—you need to figure out what you're going to need for the trip, get the skis and stuff, so you have to plan *some*. But don't plan out the whole friggin' vacation. I'll bet you've done that already, haven't you? Planned the entire thing from start to finish."

Paul was silent.

Dave sighed in exasperation. "I *knew* it. Look, if you do that, I guarantee you'll be disappointed."

"Can't help it."

"Okay, granted, that's understandable," Dave consented. "You really like Peggy. We both know that. This is like a dream come true for you. Heck, it'd be a dream come true for anybody! I know you care a lot about her, and you don't want to do anything to screw that up. That's why you're sweating this right now. But listen, good buddy, I'm telling you—the more you try to prevent this trip from turning into a disaster, the more likely it's gonna happen. Just be you, go with the flow, and you'll do just fine."

"Go with the flow?"

"Go with the flow," nodded Dave.

Go with the flow, Paul told himself for the rest of the day whenever he started to think about the trip. He imagined being on the slopes, skiing down through newly-fallen snow like a seasoned pro with Peggy and her sister close behind.

Go with the flow.

He skis down the mountain, expertly cutting this way and that way, carving smooth serpentine curves in the fresh powder, feeling the crisp breeze on his face. He can hear the girls laughing behind him, trying to keep up. As he glides through the virgin snow, it begins to change, to shift, becoming a glacier, a massive ice flow, moving with him, pushing him along, faster and faster. A rumble behind him—he turns around, looks back up the mountain—an avalanche, roiling, a massive wall of white bearing down on him. No matter, he's a pro, he can handle it—just relax and go with the flow. It lifts him up—now he's on a snowboard, surfing the avalanche like a wave, riding it straight down the mountain. Then it crests, dumping him down, down, down. *Don't fight it, go with the flow.* He ends up on top of the heap, snow in his hair, his face white with the chilly stuff, but he's okay. He brushes the snow off his eyes, looks around and sees that he's tangled with the Forsythe sisters, skis and boards and poles and legs and arms all interlocked. They laugh—*such fun! Send another avalanche! Just another perfect wintry day at Fox Hunt.*

Chapter Five

Homey

As Paul stopped at his locker after meeting with Dave, he heard a familiar voice calling out to him from down the hallway.

"Hey, Paul! Gotta talk to you!"

It was Homer Wechsler, a junior who Paul had known since elementary school. Homey, as everyone called him, was a mousy little kid with big ears that stuck way out. This was accentuated by his perpetually close-cropped hair, shaved down to the nubs like a new recruit. Homey also had a bit of an overbite, with the habit of sucking his lower lip so that he had the appearance of a little rodent. But despite his physical awkwardness, there was something engaging about him—his mannerisms were almost comical, and he took the incessant teasing by classmates in stride. It was as though he enjoyed the taunts, integrating them into his persona.

Homey reached Paul's locker, dug his hand down deep into his front right cargo pants pocket and pulled out a gray, bent piece of metal. He held it in his open palm for Paul to see. "Look what I found on the street this morning! If it's what I think it is, it's pretty valuable."

Paul peered down at the small twisted object. "What do you think it is, Homey?"

"I think it's one of those steel pennies that we minted during

World War Two," the younger boy said. "It's the right size and the right color!"

Paul picked up the coin-sized object, turned it slowly around for a closer inspection, then placed it back in Homey's palm and shut his locker. "I don't think so, Homey. There's nothing on it."

"Duh! That's because it got worn down. Goze, it's sixty years old! What do you expect?"

"Even if it *was* that old, there'd still be something left... part of the date or at least a hint of Lincoln. It wouldn't be completely blank like that."

"Okay then, what do *you* think it is, Mister Expert?"

"A slug."

Homey looked down at his palm, incredulous. "A *slug*? No way! This thing is way too old to be a slug!" He stuffed it back into his pocket. "Well, I'm keeping it. Even if it *is* a slug, it's a really old one."

"Can't argue with that," laughed Paul.

Although a year apart, the two boys had become good friends, largely because Paul took pity on Homey. He was mindful that the frail boy needed a confidant—someone he could depend on.

Seven years ago, when Homey was a fourth grader, the other students at Hatfield Elementary had ostracized him for having "cooties"—a slang term that originally meant head lice, according to Paul's dad. It struck him as odd and a bit ironic that Homey would be targeted as having lice, considering that there was no place for the lice to hide on that almost-bald head. However, the children weren't referring to actual cooties, but rather to a "condition"—an intangible stigma that made someone an outcast, a pariah. Once a student was contaminated by cooties, no one could talk to them or risk any contact with them. Anyone who dared to befriend them would become infected as well.

Paul despised this brand of social conditioning so much that he finally resolved to combat it, despite the overwhelming peer pressure. He only saw Homey once each day: during a fifteen-minute portion of outdoor recreation when the fourth and fifth grade classes overlapped. During this play period, Homey would sit alone in a corner of the playground, isolated from the others. Paul knew the story all too well—that this kid had the cooties and hence was an *untouchable*. One day, he steeled himself and walked over to Homey's corner.

"Hey, Homey, that's your name, right?" Paul asked as he approached the little kid, who was sitting on the ground organizing loose pebbles from the blacktop's asphalt.

Squinting into the sunlight, Homey looked up at Paul. "Uh-huh. It's really Homer, but they call me Homey. Why are you over here?"

"Just wanted to say 'hi'."

"You better get away. You're gonna get cooties, too."

"I don't care," answered Paul, sitting down next to the boy.

"Well, maybe *I* care," said Homey, picking up his collection of pebbles and standing. He looked down at Paul. "Hey, I know you. You're in Miss Shelmeyer's class. You're a fifth grader."

Now it was Paul's turn to squint into the sunlight. "So?"

"So, I don't know what you're *doing* here. I got *cooties*. Don't you know what that *is*?"

Paul stood up, brushing the dirt from the ground off his hands. "Yeah, I know. It means you got a disease or something."

"Yeah, and you might catch it. So you better get away from me, like quick."

Paul folded his arms. "I don't care. It's not a real disease, anyway. It's all made up. Look, I can even touch you and I won't get it."

With that, Paul reached over and touched Homey's shoulder.

Homey instinctively drew away, slapping his shoulder where Paul had touched him, as if trying to wipe it off.

"You are *nuts*, man," scolded Homey. "They *saw* you do that," he said, motioning with his head toward a group of students in the distance, who were standing in a tight group pointing toward them. "Now you got it, and it isn't my fault."

"I said I don't care. And I know it isn't your fault. I'm the one who touched you. So," Paul said, trying to change the subject, "what were you doing with the rocks?"

"Oh, nothing," shrugged Homey, opening his palm so that Paul could see the handful of stones. "Just collecting 'em."

"Awesome!" Paul said, peering down at the pebbles. "What kind are they?"

"Not sure. See, there are a few different types. There are dark ones with white specks… I think those specks are diamonds. And there are the ones that are kind of red. They might be rubies."

The two of them spent the remainder of the playtime overlap sitting at the far corner of the blacktop, comparing rocks.

On returning to his classroom, Paul quickly discovered what it meant to have cooties. Word of his misdeed had spread like wildfire, and he was now *it*, one of the outcasts, infected by Homey. For the rest of the school day, the other children avoided him, pointing at him and speaking about him in whispers. At lunch, he ate alone, the seats around him vacant, like an invisible barrier.

After school, Dave came over to his house.

"Man, what did you do *that* for?" Dave demanded. "My whole class was talking about what you did with that kid on the playground. You must be crazy!"

"His name is Homey. He's a really nice guy. I like him."

"I don't care what his name is. He gave you cooties. And the guys in my class know we're friends, so now they think that *I've* got cooties, too!"

"Well, *do* you have cooties?"

"Of course I don't!"

"Do you think that *I* have cooties?"

"Of course not! I mean, I don't *think* you do. I mean, I don't even know what cooties *are!*" said Dave, exasperated. "But that doesn't matter, 'cause everybody says you've got them!"

Dave had, as usual, hit the mark. It didn't matter how they both felt about cooties, about Homey, or about each other. What mattered was how the rest of the students felt. The rule of the masses: pervasive, persuasive, devastating. Potent enough to bend myth into truth, to twist lies into fact.

And so there was nothing to do but allow it to run its course, suffering the jeers and taunts, the isolation, the humility. For the rest of that week, Paul did his best not to let it get to him, and to behave as if nothing was amiss. This proved almost impossible, since whenever he approached his classmates they would feign hysteria and run away, screaming about the cooties. But rather than chase them around on the playground like some rabid animal or break down into tears, Paul simply shrugged it off and pretended as if nothing had happened. Unlike Homey, he didn't banish himself to the corner: he walked where he wanted to walk and sat where he wanted to sit. If the others didn't like it, well, they could be the ones to move.

Dave was not so complacent. He had his own, more direct method for quelling tormentors, and he possessed both the acerbity and the muscle to do it. Any classmate who attempted to taunt him was quickly put in his place: buried under a torrent of sharp-tongued ridicule or confronted with the real promise of pain, and to a person they thought the better of it.

Because both boys didn't play the game the way they were supposed to, either by acting the martyr or passing the affliction on to another victim, interest began to wane. Within a week, most of their classmates had tired of the sport, and by the following Tuesday the hardcore teasers had also given it up. The rest of the school slowly followed suit until even Homey was deemed disease-free. By the end of the year, as far as Paul could tell, cooties had been completely eradicated from Hatfield Elementary.

Of course, there were always other forms of ostracism—with cliques being the most prevalent. But seven years later, Paul looked back on the cootie episode with a certain degree of fondness—not only because he had found a friend in Homey, but also because he had helped to quell, at least temporarily, the vicious cycle of victimization and torment.

Chapter Six

The Visitation

Homey was a puzzle.

Mousy, big-eared, buck-toothed. Borderline pitiful: a sad-sack, a bumpkin. As Dave called him, a *nebech*. Paul didn't know the equivalent term in Kristisch, though he was certain that there must be one.

But Homey wasn't so simple. It was true that he lacked self-esteem, and he seemed to navigate life with a dark cloud perpetually hovering over him, but he compensated for this with his vivid imagination: a talent for spinning tall tales and wild stories out of thin air. He could pull contrived facts and figures from the ether so effortlessly and earnestly that his listeners couldn't help but begin to believe them, no matter how far-fetched they were.

Even so, most of the other kids dismissed the boy as a pathological liar, and there were times when Homey's assertions were so outrageous that even Paul considered following suit. Yet he couldn't help but take pity on the little guy, and he felt an almost paternal obligation to befriend him. Truth be told, Paul found Homey's proclamations uniquely entertaining: they were a refreshing spin on the mundane, a unique perspective of the world through the tinted glass of naiveté and whimsy.

In Homey's world, the stream that ran behind his house was fed by a mountain spring high in the Pennsylvania Appalachians hundreds of miles away, snaking through the richest vein of gold this side of the Mississippi. Every now and then, a small chunk of the precious metal would be pried loose from the mountainside and wind its way down through the valleys of southern Pennsylvania and western Maryland, past Leesburg and Washington, then southeast to Clifton County, and end up nestled in the soft sandy clay of the stream next to his home for him to find and bring home and keep hidden in a small shoebox under his bed: along with the yoyo with the broken string from the '72 World Championships; and the silver police whistle that was used in stopping a real burglary; and the holographic Pokemon card that was the rarest one ever made; and the meteorite that he found in his yard after the meteor shower two years ago; and dozens of other priceless knickknacks, each with its own fascinating history.

Soon after they had struck a friendship back in elementary school, Homey invited Paul to play at his house: a modest two-story colonial nestled on a wooded lot in an aging neighborhood a couple of miles from Paul's home. Up in his bedroom, after shutting and locking the door to prevent possible intruders, he showed Paul his box of treasures. Paul felt privileged, since it was apparent that Homey had never shared them with anyone else. Listening to Homey's elaborate account of the discovery of the golden nuggets, Paul was convinced that they were, in fact, priceless. It was only months later, after chancing upon a book on rocks and minerals, that he realized Homey had found iron pyrite crystals and not true gold. In a way, Paul regretted discovering the truth about Homey's treasure: the fantasy had been far richer, so to speak, and much more captivating.

Since they were a grade apart, when Paul entered Broadmore Middle School, their friendship was limited to occasional after-school get-togethers and weekend play. The following year, with

Homey also at Broadmore, they saw each other a bit more often—mostly in the hallways between classes and in the lunchroom. Since Paul and Dave already ate lunch together, it became a threesome. Dave didn't particularly care for Homey—Paul surmised that this was partly due to the cooties episode causing so many problems—but it was also because Dave found Homey's fantasies more irritating than entertaining. From Dave's perspective, life itself held enough fascination: there wasn't any need to embellish it with tall tales. Still, he tolerated Homey's ramblings because he knew they tickled Paul—all in all, he considered it a relatively harmless form of fibbing. He limited his disgust to rolling his eyes and letting out an exasperated sigh now and then.

However, every so often Homey would spin a story that was so outrageous and so preposterous that Dave couldn't contain himself, and he would take Homey to task, refuting the lie point by point. Homey would just sit there expressionless, letting Dave's harangue wash over him until it faded into the distance. When it had receded far enough, Homey would resume his exaggeration as if nothing had happened, and Dave would go back to rolling his eyes and making deep sighs.

Two years later, when Paul and Dave entered high school, Homey was once again left behind at Broadmore. Paul missed his daily servings of hyperbole over lunch, and even Dave commented now and then about how boring mealtime was without Homeboy, as he called him.

When Homey entered Forbach Valley High the year after, he rejoined the pair at the lunchroom table. Perhaps the year-long hiatus had dulled their memory, but it seemed to the two older boys that Homey's tales had become even more bizarre.

He outdid himself one day in early spring of his freshman year, entering the lunchroom appearing extremely nervous. Standing ramrod straight in the lunch line, his eyes darted about as if fearful he was being shadowed. After paying for his food, he made an almost comical dash to their usual table and sat down with his back to the wall, so that he could see the entire room. After Paul and Dave had seated themselves across from him, he half-stood, scanning the room over their shoulders. Satisfied that no one was watching, he reached down into the lower leg pocket of his cargo pants and produced a small leather pouch tied shut with red string, which he placed on his lunch tray.

The two sophomores watched silently, curious. Certain that he had their full attention, Homey pulled open the string and tipped the bag. Out tumbled a diminutive, slightly yellowed statuette of a naked woman. She appeared to be kneeling, her hands cupped under her protruding breasts, as if offering them. The tiny figurine was very smooth and worn with time, although it was still apparent that it had been intricately carved. Judging from the amount of wear on its surface and the dirt that seemed permanently etched into its grooves, Paul assumed it was very old.

"What is it?" asked Paul.

"It is…" whispered Homey, pausing for effect, "… a succubus."

Paul and Dave looked at each other and let out a laugh.

"I don't call it my 'bus", but whatever," Paul snickered.

"What the hell *is* a suck-you-whatever?" asked Dave.

"It's a demon," whispered Homey, clearly pleased that he had stumped the two older kids. "A female demon. It's made out of something called soapstone. It's really old. And it's from the Middle East. My dad got it from there."

"So, what are *you* doing with it?" asked Dave.

"I kinda borrowed it. I'm gonna return it, honest. My dad's got a whole bunch of things like this that he's collected on trips, sitting in a display case in our living room. He won't miss this one. And anyway, like I said, I'm gonna return it."

Paul reached for the little figurine, but Homey quickly snatched it up and yanked it away.

"*Don't touch it,*" he hissed.

"Okay, I won't touch it. For crying out loud, Homey, I wasn't going to hurt it!"

"No, it's not that," whispered Homey, carefully placing the smooth, milky white statue back on the table so that it was kneeling in front of the two boys. "I'd let you guys hold it, except that it's got a curse."

"It's got a *what*?" asked Dave. "Did you just say what I think you said?"

"A curse," nodded Homey. "A real, honest-to-goodness curse. That's what succubuses carry with them. They've got strange powers. My dad once told me that this succubus is three thousand years old!"

"Three *thousand* years old?" scoffed Dave. "Yeah, right, Homeboy. I'll bet this thing was made in China, and your dad got it at some sex shop. It's probably made out of plastic."

"It's *not* made out of plastic!" protested Homey, "It's heavy! And look at the way the dirt's all ground into it. That's *old* dirt!"

Dave rolled his eyes. "Things can be made to look really old. And how do we know it's heavy? You won't even let us touch it."

"That's for your own good," said Homey, his voice back to a whisper. "I don't want you to get the curse."

"Oh, shut up about the curse!" said Dave, quickly reaching over and snatching up the figurine. He had a surprised look as he weighed it in his mammoth palm. "Hey, it really *is* kind of heavy."

"Now you've done it," murmured Homey, looking down at the table and cradling his head in his hands, "You've given yourself the curse."

"Yeah, right," said Dave, scrutinizing the tiny figure. "What's it do? Turn people into donkeys? Make all your hair fall out?"

"No, it's not anything like that," murmured Homey, his down-turned head still resting in his hands.

Dave placed the succubus back on the table and Paul quickly picked it up, examining the front. "Well, if you're both cursed, I don't want to be left out. Man, it really *does* look old. Three thousand years? Is that even possible?"

"Yeah, it's possible." murmured Homey. "I'm telling you, it's real. I don't have any reason to lie. I just wanted to show it to you. Now you've both gotten cursed. You can't say I didn't warn you guys."

"Okay, tell us already," said Dave. "What's this curse thing? Oh, wait, let me guess... we get to have *cooties* all over again!"

Paul elbowed Dave hard in the ribs. "Come on, Homey. We really want to know. What kind of curse does this suck-you-thing put on people?"

Homey slowly lowered his hands and looked up at his two friends. "It's a demon. The succubus is an evil spirit, and it lives inside this statue—it's like its home—for all the ages. And when it's disturbed, that spirit haunts the person who disturbed it. When you touched the succubus, you probably upset the demon, and now she's gonna haunt you."

"*She?*" Paul and Dave asked together.

"Yeah, *she*. Can't you see she's a she?"

The two 15-year-olds looked down at the statue, then at each other and nodded, bursting out laughing. Wiping tears from his eyes, Paul stood the figurine back on the table. "You said haunt. You mean, like a ghost?"

"Uh-huh. Like a ghost. Exactly."

Dave was rolling his eyes once more and sighing. "Okay, that does it for me," he said, rising and collecting his tray. "I'm outa here. Homeboy," he pointed to the figurine, "better put that thing away. We don't want her getting loose and giving cooties to the entire school."

The two boys could hear him laughing all the way into the corridor.

Homey picked up the diminutive statue and placed it back in the sack. "Maybe this was a bad idea. I really didn't want you guys to get the curse."

"You mean you really believe that stuff about a curse, Homey?" Paul knew better than to ask that: Homey fervently believed everything he said.

"Hell yeah. My dad said these demons are powerful."

"Okay, then I believe it, too," Paul nodded, not wanting to upset his friend. "You said this thing haunts people, but what is this curse, exactly?"

Homey shrugged his shoulders. "I dunno. My dad didn't tell me that."

"Well, what kind of curse did it give you?"

"Oh, it never gave me a curse."

Paul blinked. "Didn't you just say that it curses anyone who touches it?"

"Well, yeah. That's what my dad said. And I didn't touch it for years, because I was too scared to. But then one day I bumped into the display case and I knocked over some of the statues, and I put them back on the shelf because I forgot about the curse. And then I remembered about it, but it was too late, because I'd already touched it."

"So, if you touched it, how come you didn't get cursed?"

Homey shrugged. "I don't know. I was really scared for weeks because I figured I'd get cursed, but nothing seemed to happen to me. I think maybe it's because I touched some of the other statues when I put them back in the case, so maybe that made me immune. Or, maybe it was because I was kind of doing it a favor by putting it back in the case the right way."

"Or maybe," ventured Paul, "the curse has disappeared over time and there isn't any demon inside the statue anymore."

Homey shook his head. "I don't think that's it. My dad said that it can curse people, and he knows about this stuff."

Paul had no idea what Homey's dad did for a living, or whether he was an expert in such things, but he didn't question it. Demonology was idiotic, anyway. Modern Cristicism had done away with such foolishness. The tiny statue *was* fascinating, though—Paul had never held anything that ancient before, if it really was a few thousand years old. He wanted to see it again: to do a bit of research and learn more about it.

"Hey, Homey, do you mind if I take it home with me tonight?"

"What?" asked Homey, alarmed, "Are you *nuts*?"

"I'm just curious about it is all. Look, I've already touched it, so if it's going to curse me the damage is already done, right? Maybe I can check it out, learn something about these idol things, these suck-you... what did you call it?'

"Succubus. I don't know how it's spelled, exactly."

"Succubus," repeated Paul. "Hey, who knows—maybe I can figure out a way to stop the curse. Come on... you owe me that. If I can break the curse, you've got to let me at least try."

Homey bit his lower lip. "You promise to bring it back tomorrow? Gabel your heart and hope to die?"

"I promise."

Homey handed the little bag to Paul. "Put it in your pocket and don't take it out until you get home," he instructed, "and don't let anyone touch it! Believe me, you do *not* want to give anybody else the curse!"

For the rest of the day, all Paul could think about was the carved figure weighing heavily in his pocket. It felt larger than it had appeared squatting on the lunchroom table. Walking in the corridors, he was self-conscious, wondering if the protruding figurine was evident through his pants. He thought about the famous Mae West line—imagined her grinning at him and asking: "Is that a succubus in your pocket or are you glad to see me?"

Once home, he raced up to his bedroom and turned on his PC. While it was booting up, he took the figurine out of the sack and sat it next to the keyboard, then looked in the Webster's sitting on his desk for the name of the demon. After a couple of wrong guesses at the spelling, he found it:

succubus (suk' yoo bəs) n. *a demon assuming a female form, believed to have sexual relations with sleeping men. See incubus.*

Paul chuckled to himself. *That's it? That's the curse? This idol has sex with you while you're sleeping? What kind of a curse is that? Maybe to somebody like Homey, that would be a curse. Still, the dictionary did say a demon, and demons are supposed to be evil, right?*

He logged onto the Internet, went to his regular search engine and typed in s-u-c-c-u-b-u-s.

What he found fascinated him. There were thousands of hits based on what appeared to be a whole cottage industry built around succubae and incubi: some who claimed to be possessed by them, some who purported to *be* them, and still others who specialized in hunting them. Most of those who said they were possessed were petitioning for some form of exorcism, to be administered as quickly as humanly possible. Paul couldn't decide if these writers were serious, or whether they were playing some sort of intricate game. The entire succubae-incubi network was arranged like an elaborate ruse: the hunters were trying to learn more about those who claimed to be demons—who in turn were toying with those who suffered from their charms and spells—

who in turn were pleading for the services of the hunters.

The legend of the succubus was even more intriguing. While it appeared that almost every primitive religion had some form of spirit that engaged humans in sexual intercourse, the concept of the succubus and incubus—evil demons who employed sex as a means to gain possession of a person's soul, was specific to Rhettianity and Cristicism. The legend first became popular among Cristers in the Dark Ages and then migrated to Rhettianity as that religion gained prominence. These demons were Satan's agents, enlisted to ensnare the souls of the weak-willed through erotic enticement during slumber.

The notion of succubae invading the dreams of people—and of demons in general—had lost acceptance among the Cristic people over the intervening centuries, possibly due to the maturation of the religion, as well as its transition to a minority faith. But demonology remained strong in certain Rhettian sects, especially among the German Katolish. More than half of the websites devoted to succubus hunters were sponsored by Katolish pastors serving as exorcists. Paul knew that Homey was German Katolish... he wondered if Homey's entire family believed in demons.

He studied the tiny statue kneeling next to him on the desk top. If it was as old as Homey claimed, then it wasn't made to house a succubus, since the notion of succubae was only a thousand years old. It was a demon, perhaps—more likely a spirit. Possibly a goddess of fertility, judging from the pose. If Homey's dad told him it was a succubus, that had to be a more recent attribution.

Whatever, it looks ancient.

The figurine seemed to be inviting Paul to touch her ample breasts. He reached over and turned the statue so that it was facing away from him, being careful not to touch its chest. This was the first time he had seen the backside of the figure, and he was surprised at the amount of detail—the ridge of her spine, the dimple-like indentations at the small of the back, the smooth curves of the buttocks. There were even tiny toes on the feet poking out underneath. He thought about the ancient artisan who had carved the diminutive figure... what had inspired him—or her? Was the statue unique, or just one of hundreds of made-to-order idols? Was it a hobby, or a business? And if it was a business, perhaps there were countless identical statuettes—just like the scores of little Buddhas lined up on the shelves of the tourist shop in Chinatown he'd visited during a family trip to San Francisco last year. If that was the case, did any of the others survive? Were any of them also home to a succubus?

A succubus! Right... like I really believe that demon garbage!

He flicked off the computer, picked up the figure and placed it back in the leather pouch, pulling the string taut.

Need to get back to the real world. I've got a ton of homework—why am I wasting time on this?

That evening after dinner, a warm pre-spring wind riding the jet stream from the Gulf greeted Clifton County. Paul's father opened the upstairs windows, permitting the welcomed breeze to replace the stagnant, furnace-warmed air of winter. On these first mild days of spring, the house seemed to come out of hibernation, able to breathe for the first time since Vintner.

After finishing his last homework assignment and enjoying a nighttime snack, Paul showered for bed—glad that the air in the bathroom wasn't so cold, making the transition to and from the shower stall more pleasant than it had been for months. The breeze from the open window helped dry his body like wispy fingers stroking his arms, giving him goose bumps. He felt invigorated, full of energy, as if releasing tension from a coil too tightly wound. Spring was his favorite season—no doubt about it—

with its milder, breezy days punctuated by evening thunder-showers. The emergence of verdant new life and the myriad of blossoming colors… reds, blues, purples and yellows…

Pardon: violet and gold. Some colors were a bit overdone in the spring, and not by nature.

Climbing into bed, he remembered that his homework was still in the printer tray. He crossed over to his desk and stuffed the papers and books into his backpack, and was about to tuck in the small leather bag when he had second thoughts. Instead, he opened the pull strings and allowed the small statuette to slide into his hand. Bathed by the moonlight shining through his open window, the creamy white figurine seemed almost iridescent.

He delicately placed it on the desk next to his backpack, then climbed back between the fresh linen sheets his mom had put on his bed, replacing the flannels. The ticklish sensation of the lightweight sheets floating down, caressing his chest and arms, was delicious. The soft tepid breeze wafted over him, and his mind wandered from thought to thought—about New Year's on-ly a week away, and Easter three weeks after.

New Year's, then Spring Break. He thought about how nicely the calendar marked the change of the seasons. They were near-ing the end of Ilsembre, the month named for the Virgin Mother of Goseth that signaled the end of winter and heralded the new spring. Ilsembre was, of course, followed by Gosiery, the month of her son, and Gosiery 1st—New Year's Day, the Spring Equi-nox—coincided with the first buds and early flowers. This was soon followed by Rhettag, just as the flowers reached full bloom—the birth of their messiah tied to the seasons. Why, Paul wondered, didn't the Cristic calendar do this? Why was their new year in the cold of winter? And Cristmas—it was near the end of some Cristic month, he could never remember the name— why was Cristmas always in the gray days of late Vintner or early Brie? What sense did that make? Weren't Cristers supposed to be celebrating the birth of Jesus? Spring made a lot more sense for that. Although... since Easter was all about His resurrection, maybe spring was appropriate for that, too—with the concept of rebirth and all. But rising from the grave... that seemed more like an autumn kind of thing... maybe even the end of autumn... the winter solstice... like Mithran...

As the veil of sleep softly fell over him, Paul imagined a different world, where the Cristic holidays were moved to match the Rhettian celebrations. Cristers and Rhettians shopping for presents together... visiting each other's churches and shrins... distinct, but together, their holidays equal in status and respect. No more talk about copying their celebrations... no more accusations of betraying and killing their Lord...

Paul half-opened his eyes, looking over toward his desk, partially focusing through the blue-white lunar haze on the tiny figure kneeling toward him in her submissive pose. It was bathed in a soft halo of moonlight, which made it seem to levitate from the desktop, hovering slightly in the air. A tepid breeze through the window caused the curtains to flutter. In the corner of his eye, Paul sensed a shadow move... an indistinct, nuanced form.

He sluggishly turned his head to follow, but the figure remained in the periphery: a faint presence circling the room, teasingly just out of sight. Although he couldn't see it clearly, he could sense it strongly. It was a girl, a young woman. She stole silently around the room, cat-like, seeming to move in cadence with the windswept currents streaming through the window. He could sense her enticing, sweetly alluring essence.

He lay on his back, trying to catch glimpses of her in the periphery of his vision. She came to rest at the foot of his bed, out of sight... then, slowly, her sylphid form gently crept along his legs until she was suspended above him, her long tresses brushed by the breeze. In the dim moonlight he began to make out details: the glinting golden highlights in her hair; the radiant aura of her emerald-green eyes; the soft crimson curves of her full lips, glistening. He could smell her perfumed scent as she leaned towards him, the electric tingle of her lips as they caressed his. Her soft breath was intoxicating... its misty warmth filling him with a longing to possess her. He strained to meet her, to turn her caress into a kiss, but he couldn't lift his head from the pillow... it was as if unseen hands were holding him down. Nor could he raise his arms... they seemed leaden, useless. He felt completely helpless.

The nymph was in full control, pinning him down, slowly undulating on top of him, impelling him to glide in response to the gyrations of her pelvis pressing firmly against his. He was at once filled with fervent desire and fear, wishing nothing more than to be inside of her, to possess her, yet deathly afraid of her control over him. His body was straining with a yearning he had never felt before, all of his senses fully aroused, yet he was powerless. Heavy weights seemed to press down on his chest. He couldn't breathe, couldn't reach up to push her away. He began to panic, wanted to scream, to call for help, but he was paralyzed by the sprite's suffocating power. He felt as though he was going to drown.

Another breeze ruffled the window curtains, severing the spell. Freed from its grasp, Paul snapped upright in bed, his body shaking, sweaty. He could breathe again. In the far corner of the room, a hint of shadow slithered silently along the wall, then melted away.

The torment was now a memory. But it was real, as intensely erotic as it had been terrifying. Paul was sure of it, as sure as he was of anything.

For a long while he sat there, relieved that the ordeal had ended, yet trying to remember every terrifying moment. At last he got out of bed, crossed the room and gingerly placed the statue back into the leather pouch. He pulled the drawstring tightly shut and tied it into a knot, then placed the bag in his backpack and zipped it shut.

He went into the bathroom and inspected himself in the mirror by the light of the moon. He felt oddly different, as if something had been both lost and gained. He looked the same as he always had, but something was changed deep within... a passion he had never felt before.

* * *

"Well?" Homey whispered to Paul at his locker before class. "Do you have it?"

"Have what?" asked Paul, feigning ignorance.

"The succubus! I was up all night worrying about it. I think it was a dumb move, letting you take it."

"Here," Paul said, reaching into his backpack and handing Homey the small pouch. "It's just a statue, Homey."

Homey nervously placed the pouch into his own backpack. "Well? Did you see it?"

"See what?"

"The spirit!" he hissed at Paul, exasperated. "The demon! The succubus! Did it haunt you?"

"Oh, yeah, that," Paul nodded, placing textbooks in his locker. "Sure. It was, like, really wicked. All gnarly with scales and horns and blowing fire and stuff."

"Oh, man," Homey shook his head, crestfallen. "You didn't see anything, did you?" He sighed. "Oh, well. Maybe there isn't any demon after all." He pondered this for a moment. "Or else... maybe you didn't have it long enough. You want to borrow it again? Here…" he reached back into his pack.

"No!" Paul said, stopping Homey before he could retrieve the statue. "We'd better leave the demon alone. Besides, aren't you worried that your dad might notice it's gone? You better put it back where it belongs."

"Yeah, you're right. No use taking chances. I better get it back into the display case."

Yeah, you better, thought Paul, *ASAP*.

Chapter Seven

Dorbensheyer

Forbach Valley High School had switched to an alternating schedule at the beginning of Paul's senior year, which meant that classes met for double-length periods every other day. This method of structuring the class day was catching on throughout the state because it more closely matched the collegiate system, and administrators felt that staggering the classes provided greater flexibility for facilities use. Although Paul had heard some grumbling by teachers and students alike about the change, he preferred it to the old system: the alternating days eliminated the five-days-a-week monotony, and the longer classes allowed more thorough study of each subject. Plus, it permitted better preparation for the tests.

There was a downside, however, when the teacher was either a braggart or a bore—or both. In those instances, the extended sessions became a battle to remain alert. It was common to see several students in the more tedious classes resting their heads on their desktops, snoring away the final thirty minutes. Ten weeks into the term, Paul estimated that a quarter of the students in Dr. Richter's American History were either zoning out or completely comatose midway through each class session.

The staggered school days were coded Blue and Red to make it easier to remember the schedule. Today was a Blue Day, which meant that Paul and Peggy shared the same AP English class during Second Period. Seating was not assigned, and they usually tried to sit next to each other in order to engage in a whispered running commentary about their teacher, Ms. Beckworth. Beckworth looked like she was in her late twenties: word among the students was that she had taught third grade for a few years before transferring to high school instruction this year. Lacking any secondary classroom experience, her instructional style was textbook-stiff, and her lectures were recited from rote, like the memorized (and mesmerizing) soliloquy of a museum docent or vacation tour guide. Peggy's pantomime of Beckworth's mannerisms: her ramrod straight posture; blank expression; and mechanical flap of the mouth—were dead-on perfect, and at times Paul had to clench his jaw shut to keep from bursting out laughing.

That autumn morning, try as he might he couldn't hold it in.

Beckworth had the habit of carrying a pencil around with her as she paced in front of the class reciting the day's lecture. As she talked, she would tap the eraser end against the open palm of her other hand—but occasionally she would come to a point in her lecture where she had trouble recalling her mental annotations, and she would begin to tap the eraser against her forehead, as though trying to coax the information out.

Peggy mostly mimicked Beckworth's deadpan stare, which was funny enough, but this day she picked up a pencil and began to copy Beckworth's forehead taps. Combined with the expression, it set Paul off with a barely stifled chortle, the kind that can send milk flying out both nostrils during lunch. Realizing that her pantomime had hit a particularly funny nerve and sensing that Paul was dangerously close to completely losing his composure, Peggy played it to the hilt. Flipping the pencil around so that the point was now facing her, she tapped it against her forehead a few times and then pretended to accidentally jab it into her forehead, going cross-eyed and using both of her hands to try to yank it out.

When Paul burst, it was explosive: spraying the hair of the girl in front of him with spit and a loud *snork* that could be heard in the hallway.

Beckworth glared at Paul. "Mr. Fairchild, please step up here. *Now*."

Paul slowly rose out of his seat, doing his best to wipe the spittle and embarrassed smile off his face. He walked up to the front of the class still thinking about what Peggy had done, teetering perilously on the verge of another outburst.

"Now, Paul, why don't you tell the class what is so funny. *I* certainly want to hear it."

"It was nothing, really, Ms. Beckworth," Paul apologized. "I'm sorry for the outburst, I promise I won't..."

She was doing it again.

Beckworth was tapping her pencil in her hand. Paul instinctively looked away and his eyes fell on Peggy, who was furiously tapping *her* pencil in *her* hand, giving him her best Beckworth Frown.

He lost it again. In front of the class, in front of Beckworth, in front of Peggy.

Beckworth's face flushed pink with anger. Paul thought that he could even see the vein throbbing in her temple.

"Remove yourself from this classroom, Mr. Fairchild! *Now*!"

Paul stared at her. "You mean, just stand out in the hallway?"

"That is *exactly* what I mean! No—wait... come *here*!"

As Paul watched, completely confused, she marched over to her desk and started scribbling on a notepad. He meekly walked over to her. The classroom was completely silent, each student intently watching the drama unfold.

"Here!" she declared, tearing the sheet from the pad and

thrusting it at him. "Take this to the disciplinary office! I'll have *them* deal with you!"

"Seriously? The disciplinary office?"

"Are you challenging me, Paul?" she demanded, her face still livid.

"No, ma'am," he said, taking the note from her. Beckworth folded her arms and stood ramrod straight, watching him until he had exited the classroom.

This is beyond weird, Paul decided as he walked down the corridor, *but she's the teacher—unfortunate as that is.*

Paul had never been sent to the main office for a disciplinary matter before. Straight-A students simply weren't in the habit of earning reprimands. He entered through the large glass door with the etched word DISCIPLINE and handed the receptionist the note Beckworth had scribbled. The receptionist looked it over and then paged Assistant Principal Raymond Dorbensheyer.

Dorbensheyer was a nice enough guy—a tall, slight black fellow in his late thirties going prematurely gray, sporting a salt-and-pepper moustache and goatee—old enough to have dealt with almost every crisis that high school students could concoct, yet not so old as to be burned-out or jaded. He poked his head out of his office and motioned Paul inside.

"Hello, Paul, please have a seat," said Dorbensheyer, gesturing toward the cushioned armchair facing his desk. Paul noticed that he was wearing his signature gray shirt. Dorbensheyer always wore the same clothes every day—a light gray oxford shirt with button-down collar and striped tie, with dark gray slacks and pointy black leather shoes. Paul imagined that the man's entire closet must be filled with rows of the same gray shirts, gray slacks and striped ties.

The receptionist had followed Paul into the office, and she

handed Dorbensheyer the note along with a large manila folder, and then strutted back out the door, shutting it behind her.

Paul sat down, clasping his hands in front of him. He thought about the years of studying and effort gone to waste, his desire to maintain a perfect GPA, his dream of attending Dittisham College, all lost in a single outburst.

Stupid, stupid, stupid.

Dorbensheyer scanned the note, rubbing his forehead as he read it and muttering something about "Beckworth". He tossed it onto his desk and leaned back in his chair. "I don't think I've ever seen you in here, Paul—I mean, under these kinds of circumstances. Have you ever been sent here by a teacher before?"

"No, sir. Never."

Dorbensheyer waved toward the note. "The only thing Ms. Beckworth says is that you were disruptive. Not much for me to go on. Would you like to tell me what happened?"

"That's really about it. I guess I was disruptive. I'm sorry."

"Well, were you intentionally disruptive? Did you purposefully try to interrupt her class?"

"Oh, no, no, not at all," Paul stammered. "It was an accident. Really. I just started laughing about something, and I couldn't stop. I tried, but I just couldn't control it."

"I see," said Dorbensheyer, swiveling back-and-forth slightly in his chair. "So, you were sitting in her class and something made you start laughing, and you couldn't stop. Is that about it?"

"Yeah. It was really stupid, and I'm sorry. I wish I could have stopped, but I wasn't able to. It was just too funny."

Dorbensheyer leaned forward, clasping his hands on his desk. "*What* was too funny?"

Paul looked down at his feet. "It was nothing. Really. Just a stupid thought. It just seemed really funny at the time. It won't happen again, I promise."

"Come on, Paul, you can tell me." Dorbensheyer gestured around the room. "It won't go beyond these walls, I promise. What was so funny?"

"Well, it just doesn't seem as funny now as it did then. It just seems dumb."

"And that dumb thing was...?"

Paul sighed, realizing that Dorbensheyer wasn't going to let it go. "It's the way she taps her pencil on her forehead. And the way she talks, and her expressions. It's just really funny sometimes."

Dorbensheyer watched Paul for a moment, and then he leaned back in his chair again. "But, it's never made you burst out laughing in her class before. Correct?"

Paul nodded.

Once again Dorbensheyer studied Paul. "You're not the kind of student who likes to call attention to himself. In fact, my impression of you, Paul, is that you try to avoid being the center of attention. If I remember correctly, you had a small bout of stage fright a couple of years ago during the school production of... what was it... 'Twelve Angry Jurors', I believe. Isn't that right?"

"Yes, sir," Paul nodded again.

A small bout of stage fright... yeah, right! Why in God's name did I even try out for that play? It wasn't required—but I figured it would look good on my Dittisham application. A bit of padding.

The tiny Ivy League school prided itself on being a college devoted to liberal arts, rather than a wide-ranging university like Harvard or Yale. Paul had reasoned that a drama club credit on his application would be a feather in his cap—icing on the cake— not just earning him the coveted Dittisham Scarf that all incoming freshmen proudly wore, but possibly tipping the scales on the scholarship he badly needed. Just a small part—enough to get a credit in the program, enough to say that he had a speaking role in a high school play.

What was I thinking? I knew, deep down, that I'd freeze in front of that audience, screw it up royally.

"Twelve Angry Jurors" was an adaptation of Reginald Rose's classic teleplay titled "Twelve Angry Men", revised to make the production co-ed. Paul had landed the role of Juror Number Nine, a mild-mannered elderly man who deferred to the other jurors. It seemed perfect—he could practically mumble his lines and it would seem to be in character. Plus, the old man had less dialogue than most of the other jurors, and fewer lines meant fewer opportunities to foul things up.

Paul had read the script several times over, memorizing his lines before rehearsals even began. He attended every rehearsal, knew his blocking—which was minimal, since his character remained seated throughout most of the play—and practiced his delivery so many times that it became second nature to him. He was determined to leave nothing to chance: to provide zero opportunities to initiate a panic attack.

Final run-throughs went very smoothly, and the dress rehearsal came off without a hitch. Paul even received praise from Ms. Kincaid, the drama teacher who was directing the play, on his mastery of the character. There wasn't any way he could have prepared better for the role, or have been more versed in his performance. But deep inside him, there was a tiny little clock ticking away, counting down the days, the hours, the minutes, the seconds until the moment when the curtains would part and the stage lights would isolate him in their harsh glare and he would be called upon to perform in front of a crowd.

"I see you're maintaining your four-point-oh," Dorbensheyer was saying. He was glancing over some papers in the manila folder that Paul supposed were his academic records. "Weighted with your AP credits, it's actually closer to four-point-five."

He closed the file and pushed it onto his desk. "I'll level with you, Paul," he said, leaning back in his chair and clasping his hands once more, "I've been an assistant principal for almost five years now, and I was a guidance counselor for seven years before that. I get students sent to me every day for outbursts and for disrupting classes. Some of them are intentional, and some, like yours, are unintentional. But spontaneous laughter doesn't just happen. It needs something to make it happen. Do you know what that something is, Paul—what sets it off?"

Paul shook his head.

Dorbensheyer leaned forward and whispered: "An accomplice."

The assistant principal stood up, walked around to the front of his desk and leaned against it, crossing his arms. "I'm not going to ask you who it was, but I'm willing to bet that someone in that class was making you laugh." He cocked his head slightly and looked at Paul with one eyebrow slightly raised, waiting for a response.

Paul remained silent.

Dorbensheyer sighed, uncrossed his arms and rested his hands along the edge of the desktop. "Okay. I'm not going to do anything about this, because it isn't a major infraction. We all get tickled every now and then, and we all burst out laughing sometimes. It can even be healthy to have a good chuckle. However," he leaned closer to Paul, "with that perfect record you're in line for valedictorian. I don't know whether that's important to you, but it's fair to assume you take pride in your grades. My guess is that you'd like to keep it all A's. So, my advice to you, Paul, is that you try to avoid laughing at Ms. Beckworth for the rest of the school year, especially when you're sitting in her class."

"So, I'm not getting detention?"

"Do you *want* detention? I can do that, if it'll make you feel better..."

"No, that's okay. Never mind."

Dorbensheyer slapped his thighs and straightened up. "All right then, I think we've resolved this issue. I'll escort you out."

They left the office and walked past the now-empty receptionist desk. Dorbensheyer started to open the glass door and momentarily paused, as if suddenly remembering something. "By the way, isn't Peggy Forsythe in Ms. Beckworth's class?"

Caught off guard, Paul shot a glance at the assistant principal. "Um, yeah. Why?"

"No reason. You're good friends, if I'm not mistaken. She's a bright young woman, Peggy. And very funny, too... a great sense of humor. She's a good friend to have, and probably to share a laugh with," Dorbensheyer winked at Paul, "at the appropriate time and place."

He ushered Paul out. "Now get on back to Ms. Beckworth's class. You still have half an hour before the bell."

And with that, Dorbensheyer shut the DISCIPLINE door.

Weird, thought Paul as he headed down the hallway to class. *Definitely, completely weird.*

* * *

It seemed to Paul that Forbach Valley High had geared up more for this Mithran than in years past. For the past two weeks, a large banner had hung over the main office doors in pastel letters with bold type shouting:

Merry Mithran

Underneath in much smaller black print was added, almost as an afterthought:

also Kwaanza, Cristmiss and Hanuka

On Thursday, someone dressed up as the Mithran Chipmunk visited each classroom handing out plastic "all-holiday" acorns filled with erasers, school pins and other small trinkets. At the end of the week in Advanced Ensemble Band, there was a special guest soloist from the National Opera Company: a barrel-chested baritone dressed in a concert tux, who entertained the class with popular Mithran songs, including *Mithran Parade, Goseth Rhetter Has Risen, Here Comes Chipper Fluffytail,* and *We Thank You, Goseth, for the Gabel.*

Some of the lyrics were a bit hard for Paul to stomach, considering how they dealt with the Conflagration—and all that entailed in the collective blame and persecution of the Cristic people through the ages. As he sat there politely listening to the baritone's deep, resonant voice trumpeting these songs, he wondered why the school was permitted to devote so much time and resources to Mithran...

Chipmunk visits, the Mithran trinkets, and now this Mithran songfest. This is a public school—where's the separation of church and state? Okay—the vast majority of students here are Rhettian, but not everyone is. This amounts to coercion, regardless if they decide to call it a "Winter Fest" instead of a Mithran festival. This celebration of their holy day belongs in their shrins and homes—not in a public school.

As if in answer to Paul's musings, the soloist finished his last Mithran song. As he paged through his sheet music, he announced to the class:

"Now, some of you might know that during Mithrantide, our Cristic friends among us also have a holiday that *they* celebrate. Does anyone know the name of the holiday that Cristers celebrate during this season?"

Rhettian Dunkirk raised his hand in the back of the class.

"Yes, young man?"

"It's called Cristmiss," said Rhettian, mispronouncing "Crist" with a long *i*.

"Yes, very good," said the soloist. "That's correct. But they don't pronounce it like 'Crister'. They pronounce it with a soft *i* sound, as in the word 'grist', and the second syllable uses a soft *e* sound, as in—well, as in 'mess'. Can you all say it?"

"Grist-mess," said the class, and a few students laughed at the joke.

The soloist laughed, too. "No, not 'Gristmess'… it has nothing to do with a dirty flour mill floor—it's 'Cristmas'. At any rate, in recognition of their holiday, I have prepared a special Cristmas song. The name of this song is *Walk on Water, Baby Jesus*, and I would like to sing it for you now."

Paul was familiar with *Walk on Water, Baby Jesus*. It was an old Rhettian Negro spiritual, not a Cristmas song. It was sung in Rhettian shrins, not in churches, but the soloist's decision to include it in his arrangement seemed like a sincere, albeit misplaced gesture. The song, after all, was about the birth of Jesus, so it was appropriate for Cristmas. He listened to the baritone belt out the familiar lyrics:

> *When Mary had her baby boy,*
> *Jesus was his name.*
> *And everyone did shout with joy.*
> *Jesus was his name.*
>
> *Walk on water,*
> *Baby Jesus.*
> *Make a miracle for thee.*
> *Walk on water,*

Baby Jesus.
Make a miracle for me.

A carpenter he was by trade.
Jesus was his name.
From good wood was the crux he made.
Jesus was his name.

Walk on water,
Baby Jesus.
Make a miracle for thee.
Walk on water,
Baby Jesus.
Make a miracle for me.

That was the extent of the song as Paul knew it, and he expected it to end there. But the baritone continued with an additional verse:

He told us that he'd come again.
Cristen was his name.
The True Messiah we saw then.
Goseth was his name.

True Messiah,
Baby Goseth.
Filled with love for you and me.
True Messiah,
Baby Goseth.
Filled with love for you and me.

Paul was livid with embarrassment and anger.

Is that really part of the song, or did this guy tack it on himself? True—I've only heard the song a few times... perhaps that portion was left off. Not likely, though.

He sat silently mulling this over as the soloist went on to sing what amounted to consolation songs for Chanukah and Kwanzaa. He could see other students yawning with boredom at the songs, and he wasn't listening to the lyrics either: he was still debating the surprise ending to the spiritual.

In the end, Paul decided that it didn't matter whether the lyrics were part of the original song or not—either way, they were clearly inappropriate for a Cristmas song. He resolved to talk to the soloist about it after class.

He didn't have long to wait. As soon as the Kwanzaa song was over and the music teacher had thanked the soloist for his performance, the bell sounded. Paul walked up onto the stage in the student assembly hall where the soloist had performed.

"Excuse me," he said to the soloist, who was busy collecting his music sheets and placing them in a thin, dark brown valise. "I'd like to thank you for the concert."

The soloist turned around to see who was paying him the compliment. "Well, thank you, young man," he said, smiling broadly, "though I must state for the record that it was not a concert, nor even a concertino. But I appreciate the kind words just the same." He turned back around to his valise.

"I'd like to ask you a question about one of the songs you sang," Paul continued, "if you have a moment."

The soloist turned back around to Paul and looked at his wristwatch. "Well, I do have a shuttle to catch," he said, "but what is it you want to ask me?"

"It's about the Cristmas song you sang... the one about Baby Jesus," Paul said.

The soloist was now eyeing Paul carefully, sizing him up. Paul had seen this look before—the man was tagging him as a Crister. "Yes? What about it?"

Paul cleared his throat. "Well, you had said that the song is in celebration of Cristmas, but the last part of the song isn't about Cristmas at all."

"Why, it most certainly is," said the soloist, standing up straight in a defiant pose. "The song tells the story of the birth of Jesus and the miracles he performed. That, if I am not mistaken, is what Cristmas is about."

"Yes, it is," agreed Paul, "but the last part of your song was about the birth of Goseth, and that doesn't have anything to do with Cristmas. I've heard the song before, and I don't ever re-member hearing those lyrics."

"Well then, young man," snorted the soloist, "you have not heard the entire song. Those lyrics are part of the original spiritu-al, and I always make a point of singing the entire song, not just a portion of it. It is not my place to go about editing songs."

"But that's my point," said Paul, his face becoming flushed. "The song isn't a Cristmas song, then." He could feel his ears burning from nervousness. His ears had a habit of becoming bright red when he found himself in difficult or embarrassing situations. Aware of this, he became even more apprehensive.

"I frankly do not understand what your fuss is about, young man," said the soloist, sensing Paul's anxiety. "That spiritual is an old, time-tested, highly-respected song by all people—Cristers as well as Rhettians. It tells of the baby Jesus, the miracles he per-formed, and his foretelling of the return of the True Messiah in Goseth Rhetter, as it says in the Bible. In fact, I would say that it is a uniquely Cristic song in that regard."

"But that's my point," Paul repeated. "In Cristicism, it's Jesus who will return—not Goseth or anyone else."

"I think," said the soloist, "that you need to reread your Bible, young man. At any rate, I am not going to debate religion with you. As I mentioned, I have a shuttle to catch. If you cannot appreciate my having sung that lovely and, I think, inspirational song in celebration of Cristmas, I am genuinely sorry for that. Now if you will kindly excuse me, I really must be going."

With that, the soloist strode off the stage and up the aisle toward the music teacher, who was standing in the doorway at the back of the auditorium. Paul stood on the stage watching the silhouette of the two men, and it appeared that the soloist gestured back toward him. Then the two men disappeared down the hallway. What the soloist might have said to his teacher, Paul didn't know, nor did he care.

Useless.

Why did I even approach the jerk—what in hell did I hope to accomplish? The fact that the idiot even chose that song and sung those lyrics proves that he doesn't understand or care about Cristmas, or about Cristicism for that matter.

Pointless.

The lyrics of the song plagued Paul for the rest of the day. That evening, he logged online and did a search for the lyrics to *Walk on Water, Baby Jesus*. There were a number of sites posting lyrics for the song, none of them the same. Paul figured this was to be expected, since it wasn't a recent, copyrighted song: it had been handed down orally through the generations, and variations were bound to happen. But less than half the sites had lyrics about Cristen, Goseth, and the "True Messiah"—and these were mostly fundamentalist Rhettian sites where *everything* was tied to Rhetter. So, the question remained: were those lyrics part of the original spiritual, or had they been added by whoever wrote the sheet music? After an hour paging through contradictory information, Paul let out a long sigh.

I'll probably never know... and what does it matter, anyway? If that clown feels like adding the lyrics, what's stopping him? He just shouldn't have introduced it as a Cristmas song. Besides, I've got more important matters to attend to.

It was Saturday, the 20th of Vintner, the day before he headed to Fox Hunt with Peggy and her family, and there was packing to do. Lots of it—he was going to be gone for a week. He loaded his bags with the brand-new designer clothing that his mom had helped him pick out at the mall. Trying on the cable-stitch wool sweaters and the pleated, pressed dress khakis with the cuffs, he had felt like he was prepping for an ad in GQ. Even his shoes were new. And argyle socks! Other guys at the lodge had better be wearing argyles, or Paul would never forgive his mom.

That night, Paul couldn't sleep.

He lay in bed thinking about Dorbensheyer's parting comment earlier in the week. *How could he have known about Peggy and me? Was it just an educated guess on his part— to test my reaction? Or does Dorbensheyer know more than he lets on? And if he does know— how? Teacher reports? Student gossip? Cameras in the classrooms and around the school? Maybe the guy's clairvoyant... maybe he has super-natural powers.*

Supernatural powers. Paul's thoughts wandered to that warm, windswept spring night two years ago and the still-fresh memory of the sensual, terrifying encounter with the succubus. He wondered what would have happened if he had kept the statue a bit longer. *Would my dreams have become increasingly erotic, terrifying? Could I have learned to control the fantasy—finally defeating the spirit and becoming its master... or would I have fallen deeper under its spell, until I couldn't separate fantasy from reality—becoming so fixated over the statue that I ended up with some debilitating dementia? Dementia...* Paul smiled slightly as he drifted off to sleep... *maybe that's what happened to Homey... maybe he's handled one too many of his father's demons...*

Chapter Eight

Rhettianity

The occultism that had flourished in Cristendom during the Dark Ages, fostering such notions as demons and succubae, helped create the conditions that led to the acceptance of a new messiah and the rise of Rhettianity. Just as the Essenes in Judea laid the groundwork for the arrival of Jesus of Nazareth by embracing messianic prophesies, the weighty mysticism and apocalyptic doctrines of an expanding Franciscan Order in central Europe paved the way for Goseth's ascension.

Having grown up in America, Paul knew quite a bit about Rhettianity, its history and its teachings—such was the degree of inculcation by the media, the schools and peers. Plus, he had done a considerable amount of research on his own—both in the library and on the Internet, learning many of the religion's details. Some might have termed it an obsession, but Paul saw it more as a matter of survival in a Rhettian world.

He had read about their Blessed Mother, the Virgin Ilsa. Unlike the Cristic Mary, Ilsa was a true virgin in every sense—never married, never touched by a man—flawless, immaculate and pure when she was caressed by God. Paul knew about the miraculous conception of the twins, Goseth and Cristen, and their sacred nativity under a lean-to on the banks of the River Moselle near the little town of Remich in the late Middle Ages, at the southeastern edge of the Duchy of Luxembourg—originally called *Lucilinburhuc*, though Paul had no idea how to pronounce it. At the time of their birth, the same star that had heralded the birth of Jesus appeared in the sky, and the Four Sages had traveled toward the light from the four corners of the earth in a second Epiphany, to present Goseth—and only Goseth—with gifts of gold, frankincense and deep violet myrrh.

He knew about the twins being raised by Ilsa and her brother, Selge Edel—duly rewarded by the Shrin for his selfless devotion as the first Devotee of Goseth to be canonized. Rhettians believed that the twins had a direct lineage to King David, fulfilling the ancient Jewish prophesies. But while Goseth was blessed by God, born immaculate and vested with the Spiritus Sanctus, his brother Cristen was born with mortal sin: his jealousy of Goseth ultimately leading to his brother's martyrdom, and to his own downfall.

Paul knew how Goseth's birth was presaged by the Great Famine that had gripped Europe for seven years. He knew about the legend of the despotic Pope John XXII, warned by Cristic clairvoyants at his papal palace in Avignon of the birth of a usurper in the Saar Valley near the French border, who would rise to challenge the supremacy of the Church. The evil pope, blinded by fear and rage, had ordered the death of all male children throughout the south of Saarland in a futile attempt to destroy the new Messiah.

Alerted to the imminent massacre of innocents, Ilsa and Edel fled north with the twins to the small town of Trier, just outside the dragnet of Pope John's soldiers. For more than a decade, the twins remained in hiding, until the death of John XXII in 12 JH.

In fulfillment of the prophesy, when Goseth was sixteen he revealed himself to be the Messiah, and along with this came the revelation that Cristen was the returned Crist—the fallen original son of God who, though he had failed to herald in the New Order, served as the necessary catalyst for the arrival of the True Messiah. In the ensuing years, Cristen made a sizable fortune in league with Adolph of Nassau, the Holy Roman Emperor, mining silver from the Odenwald mountains in southern Hesse. But Goseth, when he was twenty years old, enraged Cristen by entering the Great Cathedral of Speyer and persuading the Cristic silvermongers—who were using a portion of the church to mint currency for the Emperor and to serve as a treasury for the coinage—to abandon their wickedness and follow him. That led to a titanic battle between the two brothers, ending in the banishment of Cristen, who fled with his treasure to the fortress of Avignon in neighboring France, allying himself with the newly-coronated Pope Clement VI.

This was a time of social and political upheaval throughout central Europe, caused by centuries of conflict—first between the Normans and the Anglo-Saxons, then between the Anglo-Normans and latter-day Franks—that splintered most of the continent into warring nation-states that had coalesced around the remnants of the feudal fiefdoms. It was also the time of the Black Death: the bubonic plague that left tens of millions dead in its wake as it spread across Europe —transmitted by the fleas of vermin-infested Cristic cities and towns. The Cristers, however, blamed the malady on the Jews—accusing them of poisoning the well water—and they destroyed hundreds of Jewish villages in revenge. When the slaughter of these innocents didn't stem the tide of death, the Cristic people began to attribute the ravages of the disease and the seven-year famine that had preceded it to a wrathful God, and many of them began to openly question their faith. According to many biblical scholars, the very public trial of the German mystic heretic Meister Eckhart by the Catholic Church in 6 VR was the catalyst for the widespread break with the Church in Germany. Eckhart had been a forceful proponent of individual determination, and many of the people who had suffered the twin devastations of famine and plague took this to heart.

It was at the zenith of this doubt and despair that Goseth left his childhood home in the ancient town of Trier and began traveling throughout the Saar region, miraculously curing those Cristers who embraced him as the Deliverer, reborn through His Second Coming. News of these miracles and of Goseth's escalating following eventually reached his evil brother in Avignon. Cristen blamed his mother, the Virgin Ilsa, for both his own ill fate and Goseth's prosperity, accusing her of having conspired with Goseth against him.

With Pope Clement's tacit blessing, Cristen traveled north to Normandy, where he collaborated with the Elders of Rouen and the vestiges of the Danish Vikings to lead an army of Norsemen to invade Luxembourg in order to capture Ilsa. He apprehended his mother, selling her to the Norsemen for a mere twenty pieces of silver, watching from the shadows as they savagely brutalized her to force a confession of her complicity to venerate Goseth as the Messiah Returned. Suffering great agony and in the throes of death, the sweet Mother of God embraced her son Goseth as the one True Rhetter, and she died whispering his name in prayer.

Cristen then led his army of Norse plunderers, in league with French Cristic King John II, to arrest his brother in Aachen. Goseth was charged with heresy—mercilessly whipped and beaten to coerce him to renounce his messianic claims. When that failed, Goseth was forced by Cristen to hew a large Y-shaped stake from the trunk of an oak, known as The Gabel, and then humiliated by the town's Cristers as he dragged the massive gabel through the streets of Aachen, where it was erected in the town square. The mob of bloodthirsty, vengeful Cristers continued to mock Goseth as he was nailed to the gabel, surrounded by four criminals: The Liar, The Thief, The Scoundrel, and The Traitor. Viewed from above, the extended arms of the gabels formed the shape of a crux, thereafter synonymous with crime and corruption.

The Cristers celebrated throughout the night as Goseth hung there in agony, his life slowly ebbing away. In the early dawn, as Goseth was close to death, the drunken mob once more burst into dance as the Norsemen lit the stacked wood below the gabel and Goseth was slowly consumed by the fire.

Mounted on his horse, Cristen had watched the lighting of the fire and the burning of his brother. During the Conflagration, a large ember exploded, startling Cristen's horse, which bucked and flung the wicked brother into Aachen's large baptismal font, breaking Cristen's neck and drowning him in its shallow waters. Cristen's dying breath turning the Crister's "holy water" fetid and poisonous for eternity. Witnesses to the Conflagration swore that the Virgin Ilsa had appeared in an apparition formed by the smoke around Goseth as his spirit was released, her vaporous arms embracing him with the tender love of a mother for her dying child, and her image then rose to the heavens, carrying Goseth's soul with her.

Seven days after his conflagration, Goseth appeared before the Eleven Devotees suspended upon twin pillars of swirling smoke, promising to return in a third and final incarnation to deliver True Believers to the gates of Heaven after the Final End of Days and the Judgment of Souls.

To Cristers, of course, this was all nonsense. In fact, it was far more than that—it was blasphemy of the worst kind—not only an affront to their Crist, but also justification for the ensuing centuries of persecution at the hands of Rhettians. To Paul, the Story of Goseth was just that: a story. A legend. An allegory for the apocalyptic tenets of Rhettianity, which in turn was a way to rationalize the horrors of the Great Famine and the Bubonic Plague, the humiliating defeat and societal fragmentation of the late Crusades, the ensuing invasion and pillaging from the Scandinavian north, as well as a litany of incomprehensible hardships throughout an unstable and fitful post-feudal Europe.

The first of the Lorswers were codified two generations after Goseth's death. Since there weren't any contemporary accounts of his life, it was quite possible that there never was a Goseth—or a Cristen or Ilsa, for that matter. It stood to reason that these characters were created by the nascent Shrin through a merging of Norse and Cristic canon. The Rhettian saga of the emergent enmity between Goseth and Cristen had links to the mythic rivalry between two scions of Odin: the faithful Baldur and mischievous Loki. Plus, there was the ancient tale of animosity between Cain and Abel in Genesis—a rivalry that ended in fratricide. The entire narrative of Goseth's immaculate birth, his escape from a murderous tyrant and his sacrificial death corresponded so closely to the story of Jesus that Cristers considered it a blatant case of plagiarism. To Rhettians, however, the similarities made perfect sense: since Goseth was the re-emergence of the Crist, albeit in a more perfect form, his martyrdom would have followed a similar path. The obvious parallels in the two stories only buttressed their conviction that it was ordained by God: a Divine Sequel that was pointedly more profound and heart-rending than its precursor.

Suggesting that Goseth was fictitious was futile: Rhettians would have none of it, citing numerous references in the Cristic Gospels that, they claimed, both foretold and verified his existence. All of the tracts they quoted were at most vague allusions to a new messiah—but that hardly mattered, since the version of the Gospels used by Rhettians was a corruption of the Cristic original, perverted to conform to Rhettianity's version of events.

When asked why there were no contemporary references to Goseth, the Rhettians had an answer for that as well: since almost all of the manuscripts were penned by Cristic scribes, they would have been forbidden to identify the new messiah by name. At any rate, his name wouldn't have been "Goseth", but rather Yosef, which dovetailed nicely with the Rhettian belief that the returned messiah was a descendent of David, and thus kin of Yeshua (Jesus).

Ever since the time of Goseth, Rhettians had collected a host of tangible evidence of Rhetter's earthly existence—as well as his eleven martyred Devotees—in countless shards of burnt bone, singed shreds of cloth and even strands of hair that filled reliquaries in thousands of shrins throughout Europe. Paul read one skeptic's calculation that, even if one-tenth of the holy relics ascribed to Goseth were real, added together they provided "proof" that Rhetter was eighteen feet tall and weighed three tons. It was true that early Cristers had also collected and venerated relics of their saints, but that practice ended soon after the rise of Rhettianity—their adoration serving as a magnet for Rhettian contempt and retribution. Virtually all of these Cristic relics had been destroyed in pillages and pogroms over the centuries.

Even if one were inclined to believe that Goseth had existed, there were many possible explanations for his eminence: perhaps he was a devout and learned priest who had tried to spread the Gospels, only to have been mistakenly elevated by his followers to messianic status. Faced with the ravages of the plague, thousands of Cristers had embraced a virulently apocalyptic form of Cristicism, fixating on the Second Coming of the Messiah. Goseth may have been worshiped out of desperation by this rapidly growing cult, in self-fulfillment of the prophesy.

Or perhaps Goseth was one of the hundreds of false messiahs traversing Europe during the social and spiritual chaos of the Dark Ages: a madman who was convinced that he was in fact the Messiah returned, and something about his personality — possibly a natural charisma — fostered a following among the most destitute and desperate.

Then again, it could have been something more nefarious: perhaps Goseth was a sort of Rasputin — a scheming mystic who took advantage of the hysteria of the age to don the mantle of the Second Messiah in order to gain prestige and power. Perhaps his plan went awry when he became too powerful too quickly and caught the attention of the Norse army in Aachen, leading to his arrest and execution. In an ironic twist, they had underestimated the fervent effect Goseth's martyrdom would have on the cult he created, causing it to spiral out of control.

Or perhaps he was neither mad nor evil, but had intentionally and meticulously plotted his own demise based on the Cristic prophesies, cementing his immortality as the True Savior.

Whatever the true story of Goseth, his followers rapidly grew in number as the Black Death subsided and people attributed its decline to their adoration of Goseth as the Messiah Returned. His followers originally called themselves the Kristenzian (New Cristers), but this soon changed to Rhettians, from the German *Retter*, meaning "savior". Paul had read that the original name of Rhettag was *Rettertäg* — German for "Day of the Savior" — but it was Anglicized to Rhettag centuries ago, as had most of the original Germanic and Scandinavian terms.

The "New Cristers" adopted the burning gabel as their symbol, representing the Y-shaped hewn oak trunk that Goseth had been nailed to for his burning — the massive bonfires held at Mithran still spectacular memorials to this terrible event. Paintings and sculptures of the Conflagration of Goseth were idolized in their shrins. Carved into the gabel near the top of each branched stem were two pairs of letters: "YT" and "KK", which together stood for *Yosef på Trier / Kongen Kristen*: Norse for "Goseth of Trier, King of the Cristers." According to Rhettian legend, these were the words uttered by Goseth's captors as he burned on the gabel. This acronym and the phrase "King of the Cristers"—a concept stolen from (Rhettians would say in fulfillment of) the account of the crucifixion of Jesus in the Gospel of John, appeared not only in Rhettian paintings and sculptures of the Conflagration, but also on the covers of their bible. It was sung in their Rhettag and Mithran carols. It was even printed on their calendars and wedding reception napkins. And it was emblazoned in mammoth letters over their altars in their shrins. It was impossible to measure how much pain this mocking phrase had caused Cristers over the centuries—not only for the perverse implication that Cristers considered Goseth their "King"—but also for its humiliation of Cristicism.

The branching, Y-shaped arms of the gabel were everywhere: not only atop the spires of every shrin, as well as in their statues, paintings, and stained glass windows—but also on banners and currencies, billboards and posters, necklaces and bracelets, bedspreads and bath towels—even leather boots and motorcycle jackets. And, of course, the gabel served as the universal grave marker. The five gabels of Aachen—with the much taller, central one for Goseth painted white and dominating the other four— were everywhere. It was impossible to drive down an interstate without seeing this multi-story arrangement erected on some commanding hilltop, particularly in rural areas.

Natural gabel shapes were given religious significance: such as the Mountain of the Holy Gabel in Wyoming with its Y-shaped glacier, and the so-called Southern Gabel constellation, visible in the southern hemisphere and featured prominently on the flags of New Zealand and Australia. In North America, Canada geese formations—when there were several leaders in a row and it looked more like a gabel than a "V"—was interpreted as a harbinger of good fortune. For all Paul knew, perhaps every Rhettian saw it as a sign from God.

The American Red Gabel Association used it as their symbol: the bright red logo with its three short arms synonymous with emergency services and first aid. Paul knew that there was a small, independent Cristic-operated disaster response organization called the Red Crux that had petitioned for years to have its own symbol—a simple red crux with four equal arms—included with the International Red Gabel and the Islamic-based International Red Crescent, without success. The American Red Gabel chapter had been amenable to adding the crux, but both the IRG and IRC were dead set against it, arguing that adding another emblem would only cause confusion. Paul knew the real reason for its exclusion: these international organizations considered the crux to be an inappropriate symbol for aid and comfort, tied as it was to the Four Criminals of Aachen.

In fact, the Cristic Crux, along the Jewish Star of David, were considered so *mal à propos* at Rhettagtime that they all but disappeared. Even the most innocent, natural incarnations of four- and six-armed shapes were queerly converted into gabels for the duration of the holidays. Stars that were normally depicted with four or six points became three-pronged to mimic the heraldic Star of Remich that had shone down on the twin's birthplace. During the Rhettag holiday marketing blitz, even the four-petal crux-shaped flowers of the dogwood tree, with their deep red-tinted edges that many Cristers associated with Jesus' crucifixion, were redrawn with only three petals, just as it was on the Holiday Tissue Box in Paul's bedroom.

Crux bad : gabel good.

Even grotesque gabels.

Sculptures of the conflagration of Goseth—his martyrdom on the gabel—were known as conflagraphs, and some of these were so detailed that they portrayed the burning flesh peeling from Goseth's feet and legs, to better convey the suffering he had endured for all humanity: a conflagration of suffering far more excruciating and profound than the crucifixion of Jesus. After all, Rhettians invariably pointed out, not only was Goseth crucified—he was also burned alive. To their way of thinking, Jesus was second fiddle in the quest of Suffering for Mankind: a warm-up act to the real thing. It struck Paul as a sort of one-upmanship in messianic martyrdom: our Savior suffered more than your Savior.

In truth, some of the depictions of Goseth on the Gabel were beautiful, created by the greatest craftsmen the art world had ever known. Many of the paintings and sculptures of the Late Renaissance and Baroque were unmistakable masterpieces, capturing the sweet countenance of the suffering man as he was consumed by the fire, his expression a profound mix of pain, sadness and tranquility. And there were other depictions of Goseth even more moving, such as the *Pietà* by Michelangelo. Its pyramidal elegiac composition portrayed the angelic form of the spiritual Ilsa tenderly cradling the vaporous apparition of her deceased son on her lap: her delicate countenance personifying the soft radiance of absolute love and sorrow; the billowing folds of her robes a pure white cloud upon which Rhetter rested. The master sculptor's transformation of the hard Carrera marble into the corporeal and ethereal singularity of mother and child was spellbinding, providing all the proof worshippers needed that a divine hand had indeed guided Michelangelo's stonecutting tools and mallet.

There was no denying that Michelangelo had been inspired when he chiseled the extraordinary figures from the massive marble monolith. Paul could accept the notion that God had influenced the sculptor—after all, that was what the word "inspiration" meant: the breath of divine influence. But did it then follow that this flawless, entrancing, heartrending work was proof that Rhetter was the Crist returned? People of other religions had produced magnificent monuments to their faiths: the imposing austerity of the Egyptian Sphinx; the commanding authority of the Greek Colossus of Rhodes; the magnificently serene Great Buddha of Kamakura; the soaring power of Cristic painter Salvador Dali's modern depiction of *The Last Supper* and his stylized *Crucifixion*—and although Islam and Judaism prohibited depictions of divinity, what could compare in grandeur and perfection to the Taj Mahal; or in lyricism and affection to the stained glass murals of Chagall? Certainly these were all inspired, all guided by an unseen hand. If the heavens could motivate Michelangelo to create such miraculous Rhettian art, couldn't artists of other faiths be equally influenced? Could any artifact, no matter how splendid, prove the preeminence of a specific doctrine?

Whether or not divinity had intervened, the *Pietà* was light years better than the post-medieval artwork that portrayed Jesus, which had tapered from a torrent to a meager trickle after the rise of Rhettianity, finally drying up entirely—until this century, when modern artists like Dali began to re-explore Cristic art. Almost none of the wood carvings, paintings and tapestries of the Middle Ages had survived the relentless vandalism of Cristic homes and churches over the past six hundred years. As a result, historical depictions of the Crist and the crucifixion were for the most part limited to the flat, impassive tiled mosaics of late-period Roman baths and Byzantine baptismal fonts that had been uncovered during archeological digs.

Centuries ago, church baptismal fonts had done away with ornate figures of angels, seraphim and scenes of the crucifixion, to avoid attracting the attention—and ire—of Rhettian mobs. Today they were small and unadorned, and rarely placed near the altar. Although the baptismal rite remained the centerpiece of a child's entry into the Church, the ceremony was purposefully low-key, more often than not conducted by a priest or minister in the child's home instead of the church, and limited to the immediate family. Paul's parents didn't go to church that often, but in the hundred or so services he had attended since he was a child, Paul couldn't remember a single baptism performed on an infant. The baptismal font was nothing more than a symbolic relic from a bygone era.

Rhettians considered baptism by water anachronistic: an ancient, obsolete ritual. More importantly, they associated it with the drowning of Cristen in the baptismal font at Aachen, and thus a poignant reminder of his betrayal of their Rhetter. In its place, they adopted a new purification rite known as zeichism. In the original zeichisms, Rhettian infants were anointed with oil, in accordance with the numerous accounts in the Lorswers of Goseth having been doused with oil prior to his conflagration. The infants were then singed with a hot gabel-shaped iron on the sole of their left foot, leaving a small permanent scar, in memory of the burning of their Lord at the stake. In the intervening centuries, zeichism had moderated, depending on the denomination: some shrins drew a gabel in melted wax on the heel of the baby's foot, or simply applied ashes in the shape of the gabel to the underside of the foot, to avoid both the pain and the danger of infection from burning. Even so, Paul had read that there were a few sects of fundamentalist Rhettians who still practiced the searing zeichisms. Whatever the preferred ritual, unlike baptisms it was still a big event, and it was so integral to the Rhettian concept of salvation, that they felt everyone must be zeichized. One prominent Rhettian sect performed symbolic zeichisms on deceased Cristers, explaining that it was done out of compassion for the salvation of these "lost souls". Cristic groups stridently objected to the practice, considering it blatantly offensive, but their protests fell on deaf ears.

After the conflagration of Goseth, with the aid of King John II of France, the Nordic invaders reestablished their foothold in Normandy and Saxony, pushing farther south in what amounted to a pincer movement from Scandinavia and the Baltics. Taking advantage of the chaos caused by the Black Death, they were also aided by the religious and political upheaval of the Second Messianic Movement. These latter-day Vikings established military governorships in the larger towns that amounted to little more than collection depots for the plunder collected by their bands of pillaging warriors. John II—a weak commander who was better suited for political intrigue than armed conquest—soon lost control of the invasion. He was arrested and imprisoned by the Norsemen he had abetted, and ultimately conflagrated along with several hundred other Cristers in the Franconian Forest in northern Bavaria.

Taking his place was merciless Einarr the Conqueror, from the small village of Vyborg. The invaders—who became known as The New Varangians—tried to revive their Norse mythology, forcing the Cristers to adopt pagan rituals and renounce their Cristicism. Borrowing a page from the Roman occupation of the Holy Land thirteen hundred years earlier, when the Roman legions had crucified tens of thousands of Jews, the Varangians also dealt brutally with those who refused to submit, burning countless Cristers at the gabel. As passionately as Rhettians revered the gabel as a symbol of Goseth's Ardour, it was just as deeply hated by Cristers for its associations with the torture and subjugation of their own people. Paul knew that these Cristic victims, young and old, suffered agonizing deaths that were every bit as torturous as that endured by the fictionalized Goseth, but most children were never told of this carnage—only of the Conflagration of Rhetter.

The Nordic occupation, though brutal, was short-lived—Einarr the Conqueror was himself conquered, the Plague finally abated, and the Holy Roman Empire and German princes slowly managed to reassert control. Over the next century, the invading bands of neo-Viking warriors thinned and gradually blended into the populace, merging their Nordic customs and beliefs with those of the remaining Cristic people, and eventually converting to Rhettianity.

But the dissolution of Norse control left much of northern Europe in political and ecumenical disarray. As "New Cristicism" rapidly expanded, it provoked confrontation with the Cristic archdioceses throughout central Europe. The Church-controlled kingdoms responded with force, and many Kristenzians were arrested and put to death, now known as the Rhettian Martyrs.

Ultimately, the Kristenzian grew in sufficient numbers to become a political and military force of their own: through guerilla-style insurrections waged against the papal regime, the new religion gradually pushed Cristicism out of its French stronghold, and the pope fled back to Rome.

The new religion rapidly spread throughout Central Europe during the latter part of the First Century, particularly in Germany and France. It was introduced in England when Henry V converted to New Cristicism in the year 99 JH to cement his relationship with Clifford VI of France and expedite his marriage to Catherine, Clifford's daughter. Even so, Rhettianity didn't become the recognized religion of Britain for another hundred years. Due to their physical separation from the European continent, Britain, portions of Scandinavia, Spain and Portugal remained—for a time—Cristic strongholds. The escalating persecution of Cristers by the Kristenzians seemed to whet the Cristers' own appetite for scapegoats: even as Väter Hans II was massing his armies to move south toward the Vatican, Pope Sixtus IV issued the papal bull that set in motion the Spanish Inquisition of the 170's. In fact, the atrocities exacted on Jews and Muslims throughout the Iberian Peninsula by Cristers became synonymous with intolerance, and it was used by the Kristenzians as further justification for their unrelenting assaults on the remaining Cristic principalities and kingdoms. By the early 200's, England was also Rhettianized, cemented by King Henry VIII's excommunication from the Church and his establishment of the Shrin of England in 213.

Henry VIII's embrace of Rhettianity was more political than devotional: he had been at loggerheads with the Cristic pope for years over his estranged marriage to Catherine of Aragon, and a break was inevitable. With the Church's authority rapidly waning, exacerbated by the schism of the Reformation less than two decades earlier, Henry VIII saw the inexorable tide of change and acted accordingly. Establishing the new Rhettian Shrin of England gave him the means—and the authority—to accomplish everything he wanted.

To the south, following decades of turmoil between the Italian city-states and dissolution of the papacy, The Vatican and St Peter's Basilica were plundered in 188 JH by the Rhettians of Northern Italy. The Cristers of Italy entered their own diaspora... a centuries-long wandering that Rhettians attributed to God's collective punishment of Cristers for killing His True Son.

Having originated in the Saar Region of Germany and France,

the Kristenzians established The Grand Duchy of Luxembourg as their capital, governed by a council of cardinals and headed by their Holy See, called the *Heiliger Väter*, or Blessed Father. Late in the First Century, New Cristic scribes had written a codicil to the Cristic Bible, called the New Teachings, that included the supposedly eyewitness accounts of Goseth by each of his Devotees. In the Rhettian Bible, the Cristers' Old and New Testaments were combined into the Old Teachings, with many passages revised to better support the divination of Rhetter and the tenets of Rhettianity.

The New Teachings served as the basis for Rhettian religious doctrine. They included not only a history of Goseth's life, known collectively as the Lorswers, but also his teachings. A portion of these writings, called the New Revelations, talked about an End of Days similar to Cristendom's Day of Judgment, but with a Saarsenke (literally "Valley of the Saar") that was considerably more horrific and even more devastating. Salvation, according to the Rhettians, could only be achieved by accepting Goseth as the True Savior, renouncing any devotion or allegiance to, what they termed, "prior Incarnations".

The role of Jesus in Rhettian theology was abstruse—on the one hand, he was venerated as the original Savior and fulfillment of the Messianic Prophesy. On the other, according to Rhettian doctrine, Jesus was intrinsically flawed. Although he was the first Son of God, Jesus was tormented and blemished by his failure to defeat Lucifer, by his own frailties and misgivings, and by his intrinsic humanity. These failings were rectified when He appeared in His Second Coming as the diametric twins—His Goodness manifest in Goseth, and His latent Sinfulness in Cristen. He was, of course, part of the Rhettian Quadriny: the Father, the Son as Goseth, the Son as Jesus and the Sacred Spirit, which together comprised the Godhead.

According to Rhettian liturgy, the spirituality of Jesus was equally divided between the personifications of good and evil. Pressured after the Holocaust to amend this, Väter Konrad IV had issued a diktat that the "essence" of Jesus was more evident in Goseth than in Cristen. But Cristers knew that privately, in their shrins and in their homes, Rhettians were taught that Jesus was a fallen angel and that Cristen was the returned Jesus, while Goseth was the true Son of God.

By 160 JH, more than a century after Goseth's alleged martyrdom, New Cristicism dominated Europe—so much so that the Council of Cardinals in Luxembourg introduced a new calendar that was completely different from the Julian calendar. The new system had thirteen months, renamed for the Eleven Devotees of Goseth, the Virgin Mother Ilsa (Ilsembre) and Goseth himself (Gosiery). Perhaps the biggest confusion was with the month of Janiery, which sounded almost like the Cristic calendar's January but came in the summer, not the winter.

The Sabbath was moved to Monday, which Rhettian scholars claimed was the actual day on which God had rested, correcting errors in the Cristic misreading of the Old Teachings biblical text. Paul knew that the real reason for moving the Sabbath was to differentiate it from the days observed by the other major religions. In fact, the entire reason for revamping the Julian Calendar, which had worked just fine for more than a thousand years, was to realign the world to a new dating system that was tied to the birth of Goseth. As the Seventh Heiliger Väter Johanne II declared in his Oberste Lehre on the one-hundredth anniversary of the introduction of the new calendar, "The Shrin of the Rhetter, as the sole minister of God's Will, shall sever all allegiances to those within whom the Truth no longer is vested."

The new calendar was called the Erikan Calendar, named after

Erik I, the first Rhettian Väter. The years began anew, with the date reset from 1322 AD to 1 JH (im Jahr unseres Heiland—"In the Year of Our Savior"). Time before Goseth was called VR (Vorher Retter—"Before Our Redeemer"). Each month had 28 days, except for Vintner, which had 29 with the extra Monday—the "Sabbath of Sabbaths"—that was added for Mithran. Also known as "The Day That Time Stands Still", it was a practical way to align the 365-day solar year with the 364 days of the 13-month, 4-week cycle. An additional "Sabbath of Sabbaths" was added every fourth year as the last day of the year—Ilsembre 29th—to further correct differences in the two dating systems. To Rhettians, these extra Mondays affirmed the sanctity of their new calendar: it was proof that God had intentionally misaligned the solar and lunar systems to allow for the inclusion of a sort of temporal sanctum sanctorum—a special day set aside to more fully worship and appreciate His Creation.

For observant Cristers, this new calendar was not only blasphemous—it was ruinous. Not only did it change the length, number and names of the months and move the Sabbath to Monday—the addition of the extra day each year (two extra days each leap year) skewed their counting of the weeks, so that the days of the week were no longer in sync. One year, the Cristic Sunday would fall on the Rhettian Friday, and the following year it would be on Thursday, or perhaps Wednesday. Over time, it became impossible for Cristers, Jews and Muslims to observe their days of rest and still function in an increasingly Rhettian-dominated secular world. Rhettians did not tolerate laborers who insisted on resting on work days, especially when these Sabbaths shifted to a different day each year. Cristic and Jewish businesses that closed their doors mid-week suffered from the loss of revenue and fared poorly against Rhettian competitors.

By the early 400s, with European society shifting from agrarian to commercial, the pressure to conform to the Rhettian dating system became too great to resist, and it caused a schism in both Cristicism and Judaism. New "reform" movements arose in both religions that permitted modifications of past practices in order to come to grips with secular pressures. Foremost among these was the adoption of the "Secular Sabbath", which tied the observed day of rest to the Erikan Calendar. This meant that, on the Cristic Calendar, the Secular Sabbath would be designated as Thursday one year, and then Wednesday the next, and so on. Every seventh year or so, the Sabbath would land back on Sunday. But this respite was short-lived, and the following year the Sabbath resumed its trek through the days of the week.

Such accommodation was unacceptable to many Cristers and Jews alike, and they refused to acquiesce to the Rhettian system. In the orthodoxy of both religions, the Sabbath was considered sacrosanct, and it remained where God had intended. It was, after all, the Sabbath, given to them by God, inviolable—a holy day that people could not change, regardless of the circumstances. Accordingly, their cultures became increasingly self-contained, separate and distinct from the prevalent Rhettian-oriented society.

Even among those sects that adopted the notion of the Secular Sabbath, there were feelings of betrayal—a gnawing undercurrent of resentment and guilt. It was regarded as selling out one's faith, and it left a foul taste. Over the centuries, the tide of secular life enveloped most Cristers and Jews, and the Sabbath on their religious calendars was relegated to a footnote—a day to perhaps light a candle, attend an evening service or say a morning prayer—but their actual observed day of rest became the Rhettian Monday... even for Jews, as the weekend had shifted to Sunday and Monday, and no longer included Saturday.

Although Rhettians didn't give it a second thought, the power inherent in controlling the counting of the days and numbering of the years was painfully apparent to Cristers. When 2000 AD, the Cristic bi-millennium, arrived a few years ago, it was welcomed a with a great deal of fanfare among the Orthodox, Catholic and Protestant Cristic denominations, but there was barely any mention of it in the mainstream press—after all, it was 679 JH, just another year. Each of the major networks and PBS used the occasion to air Cristic retrospectives, the most controversial one being CBC's *Two Thousand Years of Cristicism—A Look Back at the Proud Parent of Rhettianity*. Protests from the Cristic community resulted in the title being amended to simply: *Two Thousand Years of Cristendom—A Retrospective*.

The Cristic calendar had undergone some changes in 250 JH, in a belated attempt to stanch the torrent of converts to Rhettianity and to reassert some control over societal time-tracking. But the effort—known as the Gregorian Calendar for then-Pope Gregory XIII—was too little too late. Rhettianity was an unstoppable force, and the new Gregorian Calendar, albeit an improvement over the Julian Calendar, only served to further confuse the observance of Cristic holidays, and it ended up hastening the demise of Cristic influence throughout Europe. To make matters worse, the Gregorian Calendar's leap year had been placed on a different cycle than the Erikan Calendar leap year. The Cristic holidays seemed to jump back and forth, so that Cristmas might fall on the 1st of Brie one year, the 27th of Vintner another year, and on the 29th yet another year.

Paul's friends would habitually ask him why Cristers didn't observe their holidays on the same day each year. At first he'd tried to explain to them that the Cristic people *did* observe their holidays on the same day each year—that since the Julian Calendar was created a thousand years before the Rhettians developed *their* calendar, it was the Rhettians who had moved the days around, not vice-versa. But he soon found his attempts to explain this to be futile, since their—and, in truth, his—only frame of reference was the Erikan Calendar. It was the center of the temporal universe, and everything else was consigned to obsolescence, hopelessly out of whack.

As the new calendar took hold in the Second and Third Centuries and the Cristic timekeeping system was purged, so too were many Cristic customs and beliefs, and the Church's influence throughout Europe vanished. In their desire to sever all ties to Cristicism, Kristenzians embraced their new name: Rhettians. The political demise of Cristendom was sealed by the revolt of Martin Luther and the Reformation in the early 200's which ruptured the last vestiges of Cristic unity and control. By the end of the Third Century JH, two-thirds of Europeans were Rhettian, only a quarter were Cristic, and the balance—something around ten percent—were other religions.

Over the ensuing centuries, anti-Cristic sentiment would occasionally flare up into riots against the dwindling Cristic communities, and in many countries the same anti-Semitic laws that the Medieval Cristic kingdoms had devised to discriminate against the Jews were rewritten to include the Cristers as well. Cristic communities were forced to live in walled-off enclaves, just as the Jews had been forced into ghettos by Cristers throughout the Middle Ages. Cristers and Jews were treated as second-class citizens, prohibited from engaging in the more lucrative trades and professions. Local laws made it a lesser crime to rob or kill Cristers and Jews than Rhettians, and their property could be legally confiscated. Cristers were contemptuously referred to as "the Jeez", a vulgar reference to Jesus. They were considered descendants of the Diaspora, and the bigotry that had originally been levied against Jews by the Cristers was now directed against them. A great deal of Rhettian anti-Semitic and anti-Cristic slander consisted of references to "the Jews and the Jeez". Cristers were commonly regarded as a disreputable people, intrinsically cheap and untrustworthy. The nefarious Shakespearean character Shyster the Crister, from his popular play *Merchant of Venice*, further exacerbated the damning stereotype of Cristers as swindlers. In lockstep with the teachings of the Shrin and the bigotry of their culture, scores of Rhettian writers followed suit—among them Charles Dickens, whose Fagin character perpetuated the image of Cristers as unscrupulous and miserly crooks. Even otherwise reasonable and responsible Rhettians found it acceptable to make references to "those filthy rich Crister lawyers" and to "the Cristic lobbyists" who supposedly controlled Congress with Cristic Money. In fact, the notion of Cristers and Jews being obsessed with money was so ingrained in Rhettian culture that the two religions had become synonymous with cheating, as in the all-too-common phrase: "That cheapskate tried to Crister me on the price."

Paul knew that other people were stereotyped as stingy—Scottish people, for example. But in their case it was considered an admirable trait: common household products often carried the "Scots Brand" label or featured the caricature of a winking Scotsman to signify good value and a wise choice. And the difference, of course, was that the Scottish people were Rhettian. They weren't derogated as a "tightfisted people" during the weekly sermons in the shrins the way that Cristers and Jews were. Scots weren't equated with the archetypal betrayers Cristen and Judas, and they weren't accused of cheating their fellow Rhettians or stealing their property.

This characterization of Cristers as penny-pinching schemers was so prevalent, that even the Cristic community accepted it as a sort of quasi-truth, ridiculing themselves in their own popular writings as opportunists preoccupied with wealth. In the United States, soon after the last wave of Cristic immigrants arrived from Europe, the newly-created theatre known as burlesque honed countless skits featuring The Close-Fisted Crister—always on the lookout for the easy mark and the fast buck. The first generation of Cristic television comedians, having cut their eye teeth on vaudeville, carried these same crass personas to the small screen: hopeless tightwads, pitiful and laughable in their obsession with dubious money-making schemes.

On the hit comedy series *The Matthews Show*, a recent episode depicted its star, Barry Matthews, being confronted with the "Donation Bucket" during a church service. The Catholic Matthews pretended to contribute to the bucket and tried to pass it on, but an eagle-eyed church employee saw the dodge and embarrassed him in front of the other worshippers, forcing him to grudgingly place several bills, one by one, into the till as the congregation guardedly watched. Before he finally capitulated, Matthews tried cadging money from the congregants sitting near him—when that failed, he excused himself from the pews, went into the confessional stall and unsuccessfully tried to negotiate a loan with the priest. The whole ordeal dragged on for the bulk of the half-hour show.

While the skit was handled humorously, the message was clear: Cristers only cared about money. Asking a Crister to make a donation was like yanking his teeth out, and the Church itself was just as obsessed with the green stuff as Matthews.

The day after the show had aired, Paul overheard a group of classmates discussing the episode:

"Man, that *Matthews Show* was a riot last night!"

"Do Cristers really *do* that—make people put money in a bucket while their service is going on? That is *so* lame!"

"And then when he went into that booth and wanted the

preesh—or whatever they call him—to lend him the money... man, I thought I was gonna lose it! I mean, how *cheap* can you *get*?"

"I love that show. It's so *funny!*"

In another popular comedy show, *Life in the Slow Lane*, the lead character—a stereotypically sad sack Crister—was attending the baptism of a newborn at a friend's home in Newark, New Jersey. Just before the ritual was performed, the character mistook the Holy Water to be used in the baptism for bottled spring water and drank it all. Completely embarrassed, he refused to own up to his mistake. Someone then had to drive to the church—which was miles away—to get another container of Holy Water while the assembled guests sat around the small inner-city apartment and stewed. When the Holy Water finally arrived, the same bumbling Crister managed to knock it off the table, spilling it all over the floor. Since nobody wanted to wait for a third jar, and the Holy Water cost money (*"Lots* of money," as the host emphasized to the assembled guests), the Cristic participants desperately scrambled to soak it up with paper towels and squeezed what they could back into the bottle to use for the ceremony. The minister was at first reluctant to use the few recovered drops of impure water for the baptism, until the baby's father begrudgingly slipped him a twenty.

Just another innocent, fun-filled slice of Cristic life.

The famous Cristic standup comic Pat Lukey, who in real life was one of the most generous celebrities of all time, having given tens of millions of his own money to charity, as well as establishing endowments for medical research, was once asked about the irony of having built his fame and fortune on the notorious skinflint Crister he portrayed on radio and television.

"You know," Lukey said, "I'd have rather played a benefactor giving his money away to good causes, but where's the humor in that? And how many Americans would accept a Cristic philan-thropist? It goes against the grain. I may not be the smartest guy on the block, but even *I* know that you can't fight city hall."

Because so many Cristic comedians successfully made the move from theater to film and television, many Rhettians as-sumed that the Cristers controlled the media and the press—a notion that was patently ridiculous, considering that almost all of the major networks and newspapers were Rhettian-owned. But nobody cared to dispute the stereotype, and it became yet anoth-er expedient prejudice in the popular psyche.

Even the Cristers' practice of penance was viewed suspicious-ly by Rhettians. Although acts of contrition, confession and for-giveness were for sins committed against God—not those against other men—Rhettians regarded Cristic priestly absolution as a devious way to nullify ethical transgressions and to escape any binding oaths or legal obligations. Even as recently as the last century, many courts refused to allow Cristers to testify or to serve as jurors, arguing that their religion permitted them to evade all moral responsibility. In a nutshell, Cristers could not be trusted.

Perhaps most damning, the Rhettian liturgy blamed the Con-flagration of Goseth on the Cristic people. This was preposterous, since Goseth was born Cristic, and his arrest and death was at the hands of an army of Scandinavian invaders and a rogue king, not the central Church. But arguing this with a Rhettian was useless, especially since they had been taught it from birth—both at home and at Monday School—and it was integral to their faith. The en-suing Cristic Diaspora was commonly assumed among Rhettians to have been divine retribution on Cristers for the sin of the Con-flagration. It was a fitting punishment, personified in the saga of The Wayward Crister.

Historians weren't certain when the legend of The Wayward

Crister began, but a German pamphlet dating from the mid-Third Century titled: *"Kurtze Beschreibung und Erzählung von einem Kristen mit Namen Metodius"* (A Short Description and Tale of a Crister Named Methodius) was widely regarded as the earliest printed reference. Whether or not this was the original source, the story quickly circulated throughout Europe, and by the Fourth Century it had become an integral part of Shrin-endorsed Rhettian folklore.

The story was about a Cristic fishmonger from the southern Slavic lands named Methodius who had journeyed north in search of fortune, ending up in Aachen at the time of Rhetter's conflagration. Methodius had joined the mob of Cristers who jeered at Rhetter as he was forced to carry the gabel and again as he burned to death in the center of the town. According to the legend, prior to the conflagration Methodius had taunted Goseth as he slowly walked through the streets of Aachen, at one point placing a garland of rotting fish heads around Goseth's neck, mocking him that it was "a gift from Our Lord to you". For his wickedness, the Wayward Crister was damned to drift the seas in search of a familiar port until Rhetter reappeared on Earth for The Third Arrival—the Savior's Final Return.

Over the years, the tale was embellished with particulars of the doomed Cristic sinner's ill-fated attempt to journey back to his homeland—first climbing through the snow-covered Alps: his iniquity a hex, sowing seeds of misfortune wherever he passed; finally reaching the Adriatic Sea and setting sail only to lose his bearings; drifting down into the Mediterranean and westward to unknown ports; never able to reach his destination, forever adrift. These supplemented details of the seafarer's endless anguish lent credence to the legend, so that over the centuries many Rhettians ardently believed that the depraved Wayward Crister truly existed and was duly punished.

The story, whose roots could be traced to ancient tales of the arduous journeys of wayfarers, as well as the Cristic concept of damnation, wasn't just an allegory for the price of wickedness—the plight of the Wayward Crister served as a metaphor for the Cristic Diaspora and the supposed sin that all Cristers forever bore for the death of Goseth. In fact, the Shrin still referred to Methodius as *Der Ewige Criste*—The Eternal Crister: a Cristic Everyman, banished by the Almighty for his insolence—lacking a moral compass, forever homeless.

To most modern-day Rhettians, The Wayward Crister was little more than a parable—an allusion to those who hadn't yet accepted Rhetter as their savior. But Cristers who bore the brunt of the demeaning stereotype saw it from a far different, less innocuous perspective: it was a damning depiction of Cristers as spiritually lost, and it served as justification for their dispersion and subjugation.

Paul knew enough about Rhettianity—he had heard enough Rhettian sermons and read enough essays by Rhettian theologians—to understand that both Cristen the Betrayer and the Wayward Crister were integral to its dogma—that the religion required both an archetypal villain on which to cast universal blame, and a perpetual scapegoat to bear the sins of the faithless.

After the Diaspora, the number of Cristers in Europe had continued to decline, due to incessant proselytizing by Rhettians, as well as the poor living conditions that came with being treated as second-class citizens, and to anti-Cristic fervor among Rhettians that led to organized pogroms and other mass-slaughters. By the mid-500's, only eight percent of Europeans were Cristic. And in the United States, even with the influx of Cristic immigrants fleeing the horrors of state-sanctioned Rhettian violence, the number of Cristers never exceeded four percent of the population. A census taken at the Cristic Bimillennium revealed that, due to low birthrates and interfaith marriages, only three percent of Americans were Cristic: about eight million people. Eight million Cristers, six million Jews, another fifteen million of other faiths... and more than two hundred and seventy million Rhettian Americans.

Chapter Nine

Fox Hunt

The snow began during the night, and by Sunday morning several inches blanketed the ground—enough to transform Paul's neighborhood into a Currier and Ives print: a Mithran picture postcard of wintry white. The flakes were still falling in the thin early light of the mid-Vintner morning, painting a serene stillness that Paul considered a good harbinger for the vacation that lay ahead.

The Forsythes arrived in their Escalade at nine sharp; the over-sized luxury SUV easily negotiating the unplowed neighborhood streets. Peggy bounded out of the car in a fluffy parka—not the ivory one she had worn to school, but another even more expensive-looking brown leather coat with plush fur trim. She and Mr. Forsythe helped Paul load his bags into the rear of the vehicle, then she bounded back into the Escalade and patted the empty seat next to her.

"You sit here, Paul, next to me. Patty gets her own seat in the back."

As Paul climbed into the spacious Cadillac, he glanced back at Peggy's younger sister. Patty was stretched out across the rear bench seat wearing a ribbed turtleneck and stretch ski pants, her feet tucked into thick fur-lined boots. She reminded Paul of a publicity photo of Lindsay Lohan he had seen in an old Glamour

Magazine a few months ago while waiting to get his hair styled—mascara and rouge and wet cherry lipstick that stood in sharp contrast to her soft lavender-blue eyes. Listening to an iPod, she was bobbing slightly to the beat in her headphones, which she lifted off one ear as Paul nodded hello.

"Hey, stranger," she smiled at him. "Welcome aboard the Fox Hunt Express. I haven't seen you in a while."

"Hey," he nodded again. "Thanks for having me along." He had trouble taking his eyes from her as she lowered the headphones back onto her ear and resumed her silent gyrations.

"Ignore her," ordered Peggy. "She's been a jerk all morning." She leaned over to Paul, whispering. "She wanted to bring somebody along too, but my folks said no, not this year. I think she has the hots for some guy at school, but Mom vetoed it. So now she's being a real bitch about the whole thing. I just hope it doesn't last the whole trip."

Paul shrugged. Patty seemed okay to him—but then again, she wasn't his sister. He wondered what it was like having a sibling, figuring there would be times of rivalry and friction. But from what he'd seen of multi-child families, there was a binding force—a cement that transcended all feuds and arguments—a confidant with whom to share all of life's moments: the joys and fears, the anger and sorrows. He wished he'd had someone like that growing up. A brother, close in age...

Like Dave.

He smiled to himself. Maybe he had it after all.

Fox Hunt was sequestered in the Shenandoah mountains midway along the western spine of Virginia. Its four-star lodge commanded a breathtaking view of twin valleys that stretched north-south between three mountain ranges. When conditions were right—when fresh powder coated the peaks to a depth of a foot or more—the slopes at Fox Hunt were said to have no rival in the Appalachians. And so, on such a week as this, with large, dry flakes having fallen for several crystalline clear and calm days, skiing enthusiasts from up and down the coast were descending on the resort, hoping to find a virgin trail upon which to carve their mark.

The ride took six hours, with stops in Fredericksburg for coffee and doughnuts, and then in Charlottesville for a deli lunch. A bit nervous at first, Paul soon relaxed in the amicable company of the Forsythes, who were doing their utmost to make him feel like a part of their family. The smooth ride and plush interior of the posh, leather-upholstered van made Paul feel like royalty, and being seated next to Peggy was pure heaven. He looked out of his window as the car traveled along a grove of white birches encased in a thin layer of ice that created a natural prism, the late morning sun having broken through the clouds, its rays cascading through their crystalline branches in dazzling staccato glints of spectral light.

"Oh, man," Paul turned to Peggy, pointing out his window. "Can you see this? The way the light's coming through these trees?"

"Where?" she asked, unbuckling her shoulder belt and leaning across him for a better view. Her breasts squeezed against Paul's chest as she peered through his window. "Oh, wow," she exclaimed, "that really *is* beautiful! It's like... like some sort of fairyland in a storybook. An enchanted kingdom right out of a dream, you know?"

He knew. And with Peggy's warm body pressing against him, too. Life couldn't get any better than this—it just couldn't.

It was hard to miss the lodge: six stories of rough-hewn timbers commanding a summit overlooking the twin valleys. But it wasn't just the lodge's imposing bulk that made it stand out. This was Mithran, after all, and the cupola that projected from the top of the lodge sported a twenty-foot-tall pastel-colored gabel at its peak that was visible for miles around.

"Look, Paul!" exclaimed Peggy as she first caught sight of the stately lodge in the distance. "I can't believe we're almost there! Oh, this is going to be so much fun! The skiing, the parties, the acorn hunt, and the *bonfire*... I just *know* you're going to love it!" she said, bouncing in her car seat like an excited preschooler. "And look at how they put a gabel on the roof. Isn't that cute?"

Paul peered out the SUV window at the building. In the afternoon light, with its giant pink and mint-green gabel, it looked like some sort of garish shrin to him. *Just great. Maybe they offer free zeichisms to vacationers.*

He chastised himself: *Stop it! Go with the flow. Try to have fun. Don't over-analyze, don't criticize. I need to concentrate on why I came along.*

And he did just that.

His room at the lodge was, in a word, opulent: a king-sized bed mounted in an elaborately-carved oak frame with soaring posts dominated the cavernous room. On one side of the bed were two tastefully upholstered wingback chairs, both with ottomans and side tables, and a bin stuffed with the latest issues of the major news, sports and fashion magazines. On the other side was a large mahogany writing desk with an oversized blotter and a classic green-glass and bronze accountant's reading lamp, complete with a broadband Internet link—it had been a good decision to bring along his laptop after all. And against the wall opposite the bed was the largest armoire he had ever seen, its massive doors concealing not only a large screen entertainment center, but also drawers filled with fresh towels and linens, and every toiletry imaginable—scented soaps, organic shampoos, shaving creams and colognes, bubble bath gels and body washes, massage oils, alcohol rubs, face creams and hand lotions, and too many dental care products to count.

The private bathroom was just as impressive, with a Jacuzzi that could comfortably accommodate two people, and an equally spacious travertine-tiled shower with multiple showerheads on the far side of the room. Sitting in-between was a curious porcelain fixture that Paul had never seen before—too low and thin to be a toilet, with a small golden nozzle pointing downward into the bowl and two bronze levers. Curious, he pressed one of the levers, causing a thin stream of water to spray from the nozzle into the far end of the bowl. Pressing the other lever startled him, as another nozzle he hadn't noticed arched a jet of water up out of the bowl and onto the granite-tiled floor. That was enough to convince him to leave the device alone for the remainder of his stay.

Over an early dinner, Mr. Forsythe reviewed plans for the week-long outing. He and Mrs. Forsythe had planned the vacation to the minute, with a detailed itinerary for everyone, including Paul. For his part, Paul was glad that they had gone to the trouble, as the resort was a bit overwhelming, and it was comforting to be able sit back knowing that all of the details had been attended to.

Patty, however, was not happy with having her activities so tightly scheduled, particularly since they required that the two sisters stay together on the slopes. Paul could feel the constant tension between the teenager and her parents: Patty's youthful craving for freedom versus their desire to set boundaries and assert parental authority. He could see why the Forsythes had to impose limits... not only was the young woman bursting with reckless energy—but at sixteen she was also drop-dead gorgeous, with a face and figure that rivaled any teen celebrity. About a year ago, Paul had read Nabokov's classic tale *Lolita*—in his mind's eye, Patty fit that vixen to a tee. He could see the young men at the resort stealing second glances at her—and at Peggy, too, for that matter. But Patty got the lion's share of stares, and she clearly relished it. She was trouble waiting to happen, and without 24/7 supervision, it was bound to.

On the other hand, Peggy seemed to welcome the carefully choreographed vacation as much as Paul did. Was this, he wondered, a sign that they were already getting old? He imagined the two of them, bundled up in large blankets, sitting in Adirondack rockers on the lodge's grand porch, idling away the vacation as Patty cavorted on the snow-capped slopes.

Well, maybe not that old.

The itinerary assembled by Mr. Forsythe included a myriad of activities—if anything, perhaps too many. Up by 7am, breakfast at 8 sharp, on the slopes by 9, then back to the lodge at noon for lunch, followed by indoor activities—and there were many to choose from at the lodge: squash and handball; weight training; swimming; aerobic classes; sauna and massage therapy—then back out on the slopes until late afternoon; returning for showering and relaxation before dinner at 7; and finally the inexorable après-ski party in the Great Room each evening. It all sounded great to Paul: it translated into being with Peggy one-hundred percent of the day—except perhaps for the early afternoon indoor activities, which of course they could do together, too... other than the sauna and massage.

Early into the first full day at Fox Hunt, Paul realized why Patty was so upset, for reasons that went beyond the strict limits on her freedom to explore. Without her own beau in tow, Patty must have felt like a third wheel: the stereotypical kid sister tagging along with Sis and her boyfriend. Paul loved it, since he enjoyed the company of both young women, but Peggy was annoyed with the arrangement, and Patty was beyond frustration.

"This totally sucks," was how she put it.

"Paul doesn't know how to ski," lectured Peggy, stating the obvious. "He can't handle the intermediates."

"Yeah, well, that's not *my* fault," Patty scoffed, stamping the snow off her skis as they waited in line for the beginner lift. She peered up toward the other skiers zipping down the higher slopes. "I'm bored stiff."

"Then go," offered Peggy.

"But Dad said…"

"Never mind what Dad said. Just go. I'll cover for you."

"You sure?"

"Yes, yes, yes. Go have fun. Just don't break anything. Plan to meet us here at eleven-thirty and we'll head back to the lodge together. Deal?"

"Deal!" Patty said. She crinkled up her pert little nose in a sweet smile at Paul. "Hey, I wouldn't mind hanging with you guys—especially you, Paul, you're such a cutie. But…"

"Just *go!*" commanded Peggy.

Paul was somewhat sorry to see her disappear into the throng of skiers, but also glad that Peggy wouldn't be distracted by her younger sister, and they could now devote their time to each other. Realizing that Peggy was also bored with the beginner slopes, he was determined to learn the basics as quickly as possible. By mid-morning on the first day, he felt that he had mastered the parallel skis, snowplow stops and side-step climbs. He concentrated on keeping his knees bent, leaning forward and using his legs as shock absorbers on the bumps. At lunch, with Patty back in tow, Peggy couldn't stop extolling his progress to her parents.

"Well, don't rush it too much, Paul," advised Mr. Forsythe between bites of his club sandwich. "We're here all week. Better to take it slow and steady."

"Yes, sir," said Paul. "It's just that I know that Peggy is a good skier... and Patty, too," he quickly added. "I don't want to hold them up while I'm busy learning."

"They can wait," said their father. "Can't you, girls?"

"Yes, Daddy," they sighed in unison.

By late that afternoon, Paul was able to negotiate some of the beginner slopes without ending up on his backside—or worse, on his face. He was feeling confident, getting his "skiing legs", and having a blast doing it. Peggy was all encouragement, trying to stifle her laughs when he performed one of his windmills on the way to the ground, and helping him back up onto his feet, which was often the hardest part.

Patty had immediately taken off to the more advanced trails, and they didn't see her again until dusk had fallen and it was time to start back to the lodge. This time, she had a young man in tow.

"Hey guys, this is Rhett," she said.

Now that's an original name, Paul thought. A quarter of the guys at school were named "Rhett", "Rhettian", or some variation. And there were even more girls named after Rhetter—"Rhettine" and "Rhettiana" and "Rhetina" and the insufferably cute "Rhettie".

That seemed so odd to Paul—choosing to name your child after your religion. *Cristers don't name their children "Crister". How weird would that be! Weird and demeaning: "Hi, my name is Crister!"*

But it went beyond that... the inevitable contempt, the disparagement or, as happened throughout Nazi-era Europe, the harm that would befall someone unfortunate enough to have been named "Cristiene", "Cristine" or even "Cristopher": too close to Cristen, the traitorous brother who had sold his own mother to the Norsemen for twenty pieces of silver, then conspired with them to conflagrate their Lord.

Similarly, "Goseth" was popular with Rhettians, especially among Hispanic Anointists, who spelled it "Goseh" and pronounced it "Go-SAY". It was so popular that Paul guessed most Latinos used "Goseh" as either their first or middle name. But a Cristic family naming their child "Jesus" or some variation of this was unthinkable, since it would automatically brand that child as a Crister. Even though Rhettians knew who Jesus was—after all, He played a prominent role in their liturgy—any mention of Him in conversation immediately solicited the admonition: "Oh, you mean Cristen"... so deep was His association with this scoundrel of scoundrels. Thus, naming a child "Jesus" was out of the question in the United States—or in any other Rhettian country, for that matter.

Paul took off his glove and extended his hand to Rhett. "Nice to meet you."

Rhett made a fist without removing his glove and tried to do a knuckle-knock with Paul's open hand. "Yo. S'up, Dude?"

A real classy guy, this one, thought Paul, putting his glove back on.

"Rhett's a boarder," said Patty, by way of introduction.

That explains a lot. Snowboarders are a different breed, for sure. Anybody who jumps on a board and goes barreling helter-skelter down a hill at fifty miles an hour has to have the intelligence of a... of a Rhett.

"Are you from around here, Rhett? Do you live in Virginia?" Paul asked the boarder, mostly out of politeness.

Rhett chuckled, "Nah, dude!"

"He's from California," volunteered Patty.

That explains even more. Yes, indeed, ladies and gents, we have a wiener. Thank God this California "dude" is a man of few words. Who knows what sort of profundities emanate from that keen mind? With any luck, maybe he'll snowboard into an oak tree...

Paul caught himself. *Where did that come from? What has this boarder ever done to me? I just met the guy. Sure, Rhett seems dense as dirt, with the manners of an ape, but that isn't any reason to wish he'd slam into a tree. Is it just his name? Does that automatically make him a jerk? What else could it be? That he's tall, blonde-haired and blue-eyed with perfect teeth? That he snowboards?*

"Well, it was nice meeting you, Rhett," Peggy smiled.

Why did she smile at him?

"Later," Rhett said, with a little flip of the wrist and finger-point that Paul surmised must have been the latest cool way to wave in California. Then he turned and gave Patty a lingering kiss on the lips before heading back off to the mountain. Patty lingered too, murmuring a soft "mmm..." during the seemingly endless lip-lock, as Paul and Peggy shot each other awkward glances.

"What was *that*?" demanded Peggy after Rhett was out of ear-shot.

"What was what?" asked Patty, all innocence.

"You know perfectly well what 'what' is!" Peggy snapped back. "You just met the guy, for Rhetter's sake!"

"Look, it's just his way of saying 'goodbye', okay? It's no biggie."

"Yeah, right... and his way of saying 'hello' and 'nice day' and 'please pass the sugar' too, I'll bet."

"What are you—Mom all of a sudden?" snapped Patty. "You got to bring Paul here and I didn't get to bring anyone, so butt out!" And with that, she turned, stabbed her poles into the snow and propelled herself toward the lodge.

Pointing at her departing sister, Peggy turned to Paul. "Did you *see* that?"

"It's this younger generation," sighed Paul. "What can you

do?"

"Yeah, go ahead and make a joke. I have half a mind to tell Mom."

"Well, you might want to listen to the other half," advised Paul. "Remember—she was supposed to be with us on the beginner slopes the whole time. How are you going to explain her hanging with Mr. Snowboard?"

"I don't know," admitted Peggy, biting her lower lip. "But she's my kid sister. I have to keep her out of trouble."

"Which means the sooner we join her on the intermediate slopes, the better," offered Paul. And he made up his mind to progress beyond the beginner slopes as soon as possible, for the sake of both sisters.

"Yeah, well, I'm not going to worry about it tonight. It's Mithran Eve. Oh, Paul," Peggy said, her mood suddenly brightening, "This is just going to be so *fantastic*! Can you imagine, Mithran Eve here at Fox Hunt? It's supposed to be the absolute *best*! And you've never even been to a Mithran bonfire, have you? Oh, God, you're in for such a surprise—you've never ever seen anything like it, I bet. They're always so much fun, and this is going to be the most wonderful one ever!"

She grabbed his arm with excitement and did a little dance with her skis. "Come on, I'll race you to the lodge. Last one there's a rotten acorn!"

She dug her poles into the packed snow and skied toward the mammoth, brightly-lit building in the distance. Paul did likewise, falling twice along the way.

* * *

Peggy was right: he'd never ever seen anything like it—at least, not in person. He'd seen Mithran bonfires before, of course, including the one at the Clifton County courthouse. That one hadn't been called a Mithran Bonfire for several years, ever since the local paper ran an editorial challenging whether county sponsorship of a Rhettian holiday violated Constitutional guarantees of the separation of shrin and state. However, instead of cancelling the ritual or moving it to another location—for example, to one of the dozens of shrins in Clifton—county supervisors simply renamed it The Annual Winterfest Bonfire. Paul realized that the name change was simply political cover, since no other religion used bonfires in their holiday celebrations, but changing the name seemed the perfect solution in the minds of county legislators and executives. And it wasn't just the bonfire—all of the "Winterfest" festivities at the courthouse were devoted to Mithran: the Clifton County Choir sang Winterfest Carols, there was a Winterfest Acorn Hunt, and a Winterfest Acorn Roll. Since Cristmas, Chanukah and Kwanzaa occurred around the same time, there was some obligatory mentioning of these festivals, but it was only tagged on as a patronizing, politically-correct postscript.

The federal government made no pretenses about honoring the spirit of the First Amendment, either. Instead, on Mithran Eve there was always a spectacular bonfire in the center of the Ellipse near the White House, with the president given the honor of lighting the first ember. The following day, there was the annual Mithran Acorn Hunt and Acorn Roll on the south lawn of the White House, once again with the president presiding over the festivities.

True... in response to petitions from Cristic, Jewish and African-American groups, the government had added a token set of Cristmas luminary bags, a Chanukah menorah, and a Kwanzaa candelabra on the Ellipse, all at a safe distance from the Official White House Mithran Bonfire. These competing symbols were fairly large—in fact, the luminary bags looked like a row of giant shopping bags, which seemed to defeat the intent—but they were still dwarfed next to the massive pyre, and they seemed like nothing more than hollow gestures—conciliatory booby prizes for those *other* Americans. Most visitors who saw them didn't even know what they were: on a class trip to Washington around Mithrantide, Paul remembered overhearing one tourist wonder aloud whether the decorated Cristmas luminary bags and the candelabras were some sort of primitive sculptures on loan from the Smithsonian.

A few years ago, one of the thousands of photographs taken of the White House Mithran Bonfire was snapped at just the instant when the pattern of flames seemed to resemble the shape of a person with an outstretched, waving arm. A similar pose had been the trademark of Heiliger Väter Jan Edel II, possibly the most beloved Holy See in modern times, who had died earlier that year. To Paul, the outline of the fire vaguely suggested any number portly waving fellows: Winston Churchill, Walt Disney, Mickey Mouse or one of the Selgas; but many Rhettians took it as a sign that the federally-sanctioned bonfire had received the Almighty's Seal of Approval.

Paul had, of course, seen the White House Mithran Bonfire on television, but the Fox Hunt celebration would be the first time he had ever personally witnessed a bonfire of that scale—and according to Peggy, the lodge's bonfire dwarfed even the one on the Ellipse.

The Forsythes and Paul arrived at the Great Circle a short while before the bonfire began, and a large crowd of revellers had already formed a wide circle in the snow-blanketed field around the immense pyre—a monstrous pyramid of stacked logs that seemed to climb forever into the starry sky, awesome and fearsome in its sheer bulk. On seeing it, two thoughts immediately crossed Paul's mind: *How do they manage to construct such a massive tower of logs, and what keeps it from collapsing from its own weight?*

"I know what you're thinking, Paul," Mr. Forsythe said. "You're wondering how they did it. I used to wonder the same thing as a child. They start from the bottom and build their way up, obviously. The trick to keeping it from falling down is the way they're stacked. It's a fairly intricate system of interlocking timbers. The logs are pre-notched—similar to the old Lincoln Logs that children used to play with—but at specific angles that allow them to form the pyramid shape. It's rock solid... even a hurricane wouldn't knock it down. And it stays together through almost the entire burn. Really quite fascinating. Rhettian ingenuity at work."

He paused, studying Paul.

"Cristicism doesn't have anything like this, does it? I mean, I know about how you gather around trees at Cristictide and you light candles, but there aren't any bonfires, are there?"

"No, sir," Paul answered. "We don't do anything like this. And it's called Cristmas, not 'Cristictide'."

"Crismess," Peggy's dad nodded. "Yes, I knew that. My apology. Crismess."

Whatever, thought Paul. He really didn't want to get into a discussion of Cristmas with Mr. Forsythe right then. But he was thinking to himself: *We don't create stupid bonfires, and we don't chop down trees and stick them in our homes to dry out and die like Rhettians do at Rhettag, either.*

A Fox Hunt employee bedecked in a Mithran pastel-colored fur-lined coat was serving hot amber-colored drinks in clear glass mugs. She came over to the Forsythes and Paul, and each of them took a steaming mug from her tray.

"Ah, Mithran Nog!" exclaimed Mr. Forsythe. "This will warm

your soul. Hot cider and cinnamon with nutmeg. You know, Paul, traditional Mithran Nog is spiked with rum... quite a bit, too. Now, that's a *real* nog."

"This *is* spiked, Dad," said Peggy, taking a sip.

"It is?" asked Mr. Forsythe. He sniffed his cup. "Well I'll be."

"Patty give me that," instructed their mother, reaching for the younger sister's mug. "You're not old enough to have this."

"No way!" shouted Patty, who turned and ran off with her cider nog. Mrs. Forsythe watched her disappear into the crowd, then she turned back to her husband.

"Honestly, Jim, I can't believe they served her that!"

"Well, Amanda, she looks older than sixteen. Besides, it's Mithran. I think we can bend the rules a little just for tonight."

The circle around the pyre was becoming immense, with several hundred revelers joining hands to make an unbroken chain, large enough to stand a couple of hundred feet from the logs—a safe enough distance, at least at the start of the conflagration. As if on cue, as the last few broken links of the human chain were filled with latecomers, the throng burst into song as a Fox Hunt employee ran up to the base of the pyre with a flaming torch and touched it to some of the kindling at the bottom, igniting the bonfire. Paul had heard this Mithran carol many times—too many times!—but he didn't know all of the words. He had no intention of joining in, anyway: the song was a paean to the Conflagration and to Goseth's supposed rise to Heaven as the True Messiah.

In the not-too-distant past in Europe, the bonfires and drinking and song were the warm-up act to a night of attacks on Cristic and Jewish villages, of vandalism of businesses and homes and churches and synagogues and, in some instances, state-sanctioned pogroms with their brutal rapes and murders. The bonfires were used to burn Cristic bibles and Torah scrolls, and sometimes people, too. It was small wonder that many Cristers and Jews still dreaded this ritual, and the unabashed merriment and joy of Rhettians at Mithran wasn't enough to offset the memory of the pain, the suffering, the fear and the horror it had meant for others who became perennial scapegoats for the death of the Rhettians' Lord.

The circle of people singing the Mithran hymn brought back memories of the time Paul's parents had enrolled him in a YMRA summer camp. The "Y" as it was popularly called, with its direct association to the gabel, was a Rhettian missionary movement founded in England for the purpose of spreading the word of Rhetter through bible study and prayer meetings to the young men who made use of its social and athletic club activities. After it had crossed the Atlantic to America, the "Y" became a fixture in almost every major city, and it branched into other activities to achieve a greater outreach. Although the organization continued its proselytizing mission, this was not widely advertised, and most people no longer associated the "Y" with Rhettianity. That was the case with its summer camp program.

Paul's parents had assumed that, because there was no mention of Rhettianity in the brochure and since it was open to the general public, the YMRA camp was nondenominational. It was a day camp located almost thirty miles from their house. Paul, who was ten at the time, had to get up very early in the morning and walk about half a mile to the main highway in order to board the bus to camp. This was not how he had planned to spend his summer: from his perspective, there were already two strikes against the camp before he even got there.

On arriving at the camp, things got progressively worse—a lot worse. First, he discovered that his juice pack had sprung a leak in his thermal-lined lunch bag and saturated his baloney sandwich, his chips, and even his cookie snack. Then his left shoelace broke and he had to unthread it from the top two sets of eyelets in order to retie it, which meant that it didn't fit securely on his foot anymore and he had to spend the rest of the long day with his toes scrunched up in order to keep the shoe from falling off.

He was not a happy camper.

His camp counselor was a young muscular fellow with a flat-top haircut wearing a white t-shirt with a large burning "Y" logo in the center. Imprinted on the two angled arms of the flaming gabel were the words HONOR and FAITH, and a third word, DEVOTION ran along the gabel's stem. The guy looked like a drill sergeant.

"Alright campers!" he barked at Paul and the other kids who had just stepped off the bus, "Front and center!" He pointed to the ground just in front of him. "Form a line right here! On the double! Move it! HUP, two, three, four!" The drill sergeant suddenly pointed over to the side of the bus. "Hey, *you* there! You with the red pants on!"

Paul looked over where the jarhead was pointing. A small mousy-looking kid with dark-rimmed glasses and wearing red shorts was drinking from a canteen. The boy stopped drinking and pointed to himself, mouthing the word "Me?"

"Yeah, *you!*" bellowed the drill sergeant. "No drinking unless I give the order, so put that away! Put it away *now!*" He stared at the kid's pants. "And what kinda pants are those? Who in hell wears red shorts anyway? Only *Commies* wear red shorts! From now on, your name is 'Pinky', you got that? Now get over here Pinky, and that goes for the rest of you, too!"

Paul hurried over with the dozen other boys to the designated spot in front of the drill sergeant, fearful of being singled out the way "Pinky" had.

"Okay now, listen up!" barked the young man after the new arrivals had formed a line. "I am your leader at this camp! What I say goes! Is that understood?"

"Yes, sir!" responded Paul and the others.

"*What* did you say?" bellowed the crew-cut. "Do you think you're in the goddamned Army? Don't call me 'sir'! My name is Nick! You got that? Nick! Let me hear you say it!"

"Nick!" shouted the line.

"Damn right!" shouted Nick back at them. "You remember that! Now, if you have a problem, you come to me! Don't go off looking for some other counselor to cry to. You come to *me!* Understood?"

"Yes, sir…. Nick!" responded the line.

"Nick! Just Nick! No 'sir'—just 'Nick'! Remember that! Say it again!"

"Nick!" shouted the line in unison.

"What, Nick?" demanded Nick.

This was met with the silence of confusion.

"*What* Nick?" repeated Nick.

The line of kids glanced at each other and then shouted "*What* Nick!"

"*No, No, No!*" berated Nick. "'*Yes*, Nick'. You were supposed to answer 'Yes, Nick'! *Understand?*"

"Yes, Nick!" answered the line.

"Good!" said Nick. "Okay, then! Now, everybody at this camp gets a nickname! Mine's Nick—see? My nickname's Nick, 'cause Nick's my name! Get it?"

"Yes, Nick!"

"Good! Now, I already gave Pinky *his* nickname. You!" Nick said, pointing to the boy at his far left, "Your nickname is… Slim, because that's what you are! And you!" said Nick, pointing to the next boy, "Your nickname is… Four Eyes! And you… *damn*, you got big ears! Your nickname's Dumbo!"

And so Nick went down the line, pointing and naming. When he got to Paul, he quickly scanned him, looking for something to hang a handle on. "You! Your nickname is..." Nick made a second sweep, noticing the broken lace. "Shoo! Your name's Shoo! *Got* it?"

Suddenly, a loudspeaker squealed to life and a man's voice barked across the campsite. The words were muffled, but Nick had no problem deciphering the message.

"Okay troops, we'll finish this later! Form a single file and follow me! We've got to get to Camp Circle!"

They set off in a haphazard march behind Nick through a wooded area toward the center of the camp. Camp Circle was a large clearing, with a wide pit in the middle filled with charcoal and burnt wood: judging from its size and the amount of coal and ash, Paul assumed that it must have been used for dozens, maybe hundreds of bonfires. Standing some distance from the pit were three poles: one looked like a telephone pole with a loudspeaker mounted at the top. At a distance, the sounds that emanated from it were simply unintelligible: up close, it was both unintelligible and deafening. The second post was a large flagpole, perhaps forty feet tall. And the third was a giant "Y", fashioned out of three thick timbers. Paul assumed that it stood for the name of the organization that held the camp. Several dozen boys were already standing around the three poles in a large circle and more were joining the circle. From their movements Paul could tell that many of the boys had done this drill before. He knew that his parents had signed him up for the shorter camp term (thank goodness for that!), so those kids must have started a couple of weeks ago. Either that, or they were repeat campers.

Nick ordered Paul's group to join the circle, which now consisted of close to a hundred campers. When the circle was finished, Paul found himself almost directly in front of the loudspeaker—a bad position, as he discovered when the speaker squealed to life again, forcing him to wince in pain and cover his ears.

"WELGM GAMFRZ ZU GAM FRNZHP," the voice said; or at least that was what it seemed to say. "BLZAND ADADNZHN FRDEE VLAGRZNG."

Half of the campers around the circle turned toward the pit, and Paul and the rest of the kids copied them. From that direction marched three campers carrying folded flags. They proceeded up to the base of the flagpole where one of the counselors was standing. They handed their flags to the counselor one by one, as he attached them to the halyard and then pulled on the rope to raise them to the top. As they lifted into the air, Paul saw that the topmost was the United States flag, the second was the flag of Maryland, and the third was a large purple "Y" on a yellow field.

Half of the kids around the circle saluted as the flags climbed the pole. The rest then saluted, too.

"WEEWLNOW RZEIDA BLEJZLEEJNZ."

Half of the kids placed their hands over their hearts, and the remainder aped them as they began to recite the Pledge of Allegiance. Well, thought Paul, this was no different than the start of each school day. He had always dreaded being sent to Summer School—even at ten years old, he considered that to be the ultimate disgrace. Only bad kids and flunkies had to go to Summer School. It was the greatest insult he could imagine, a form of personal hell. But this wasn't Summer School. It was camp, and his parents had told him how much fun he'd have— swimming and canoeing and archery and nature hikes and making key chains and other cool stuff. It did sound like it could be a lot of fun, and he was trying to keep a positive attitude.

The circle finished reciting the Pledge, and the loudspeaker barked again:

"WEEWLNOW ZNGDA GAMZONG GOFRTH RDEEIN WORYRZ."

This was followed by the harsh, squealing notes of a tune that was completely unfamiliar to Paul. It seemed to be a marching song, but not lighthearted like the John Phillip Sousa marches at the Twenty-Third of Pendiery parade last year. This sounded more like the forceful hymns emanating from shrins on Monday mornings. Although the tune was foreign to him, almost every other kid seemed to know the song by heart—even those who were apparently new to the camp.

Not wanting to appear different and hoping to fit in, Paul strained to hear the lyrics that the others were singing, and he tried to mouth along.

> *Go forth, Rhettian Warriors*
> *Marching as before,*
> *Goseth's burning gabel*
> *Leading as to war.*
>
> *Goseth, royal Master,*
> *Fights against our foe,*
> *Forward into battle*
> *See our banners go!*

Paul stopped mouthing the words. His face became flushed. What sort of camp song was this? Goseth, royal master? Leading to war? Forward into battle? He glanced around the circle at the other campers, all of them standing at attention, almost shouting the song:

> *Castle walls may perish,*
> *Kingdoms rise and fall,*
> *But the Shrin of Goseth*
> *Does outlive them all.*

Enemies can never
'Gainst our Shrin prevail;
We have Goseth's promise,
And we will not fail.

Enemies against their shrin... what enemies? Who is this foe their "Master" *is leading the Rhettians to battle against?* Paul thought about the Holocaust. At ten years old, he had heard about the Nazis. He didn't know a lot about them, but he knew that they were Rhettians and that they had considered Cristic people to be their enemy and had killed many Cristic and Jewish children. The Cristic people didn't have any songs like this where they glorified war and called other people their enemy.

Why are these Rhettians now singing about going to war? And all of these kids know this song... they know it by heart! Are these all Nazis? Is this a Nazi camp for children?

Go forth, Rhettian Warriors
Marching as before,
Goseth's burning gabel
Leading as to war.

Paul turned pale.

Do they know I'm Cristic? Are they testing me? Are they having fun with me, making me feel different and afraid and alone before they torture and kill me, the way the Nazis did to the "Dirty Cristers"?

Why did my parents send me to this strange, God-forsaken place so far from home? Did they know about this? They must have known. Are they testing me? Is this their way of showing me what Rhettians are really like? No... that doesn't make any sense. They must not have known about this. They must not have known that this was what Rhet-

tians do at YMRA camps—that they sing about going to war and marching behind banners to fight their enemies.

It went on, verse after verse, for what seemed like an eternity. *This is what purgatory must be like,* he thought to himself, as the Rhettian kids surrounding him passionately belted out the song. He tried to mentally steel himself for the attack that he was certain would follow the song. He would not cry, he told himself, he would not scream. He would die reciting the Lord's Prayer—the only prayer that he had memorized. Perhaps that was what the pit was for... perhaps they would move that "Y"—that giant gabel—into the pit and lash him to it and burn him, like they used to do to Cristic people. Perhaps this was part of a beastly ritual that these Rhettians did each summer.

Despite himself, Paul started to tremble in fear.

Then the song ended.

The circle of campers disbanded.

Nick marched up to his group.

"Alright you guys, line up again! I didn't finish giving you your nicknames! Line up in the same order so I don't lose track! Come on, HUP, two, three, four! Get a move-on!"

No attack, thought Paul. *No torture, no fire. Maybe they don't know I'm Cristic after all.* He looked down at his hands which were aching... he had clenched his fists so tightly, his fingernails had left marks on his palms. He wished he was somewhere else—anywhere but there.

The rest of the day was fairly uneventful. The swim in the lake was fun, but his feet kept getting stuck in the bottom muck, and bluegills would swim up to him and peck at his belly, which pinched a bit. And during the canoe outing, the boy in front of him kept splashing his paddle in the water, drenching Paul and once giving him a mouthful of lake water. But for the most part the camp activities were okay, and for a while Paul even started to forget about the events of that morning.

But he never fully forgot, and on the long ride home he played it over and over in his head, trying to make sense of it. At ten years old he could not fathom that Rhettians would sing such a song and consider it routine, inoffensive, harmless. Only later did Paul begin to grasp that some religious beliefs could be so ingrained in people that the extreme could become commonplace, bigotry the rule, and intolerance second-nature.

When he arrived home, he told his parents about the morning sing-along.

"Shoo" never went back to that camp.

The loud report of an exploding ember snapped Paul back to the bonfire, just as the last words of the Mithran hymn rose to a crescendo. The fire had spread almost to the top of the pyre, casting a harsh yellow glow on the upturned faces of the assembled revelers. It was so very odd watching hundreds of Rhettians sing their praises to the inferno: the overwhelming tide of unabated, innocent joy, with an unsettling undercurrent of mass inculcation. It would have been engaging enough and cause for merriment, if there wasn't such a gruesome history of these passions being sated with rampages of hatred and vengeance—a catalyst for the senseless, brutal murders of hundreds of thousands, perhaps millions of Cristic and Jewish sacrificial lambs to appease whatever demons Rhettians harbored in their lives.

The hymn finally ended and the circle began to break apart, with neighbors shaking hands and wishing each other a Merry Mithran. As Paul joined in the good tidings, he felt a pang of guilt for agreeing to come on this trip, for joining in these festivities when so many of his ancestors had feared them, and with just cause. Was he being a traitor to their memory, disrespectful of their suffering by standing in this circle in the snow, holding hands and paying homage to the Rhettian Conflagration? Or was there a point where you move on, accepting the olive branch offered by people who weren't responsible for those past horrors, hoping that through bonds of friendship such bigotry born of ignorance could be banished?

Another loud bang—like a cannon shot—sent a plume of sparks arching toward a knot of people, almost reaching them. Nervous laughter arose from the crowd.

"Pretty wild, eh, Paul?" asked Mr. Forsythe, patting him on the back. "Yes indeed. Nothing like a big Mithran bonfire to welcome in the holiday."

The pyre was now totally enveloped in flames, their dull roar like that of a rampaging river as they hungrily licked at the crackling, sizzling logs, consuming everything. The fire lasted for hours, and the revelers basked in its warmth and glow, wishing each other comfort and joy, making toasts over spiked cider and hugging and dancing and bursting into song as the moment seized them.

Chapter Ten

Mithran

T he Lord is watching over you!
His Son and Savior is watching over you!
Embrace Goseth! Take Him into your hearts!
Goseth died on the gabel for your sins!
He gave us all His love, His pure, unselfish love!

Who's shouting?

He wants to take you into His House!
Into the Lord's House!
Into the House of the Blessed and the Faithful!
Accept His offer, and accept Him into your hearts!

House of the blessed and the faithful?
He struggled to open his eyes.

The sinner turns away, the sinner lives in hate!
The sinners burned our Lord at the gabel!
The gabel of our faith.
We carry the gabel as He did, in love!
Not with hate.
Not with vengeance.

But with pure and unconditional love!

He managed to open one eye, turning toward the shouts.

On this special day, this Holy Day, we turn to Him!
As He taught us in Vinten 3:14—
Do not turn from Me, for I am...

Paul hit the snooze button and peered at the clock.
What time is it? Seven already?

He sat up in bed, forcing the cobwebs away, then turned the selection knob to OFF. The last thing he wanted was to fall back asleep and have to wake up to *that* again. He remembered last night trying to find a good station to wake up to, but found that out here in the boondocks there simply wasn't anything.

Rhettian Lorswers and country western—that's all there is. He laughed to himself: *Vince would be right at home out here. Can he ski? Is there any place to ski in Texas?*

He tried to picture a map of the state...

Maybe some mountains way out west, beyond the panhandle. Do they get snow in the winter? Then again, Vince could have travelled farther west or north, into New Mexico or Colorado. It's probably a plane trip either way, but it's still Country Western Territory. Is there something about the mountains that makes people addicted to country western music? Could be the thinner air...

Curious, he switched the radio knob back to ON, then slowly turned the tuner:

... He said to them, "Give unto them that which they..."

... when the Lord shone His Countenance upon them...

... and the faithful came to see His...

... on this Monday, this special Sabbath of Goseth's Conflagration, we...

Incredible, Paul thought. *Not even any country music this morning. Just wall-to-wall sermons. Is that all these hicks listen to out here?*

He turned off the radio, stretched his arms and legs and headed into the bathroom.

Maybe just on Monday mornings. Or, maybe just on Mithran. That must be it—just on Mithran Monday.

Mithran Monday. The Monday after Monday—the Sabbath of Sabbaths, as Rhettians called it. The one time of the year when there were two Mondays together. According to Rhettianity, Mithran Monday was the Day That Time Stood Still: when Goseth Rhetter's immeasurable suffering and his conflagration caused God to stop time in His Grief, to extend the Sabbath for an extra day.

Paul realized that the real reason for the extra Monday was, of course, to rectify the calendar's fifty-two weeks with the 365-day solar year. Fifty-two times seven was 364, so another day had to be added in order to keep the days of the week consistent—otherwise the days would keep shifting, like they did on the Cristic calendar. By adding a second Monday, that meant that Vintner 23rd always came on a Monday, and that Rhettag—Edel 1st—fell on their Sabbath, too. And New Year's Day, Gosiery 1st, would always be on Monday as well. Every date was always on the same day—Paul's birthday, Franzen 17th, was always on a Wednesday. Independence Day, Pendiery 23rd, was always on a Tuesday.

He knew enough about the Cristic calendar to know that this

wasn't the case. Cristmas fell on Vintner 27th, 28th, 29th, or even Brie 1st, depending on the year, although according to the Cristic calendar it was always on the same day—he couldn't remember the name of the month—Dee-something. But even though it was on the same Cristic date, the day of the week kept jumping around, so that sometimes Cristmas was on the Cristic Monday, or Thursday, or Saturday, or Wednesday. It could land on any day.

It was pretty screwed up.

Easter was different—it was always on a Cristic Sunday. In fact, Cristers called it "Easter Sunday". But Easter hopped all over the actual calendar... it could be weeks before Rhettag one year and then weeks after it the following year. Sometimes it landed almost on top of Rhettag. Inevitably, every year some of his classmates would scoff that the Cristic holidays were just plain weird because they jumped around so much.

Adding the second Monday at Mithran—and yet another extra Monday every four years at the end of Ilsembre for the leap year—helped to establish order to the calendar. But Cristers and Jews both considered it blasphemy, a violation of God's sacrosanct seven-day week, tied to Creation. Seven days was seven days, according to Cristic and Jewish theologians. You don't go tinkering with God's rules just to even out the days and dates. Of course, to Rhettians it *was* God's rule: the fulfillment of a new Commandment ordained by God, part of mankind's journey down the pathway to enlightenment.

Paul turned on the shower, waited a moment for the water to heat up and then stepped in.

His granddad used to like to listen to Kristisch folk music while lounging in the bath on Sunday mornings. This was possible because there used to be a Cristic radio station in Anne Arundel County where his dad grew up. Anne Arundel had the largest Cristic population in the Washington metro area: big enough to support several churches, a few Cristic ethnic restaurants, and that one radio station. The schools there even closed for Good Friday and Easter. As far as Paul knew, the Anne Arundel schools still closed for Easter, but the radio station was long gone.

Dave's family had migrated down to Clifton from Montgomery County. Most of the Jewish families in the D.C. area lived around there. It was kind of an unwritten rule: Cristers in Anne Arundel, Jews in Montgomery.

And Rhettians everywhere.

As Paul headed down to Mithran Breakfast, he peered through one of the lodge's immense picture windows up the mountain toward the spot where the bonfire had burned the night before. There were still faint wisps of smoke rising through the trees. The Forsythes had stayed at the bonfire until the flames had subsided into a twenty-foot pile of undulating, radiant embers that seemed to have a life of their own, constantly shifting from iridescent gold, to orange, to a searing red. On the way back down the mountain, Paul kept looking back at the glowing mound, trying to fathom its primal, almost visceral allure.

The Forsythes had invited him to join them at Mithran Feier the following morning, and he had graciously accepted their offer. After breakfast, the five of them climbed into the Escalade and set off to a Paxist shrin in the nearby town of Grangeville. It had seemed impolite to decline the invitation, and besides... he was curious to see how a Feier was conducted in a shrin.

The Rhetter Our King shrin in Grangeville was small compared to the ones in Clifton County, but still bigger than the church his family belonged to. Its large oak door sported a Mithran wreath—unlike the Rhettag wreath with its garish purple and yellow pansies, the Mithran wreath was all earthy hues, made from intricately woven willow branches and clusters of acorns, with pastel ribbons intertwined.

Seeing it reminded Paul of a newspaper article he saw a couple of years ago about a Mithran wreath featured in a Playboy centerfold—lovingly embraced by the beautiful and naked Miss Vintner—that was supposedly adorned with acorns. However, although the article didn't include the picture, it claimed that on closer inspection the acorns weren't acorns at all, but rather bunches of brown plastic knobs that, according to some readers, resembled the tips of penises. Allegations that the magazine had substituted erotic symbols for acorns on a Mithran wreath caused an uproar—the immediate result being that the Vintner issue sold out within days.

Paul and Dave, after a great deal of effort, had managed to acquire a worn copy, and they carefully examined the centerfold—after carefully examining Miss Vintner—to see for themselves whether it was true. Even using the magnifying glass from his dad's stamp collection, Paul couldn't tell for certain.

Granted, they don't look like acorns, and with a little imagination they could look a little like… well, like that other thing, but not definitely.

After a minute of staring through the loupe, Dave looked up, blinking several times to clear his eyes, then shrugged.

"Well?" Paul demanded.

"Based on my very detailed analysis, I'd have to say that her tits are big enough without magnification."

Paul punched his arm.

"Not *her*… the *wreath*!"

"The wreath? What wreath? Oh… you mean the schmuck schmorgasbord? Yeah, those are dick heads all right. All of them circumcised, too, as a matter of fact. Curious thing, that."

"How can you be so sure?" Paul asked, grabbing the magnifier from Dave and peering once more.

"I thought we decided that they definitely weren't acorns."

"Yeah, definitely not acorns," Paul agreed, still peering.

"So then, Sherlock, what are they?"

Paul looked up. "Honestly, I don't know."

Dave eyed his friend. "Is this or is this not a sex mag?"

"Well, I think they call it a 'gentleman's magazine'..."

"Yeah, right. Selling what?"

"Um... sex."

"Duh. It's a magazine whose main business is selling sex. And this extremely talented young lady in the centerfold represents—what?"

Paul sighed. "I suppose you want me to say that she's every guy's sexual fantasy."

"Well, maybe not *every* guy, Four-Oh, but a helluva lot of guys. So we're agreed that she's a sex symbol. And what is she hugging and fondling there?"

"A Mithran wreath."

"Okay, superficially, yes. But in most every guys' dreams, what is she fondling?"

He sighed again. "Our dicks."

"Bingo. So why is it so hard for you to accept that the folks at Playboy assembled a garland of dick heads for this amazingly naked creature to caress?"

Paul frowned. "It's just so... perverted."

"I think that's the point."

"But on a Mithran wreath? I mean, that's just too obscene!"

Dave leaned back, locking his hands behind his head. "Uh-huh. Too obscene. I see. Isn't this the same religion where half the pastors were fondling and screwing kids while the Shrin looked the other way? Which is more obscene—shrin-protected pedophiles raping children, or plastic dick heads stuck on a wreath in a girlie magazine?"

Paul smirked: Dave had a point.

Inside the Rhetter Our King shrin, the Forsythes and Paul sat in a large balcony reserved for non-parishioners, along with several other families he recalled seeing at Fox Hunt.

Parts of the service were similar to the Cristic liturgy—such as the use of an altar on a rostrum that Rhettians called the *kanzel*, the sacramental robes, the burning incense, and the choir. But other elements were completely foreign, and Paul had no idea what their function or purpose could be. The elder's hat was white and shaped like a floppy triangular mortarboard, with a purple gabel imprinted on the top of the hat connecting the three corners and purple tassels dangling from each point. It not only looked ridiculous to Paul, but also uncomfortable.

The centerpiece, of course, was the gabel: in this particular shrin, it was portrayed in a large ocular stained glass window above the altar, surrounded by angels. The gabel in this dazzling multi-hued window seemed to be perpetually aglow, as if on fire—whether this was a trick of the sunlight filtering through the colored glass or due to some artificial enhancement by hidden lights, Paul wasn't certain, but it was an impressive illusion. Paul also noticed that there were no representations of Goseth burning on the gabel anywhere in the shrin. This was, of course, because it was a Paxist shrin. Conflagraphs—with their serenely countenanced, suffering Goseth, were only found in the Katolish, Anointist and other fundamentalist denominations. But even without Goseth, there were the same four carved letters on the branches of this stained glass gabel: YT / KK—"Goseth of Trier, King of the Cristers".

King of the Cristers! Crap on that.

Midway through the service, the Forsythes left their seats to traverse the kanzel to receive their Holy Communion. They didn't call it that, of course—in Rhettianity, it was called the *Divine Affinity*—but it was pretty much the same ritual as the Cristic Eucharist. Instead of a sacrament of wine and wafers, the Rhettian Eucharist used consecrated virgin spring water and pieces of soft bread pulled from the interior of a large loaf, called the *wamme*, or "womb". Paul remembered reading somewhere that the pieces of bread had to be torn by hand and not cut with a knife or other mechanical device, though he didn't know the reason for this proscription.

Paul did know that the virgin spring water used for the Eucharist came from a single source in Élies, France where, according to legend, a young girl was visited by the Virgin Ilsa soon after the conflagration of Rhetter and told of a secret spring that flowed with the blood of Goseth, a single sip of which could cure the faithful who had fallen victim to the plague. Following the Virgin's clues, the child found the spring, its water gushing from the crevice in the middle of a granite boulder that appeared to have been cleaved by a giant sword, forming a massive gabel. According to the girl's testament, the water that burst forth was a deep scarlet, but when she cupped her hands under the spray, the water that filled her palms was miraculously crystal clear.

As the legend went, the girl ran pell-mell to nearby Élies and told the villagers of her meeting with the Virgin and of her discovery. By the time they arrived at the spring, the water had clarified to just a hint of red. The remarkable sweetness of the water and its alleged curative powers were quickly embraced by the Kristenzian as proof that it embodied Rhetter's blood, and it became an integral part of the liturgy for the fast-growing religion. Many of the millions of Rhettians who made the annual pilgrimage to Élies to see the gabeled-stone spring swore that the water that issued from the rock was tinged with a reddish hue, though geologists had long ago determined that this was simply due to reflections from red mica schist embedded in the granite stone.

As Rhettianity grew, so did the enterprise built around the Virgin Spring at Élies. Today, the spring was surrounded by a massive bottling plant, its operation supervised by three Rhettian bishops appointed by the Heiliger Väter. Each container was inspected prior to bottling, and secured with the official seal of the Väter before being shipped to the tens of thousands of shrins around the world for use in their sacraments and other holy rites. Cristers disparagingly referred to it as Väter Wäter, since they regarded it as nothing more than a cheap imitation of their sacramental wine. Paul knew that the elder of each shrin was under strict orders to account for every empty bottle and to ship it back to Élies, but that every now and then one or two "empties" would be misplaced and wind up in the hands of a collector. Sometimes one of these would surface on eBay, and bidding could reach several hundred dollars for a single bottle.

He thought about the episode of *Life In The Slow Lane* with the baptism at the apartment in Newark and the spilled Holy Water, the host despondent over its cost and the mad scramble to soak it up with paper towels in order to proceed with the ceremony. A similar skit could just as easily have been made around Väter Wäter, with a group of Rettians desperately trying to sponge up their holy water in order to save money while receiving their Divine Affinity.

Yeah, right. Not in a million years.

Watching the procession of worshippers beneath him, Paul saw that they were given the Affinity Water in individual paper cups from a silver tray held by one choirboy—the cups were then discarded in an ornate silver receptacle that looked a bit like a spittoon held by another young boy. At first, he assumed that this was for hygienic purposes, but he then noticed that the elder placed the pieces of *wamme* bread directly into the mouth of each worshipper with his bare hands: hardly a sanitary way to administer the yearning. Well, Paul surmised, if Goseth had the power to cure them of the Plague, he could certainly dispel a few pesky germs from the elder's hand.

Even if the hand-delivered *wamme* bread wasn't unsanitary, the Affinity Staff certainly was. The long golden rod, held by a shrin rector, was topped with a tiny bust of the Baby Goseth, patterned after a darling sculpture of an infant child by the Northern Italian sculptor Desiderio da Settignano in 139—Paul knew this because he had seen the original bust at the National Gallery of Art. The delicate, innocent features of the child's cherubic face struck an emotional maternal chord, and Paul knew that the Holy Shrin must have chosen it for this reason, as a way to enhance the worshippers' empathy and love for Goseth.

As each parishioner approached the altar, they knelt in front of the rector, who lowered the end of the staff so that they could kiss the bronze head of the child on the lips. Paul had read that Katolish Rhettians believed that the bust became actual flesh at the moment of the kiss—a process known as *The Transformance*—its evident origins in the Cristic transubstantiation of wafers and wine into the flesh and blood of Jesus—which in turn was the basis for the detestable Flesh and Blood Libel. How ironic that the miracle that represented thanksgiving to Cristers was the basis for such grotesque defamation by Rhettians—and yet the Rhettians themselves plagiarized the same miracle, worshipping a bronze head! Images of the Golden Calf entered Paul's thoughts...

With each parishioner kissing the bronze bust in turn, germs were bound to be transferred... in fact, it was suspected to have contributed to some of the most serious outbreaks of influenza in

Europe during the early centuries. To help remedy this problem, Shrin Elders had adopted the practice of anointing the lips of the sculpture with *sanctified spirits*—distilled grain alcohol—between kisses, and Paul noticed that a choirboy quickly dabbed the lips with a small cloth after each peck.

After kissing the Baby Goseth, the Forsythes reached the two choirboys holding the silver trays of Affinity Water and *wamme* bread, and they again knelt at each in turn to receive the sanctified gifts—Mrs. Forsythe in the lead, followed by the two girls and then their father. The act of kneeling was accompanied by a gesture wherein each parishioner would bring their arms together in front of their chest with their hands opened palms up beneath their chin, so that the touching forearms formed the stem of the gable and their hands were the branches of the "Y". This action was called bigenection, from the German term *VerbiegenKnien*, or "bended knee". Peggy was the first of the sisters to receive the Eucharist, and she went through the well-practiced motions—bigenect, receive, drink, discard, stand, step, bigenect, tongue-out, tongue-in, stand, proceed off the kanzel—with an automatic precision that, from Paul's vantage point on the balcony, suggested the robotic routines of a manufacturing assembly line. He wondered whether he also seemed so mechanical when he received communion at his church. The bigenecting reminded Paul of the kneeling gesture traditionally done in Cristic Catholic churches called genuflection, but Catholics described a crux shape with their hand instead of the gabel. Which came first—the gabel or the crux hand gesture? Paul made a mental note to log onto Wikipedia to check it out when he got back to the lodge.

Patty followed her older sister onto the kanzel to the tabernacle. Paul watched her intently as she knelt and drank the holy water. As she again knelt and stuck out her tongue for the bread, she looked up at Paul—even at that distance he saw her wink at him and smile, her eyes fixed on him as she stood back up. There was something about the way she had slipped the small piece of bread into her mouth on the tip of her tongue that was sensuous, arousing—maybe it was just the way she was looking at him—maybe he had imagined it all. He must have imagined it. This was their Divine Affinity, for Rhetter's sake! He chastened himself for thinking such thoughts in a holy place.

On the ride back to the lodge, Patty leaned forward from the back seat and playfully poked Paul's shoulder. "I bet you're wondering what the holy virgin water tastes like, Paul," she teased. "Too bad you couldn't try it."

Mrs. Forsythe spun around and glowered at her younger daughter. "Patricia Lynn Forsythe! That's not a proper thing to say to Paul. You should apologize to him."

"It's okay," Paul interjected. "We do pretty much the same thing in our church."

Mr. Forsythe half-turned around in the driver's seat. "That's right. You do have something similar to the Divine Affinity. You call it by some other name... what is that thing called..."

"We call it the Holy Communion. But we use wine... well, juice for younger people... and a kind of wafer instead."

"Copy Cat," said Patty, sitting back in her seat and folding her arms across her chest. "Holy water and holy bread make more sense."

"I don't think they're copying us," her dad said. "The Cristers—I mean, the Cristic People—have been doing their rituals for a long time. I'm guessing that your ritual goes pretty far back... is that right, Paul?"

Paul had no idea how long Cristers had been practicing the sacrament of the Holy Communion, but he knew that it had to pre-date the Rhettian Affinity by several centuries at least—

perhaps as far back as the early days of the Church. *Another topic for Wikipedia.* "Yeah, it goes pretty far back."

"See, Patty?" Mr. Forsythe scolded. "You shouldn't rush to conclusions like that. Remember what Goseth taught us: 'Do not pass judgment lest ye be judged.'"

Hold on, thought Paul... didn't Jesus say that first? "I think the Crist said that," he volunteered.

Mr. Forsythe glanced back again. "Well, I'm not surprised if he did. The Old Teachings are filled with stories and lessons that Goseth built upon. In fact, I think Isaiah also said something along those lines."

"Isaiah?" asked Peggy. "Who's that?"

Yeah, wondered Paul, who was that? The name sounded familiar.

"He was one of the Hebrew prophets," explained Mr. Forsythe, "Also from the Old Teachings."

"Well, if everybody said it," asked Peggy, "who said it first?

"Wait a minute," Patty chimed in. "Why would Cristen say something like that? Cristen was the bad guy!"

Mrs. Forsythe shot her daughter a look that Paul easily deciphered as *shut up*! Noticing that Paul was watching her, Mrs. Forsythe gave him a weak smile and turned back around in her seat.

"Not Cristen, Patty," corrected Mr. Forsythe, oblivious to the exchange between mother and daughter. "Paul said the Crist—Jesus. You know who Jesus was."

"Yeah, whatever," said Patty. "Cristen—Jesus... what's the difference?"

Mrs. Forsythe spun around again, her eyes glaring. "That is *enough*, young lady! I don't want to hear another word out of you, do you *understand*?"

"Well, it's true," murmured Patty.

Peggy looked back at her younger sister, and in a lecturing tone said: "Cristic people don't believe that Cristen was Jesus, and they don't accept Goseth Rhetter as the True Savior, either. Isn't that right, Paul?"

Paul didn't want to be drawn into this discussion—not in this car with her parents and Patty, not in the midst of his Fox Hunt fantasy. He meekly nodded, hoping that would be the end of it.

"Well, not exactly," said Mr. Forsythe, unaware of Paul's nod. "Forgive me for answering for you, Paul, but as I understand it, Cristic people know that Goseth was chosen by God, but they don't accept Him as the Lord. They still think that Jesus was the Messiah. In all honesty, I'm not sure how they feel about Cristen. Maybe Paul can explain that better."

Oh, Lord, please make this just go away, thought Paul. But it wouldn't go away—the Forsythes were watching him, waiting for his response. He sighed, rehearsing his answer in his mind before replying. "I, uh—the Cristic people—we don't really think too much about Cristen, or about Goseth. I mean, it's not part of our faith."

"But you don't accept Goseth as your Savior, right?" prodded Peggy.

"Um... yeah, we don't," Paul nodded, then shook his head. "I mean, no, we don't."

"That's all right, Paul," said Mrs. Forsythe. She gave him a consoling, almost pitying smile. "Goseth still loves you just the same."

That's just goddamn wonderful, thought Paul. He smiled wanly back at her and nodded a little appreciative thanks.

* * *

By the time they arrived back at the lodge, the Mithran celebration was in full swing—the snow-covered lawn surrounding the lodge gaily decorated with large poles wrapped in pastel ribbons, the loose ends at the top of each pole playfully fluttering in the thin winter breeze. Pale multicolored streamers hung from poles projecting from every gabled window and from the twenty-foot pink and green gabel on the spire, giving it the appearance of a medieval castle at tournament time.

In the large gazebo out front, a small brass band was playing a medley of popular Mithran songs. Paul could make out portions of *Mithran's On Its Way, Here Comes Chipper Fluffytail,* and *Mithran Parade.*

Peggy was fidgeting in her car seat like an eager six-year-old, glancing out of her car window at the festivities.

"What time is it, Dad?"

Mr. Forsythe glanced at his watch. "Ten-thirty-three."

"Oh great, just enough time!" she cried. "Come on, Paul, let's do the Acorn Hunt! You've never done an acorn hunt, have you?"

"Peggy, dear," Mrs. Forsythe admonished her daughter from the front seat, "I'm sure that the Acorn Hunt is for the younger children. You and Paul are a bit too old for that."

"Well I'm sure we can do *something*," Peggy protested. "I don't want to spend Mithran at Fox Hunt just sitting around on my butt, and Paul's not going to, either. Come on, Paul," she commanded, grabbing his hand as the car slowed to a stop in the valet parking line. "Let's see what's still okay for us *older* kids."

"Patty, you go with them," instructed Mr. Forsythe. "You know the rules."

Patty rolled her eyes, departing the van with the other two.

As soon as the trio had traveled beyond sight of the elder Forsythes, Patty waved goodbye to her sister.

"*I'm* heading out to the slopes," she announced. "It's way too nice a day to spend it looking for acorns."

You got that right, thought Paul.

After Patty departed, the pair walked together along the shoveled pathways around the lodge, taking in the sights and sounds of Mithran merriment. Easter, the Cristic equivalent of Mithran in the springtime, didn't have anything like this. It was a much more serious holiday, focused around worship services at the church on the Cristic Good Friday and Easter Sunday. The Eucharist… visiting the Stations of the Crux… the Easter Mass… the Easter meal featuring egg dishes… that was about it. None of this superficial frivolity.

Approaching them along the path was the embodiment of Mithran silliness—a Fox Hunt employee dressed in a Chipper Fluffytail outfit, looking like a character from Disney World. The chipmunk carried a large basket of oversized pastel-colored acorns and was passing them out to people along the pathway. There was something surreal and disconcerting about a human-sized chipmunk trudging along a snow-covered pathway, basket in hand—but no one else seemed the least bit bothered by it. In fact, children were running up to the creature and hugging it before receiving an acorn.

As it passed by Peggy and Paul, the chipmunk handed each of them an acorn. Peggy immediately snapped the top off hers to see what was inside, and held up the foil-covered treat.

"Oh, my, a Dove Mithran Acorn! They're my absolute favorite!" she exclaimed. Without hesitation, she expertly unwrapped the pink foil and bit off a portion of the chocolate acorn, closing her eyes with rapture. "Mmmm… this is absolutely heavenly! What'd you get? Open it! Open it!"

Paul tried to comply, but he wasn't able to snap his acorn open the way Peggy had. He then tried twisting the top off, also to no avail.

"Silly," she scolded, snatching it from him, "this is how you do it."

With one deft motion of her gloved hands, she had the acorn opened and upside down, the prize tumbling out into Paul's palm.

"Oh, Paul, you got a Jenny Lou Mithran Acorn! They're my absolute favorite!" she cried. "You lucky S.O.B.! Oh, I just *hate* you!"

"You just said that Dove thing was your absolute favorite."

"Well, they are... but Jenny Lou's are *really* my all-time absolute favorite!" She made a grimace. "Oh, Paul, you're not going to eat that, are you?"

"I don't know," he said, holding it up in the sunlight and turning it around. "What's in it?"

"It's divinity and caramel covered with crushed walnuts. It's fantastic!"

"What's 'divinity'?"

"Divinity! You know... you really don't know what divinity is? What planet are you from?"

"Hey, I don't know, okay? Give me a break. We don't have stuff like this."

"You don't have Mithran acorns?" Peggy asked, incredulous. "How is that even possible? They're everywhere you look! The supermarkets are full of them!"

"I never go into supermarkets. My mom does all the shopping. And she never buys this stuff."

"Oh, poor baby," Peggy sympathized, taking off her glove and softly rubbing Paul's cheek. "You've had a really deprived childhood. You know, I was hoping you'd give it to me, but seeing as how you've never had one, you should try it. Besides, I'm getting fat."

Paul looked at her. There wasn't an ounce of fat on that perfect body.

"No, here," he said, handing it to her. "Take it. I've gone seventeen years without one—I can wait a bit longer. You want it more than I do, and besides, it's your holiday. And you're *not* fat."

She took it from him, and before he knew it the candy was unwrapped. "You're such a sweetie," she said, wrinkling her pert little nose at him. "Tell you what. It's big enough to share." She bit off a piece and handed the Jenny Lou back to him. "Here, if you don't mind sharing germs."

Paul took the nut-encrusted candy acorn and also bit off a chunk. It was good. Really good. And he didn't mind sharing germs at all. He had hoped they'd share germs for a long, long time.

After finishing the treat, they went off in search of the Mithran activities for young adults. These included a silly contest where couples had to grasp the handle of a spoon in their mouths, one person carrying a plastic acorn in the bowl of his or her spoon and transferring it to the other's spoon, all without using their hands. Another game was based on the classic three-legged race, but in this one the couples had to wear snow shoes and stay on top of the snow without breaking through the top crust and falling down—much harder than it looked, especially with one bound leg and having to negotiate the enormous meshed paddles of the shoes.

Although they didn't participate in the Acorn Hunt, Paul and Peggy did help the Fox Hunt staff search for unclaimed acorns after the children had finished their game. It was more fun than Paul had imagined, trying to find brightly-colored acorns half-buried in the snow. Maybe it was simply the joy of the hunt, or perhaps the promise of the sweet surprise that came with each discovery. He found several acorns: together, he and Peggy filled a small basket, and they ran off to her room to share their booty.

With Patty on the slopes, they had the room to themselves. Sitting at the edge of Peggy's bed, they spilled the basketful of acorns onto the bedspread like pirates spreading out loot from a recent plunder and popped them open. The gilded candy wrappers shone in the late afternoon light, each one beckoning to be the first one tasted. Peggy made the first choice for them, slowly unwrapping the delicate foil to reveal the creamy chocolate treat inside. Instead of biting it, she licked one side of it, then passed it to Paul. Copying her, he licked the other side and passed it back.

"It might take a while, at this rate," he said.

"So what? Are you in a hurry?" Peggy teased, taking another lick. "Let's see how many licks it takes."

Paul took the candy from her, licking it again. "Mmmm, it *is* good. I just don't know if I can stick to one lick."

"Then take another lick," she said, smiling. "I won't tell."

He took another lick and passed it to her.

"Now I get to take two licks," she said. "It's only fair."

She slowly took two long licks, Paul watching her tongue stroke the surface of the wet candy. Then she took a third lick, giggling. "Oops. I cheated," she whispered. "I'm being a bad girl."

She brought her face close to Paul's, the candy between them.

"Let's lick it at the same time."

As she held the candy, they both licked at it. Paul could feel her breath: mixed with the sweet scent of chocolate, it was intoxicating. Her lips were entrancing, moist cupid bows of glistening pink lipstick. He could think of nothing else but those lips, and before he knew what was happening the candy had slipped into her mouth and his tongue had followed it, touching hers, the taste electric, his lips meeting hers, warm and soft and wet and firm, and the chocolate now pushed by her tongue into his mouth, their lips still locked, their tongues dancing together as the sweetness and saltiness mixed, and he wanted it to last forever, this first kiss, this perfect moment...

Someone was knocking.

Insistent raps.

"Damn it!" Peggy whispered, breaking away, standing up and straightening her shrin dress. She crossed over to the door as Paul swallowed what remained of the chocolate.

She opened the door to a perturbed Patty.

"What the hell is this door locked for? My passkey wouldn't even work!" Patty stormed into the room and spied Paul seated on the bed. "Oh... hi, Paul." She turned back to Peggy. "You could've told me..."

"How could I tell you?" demanded Peggy, combing her fingers through her hair in frustration. "Post an announcement on the door? What are *you* doing back so soon? What happened to Rhett?"

"Rhett's history. He left without telling me. The jerk. Hey, is that a Jenny Lou?"

"It's mine!" shouted Peggy, rushing over to the bed and snatching up the one Jenny Lou Mithran Acorn before Patty could touch it. "Go get your own!"

Patty looked at her sister, disgusted. "What a brat!" She turned to Paul. "I hope she isn't that greedy with you, Paul. If *I* had that candy, I'd share it with you."

Paul thought he saw her wink at him as she turned away and headed to the bathroom, unzipping her ski parka on the way.

"Anyway, it's almost three. You two lovebirds might want to get some skiing in before dinner."

As Patty shut the bathroom door behind her, Peggy sat back down on the bed beside Paul.

"Sorry about that," she whispered.

"Hey, don't worry about it," Paul whispered back, taking her hand in his. "That was great... I mean, it was the greatest. Fantastic. Thanks, really."

"It *was* great," agreed Peggy. "I just wish we hadn't been interrupted."

"Yeah, me, too," Paul nodded.

He wanted to kiss her again, to pick up where they had left off, but he knew that she couldn't, not with her sister there. Peggy read his thoughts.

"Again, soon," she whispered, kissing him on the cheek.

Very soon, Paul prayed silently. *Please make it very, very soon.*

Chapter Eleven

The Fall

The shaft of sunlight struck Paul full in the face, evaporating the dream.

He'd had this dream before, or at least thought he had. Perhaps it was only déjà vu—but it seemed to him that it recurred every so often, with only slight variations.

He was at home in the dream, or something like home... in truth, it wasn't like home at all, not in appearance, but it felt like home. He was lying on a small leather sofa, reading a magazine or watching TV or something—it didn't really matter. What mattered was that the sofa was warm, inviting, it seemed to nestle him like a womb, and he felt secure and protected. At some point he looked up and saw her standing behind the sofa, smiling down at him. She was wearing a gown, or perhaps a long robe, and the light was behind her, enveloping her in a sort of soft halo. *She said something—what was it?* Paul didn't know, or he couldn't remember... it was something like "Hi, stranger" or "Hey"... just a simple greeting. But it meant everything—it meant "I'm here", and she moved to the other side of the sofa and lay down beside him, snuggling next to him, and the robe parted or the gown simply faded away and he could feel her suppleness and smell her delicate perfume, and when he kissed her warm, soft lips, the two of them became one, and there was nothing in the world as sensuous and satisfying and right.

But it had vanished into the morning light.

He was momentarily disoriented, aware that he wasn't in his own bedroom, but not yet remembering the lodge. An instant later the cobwebs cleared and he had his bearings, jumping out of the king-sized bed and heading into the bathroom. He reminded himself of the resolution he had made before going to bed:

Today's the day I'm moving on, leaving the novice runs and heading up to the intermediates. I've held Peggy back long enough… the vacation's almost half over—it's time to start skiing for real.

After breakfast with the Forsythes, Paul and the girls grabbed their skis and journeyed out to the slopes. But as they traveled out of view of the lodge and Patty was saying her goodbyes, Paul interrupted.

"We're going with you."

"Where?" Patty asked, surprised.

"Up to the intermediates."

The sisters exchanged glances.

"You're not ready, Paul," Peggy said. "You need more practice. It's too dangerous."

"I'll take it slow," Paul assured her. "Look, I was okay yesterday afternoon. I was skiing all the way down, no problems."

Peggy made a frown. "You know what my dad said. Take it slow. You could really hurt yourself if you don't know what you're doing."

"Well, *I'm* going," announced Patty, turning and walking off toward the trails to the intermediate lifts. "Later."

"Come on," Paul pleaded with Peggy. "Let's go. I know you're bored stiff down here. I'm just holding you back."

"I don't care where I ski. I can have just as much fun down here as up there."

"I don't believe you," Paul countered, starting to follow Patty's footsteps. "I'm going to try it. You can come along if you want."

Peggy huffed, catching up with him. "This is really boneheaded. If you break your neck, it's not my fault."

"Duly noted. At least if I'm boneheaded, I won't crack my skull."

"Not funny," she said. But Paul saw she was smiling. "You just have to promise me that you won't try any crazy stuff."

"I'll take it slow, I promise," he said, tracing a Y mark with his index finger on his chest. "Gabel my heart."

He did take it slow, and not just because he had promised. The intermediate slopes were nothing like the beginners: they seemed to Paul to plummet down in nearly vertical drops, like skiing off a cliff. He was petrified, and he swore at himself for being so rash and not spending another day practicing below. Having spent most of Mithran Monday off the slopes, he was still experiencing difficulty with his stops and turns. But he didn't have any difficulty falling, which he did constantly. On Peggy's insistence, he was following her down the hill, staying as much as possible in her tracks, and he knew that she was trying to take it as slowly as she could, cutting back and forth across the hill in smooth, wide turns. It was second nature to her. Watching her leisurely glide back and forth, Paul was convinced that she could have done it blindfolded on one ski, without poles. He felt like he needed a third ski at least—some cleats would have been nice, too.

"Whoa! Whoa!" he shouted, not for the first time, as his legs threatened to slide out from underneath him.

Peggy turned to look back and slackened her pace even more. "That's okay, I'll go slower. Bend your knees more. Use them like shock absorbers. Find your center of balance. Lean forward. Tuck your poles under your arms. Snowplow if you feel like you're going too fast."

He followed her directions as closely as he could. Other skiers were whizzing by him, kicking up small jets of spray, leaning to and fro in perfect balance, using their poles for propulsion, not props. He felt completely embarrassed.

Enough of this! he admonished himself. *Mind over matter! Master the snow—don't let it master you! The only way to do this is to overcome your fear of failure, take a few tumbles and learn from the experience. Toddlers don't learn to walk by staying on all fours—they fall, get back up, and do it better the next time.*

He let himself glide and concentrated on looking several yards ahead, anticipating the turns, feeling the movement in his feet and legs and compensating by using his knees to control his position. Simple physics: the more he positioned himself parallel to the slope, the faster he went—the more perpendicular, the slower he would go. He sped up on the turns, then slowed during the slide across the open hill, then gained speed once again during the turn the other way.

By the time he reached the bottom of the hill, he was feeling more self-assured. By the time he finished the second run, he was beginning to enjoy himself.

Peggy noticed. "You're doing much better, Paul," she said, adjusting her gloves as they waited for the lift for their third run, "but don't get over-confident. We're still going to take it slow today."

"Yes, ma'am. You're a very good teacher, you know."

"Thanks," she said, wrinkling up her nose in her cute smile. "I charge a hundred bucks an hour, by the way."

"Put it on my tab."

The rest of the day was pure pleasure, as Paul became increasingly adept at making turns and controlling his speed. He could think of no better way to learn to ski than following Peggy down the hill, watching her lithely move her hips in a sleek, graceful dance with each turn. Every now and then she would look back and smile at him: whether it was for encouragement, or because she knew he was staring at her, he couldn't tell.

When Paul awoke the following morning, the disorientation that gripped him on the previous mornings had lessened. He was becoming acclimated to his new surroundings, even beginning to feel at home. Part of this had to do with the end of the holiday. By yesterday afternoon, all vestiges of Mithran—the pastel ribbons, the large gabel on the roof, the omnipresent baskets of acorns and the giant cardboard chipmunk in the lobby—had vanished. Best of all, the incessant Mithran background music piped through the lodge's PA system was gone, replaced by the easy-going secularity of soft jazz tunes. It was as if the holiday had never occurred, which was fine with Paul. The transition to normalcy was a relief, as if a weight had been lifted.

Mr. Forsythe's family itinerary was so packed that Paul hadn't had a chance to be alone with Peggy the previous night. After skiing that afternoon and attending the après ski party, the family had driven to a restaurant on the eastern side of the mountains renowned for its prime rib. It was very good—although a bit rarer than Paul preferred. The best side dish was julienned green beans sautéed with dill and almonds. He had never liked green beans, but these were thin-cut and still crisp, and the sharp nutty taste of the toasted almonds blended perfectly with the beans. He made a mental note to mention them to his mom in his next e-mail.

It was over an hour's drive to the restaurant, and the meal had lasted so long that when they arrived back at the lodge, it was time for bed. Paul was exhausted from the full day of skiing—his aching calves reminded him that he wasn't used to that kind of activity. He had stopped by the indoor whirlpool hoping to get a few minutes of massage under the warm jets, but it was filled with older people sharing jokes and conversation, and he didn't feel like crashing their party.

He settled for a long soak in the Jacuzzi in his room, which was nearly as good. The oversized tub allowed him to stretch out, and as he let his legs bobble in the rapidly churning spray, he imagined sharing the bath with Peggy—her seated at the other end, their legs interlocking among the millions of bubbles. He wondered if she was also bathing in her Jacuzzi, thinking the same thing. He closed his eyes and floated with the fantasy that they could read each other's thoughts... in a single, fluid motion, she was stepping out of her tub... wrapping herself in an oversized towel... tiptoeing out of her room... lightly running barefoot down the hall... using the keycard he had given her to enter his room... walking into the bath... without a word, letting the towel fall from her and stepping into the bath across from him...

He opened his eyes, half expecting that the fantasy had come true. He let out a long sigh, stepped out of the Jacuzzi, toweled himself off and climbed into bed.

At breakfast, things were unusually quiet. Perhaps, Paul surmised, Post-Mithran Letdown had set in. He had read about this syndrome in *Newsweek*—or maybe it was in *Time*. Although he didn't think that it amounted to full-blown depression, he had seen enough of a change in mood among Rhettians in the days following Mithran and Rhettag to know that there was some truth to it.

Also, with all three of them now stealing off to the intermediate slopes, it was possible that the girls didn't want to let something accidentally slip out in conversation, knowing that the news would be met with angry disapproval, and perhaps even an outright ban on skiing the intermediates for the duration of the vacation. Instead, the sparse conversation centered around their parents' pleasure with the offerings throughout the resort: the mud baths; handball and racquetball courts; weight-training rooms; aerobics classes; indoor track; two indoor pools and one heated outdoor pool; a Swedish sauna and massage therapy; and a wealth of other amenities.

"Patty and Peg—they have an Olympic-size pool here. You could do your laps to keep in shape," their dad said between bites of salad. "And Paul, we should have a game of racquetball while you're here."

Mr. Forsythe looked in pretty good shape for a guy approaching fifty. The older man was fairly muscular, trim and agile. Even with his youth advantage, Paul doubted he could best the girls' father at racquetball, especially since he'd only played it a few times. It would definitely be a fun challenge.

"I'd like that," he said.

"Good," said Mr. Forsythe, dabbing his mouth with his napkin. "I'll sign us up for tomorrow morning—say, ten o'clock?"

"Fine," agreed Paul. He was actually looking forward to it.

With breakfast finished, the teenagers headed out to ski. As they had the day before, once they were out of sight of the lodge, all three trekked over to the more advanced slopes. Goggles perched on his forehead and skis slung over his shoulder, Paul felt like a seasoned pro. His increasingly successful runs from yesterday filled him with confidence. He imagined that he was at the Olympics in Salt Lake City, walking over to the lift for the conclusion of the Super G...

Screw that—this is the Downhill.

He was in third place going into the final run, behind the favored Austrian Franz Hoffenmeier and World Finals Champion

Jan Störmgen of Norway. He had surprised everyone: although he was considered the United States' best chance, nobody had expected him to be in medal contention. But he wasn't interested in the bronze: he wanted gold. Nothing else would do. He had devoted every waking minute over the past few years to reaching this point: the countless, grueling hours of physical training and diet regimens; globetrotting to the world's most challenging courses; employing bio-mechanical computer analysis to perfect his form; rehearsing every nuance of this run in his mind's eye—the most efficient turns, the most controlled jumps, the optimal streamlined tuck on the final straightaway to the finish. In a sport of microseconds, only .620 separated him from the leader. He could do it. He just knew he could do it.

The rude bump of the lift seat striking his backside jerked Paul from his reverie, but only for an instant. As he took the slow ride to the top, he imagined the tension at the starting gate, gripping the handles of his poles as the seconds ticked down, waiting for the moment when the harsh blare of the starting buzzer and the green GO light made him to snap out his taut crouch like a tightly wound spring, digging both poles into the packed snow, starting down the steep unforgiving hill to the waiting crowd and fame.

"Follow my path," Peggy told him. "I'll try to take the turns slow, okay?"

He nodded, lowering his goggles over his eyes. He got into his crouch as Peggy started her run.

3... 2... 1... BEEEEEP.

He dug in with both poles, pushing off. Nothing to it. Just keep the knees bent and control the ankles. Following the newly-carved channels from Peggy's skis as best he could, he imagined that he cut an impressive figure heading down the mountain—a sleek dash of blue and green in his brand-new ski outfit. Gaining speed, he crouched even more. Lower wind resistance—that's the key. Keep those poles tucked tight under the arms. Concentrate on the turn—good! Now gain more speed on the straightaway.

Peggy's line was too shallow—she was practically skiing sideways along the hill, losing momentum. He could see her farther ahead, slowly swishing back and forth in a loopy, lazy pattern.

Why is she taking it so slow? Doesn't she know I can ski better now? Maybe I should show her. Heck, I can beat her down the hill—that would surprise her!

He left her tracks and took a steeper angle down the slope. Ahhh... this was more like it! More speed, baby! Now *this* was skiing!

He took the next turn, a bit wider than usual because of his speed, slipping a little, his right arm instinctively snapping his pole out, stabbing the ground to catch himself.

Everything's fine—just a tiny slip, maybe some ice.

Out of the turn, he angled downhill even more. He could feel the wind chafing his cheeks.

Exhilarating! What am I going now—twenty miles per hour? Thirty? Maybe a little too fast. Maybe time to put the brakes on a bit.

He tried to snow plow, but it wasn't much help.

Need to slow down some. Definitely too fast now.

He tried to turn his skis into a less steep angle, without success.

He started to panic: the turn was coming up, and he realized that he was going too fast to negotiate it.

Then he noticed the trees.

The trees! Where the hell did they come from? Three—four big pine trees!

He stuck out both poles as if to fend them off, forced his ankles to turn hard left, losing his balance, the sickening feeling of the skis slipping out from under him, knowing he was falling hard, spinning around, a hard crack as a ski left his boot, tumbling, tumbling, ice smacking his face, burning his ears, somersaulting, his shoulder slamming into the snow, sliding some more, then finally stopping, splayed out like a snow angel, looking up into the blue sky.

An eternity seemed to pass. It was actually kind of tranquil, lying there on a blanket of crystalline white powder.

Should I move? Can I move?

Paul tried to get up, but something wouldn't let him. He managed to force himself up onto his elbows, looking down at his left foot. It was at an odd angle. Definitely not a normal angle. He tried to move it but couldn't.

He could hear Peggy shouting at him. Then the swishing sound of someone approaching from above—a moment later, a guy in a Fox Hunt jacket with a red gabel in a white circle on an armband was looking down at him. The blessed ski patrol.

"Hey, buddy, you okay?"

"I'm not sure," Paul answered, gesturing toward his leg. "I can't move it."

The patrol knelt beside Paul's leg and expertly, gently fingered it above the ankle. "Yeah, looks like you did a number on it. Anything else hurt?"

Paul shook his head. "Not really. Maybe my shoulder a little."

"How about your other leg?" asked the patrol. "Can you move it?"

Paul dutifully moved his right foot.

The patrol nodded. "Okay, good."

He pressed a button on his shoulder-mounted walkie-talkie. "Center, this is Brad."

A moment later, the radio crackled back. "Go ahead, Brad."

Brad pressed the button again. "Yeah, Center, we got a 10-52 on Run 17. Possibly a break. Need a crew near the top."

A pause, then a burst of static, followed by "Okay, Brad. On its way."

"Roger, out."

Brad looked down at Paul, patted him lightly on the shoulder. "Okay, buddy, just hang loose. We'll get you off this hill soon."

By now a small knot of skiers had formed around Paul, including Peggy. She looked down at his twisted left foot.

"I think it's your ankle, Paul."

"Yeah, looks that way," he nodded.

"I was trying to go slow," she said. "I guess it was still too fast, huh?"

Paul looked up at her. He wanted to admit that it was all his fault. That he was stupidly trying to beat her down the hill. Instead, he shrugged. "Guess so."

The rescue team was there within minutes, and before the hour was out Paul had been bundled onto a special stretcher outfitted with skis and transported down the mountain to the medical facility, where his foot was immediately X-rayed and tightly taped. From the matter-of-fact efficiency of the EMT team, Paul could tell that this was a common ritual at Fox Hunt.

It turned out to be a badly sprained ankle—not a break.

When Peggy's parents were notified of the mishap by the Fox Hunt management, they were less than pleased.

"What did I tell you, young lady?" Paul heard Mr. Forsythe scolding Peggy outside the examining room door as the doctor checked his foot. "What did I say? I told you to take it slow. You knew that you were supposed to stay on the beginner slopes. Why is it you girls never listen to me?"

"That was like back before Mithran!" Peggy protested. "Paul's been skiing for three days. He was doing really well, too."

"Obviously not well enough. Who's going to pay this bill? I

can't go to his parents. Are you going to pay for this?"

"I'm sure his parents have insurance," snapped Peggy. "All you care about is the money."

"That's not fair, Peggy," interrupted her mother. "We're glad Paul wasn't hurt more than he is. He's a nice young man. But now he's bedridden for the rest of the vacation, and it's because you didn't listen."

"Dad broke *his* leg skiing," argued Peggy. "You told me he did soon after you got married. Maybe *he* doesn't listen, either."

"That was different," said Mr. Forsythe. "I'd been skiing a long time before that happened. It was a fluke. *This* was avoidable."

"Where's your sister?" Mrs. Forsythe asked. "Wasn't she with you?"

Oh gopes, thought Paul in the next room. *Patty! How is Peggy going to explain that?*

"I dunno," Peggy mumbled. "She… she went down the mountain ahead of us. I guess she didn't see what happened."

Good save, he thought.

A few moments later, the three Forsythes came into the examining room. "So, how are you feeling, Paul?" asked Peggy's dad. "Took quite a tumble, I understand."

"I'm okay, Mr. Forsythe," Paul sheepishly smiled. "Sorry about all this."

"Don't worry about it, son," Mr. Forsythe said. "These things happen all the time at ski resorts. We're just thankful that you didn't injure yourself any worse than this." He turned to the physician, who was holding Paul's X-ray up to the fluorescent light box. "What's the prognosis, doctor?"

"The X-ray doesn't indicate a fracture. Just trauma to the ankle region due to sudden torsion." He snapped the large, ghostly image into the clip at the top of the light box, then turned around to the Forsythes. "He's got a bad sprain, probably a grade three. We'll need to set it to immobilize it."

"Hear, that, Paul?" asked Mr. Forsythe. "You're going to get to wear a cast."

"I guess I won't be able to play racquetball after all."

"Ah, so *that's* it!" Mr. Forsythe grinned. "This was all so that you wouldn't have to play me in racquetball? You needn't have gone to the trouble, son," he said, playfully punching Paul's arm and giving him a wink. "I was going to go easy on you."

After the cast had hardened, Paul was given quick instructions on its care and the use of crutches and released from the infirmary. As soon as he had settled into one of the overstuffed reading chairs in the Great Room, his cast propped on an ottoman, the elder Forsythes headed back to their scheduled activities. Soon after, Peggy headed back out to the slopes—Paul knew it was to find Patty, in order to synchronize their stories before lunch.

He had a pile of magazines, courtesy of the lodge, and a good paperback he had been meaning to read. The Great Room was pleasant enough: a cavernous space with a soaring three-story ceiling, brightly lit by immense picture windows that offered a spellbinding view of the mountains and valley. It was very quiet: only the muffled, slightly echoing voices of distant conversations. They reminded him of the softly reverberating sounds he had heard in the rotunda of the United States Capitol on that winter field trip to Washington.

Try as he might, he couldn't concentrate on reading. His mind kept wandering, flashing back to his tumble on the mountain: his overconfidence and subsequent panic. He thought about his Olympics fantasy, convincing himself that he was a world-class downhill racer after three days of fitful skiing.

How could I have been so stupid? What was I thinking? If I'd just listened to Peggy, taken it slow, acted sensibly, I'd still be out there with her... enjoying this perfect day of this perfect vacation on the perfect mountain with the perfect girl.

He had a real knack for screwing things up. Things that were handed to him on a silver platter, he'd ruin, tarnish, spoil. He remembered begging for a lizard when he was eight years old, and his parents finally consenting and buying him a chameleon in a nicely-furnished five-gallon terrarium, with strict instructions that he had to feed it occasionally and give it water every day. His dad would keep the cage clean—all Paul had to do was make certain that it always had fresh water to drink. And he had done so, religiously, every day for the first month. Then every other day for the second and third month. Then a couple of times each week. And then once a week.

And then, he forgot.

When something finally sparked his memory, two weeks had gone by. He had raced up to his room, two steps at a time, to check on his pet. The poor lizard was leathery-looking, desiccated and stiff, the eyes dull and hard like tiny raisins. Paul remembered the feeling of panic: his heart pounding, forehead throbbing, ears burning, as he picked up the stiff creature by its tail—it was light as a feather—and ran into the bathroom, placing it in his sink, closing the drain and filling the sink with water, hoping beyond hope that the water could revive him, reconstitute him like a sponge.

He remembered the sense of helplessness, the emptiness and loss and guilt. The anger with himself.

He turned back to his book, put it down and picked up a magazine.

No good. He put the magazine down, looking out the window at the mountains blanketed in white. Peggy was out there somewhere. Had she found her sister? Were they skiing together? Had Patty found another Rhett? Maybe they had found two Rhetts.

Two Rhetts with two good legs each. The foursome skiing and boarding together, doing turns and jumps and hot-dogging together, having a great time.

He picked up a different magazine, flipping through it.

It's probably for the best. Let her have fun. It's really her vacation, anyway—I'm only along for the ride. Why did I even come along in the first place? She can ski, I can't—obviously. Why did she invite me? Was it out of pity? Did she feel obligated?

This is torture.

He put down the magazine. His foot was itching.

Chapter Twelve

The Game

They had a discussion over breakfast the following day.

"I think," Mr. Forsythe began, "that it would be best for you girls to take a break from skiing. This lodge has so many things to offer, and you should be taking advantage of it. How about we visit the spa this morning? Nothing like an early sauna and massage to limber you up for the day's activities. Paul took quite a tumble yesterday—a massage will do him a world of good. After that we'll have our racquetball game, followed by lunch, and that will still leave the entire afternoon for skiing."

"Um, Dad... Paul can't play racquetball now," Peggy reminded her father.

"I'm not talking about Paul," Mr. Forsythe replied, spreading a thin layer of marmalade on his English muffin. "I'm talking about the two of you. Against me."

Peggy and Patty looked at each other and then back at their father.

"You can't be serious," Peggy said.

"Completely serious. I've got the court reserved, so let's make use of it. Paul can watch and cheer you on." He winked at Paul. "Or cheer *me* on, if he wants to root for the winner."

"That sounds like fun, girls," their mother said. "I think I'll watch, too."

"Oh, brother," Patty moaned, rolling her eyes. "Another great Forsythe Family Activity. Do Peggy and I have a say in this at all?'

"No," their father replied.

"But Patty can't even hit the ball," complained Peggy. "It's not fair!"

"*Me*?" retorted Patty. "*I'm* not the spastic one! *You're* the one who can't play racquetball! The last time we played, I beat you to a pulp."

"Like in your dreams! You have a pretty bad memory, little sister. You were practically crying, I beat you so bad."

Paul imagined the two of them bouncing around the court in their tennis skirts, smacking the caroming little rubber ball with their racquets. He was going to enjoy watching them play their father.

Patty sneered at her sister. "Oh, get real! *You* were the one who was sobbing out there. I even had to go get you a towel so you could wipe your tears."

"Okay, enough," interrupted Mr. Forsythe. "We'll find out who the better player is after the sauna. Now we need to discuss another, more serious matter. In light of recent events, perhaps we should consider cutting short our vacation."

Patty stared open-mouthed at her father, letting her fork drop onto her plate with a clatter. Peggy was also nonplussed.

Mr. Forsythe concentrated on slicing his sausage links into bite-sized bits, aware of their reaction. "I'm just tossing it out there for discussion," he said, taking a bite of sausage.

"It's only Thursday!" protested Patty, almost shouting. "We're supposed to be here until Sunday!"

"It's not fair!" Peggy joined in. "I've been looking forward to this trip for months!"

Their dad looked up, munching his breakfast. He took a sip of his iced tea. "We've all been looking forward to this trip, girls. But we need to consider what's best for everyone."

The girls turned and stared at Paul. So did their parents.

Paul fidgeted, looked around the table and shrugged. "I'm fine here," he said peevishly. "I don't mind staying."

It was only half a lie, really.

Mr. Forsythe took another bite of sausage. "But your mishap does change things, Paul. You can't be happy sitting around here. The entire lodge is set up for activities."

"No, really, I'm fine. It's a great place to just relax. That's all I'd be doing at home, anyway."

"Are you sure, Paul?" asked Mrs. Forsythe. "You *are* our guest. If you feel that you should go home, that's fine."

The girls glared at their mother, but she ignored their daggers.

"No, no, it's really okay, Mrs. Forsythe," Paul assured her, smiling. "I'm sure I'll find things to do. This is a great place... great scenery, great food, and my room is great, too. I really didn't come here to ski, anyway."

As soon as the words left his lips, he regretted it.

"You didn't?" asked Mrs. Forsythe, surprised. "But that's what this is—a skiing resort, Paul."

"You didn't want to learn to ski?" asked Mr. Forsythe. "I don't understand..."

"No, it's not that," Paul said, desperately trying to regain his footing. "I mean, I *did* want to learn to ski. But I also wanted to just see Fox Hunt—you know, since it's so famous—and also with it being Mithran and all, I wanted to see the bonfire and learn about that, and the Acorn Hunt and stuff."

"Oh?" asked Mr. Forsythe, raising his eyebrows in surprised admiration. "So you're interested in Rhettian traditions? Very admirable." He gestured with his fork toward his daughters. "I think that these two would benefit from learning a bit about Cristicism, too. There's that Cristic holiday coming up soon... wait... I forgot—*Crismess*, right? You corrected me before and I've forgotten. Excuse me. Crismess always seems to follow Mithran by several days. Perhaps you could tell them a bit about that. When is it, exactly?"

Oh God, Paul thought to himself—Cristmas! He'd forgotten all about it! It was coming up soon. Did he miss it? He counted the days in his head... Mithran was, what—three days ago? Cristmas always followed it somewhere between four and seven days, so it hadn't come yet. But this year, was it four, five, six, or seven days after Mithran? Paul didn't have a clue.

He shook his head. "Actually, I'm not sure. It's coming up soon, I know that."

"You don't even know when your holiday is?" Patty asked incredulously. "Man, that is some weird religion you got there!"

"Well, it jumps around a little bit," Paul tried to explain. "It's based on the Cristic calendar, not the Rhettian calendar..."

"The *Rhettian* calendar?" asked Patty, making a face. "What the hell is *that*?"

"He means the normal calendar," explained Mrs. Forsythe. She turned to him. "Is that what you meant, Paul?"

Paul could feel his stomach knotting. The *normal* calendar.

Mr. Forsythe joined the conversation. "It just occurred to me," he said, pulling out his BlackBerry and tapping on the keys, "that my calendar probably has Crismess listed. Wait a moment."

He typed in a few commands, then looked up at Paul. "I must be spelling it wrong. Is it C-R-I-S-M-E-S-S?"

"Cris-MESS," giggled Patty. "That's funny!"

Paul could feel his ears turning red. "No, it's Christmas," he said. "It means the mass for Crist. We call our Savior the Crist."

"Yes, yes, I know that," said Peggy's dad. "That's where 'Crister' comes from, of course. Ah!" he remarked, suddenly remembering. "Mass! Of course! That's what you call your services. Instead of Feiers, you call them Masses, right?"

Paul nodded.

"So, it's 'Crist-*mass*'," Mr. Forsythe said, "with a tee after the 'Cris' part. But you pronounce it with a short 'i'—'Crist', as in Cristic—not 'Crist', like the name."

"They pronounce it like *Cristen*?" Patty asked. "Why would anybody name their holiday after *him*? That's beyond weird!"

"Patricia Lynn! I'm sure it's not for him!" Mrs. Forsythe scolded her younger daughter.

"I suppose it's like 'Cristicism'," Mr. Forsythe observed. "Alright then, so Crist-mass it is. You learn something new every day. Let that be a lesson to you girls," he said, pointing his finger at them. "You're never too old to learn something. Now then," he said, tapping the keys on the BlackBerry again. "C-R-I-S-T-M-A-S-S..."

"Just one 's' at the end," Paul corrected.

"I've seen it with two, I think," Peggy remarked.

"That's right," agreed Mrs. Forsythe. "I'm sure I've seen it with two esses, too. In a holiday catalogue I was looking through just last week, in fact. They had a picture of some Cristic gift wrap paper and it had the holiday name printed on it, with two esses."

Paul had seen it spelled several different ways: as "Cristmass" and Kristmas", and even "Christmas" with an "h" added after the "C". He wasn't sure why some people spelled it with the "h", since that made it even more confusing. From what little he had read, apparently there was a period in the Third Century when the newly-formed Protestant church changed the spelling of Crist to "Christ", to tie it to the Greek letter "Chi", which was the first letter in the original Greek word for "anointed". This spelling change didn't stick for Crist, Crister or Cristicism, but for some reason the holiday name had retained that odd variant among a few observers.

Mr. Forsythe was feverishly tapping at the BlackBerry. "'Crist' with a 't'... C-R-I-S-T-M-A-S-S... my mistake—force of habit—only one 's' at the end... C-R-I-S-M-A-S... no... C-R-I-S-S-M-A-S... no, nothing."

He sighed, turned off the BlackBerry and tucked it back into his jacket pocket.

"No matter. We'll find out when it is later. If we're still here when the holiday arrives, we'll have to remember to do something special for you. Is there a particular song you sing for Crismass? A certain food, perhaps?"

"That's okay," Paul said. "It's kind of a private holiday. A family thing."

"Well then, that settles it," Mr. Forsythe said, picking his fork back up and stabbing another piece of sausage. "We'll find out when it is and make certain you're home for your holiday, so that you can celebrate it with your family."

Across the table, Patty let out a long, audible sigh.

*   *   *

Mr. Forsythe's suggestion that they visit the spa was spot-on. Paul hadn't realized how stiff he'd become from his tumble until the masseur went to work on his shoulders and back. By the time he was finished, Paul felt rejuvenated—if it hadn't been for the cast, he would have tackled the intermediate slopes all over again.

After the sauna and massage, Mr. Forsythe and his two daughters left to dress for their racquetball game.

Paul was already getting used to the crutches, able to balance himself for a moment with both feet off the ground, like a human pendulum. Because crutches and wheelchairs were not uncommon at ski resorts, Fox Hunt had been designed to accommodate them. Most stairways either had an elevator convenient or an adjacent handicap ramp.

"How are you feeling, Paul?" asked Peggy's mom as they slowly made their way over to the handball courts. "It's such a shame you had that fall. For the life of me, I don't know why Peggy had you skiing on those slopes."

"It wasn't her fault, Mrs. Forsythe. I'm the one who wanted to try them. I talked her into it."

"Even so, she should have known better. She knows how treacherous those advanced slopes can be. You couldn't know, because you haven't skied before. She's the one who should have been more responsible."

More responsible. Did they consider me to be a less responsible person?

"I have a question I'd like to ask you, Paul," Mrs. Forsythe continued, after they had walked for a bit in silence, "but I don't know if it's appropriate to ask. I don't mean for it to be offensive, but I am curious…"

"Go ahead, Mrs. Forsythe. I'll try to answer it if I can."

"Well," she began, "you see, Mr. Forsythe and I have been going to ski lodges such as this one for many, many years. I don't know if Peggy's told you, but we met each other on a ski outing while we were in college. In fact, Jim—I mean, Mr. Forsythe— had broken his leg on our first ski vacation after we were married. Come to think of it," she said, studying Paul on his crutches, "he looked a lot like you do now. Isn't that interesting! But he was an accomplished skier even then. However, like you, I was a bit of a novice. Over the years I became a rather skillful skier myself, with my husband's help.

"Anyway, Paul," she continued, "my point is that we have always enjoyed skiing, and each year we always plan a trip or two to a ski resort. We've done this for, oh my, let's see... I suppose it's been twenty-five years. And in all those years and those many trips, something has struck me as rather odd—and please understand that I don't mean to offend you by this—but I couldn't help but notice that there aren't any Cristers—I mean, Cristic people—at these resorts... or very few of them. Obviously I don't go up to everyone and ask them if they're a Cristic person or not. But over the years I have gotten this impression. No Jews either, I think. Do you know why this would be? Do Cristers not like to ski?"

Good Lord, thought Paul, his ears turning red. *What sort of question is this?*

"Gosh, Mrs. Forsythe, I dunno," he shrugged. "I never really thought about it."

"Oh my—perhaps I shouldn't have asked that. I'm so sorry, Paul—I didn't mean to embarrass you. I was just very curious."

"Maybe it has to do with the whole social strata thing," he offered. "You know, the landed gentry and all that."

"The 'landed gentry'? You mean, as in aristocratic? Oh, my—I never thought of myself that way. But the lodges we go to aren't exclusive. I mean, they *are* privately owned, but they aren't private clubs. They don't limit their membership." She stopped walking and looked at Paul with a serious expression. "We would *never* belong to any club that discriminates against other people."

"I didn't mean that, exactly. I meant more along the lines of being... posh. These ski resorts are unbelievably expensive."

"Well, yes, they are expensive," agreed Peggy's mother, "but that shouldn't be a problem for Cristers. The Cristers—excuse me, I mean Cristic people—certainly aren't poor, what with all of the banks and businesses they own, and the media empire they control, and so many of them being lawyers and such..."

Oh, Goseth Rhetter... the Banks-and-Media-Controlling-Cristers Myth. Even Peggy's filthy rich parents believe it!

"Perhaps it's just a cliquish thing, then," he suggested. "Maybe most of the people who first started skiing these mountains were Rhettian, and they bought the land and built the lodges, and their circles of friends started going there and, like with you and Mr. Forsythe, it became sort of a tradition, and non-Rhettians just never picked up on it."

He thought about the giant gabel on the roof of the Fox Hunt lodge, and the Mithran Bonfire and Acorn Hunt and Chipmunk. *Cliquish didn't even begin to describe it.*

"Perhaps you're right," said Mrs. Forsythe. From her tone, he could tell that she wasn't satisfied with his explanation.

What is she looking for? Some sort of confirmation for her prejudice? That Cristers inherently don't like to ski, or can't ski? That there's something in our liturgy that forbids skiing? That a lack of skiing activity is one of the punishments levied on Cristers for not worshipping Goseth?

Perhaps Cristers do ski as much as Rhettians, and she just doesn't know it. After all, Cristers are less than three percent of the population. Like she said—she doesn't go around asking people at the lodges what faith they belong to. It's possible that, like me, some of those people attending the Mithran Bonfire were Cristic. They just weren't wearing their Cristicism on their sleeve.

"Well, never mind," said Mrs. Forsythe, giving him a quick hug. "You're here now. Perhaps, even with your mishap, you'll have enjoyed skiing enough to start your own tradition."

Does she mean with her daughter? Or am I reading too much into that?

They resumed walking and soon arrived at the courts, taking the elevator up to the viewing deck: a narrow walkway around the perimeter of each court lined with benches, and a plexiglass window to protect spectators from high-bouncing balls.

"They said they were playing on the third court," said Mrs. Forsythe.

Each court had a large number painted on its whitewashed wall that could be easily read though the plexiglass. They found Court Three and settled onto one of the benches at the front end of the court, so that they could see the players' faces.

After sharing a bit of small talk that was mercifully free of any more queries and comments about Cristers, Mr. Forsythe and the girls entered the court below. They were all dressed in white: Mr. Forsythe in a white polo shirt and workout shorts, white socks and sneakers; and both girls in white tennis blouses and skirts, with their hair pulled back in ponytails with white scrunchies. They looked like twins—the only obvious differences at that angle being Patty's blonder hair and fuller breasts. She had left her blouse unbuttoned enough to display her cleavage, and Paul had a clear view from his perch above the court.

Did she do that on purpose?

If Paul and Mrs. Forsythe had come expecting to see a good game of racquetball, they would have been sorely disappointed. Mr. Forsythe was by far the better player—it was doubtful that the girls even knew the rules of the game beyond which direction to try to hit the ball. Their play was utterly uncoordinated, and they spent more time berating each other's missteps and errors than they did playing the game. This in turn perturbed their father, who was constantly stopping play to lecture them on game etiquette.

It seemed to Paul that the entire affair would have been far more enjoyable if the three of them had taken a lighter attitude toward the game and just played for the fun of it. This was, of course, impossible, with their father's incessant perfectionism and their own ceaseless sibling rivalry. It created a sort of vicious cycle of errors, accusations and admonishments. Still, every now and then there were some lighthearted moments, when both girls completely misjudged the ball and ended up splayed on the floor, laughing at their own ineptness.

Despite the heated exchanges and name-calling, Paul enjoyed watching the game. Even with their lack of coordination and their difficulty hitting the ball, the two young women were charming—gliding about the court, stretching and twisting and diving. He imagined watching them in slow motion, their pony-tails flowing behind them, the muscles in their thighs and calves taut and smooth, their chests bouncing in cadence with their footsteps.

"Oh, dear," remarked Mrs. Forsythe after a series of especially awkward moves by her daughters, "they aren't very good, are they?"

"They're a lot better at skiing," Paul admitted.

"I should hope so," their mother replied. "Otherwise they'd be on crutches, too. Oh, I'm so sorry," she quickly added, patting Paul's knee, "that was very insensitive of me. Anyone can have an accident."

Anyone who's a klutz, he thought to himself.

After their racquetball session and lunch, the entire Forsythe family headed out to the slopes for a few hours of skiing before dinner. It occurred to Paul that his injury was responsible for the family getting together—that his being sidelined freed Peggy and her sister to use the intermediate slopes, and this in turn permitted all four of them to ski the slopes together. Conversely, his coming along on the trip had prevented any family outings—the kind of Kodak moments the Forsythes had undoubtedly enjoyed on every prior vacation.

He felt like a fifth wheel, completely out of place. *Maybe Peg-*

gy's mom was right—maybe Cristers didn't vacation at ski lodges. Maybe that was the reason they avoided them: because they didn't fit in.

Once again left alone in the Great Room, he thumbed through his small pile of magazines. A half hour later he couldn't take it anymore, his mind too preoccupied with reliving past missteps and missed opportunities to concentrate on reading.

He slowly worked his way up to his room, turning on the television and channel-surfing for something of interest. But it was early afternoon, and all the satellite feeds offered were vapid talk shows, overacted soaps, a hodgepodge of old reruns and a bottomless barrel of bland cartoons and children's programs.

He turned it off, stretching out on his newly-made bed. Maybe he should take a nap.

He couldn't sleep.

He hobbled over to the window overlooking the wintry vista—the white, glistening valley and the majestic mountains that framed it on either side. Far off to the right he could see one of the slopes and the tiny black dots of skiers zigzagging down the powdery face.

Looking out at the snow-covered expanse, he recalled the blizzard of '78 when his neighborhood was blanketed with over a foot and a half of snow, and he and Dave had spent the entire weekend shoveling driveways and walkways. They had earned quite a bit of money between the two of them—a lot for a couple of 13-year-olds, anyway. Looking back on it, Paul realized that Dave had done the lion's share of the work, although they had split the proceeds 50-50. He remembered how he was hot and cold at the same time—sweating under his layers of shirt, sweater, scarf and heavy winter coat, while his gloved hands became stiff and frozen from holding the shovel. After a couple of houses they would take a break, retreating to either his or Dave's house where a hot mug of cocoa and a little snack would recharge their batteries, and then off they went once more to clear another pathway for a neighbor.

He remembered one house in particular: Mrs. Hereford, an elderly woman who lived alone. She must have been in her eighties, possibly her nineties. Paul and Dave negotiated a price to shovel both her walkway and drive, but even before they tackled the driveway they had decided not to charge her, since they had already made a bundle.

When they finished, they refused the money that she offered them from her purse. Mrs. Hereford thanked them profusely for their help, and then she said something that Paul had never heard before:

"It was very Rhettian of you boys to have done that for an old lady like me."

Paul and Dave had looked at each other, then Paul turned back to her and said "Thank you, ma'am. But actually, it was very Cristic of us."

"And Jewish of us, too," Dave added.

The woman gave both boys a perplexed look, then muttered something under her breath and shut the door on them.

Over time, Paul came to understand that Rhettians used "Rhettian" as an adjective for kindness, consideration, giving and caring—and all manner of other good traits. And they considered these traits to be the exclusive province of Rhettianity: "If only people behaved more Rhettian toward each other"; "Those blood donors were truly Rhettian". They couldn't—or wouldn't—accept that the same ethos applied to Cristicism, to Judaism, or to any other religion. The phrase "to be Rhettian" went beyond simple pride: it accorded a moral superiority to Rhettianity, and it relegated other religions to a decidedly less virtuous station.

That's why Mrs. Hereford was so befuddled by their response: using the term "Cristic" to be synonymous with "righteous" simply wasn't in her lexicon.

Just chalk it up to one more lesson in life.

Thinking of his neighborhood, Paul felt homesick for the first time. *What is everyone doing right now? Dave's family must have finished celebrating Chanukah—we went over to their house for the first candle lighting over two weeks ago. Now my family's preparing for Cristmas. When is it this year? Have I missed it already?*

He sighed.

It doesn't really matter anyway... all we do is that ritual with the paper bags, attend evening services and give each other gifts.

Gifts!

He turned from the window, hobbled over to the dresser, grabbed his wallet and headed for the door. There was a small gift shop down in the lobby. He should have something to give his folks besides an overstuffed bag of dirty laundry.

*   *   *

By the time of the après-ski party, he had finished his shopping: a fluffy faux-rabbit fur hand muff for his mom, and a navy blue polo shirt for his dad with the classy Fox Hunt logo embroidered on the pocket. The salesgirl had taken special care to package the items in white cardboard gift boxes with loads of tissue, and had wrapped them in colorful foil—all she had was gift wrap in Mithran pastels, but at least it didn't have "Merry Mithran" printed all over it. Paul also bought something for each of the Forsythes: an apple blossom and cinnamon sachet for Mrs. Forsythe; a figure puzzle made out of wrought iron geometric shapes for Mr. Forsythe; a delicate ceramic bell for Patty; and for Peggy, a small anthology of poetic works by Byron.

The Forsythes were in high spirits at the après-ski party: the family outing had done them a world of good. Refreshed and energetic, their cheeks slightly pink from windburn, they were laughing and joking together. Paul imagined it was the way they acted on every other vacation, before he had come along.

As he made his way into the Great Room, all of the hotel guests in attendance turned and gave him a round of applause — a tradition at Fox Hunt for anyone who ended up on crutches. It wasn't so much out of sympathy as empathy, with a bit of light-hearted ribbing as well. He saw the Forsythes waving to him at the far corner of the room.

"I found out when Crismass is, Paul," said Mr. Forsythe. "It's on Saturday. So, we'll be leaving immediately after dinner tomorrow. That will get us home late Friday evening."

"*Tomorrow?*" Patty shrieked, "You're like cutting out *two whole days!*"

"That's enough, Patty," Mr. Forsythe chastened his daughter. "We made a promise to Paul, and we're going to keep it."

"But two whole days!" she loudly protested. "It's not fair! All because of some stupid Cristic 'holiday'!"

"I said that's enough!" her father was practically shouting himself. Some of the other hotel guests turned to look at him. He caught himself, lowering his voice. "You will behave yourself, young lady. We've already been over this. Paul's Crismass is on Saturday, and we are going to make certain that he is home for it. End of discussion."

"Nobody ever cares about what *I* want," Patty sulked, and she stormed out of the Great Room.

Mr. Forsythe watched her depart, and then he turned back to the others. "I apologize for that, Paul. She can be rather high strung at times."

"It's okay. I'm just sorry that I'm making you leave early."

"It's probably for the best," Mrs. Forsythe assured him. "I think we've all had enough vacation."

Mr. Forsythe reached into his left jacket pocket and pulled out his wallet. "Listen, Peg... your mother and I talked earlier, and we decided to give you and Paul a little treat, so to speak. Since this is to be our last full night at Fox Hunt, we thought it would be nice to let the two of you have dinner together in the Steeplechase. That is, if you'd like to."

Peggy and Paul looked at each other and nodded in unison.

"Good," Mr. Forsythe said. "We thought as much. We made reservations for you at seven-thirty."

He removed the Fox Hunt key card from his wallet and gave it to his daughter.

"Just pay with this. If they ask which room to bill it to, we're in 328."

After a few more minutes of conversation, Peggy's parents excused themselves and left the Great Room. When they were out of earshot, Paul turned to Peggy. "Hey, that was really nice of them. I was hoping we'd get another chance to be alone before we left."

"Yeah, I think they figured that," Peggy nodded, "but I think they did it for themselves, too. They always take one night on vacation to have dinner together without Patty and me, and this gives them that chance."

"What about Patty? She doesn't have anybody to eat with."

Peggy shrugged. "So? She's a big girl. She'll probably order a pizza from room service and watch MTV and be in fat heaven. Plus, it gives *her* a chance to be away from the folks and from *us*, and I think right now that's perfectly fine with her."

"Your dad said we're eating at the Steeplechase. That's awesome!"

Fox Hunt boasted a trio of restaurants, all of them upscale, but the Steeplechase was the best of the three. Elegant ambience, exquisite cuisine, exorbitant prices: the kind of restaurant that Paul could only dream of taking a girl to. True... he wasn't taking Peggy—it was on her father's tab, so in a way she was taking *him*—but that was even better.

They parted company to change for dinner and met at the restaurant at seven-fifteen sharp. Seated at a cozy table in the back of the dining room, they had an entrancing view of the moonlit slopes under a canopy of stars. The table was adorned with a single candle—its soft warm light dancing over Peggy's captivating face. She had dressed up for the dinner, wearing an ivory-colored cardigan draped over a cream-colored sleeveless gown, and high heels with matching purse. Her silky auburn hair cascaded over her shoulders, each strand perfectly in place. She was also wearing lip gloss—a pink-peach color with a thousand sparkles that defined her full lips. The candle's glow bathed her entire body a deep bronze tan, offset by the almost iridescent glow of her lips.

He was having difficulty concentrating on the menu, finally setting it down and gazing at her. "You are absolutely lovely!"

"Oh, how sweet! Thank you. And you're very handsome."

Compared to her, he knew that he looked like trash. His cast had prevented him from wearing the one suit he had brought along for the Mithran services. Instead, he wore the only long pants he had that fit over the cast: a pair of maroon jogging sweats with white stripes along the sides. He was wearing the white cable-stitch sweater that his mom had bought him for this trip, which was passable, but it didn't come close in class to Peggy's attire. And he had forgotten to use conditioner—in the dry mountain air, his hair was beginning to frizz at the ends. He felt like a bum.

"I wish you could have been out there," Peggy said after they had ordered. "It was fantastic! The sky was this amazing blue and there wasn't any wind... I just felt like I could ski forever. Patty and I were doing this sort of crisscross pattern and sometimes she'd be in the lead and sometimes I would—like we were doing some kind of exhibition skiing, it was so cool!"

Paul wondered whether two of the dots he had seen from his hotel window had been the sisters. "Sounds like fun," he said. "You know, maybe it's for the best that I twisted my ankle. I mean, there's no way you could have done that if I was out there."

"Oh, silly!" Peggy insisted. "We missed you! Patty kept asking me if I thought you were okay. I told her to get her own boyfriend."

"She asked about me?"

"Yeah... I think she was just trying to make me feel guilty, what with you being stuck back here. But, you know something?" she smiled smugly at Paul. "It didn't work! I had a great time anyway!"

"Well, good for you! I'm sorry about making your dad cut the vacation short."

"Hey, it's only a couple of days," she said, smiling. "And it's not like you purposefully tried to hurt yourself. At least, I *hope* you didn't do it on purpose. And besides, you've got your holiday on Saturday and you really should be home with your family for that."

"Yeah, that'll be nice, I guess."

"You *guess*? What... you don't want to spend Cristmas with your family? Don't you celebrate it together?"

"Sure we do. But it's not the same as, like, Mithran or Rhettag. It's not all blown up into a mega-event. It's more like a small religious holiday. We go to the church, we have a short service outside, we exchange gifts, and maybe have a special meal."

"Well, we go to shrin on Mithran, too," Peggy reminded him.

"You know that. It's not like all we do is party."

"Yeah, I know, but a lot of the stuff with those holidays is just crass commercialization. You've got to admit that's true—with the Mithran Bonfire and the Chipmunk, and the Acorn Basket, and the Three Selgas, and Gluecken the Gold-Nosed Pony... I mean, it's just too much. It's overkill."

"You seemed to enjoy yourself at the bonfire," she pouted. "I'm sorry if having a good time during holidays offends you. Maybe you should go live in a monastery."

"No, you're right. I did have a good time at that bonfire... and I liked doing the acorn stuff with you. It was a lot of fun, really. All I'm saying is that Cristic holidays aren't like that. They're more... subdued."

"I'll bet if most Americans were Cristic, it wouldn't be like that. I bet you all would have big parties and celebrations and the stores would be filled with Cristic holiday stuff!"

"You may be right. I guess we'll never know."

The dinner arrived soon after. Unfamiliar with restaurants with more than one fork, Paul was at a loss as to how to comport himself. Seeing how Peggy was completely at ease in these surroundings, he became painfully aware of the difference that money and social status made. He took his cues from her actions and gestures, trying to mimic them without being obvious.

With the exception of his own awkwardness, the dinner went splendidly. Once their conversation left matters of family and religion behind, it flowed seamlessly, and the two teenagers returned to a more innocent time, when they had enjoyed each other's company as friends and nothing more.

Chapter Thirteen

The Pool Party

He awoke with a start. Something was holding his foot down. He couldn't move it, couldn't feel it. His thoughts flashed to the succubus. *What was it I was thinking, dreaming? My foot!* He lifted the covers, looked down at his foot and suddenly remembered the cast.

He slowly got out of bed, gingerly swinging his clubbed foot over the side. Events from the last couple of days came rushing back to him: *my fall... the examination in the clinic... this cast... that racquetball game yesterday... the après ski party... the dinner...*

The dinner.

She was dazzling.

He recalled watching her gloss-covered lips—how they moved when she talked, when she took a bite, when she chewed, when she drank, when she smiled and when she pouted.

All he had wanted to do during dinner was to kiss them.

Three feet away—it might as well have been three thousand feet.

Thoroughly enjoying their candlelit dinner, he had imagined how their evening together would progress:

We'll sit and chat over lattés on a sofa in the Great Room; then go for a walk around the lodge—perhaps taking a quiet stroll outside in the crisp evening air. Peggy will gaze in wonderment at the ocean of glimmering stars... an infinite seascape. Out here in the mountains on a clear night, it seems as though the world itself is a ship, sailing an un-charted path through the cosmos. Under this canopy of a billion points of light, she'll turn toward me, holding my hand, and words will cease to matter, and slowly, inexorably, we'll drift together…

"How is everything? Almost finished?" Mr. Forsythe asked. He had appeared out of nowhere, just as they were finishing dessert. It was as though her dad had been watching them, timing his arrival to coincide with the end of the meal.

"Mind if I join you?" Not waiting for a response, he sat down in one of the two empty chairs. "Peggy, why don't you give the card back to me—I'll pay the check when the waiter returns."

Peggy reached into her purse and pulled out the key card, handing it to her dad.

"Listen, kids. Since we all dined apart, Peggy's mother and I decided it would be a good idea for the family to do something together tonight. Patty suggested we go for a swim."

A swim! Other parents might suggest taking in a movie, or going bowling… Paul wondered if there even was a movie theater with-in fifty miles of Fox Hunt—or a bowling alley, for that matter. *Maybe the only family-oriented thing to do at Fox Hunt in the evening is go swimming.*

Mr. Forsythe looked at him. "I realize that you can't go in the pool, of course, Paul… we'd like to have you join us at poolside, although we certainly understand if you'd rather spend your time elsewhere. The Great Room is a nice place to relax, as you know—I believe there's a jazz ensemble in there tonight."

"No, that's fine," Paul assured him. "I'd love to join you at the pool."

They met at the larger pool at a quarter-to-nine. Perhaps twenty other people were there: a couple of families with young children occupied the shallow end; while in the middle section some teenagers and paired-up twenty-somethings were playing with a water polo ball; but the Olympic-size pool was so large, it seemed practically empty. Paul hopped over to one of the loungers and sat down, gingerly placing his cast-encased foot on the padded vinyl cushion of the chair. He had brought a book along, but as soon as the Forsythe girls emerged from the women's changing room, he knew it would remain unread.

Crossing over to the pool area in their swimsuits, the two girls were absolutely stunning: Peggy was wearing a tie-dyed blue and green one-piece with a plunging neckline practically down to her navel and Brazil-cut thighs, while Patty flaunted a bright yellow spandex bikini with tie-strings on each hip. They ignored the NO RUNNING signs stenciled on the cement and chased each other to the pool's edge, laughing and diving into the deep end.

Paul considered himself to be a good swimmer, having earned his senior lifesaving certification a couple of years ago—but he was not in the same league as the girls, both of whom swam competitively. They were at home in the pool: their toned bodies effortlessly gliding through the turquoise water with a dolphin-like ease. It called to mind Peggy's description of them skiing together earlier, carving figure eights in the snow on their slalom runs.

The sisters found an unused polo ball floating in the pool, and they decided to play a game of "keep-away" with their parents: Peggy and her father on one team, Patty and her mother on the other. Eventually this turned into the daughters versus the parents—which would have been decidedly lopsided if the girls hadn't intentionally restrained their play. Keep-away was followed by a sportive competition on the diving board, with each Forsythe taking a turn while the other three served as judges. It was apparent that Mr. Forsythe's favorite was the swan dive, which he executed perfectly every time. The most accomplished diver by far was Patty, who could get an amazing amount of spring off the board—almost losing her scanty top more than once in the process.

They played in the pool until everyone else had left. By ten-thirty, the elderly Forsythes had also called it quits, and they left reminding the girls not to stay up too late. Peggy and Patty played a bit longer, pretending to be synchronized swimmers practicing new moves. Paul was transfixed, watching the two of them work through their routines, doing coordinated hand-stands, pirouettes and back-to-back leg kicks, their arms linked at the elbows.

Close to eleven, Peggy announced that she had had enough.

"I feel like I'm totally waterlogged," she said. "I'm going to shower off and head to bed. Let's go, Patty."

"You go ahead," her sister replied. "I'm going to do a few laps. I'll be up soon."

"Suit yourself," Peggy said, climbing one of the aluminum ladders and pulling off her bathing cap, shaking her hair loose. She walked over to Paul.

"Did you enjoy the show?" she asked, smiling.

"It was excellent, like you'd practiced it."

"We have, in a way. It's not the first time we've played around like that."

"Maybe the two of you should join a sync swimming team. You're both good enough."

"Thanks but no thanks," she said, selecting a towel from the nearby rack and dabbing her ears. "It's fun to play at it, but we'd kill each other if we tried to do it on a team."

Paul thought about the racquetball game. "Yeah, I see what you mean," he agreed.

Peggy pulled another lounger over to his and sat close to him, whispering.

"Hey, you want to come up to my room?"

"Now?" Paul asked, watching Patty swim her laps in the distance. "What about your sister?"

Peggy looked over at the pool. "Maybe she'll be here a while."

"Think so?"

Peggy sighed. "No. As soon as she sees us leave, she'll come up. I know her. Bitch!" she quietly sneered at her sister. She looked at Paul. "We could go to your room…"

Paul's heart was pounding, thinking of Peggy and him alone in his room. "Won't Patty wonder where you were? Will she tell your parents?"

"I'll threaten to kill her if she did."

"Would that work?"

"No," she sighed again. "She'd tell. Oh, I *hate* her!" Peggy stood up. "This stinks. I'm going to bed." She leaned over and gave Paul a kiss on the cheek. "It was a nice thought while it lasted."

Paul watched her slowly walk away toward the changing room. He wanted to be with her so much it hurt. He looked down at his plaster-encased foot, cursing himself for his stupidity, his rotten luck.

Patty continued swimming laps—a leisurely crawl, gliding powerfully, effortlessly through the water. He watched her, all the while trying to hide the fact that he was staring. How could someone so incredibly sexy be so strong? On each turn, he thought he saw her glance over toward his chair. *Is she watching me, too? Just my imagination…*

Ten minutes later, he decided it was time to call it a night. Collecting his book and crutches, he slowly stood to go. As he started hobbling toward the changing room door, Patty called out.

"Paul! Wait a minute!"

He turned back toward the pool. Patty was swimming over to the edge. He limped over to her.

"Paul, I've got to shower off, and I'm scared to be here alone. Can you wait just a minute until I'm done?"

He shrugged. "Sure."

"Thanks."

She planted her hands on the tile edge of the pool and lifted herself out of the water in one smooth move. Standing there dripping and glistening in her taut bikini, she pulled off her cap and shook her hair free, just as her sister had done.

Oh, Lord, she's amazing!

"Alright... I'll just be a second. Wait for me here, okay?"

She snatched a towel from the rack and skipped into the women's changing room.

A moment later, Paul could hear the shower running. It sounded like she was humming.

A few minutes went by as he stood dutifully outside the changing room, listening to the white noise of the shower and Patty's lighthearted humming resonating inside the changing area. He wondered what Peggy was doing up in her room... *reading in bed? Watching television? Painting her nails? Doing whatever girls do with their hair? What do women do before they go to sleep?* He had no idea.

"*Ow!*"

The humming stopped. Another shout: "*Ouch!* Dammit!"

Paul shouted into the changing room. "You okay in there?'

No response. The shower water stopped.

"Patty?"

There was a loud moan.

"Patty?"

There was a pause. Then: "*Shit!*"

"You okay?"

"No. It *hurts*."

"What hurts? What happened?"

"I think I twisted it. *Ow!*"

"I'll go get someone," Paul shouted.

"No, wait. It's not that bad," Patty hollered back. "Hold on."

He heard the shower curtain sliding, followed by a series of little *ows* and oaths. Then—

"Paul, I need your help."

"What do you need?"

"I can't put any weight on it. It really hurts. Can you help me get over to the changing stall?"

Paul hesitated. "Maybe I should get someone..."

"No, it's not that bad. I just need some help getting over there."

"But I can't..."

"Yes, you can. There's nobody else here. It'll just take a second. Please?"

He looked around, though he already knew that the pool area was vacant. He swiveled about on his crutches and quickly hobbled into the changing room.

It was a strange feeling, entering the women's side of the changing area. A strong sense of taboo, of impropriety pulled at him, like invisible hands. The strangeness was accentuated by the steam wafting through the room. She must have taken a very hot shower, he thought.

Through the mist, he saw her standing next to the shower, holding the edge of the stall with one hand, the other grasping the ends of the large knotted bath towel wrapped around her body. She was standing on one foot, watching him.

"Hi," she said, somewhat embarrassed.

"What happened?"

"I just kinda slipped in the shower... think I twisted my ankle a little. It really hurt. It's not so bad now, but it still hurts to stand on it."

She made a little pout that was both heartbreaking and madly alluring.

"Maybe if I just lean on you for support, you can help me get to the changing area. My clothes are in there."

"This is like the lame helping the lame," Paul laughed, trying to put himself at ease.

"Yeah," she laughed, too. "Except that you've got crutches and I don't."

"Alright," he said, hopping up next to her. "Just hold on to my shoulder, and we'll take it slow."

"Okay," she nodded.

They gradually made their way across to the changing rooms, one step at a time. He could easily tell which stall was hers, since it was the only one with clothing. Her tiny yellow bikini was hanging on the hook inside the stall, along with a pair of faded blue jeans, panties, a bra and a sweater. When they reached the stall, Paul stopped.

"There you go, I..."

Before he knew what was happening, she grabbed him by his shirt collar and pulled him to her, kissing him hard, her tongue quickly darting between his lips into his mouth. Instinctively, his arms flailed, dropping his crutches. As he lost his balance, he felt Patty guiding him into the stall and he landed sitting with a loud thump on the bench with her on top, straddling him. Immediately, she bent over and kissed him again, passionately, and his arms reached up and pulled her to him—at that moment he wanted nothing else in the world than to keep kissing her. The amorous feelings that he had been keeping in check all evening came flooding out, and he was helpless to arrest his desire for her even if he had wanted to.

And he didn't want to.

They kissed for what seemed like an eternity, each press of their lips igniting a deeper, more passionate embrace. When they finally released each other to catch their breath, Patty sat up and, with a coquettish smile, undid the knot of her towel and let it fall away. Paul reached up and lightly touched her nipples. She grasped his wrists and pressed his hands firmly against both of her breasts, moaning, her back arching in pleasure.

As they made love in the women's changing room, he knew that he was not her first—

Can she tell, he wondered, *that she's mine?*

Chapter Fourteen

Cristmas

Their little secret.

For Paul, it was a no-brainer: there was nothing to gain and everything to lose by letting the truth slip out. As for Patty, the advantages of keeping mum were less obvious. He supposed that, on balance, the smug satisfaction she gained from possessing this secret reaped far more dividends for her than the emotional shock and reprisals its revelation would cause. Perhaps at some point Patty would decide to use it as leverage against her sister—but not now. Paul didn't relish that prospect, but keenly aware that he had no choice in the matter, he was resigned to it.

What he found truly amazing—and a bit disconcerting—was Patty's complete nonchalance about their steamy, passionate soirée in the changing room. Throughout the following day and even during the long drive home that evening, she treated him as she had before, with the same flippant attitude and occasional wisecracks: no fawning, coy looks, pining or knowing smiles. Paul, on the other hand, couldn't help but feel differently about her. As much as he tried to conceal it, he kept stealing glances at her, searching for some indication of how she felt. At one point during the long ride home she shot him a stern frown from the back seat of the Escalade as if to say *shut up*! She was right, of course, but it still bothered him that she could handle it with such insouciance, while he was wrestling with it so badly. Perhaps it was because he was the one who had lost his virginity and not the other way around.

Peggy, thank goodness, seemed clueless. At first a bit down-hearted over the end of vacation, she had gradually cheered up during the day. Paul worried that he was the one acting different-ly—fearful that he was projecting some kind of subconscious au-ra that signaled something was amiss—that their relationship had been thrown an unexpected curve. He still felt the same way toward Peggy he always had, but there was no denying that, un-beknownst to her, things had changed profoundly last night.

After lunch she had taken him aside.

"I had a great time at dinner last night," she confided. "It's a shame we couldn't spend more time together, just the two of us."

"Hey, it's okay. Those things happen."

He felt like a primo jerk.

"I'll make it up to you," she said. "Maybe I'll even ask you out!"

He imagined the two of them going to a movie and ending up together in a stall in the ladies room.

At one point, Peggy mentioned that Patty had come back to their room very late, and she asked Paul if he had seen her leave the pool.

He shrugged. "Actually, I got up to go a little while after you left." Technically, it wasn't a lie: he *had* gotten up to go, even if he didn't end up leaving right then.

And that was that... no doubtful looks, no follow-up ques-tions, no third degree.

It was nice to be home for Cristmas. As much as Paul hated be-ing responsible for the abbreviated vacation, he was thankful that

Mr. Forsythe had insisted on getting him home for the holiday.

They arrived back in time for him to go to the midnight Cristmas Eve Mass with his parents. Having attended the Mithran Morning Feier with the Forsythes, Paul found himself comparing the rituals at their shrin with those of his church. The two had quite a bit in common: there were more similarities than he had supposed. But he found the Cristmas service to be far more reflective and introspective. Obviously he was biased, but it was something else—something only those with a legacy of hardship could understand—an abiding appreciation for the centuries of sacrifices made by past generations in the face of unspeakable persecution and pain, and an enduring dedication to keep the sacraments holy and pass them on to their children. Because of this, the rituals were not just hollow gestures, but rather testaments to a faith that transcended the eccentricities of cultures, countries and time.

This was what he liked about the simple, understated rites of Cristmas: the quiet songs during the candle lighting; the tray of shortbread cookies his mom baked; the gift exchanges before breakfast. They didn't need public bonfires and pastel-colored gabels on rooftops and shouting preachers on the radio and super sales events at the mall and people wearing chipmunk costumes handing out hundreds of candy acorns. Cristic holidays were completely different... unassuming, unpretentious, unadorned.

Religion without the kitsch.

Chapter Fifteen

Cristers for Goseth

Lost opportunities. Things he should have done.

He thought of Avie. She wasn't well.

Truth was, she hadn't been well for years—although Paul was too young, and he saw her too infrequently, to notice the impairment. His mother detected the changes almost immediately: the fleeting forgetfulness, the agitation and accusations, the loosening of her once indefatigable grip on the simple chores and daily rhythms of life.

Eventually, as he entered his teens, he had noticed it too, though he didn't want to admit it. It was true that she forgot his name every now and then—but she had a half-dozen other grandchildren, of which he was by far the youngest—she could be forgiven for not always remembering. And sometimes on her visits she'd become disoriented, wondering where the bathroom was, or why the grocery store wasn't within walking distance. But this wasn't her home, so it seemed to Paul completely understandable that she might occasionally become confused. It was just part of getting old.

And besides, her memory of past events was as sharp as ever. He loved hearing Avie—Kristisch for *grandmother*—tell stories about his own mother growing up. Avie could remember every detail about his mom as an infant and as a young child: the soft and warm bright yellow fleece cloth in which she used to swaddle his mother; how his mom hated the bottle and would only breast feed; the time his mother hurt her knee riding her bike and needed sixteen stitches; the pink taffeta gown she wore to the prom.

Paul's mom was the youngest of four children: three boys grouped closely in age, and then her. Twelve years separated her from the next youngest, Paul's Uncle Andrew, and the running joke in the family was that Mary was a mistake—to which she would invariably retort that a girl was always a blessing, *never* a mistake. Avie was forty years old when she had Mary, and since Paul was also a late arrival, his grandmother was almost seventy-five when he was born. She was from a completely different generation—literally from a different world—having been born in Lithuania and coming to America as a young child at the very end of the Sixth Century, during the last major wave of Cristic immigrants fleeing the Cossack-led pogroms of Eastern Europe. Every now and then Avie would insert a Kristisch phrase into her storytelling, and Paul would stop her to ask what it meant. He wished that he could remember the phrases in order to incorporate them into his own conversations.

Whenever Avie visited, she would bring Paul a gift: a little toy or trinket that she had picked up especially for him. Like his mother before him, Paul had fought bottle-feeding, and as a toddler he continued to refuse to drink milk. On one visit, Avie brought him a little mechanical wind-up bear with a bottle of milk in one paw and a tiny silver cup in the other. When wound, the mechanical bear would play the tune *Picnic Time for Teddy Bears*, pour himself a cup of milk and then lift the cup to his mouth to drink. It was Paul's favorite toy, and soon after he received it he was asking for milk with every meal and snack.

Avie still brought him gifts, but they hadn't matured along

with him, so he continued to receive toy cars, action figures, and youth-sized T-shirts. At first he loudly voiced his disapproval, but over time he came to know better and graciously accepted each gift. On her last visit, when Paul was sixteen, she brought him a Scooby Doo coloring book.

She had it in a bag, unwrapped, and she walked up the front steps haltingly, holding onto his mother's arm with one hand and tightly grasping the handles of the bag with the other. She needed a cane, he decided, or perhaps one of those aluminum walkers he saw elderly people use at the mall.

As she entered the house, she glanced down at the bag she was holding and then looked around, confused. She turned to her daughter.

"*Wou ist das parvuleh*?" she asked.

Paul's mother looked at Avie, then pointed to Paul.

"He's right here, Mom. He's standing right in front of you!"

Avie followed her gesture, looked at Paul, shook her head and waved him off.

"*Diese ist nicht ein parvuleh!*" she retorted.

"What's she asking?" Paul inquired.

"Nothing," his mother said, exasperated. "She's asking where the little one is. The little child. She means you."

"Me?" asked Paul incredulously. He laughed. "She knows who I am, Mom. I think she's just kidding you."

"I wish she *was* joking, Paul." Mary turned back to her mother, pointing at Paul again. "This is *Paul*, Mom. This is your *grandson.*"

Avie looked at her daughter and then up at Paul, almost fearful. She timidly extended the bag to him. Paul took it graciously. "Wow, for *me* Avie? Thanks very much! What is it?" He lifted the coloring book out of the bag. "Awesome! A Scooby Doo coloring book! Thank you so much!"

He leaned down and gave his grandmother a hug. As he stood back up, he saw a change in her expression—a sudden look of recognition as if a veil was being lifted. "Paul!" she said, suddenly very happy. She turned to her daughter. "This is Paul!"

"Yes, Mom," Mary said, sighing. "That's Paul."

"Paul! How are you, Paul? My oh my you've grown! I thought you were somebody else, you've grown so much! Have you eaten? Let me make you something. Where's the kitchen?"

"This way, Mom," said his mother, helping her down the hallway.

Avie stayed with them for several days—Paul's mother taking a short leave from her part-time job to care for her. From what he could gather, Avie's apartment in the assisted-living community outside Camden was being refurbished, and she needed a place to stay until the work was completed. By the middle of the following week the refurbishing was finished, and it was decided that Paul would accompany her on the train back to Camden to make certain she arrived safely back home.

His dad drove them to Union Station in Washington on his way to work. Paul had worried all week about the trip, wondering whether Avie's Alzheimer's would stay in check. The onset of her dementia—which ranged from mild forgetfulness, to mood swings, to complete disorientation and panic—was unpredictable. Fortunately, she seemed especially clear-headed this morning, excited about returning to her apartment.

Paul purchased their tickets and together they walked through the cavernous station lobby to the boarding tracks. He had only been inside Union Station a handful of times over the years—most of them as a child—but the place never ceased to impress him. He loved the omnipresent hollow booms made by the footsteps of hurrying passengers; the deep echo of the woman's voice

announcing arrivals and departures; the lingering scents of decades of cigars and diesel and shined shoes and coffee; the play of
sunlight from the stories-high windows filtering through perpet-
ually-suspended dust. He'd ridden Metro dozens of times, but
the sterile concrete honeycomb of those stations didn't compare
to a real railroad station such as this.

He would never forget that train trip to Camden, sitting in the
wide upholstered seat next to his grandmother. For three hours,
she regaled him with tales of his mother and his three uncles—
stories which, if he'd heard them before, still sounded fresh and
new in the retelling. Woven into the anecdotes were insights into
death and life, history and family—lessons that only a grandmother who had lived through immigration to a new world, a
depression, a world war, a social revolution, and the dawn of a
technological society could provide. As she talked, he studied her
sweet countenance, her weathered hands tenderly holding his,
the wisdom she imparted over the soft clatter-clack of the train.
Listening to her, Paul hoped that he would live long enough to
raise a family and watch his children raise their families, so that
he in turn could share with them the stories of their parents and
the times they had experienced.

He would never forget that trip because it would be the last
time they ever talked together, face to face.

After the train arrived in Camden, after the taxi ride to the
nursing home, after she was settled back into her apartment, after
the assistant manager had called for a cab to meet him in front of
the high rise, he saw her tiny figure waving to him from her balcony as he got into the taxi.

A few months later, she fell in her apartment and broke her
hip, and her health rapidly deteriorated. On the phone after the
accident, even though he only spoke to her for a few seconds, she
sounded frail and distant to him, and in retrospect he realized

that she was ebbing away.

During the entire train trip, the ride through Camden in the taxi, the short visit in the apartment, the cursory wave from the street... he never told her how much he enjoyed her stories, how much he appreciated having her as his grandmother, how much he admired her, how much he loved her. Not once.

He took the bus home, his parents deciding that he should do this for several reasons: it was cheaper than the train; the station was closer to the nursing home; and it would take him to Sg. Clifton, only fifteen miles from their house. The train trip north had been for Avie's benefit, not his.

As soon as he boarded the bus, he regretted having agreed to the plan. It was not nearly as pleasant as the train: cramped, dark, grimy and permeated with the stench of chemically-treated waste from the tiny restroom in the rear. And even though smoking was prohibited, the reek of stale cigarettes still wafted through the cabin—either the lingering remnant of past abuses or the vestige of some recent scofflaw.

He couldn't stretch out the way he had on the train's oversized seats. Plus, the reclining button didn't work. And the "sanitized" cloth draped over his headrest was highly suspect, speckled with assorted light-brownish stains from God-knew-what.

But that wasn't the worst part of the six-hour ride home. Not by a long shot.

"Is this seat taken?" asked the smiling young man with the perfect teeth and moussed hair, who had boarded the bus at the next stop.

"No," Paul said, looking up from the book he was reading. "It's yours."

Why hadn't he said yes, it was taken, or simply nodded?

"Thanks," the moussed fellow replied. "By the way," he said, extending his hand to Paul as he sat down, "my name's Eric."

"Paul," Paul replied, shaking Eric's hand.

"Nice to meet you, Paul. Where are you heading?"

"South."

Eric laughed. "Yeah, I figured that. Unless, of course, I'm on the wrong bus." He laughed again. "What I meant was, where are you heading *to*? What's your destination?"

"Sg. Clifton."

"Sg. Clifton. I'm afraid I haven't heard of that. Is it a private school?"

"No, it's a town. In southern Maryland."

"Ah," Eric nodded. "A town, not a school. I thought by the name that it might be, you know, a Rhettian school. Are you Rhettian?"

Paul hesitated. *Why is this guy asking that?* He tossed it around in his mind and decided that there was no harm in answering. "No, I'm Cristic."

Eric's eyes suddenly lit up. "Really? Hey, I'm Cristic, too!" He extended his hand to Paul again. "Glad to meet a fellow member of the Cristic faith."

Paul shook Eric's hand again. *Sure is a friendly fellow,* he thought.

"What branch of Cristicism do you belong to?" asked Eric. "Orthodox? Catholic? Protestant?"

"Protestant... Methodist, actually."

"Methodist? Great! Is there a Methodist church in Sg. Clifton?"

"Yeah, one. It's a bit of a drive from home."

"Understandable," nodded Eric. "There aren't too many of us. I don't know how big Sg. Clifton is, but it doesn't sound like a very large town. I'm surprised you even have a church there at all. Do you go to services a lot?"

Paul shook his head. "Nope. Just a few times a year. The major holidays, or if somebody's getting married. That's about it."

"You should go more often. It's important to stay active in our faith. I'm fortunate to have my church close to where I live outside Atlanta."

"Are you Methodist, too?"

"No, not Methodist," Eric said. His smile seemed plastered on his face. "Actually, I belong to a fairly new branch of Cristicism. You might have heard of it—it's called Second Coming Cristicism. We used to call ourselves Cristers for Goseth."

Cristers for Goseth! Oh Good God, thought Paul, *now this is making sense—the handshakes, the inquiries about religion, the perpetual smile. This guy's a Goseth Freak. And the worst kind of Goseth Freak— one who pretends to be Cristic.*

"Wait," said Eric. "I bet I know what you're thinking. You're thinking that there's some crazy nut sitting next to you, and that he's trying to sell you something. Well, you're half right," he laughed. "I'm definitely *not* crazy, but I *am* going to try to sell you on something, and that something is Everlasting Life."

"Thanks," said Paul, turning back to his book. "Not interested."

"Not interested. You know, I wish I had a dollar for every time I've heard that. I'd be a millionaire. But you know what? If I could then give all of that money back just to help *one person* see the light of truth, I'd do it in a heartbeat. Because that's what it's all about. Helping people. Bringing everyone into the sunshine of God's good graces and onto the pathway to salvation. Let me ask you something, Paul. Do you believe in God?"

Cristers for Goseth. Second Coming Cristers.

The hard-sell by these fanatics was bad enough, but what really angered Paul was their name and the implication of their movement: that Cristicism was an incomplete, obsolete religion, and it was ordained that Cristers would relinquish Jesus and accept Goseth as the True Messiah. It was an affront to every truly Cristic person—a deeply insulting premise. Since Cristicism was based on the belief that the Crist was the only Savior, anyone believing otherwise was, by definition, not Cristic. "Cristers for Goseth" weren't Cristers—they were Rhettians. They had abandoned Cristicism for another religion. If these poor souls no longer accepted Jesus as their Savior, fine—whatever turned them on was their own business. But they should call themselves what they were: Rhettians, and leave Cristicism out of it.

Paul knew something about the proselytizing history of Cristicism, although the textbooks at school barely touched on it, and they certainly didn't teach about it in his Sunday School classes. But through his own reading he knew that, during its first thousand years up to the advent of Rhettianity, the Cristic people had been militantly missionary, at first actively seeking converts among individuals—both pagans and marginalized Jews—then later compelling entire communities to accept the Crist, and finally forcing conversions on pain of torture and even death. This reached its zenith around the time of the rise of Rhettianity: the most notorious instance being the Spanish Inquisition, when hundreds of thousands—perhaps millions of Jews and Moors—were either involuntarily converted or forced to flee the country. The practice of forced conversions continued well into the rise of Rhettianity and the corresponding fall of Cristic influence. Ironically, the brutal techniques employed by Rhettians to force the Cristic people to embrace Goseth as their Lord were based on lessons learned from the Inquisition, the early slave trafficking in Africa, the Crusades, and other past proselytizing efforts by Cristers. *As ye shall sow, so shall ye reap*, thought Paul. *They who liveth by the sword shall surely perish by it.*

Eventually, Cristic sects ceased actively seeking converts. This was due in part to early decrees in many Rhettian countries that had made proselytizing by Cristers a punishable offense. But more importantly, having been subjected to coercion themselves, it became clear to Cristers that forcing people to convert—and even aggressively proselytizing others—was a sin. That to be sanctioned in the eyes of God, the act of embracing a new faith had to come from the heart and soul of the converted—willingly, free of intimidation or threats of punishment.

This incessant badgering by the obsessed fellow seated next to him on the bus was a real nuisance, and it was giving Paul a major headache. He decided that he had to do something—to go on the offensive, to show this Crister for Goseth just how obnoxious it was to force personal beliefs down someone else's throat.

"Hold it," said Paul, cutting off his seatmate in mid-sentence as he was citing Konrad 3:17, about how the unwashed—in other words, the Cristers—became cleansed after embracing the purifying light of Goseth's teachings. "You just mentioned Goseth's Perfect Lesson."

"Yes, yes!" Eric said excitedly, thinking that he had finally found a crack in this Crister's armor, a way to introduce him to the revelations of Goseth. "Exactly! In Franz 15:23, Goseth teaches us that we must love others as much as we love ourselves, that we must see God as a God of love, not hate, that it is through love…"

"Wait a minute, okay?" interrupted Paul. "Now listen to me. This Franz 15—whatever. This Perfect Lesson. It's just the Ethic of Reciprocity… that same thing is found in every religion. How is that unique or special to Rhettianity?"

"Reciprocity? I don't follow…"

"Yes, reciprocity. Like in our Gospels—it says that you should love your neighbor as yourself. It's the same thing."

"I'm not sure I follow…" mumbled Eric.

"Okay, then, how about the Gospel of Matthew? How is it any different from that?"

Eric for the first time was flummoxed, staring blankly at Paul. Finally, he said, "What about Matthew?"

"Surely as a former Crister you know about what it says in Matthew, don't you?"

Eric rolled his eyes, bothered by the interruption. "I *am* a Crister, not a 'former Crister', as you put it. But anyway, go ahead and humor me. Tell me what it says."

Paul continued: "I think it's Matthew 7—something. It says we should treat others the way that we expect ourselves to be treated. The same thing Socrates said back in, I dunno, two thousand VR. How is that any different from your Perfect Lesson?"

Eric's eyes lit up. He had prepared for this one after all. "Oh, yes, now I remember! The Cristic 'golden' rule! Yes, yes, it's certainly a good rule, I mean, it's in the Old Teachings. And I'm not saying that Jesus was in any way evil, don't get me wrong—but don't you see, the Perfect Lesson takes it further in the True Teachings by teaching us that the way to God is through the *love* of Goseth and that embracing the love of others is the key, not just how we treat them. In Rhettianity we learn that God is a God of love, not hate—not vengeful like the Cristic God…"

"Whoa! Hold it," Paul interrupted. "You're saying that Cristicism teaches that God is *hateful*?! Where do you get off saying that?"

Eric gave Paul a sad, pitying smile. "It's all throughout the Old Teachings, Paul. The threats of retribution and eternal damnation—how can you get more vengeful than *that*? I mean, *eternal* damnation… think about it. No chance for salvation, *ever*? Goseth our Lord in Heaven remedied that, opening the door to salvation even after death. It's a tough, long climb to rise from purgatory, but it can be done, through accepting the love of Goseth Rhetter that He gave the world through his Conflagration."

"But that's what we say about our Crist," insisted Paul. "All this stuff is just taken from our bible and twisted around. *Jesus* is the one who died for our sins, not Goseth. *Jesus* is the one who preached about the love of God. This Goseth is a carbon copy, a Johnny-come-lately. There's nothing new in what he said. He just repeated what was already there."

Eric was gazing at Paul with the same pitiful smile plastered on his face, slowly shaking his head. "Paul, my friend," he said, "you're almost there. I can tell. I can feel it in you. You want to believe but you just can't take that step. You need to cast aside your doubts and your fears. Goseth is no 'carbon copy'—He's the *real thing*, the true Lord returned to save us all. Remember how He showed the Cristic silver mongers in the Cathedral at Speyer the truth and made them abandon their sinful ways, the same way your Jesus had done at the Temple in Jerusalem? It was fore-told in the Old Teachings—in the Book of Revelation, you know that as well as I do—that He would return to Earth to finish his work, to save mankind. You feel that by embracing Him you're being unfaithful to your Jesus, but you're *not*—Goseth *is* the Sav-ior returned, the Rhetter of Love. You want to believe this... let yourself go, accept His return and embrace Him."

Paul thought about his own recurring uncertainties—about whether Goseth *was* the Messiah returned, and whether the prophesies of the Gospel had been fulfilled by his birth. *Two bil-lion Rhettians worldwide—two <u>billion</u>! All embracing Goseth, all wor-shipping the Second Messiah, the Crist-returned, the Rhetter. Can so many people be wrong? How could God bestow so many blessings, so much power on the Rhettians... permit so much persecution and suffer-ing of the Cristic people, if Goseth wasn't the Son of God?*

And then Paul reminded himself that popularity and wealth mean nothing in matters of faith. That the very act of being vastly outnumbered in a Rhettian world, of carrying forward one's beliefs in the face of constant prodding and poorly-masked ridicule actually made it more personal and profound. That it was just as reasonable to argue that the few who had kept the faith were chosen by God to keep the flames of truth burning... that they were guardians of the light, special and loved.

"He died on the gabel for your sins and mine," Eric was saying, "for the sins of the entire world. And you should feel especially blessed, Paul. Rhetter is *your* king."

"*My* king?" asked Paul. "What do you mean he's *my* king?"

"Of course he is! As it was prophesied in the Old Teachings—forgive me, I mean in your Gospel: 'Lo, there shall return the King of the Cristers, Our Savior'. You can't deny it. The New Teachings themselves declare it, in Jurges 16:26, '... and they burnt him until his flesh fell from his body and in rancorous glee declared that here was their beloved king, the King of the Cristers!'"

"That is total crap," said Paul. "This is utterly asinine." He pointed his finger at Eric. "You keep talking about love and respect and all, but everything that comes out of your mouth trashes Cristicism. I'll bet you say the same crap to Jews—that *their* God is *also* hateful and vengeful and without love."

Eric started to reply, but Paul cut him off.

"Listen, I've had it. Just shut up! I'm not going to convert you, and I sure as hell don't want you trying to convert me! Thousands—no, make that millions—of Cristers and others have been forced by Rhettians to convert throughout history. Many were persecuted, many were killed. If you really *were* Cristic like you claim, you should be ashamed of yourself for abandoning your faith. You are beneath contempt, beneath my tolerance level now. Don't say another word to me for the rest of this trip. Go read your Lorswers and don't say another *word*. I *mean* it."

Eric looked at him wide-eyed. He had never before encountered a Crister as rude as this one. He started to speak, thought the better of it, sat back in his seat and with an obvious pout stared down at his Rhettian Bible, muttering prayers to himself.

This half-whisper was clearly intended to bother Paul, and he was going to tell the Goseth Freak to cram it, but decided to let it be. Maybe this was a test by God, seating him next to a Crister for Goseth. He resolved to ignore the mumbling and relegate it to the background noise of the bus as best he could for the next five hours.

Chapter Sixteen

Dr. Richter

D r. Richter was, by everyone's estimate, ancient. None of the students at Forbach Valley knew how old he was, but the one thing they did know was that he had been teaching there forever. There were rumors that he had even taught the parents of some of his students. He taught American History, and the joke around school was that his knowledge of the Civil War was based on personal experience. Midway through the second semester of Paul's senior year, Richter had just completed Reconstruction in the South and was now lecturing on the Industrial Revolution and the rise in European immigration.

Paul was only half-listening, partly because Richter had a monotonous drawl that put half the class to sleep, and partly because he already knew a good deal about the waves of Cristic immigration to the major urban centers along the East Coast. Since all eight of Paul's great-grandparents were part of that tide, the subject held quite a bit of interest for him. He had read several books on the subject, watched countless PBS documentaries and spent many hours on the Internet researching Cristic refugees from Eastern Europe (his mother's grandparents) and Western Europe (his dad's side)—particularly from the British Isles, France, Germany, and Scandinavia. However, even with all his research, he had only a vague idea of where the name Fairchild came from. He really ought to ask his dad about it—and ask his mom about her ancestors, too.

Dr. Richter was droning on about immigrants arriving in New York before the turn of the century, and he was a bit more animated than usual. It was clear that he fancied himself to be an accomplished orator—*he's certainly had enough experience*, thought Paul. And there were times when Richter did almost wax poetic, especially during his lectures on the Civil War: one of his relatives apparently had been wounded at the Battle of Bull Run. *A sibling no doubt*, Paul chuckled to himself.

Now Dr. Richter was at the board, writing the last part of a poem in chalk. Richter's hearing had evidently lost its sensitivity to high-end frequencies, because he invariably screeched the chalk on the board with each stroke, causing some of the students to clench their teeth and wince in pain. Practically all of the classrooms in the school were equipped with whiteboards, and a few were experimenting with the new interactive LED displays, but Richter had insisted on keeping his blackboard and chalk. *Old dogs and new tricks*, thought Paul.

Dr. Richter finished his scratching and turned to the class.

"… 'Send these, the homeless, tempest-tost to me; I lift my lamp beside the golden door!'—those uplifting words of promise at the base of the Statue of Liberty are by the gifted poet Emma Lazarus. Lazarus was a Jewess who was born in the United States, and those words are from her poem, *The New Colossus*. Her family had preceded most of the other Jewish immigrants to our shores by four generations—indeed, they were one of the oldest Jewish families in New York City. She wrote this poem in part because of the *pogroms*, which were attacks against the Jews in Russia, Poland, the Ukraine and elsewhere during the second half of the Sixth Century. She was hoping that her fellow Jews could escape from these countries to the safety of America."

Dr. Richter paced at the front of the class, holding the chalk between his thumb and forefinger and making little stabs in the air
with each remark. "Now, another influential poet from around
this time, and from a different minority, was a young fellow
named Ezra Pound, a Presbyterian Crister."

The word "Crister" caught Paul's attention.

Dr. Richter continued: "Every year I invariably get papers
turned in to me claiming that Ezra Pound wrote the poem at the
Statue of Liberty. Perhaps it's because 'Ezra' sounds a little like
'Emma', and also a little like 'Lazarus'. Or, maybe it's because
they were both from minority races..."

Races? Did he just say that? Paul could have sworn that both
poets were white.

"... or perhaps it's because Pound is a more famous poet than
Lazarus. But Lazarus wrote that poem before Pound was even
born—she died in 565, just two years after Pound's birth. As a
matter of fact, the two of them were like night and day: Lazarus,
being a Jew, must have had relatives back in Europe who became
victims of Nazism and Fascism. Pound, on the other hand, although he was born in America like Lazarus, moved to Italy in
600 and actually became a propagandist for Mussolini and for
Fascism—that is, until the Italians turned on their Cristic sup-
porters and started sending them to the concentration camps
near the end of the war. Still, as poets and writers, both Lazarus
and Pound were clearly a credit to their respective races."

Races!

"Their rapid rise to prominence proved that, here in America,
even the Jews and the Cristers could achieve their dreams."

As if on cue the bell sounded, waking those students who had
cradled their heads on their desktops and signaling the exodus to
yet another class. Paul waited until the last students had filed out
of the room and then walked up the front desk, where Richter

was busily grading the previous night's homework assignments.

"Excuse me, Dr. Richter," Paul said, "May I speak with you for a moment?"

Dr. Richter put down his pen and took off his reading glasses as he looked up from the homework sheets. "Why, of course, Paul. What is it?"

"I uh, I just wanted to ask you about something you said at the end of the class, about Ezra Pound. You know, when you were talking about him and, uh, Emma... Emma..."

"...Lazarus." said Dr. Richter. "Yes, what about it?"

"Well, you mentioned that Pound was a Presbyterian, and then I think you said something about him being a credit to his 'race', or something like that." Paul felt uncomfortable having to talk about this with his teacher, yet he was determined just the same.

Dr. Richter looked off to the right, trying to recollect that part of his lecture, then he smiled up at Paul. "Why, yes, I remember. Yes I did." Suddenly, his eyes brightened. "Ah! That's right... you're a Presbyterian Crister, too, is that correct? Are you interested in learning more about Ezra Pound? He was a truly gifted poet, a remarkable man. A real credit to your people, despite his political leanings..."

"Actually, sir," interrupted Paul, "I'm Methodist, not Presbyterian."

"Ah..." said Dr. Richter, "yes, of course, my mistake. But you're still both Cristic, so you have that kinship. Something to be proud of. A remarkable people, the Cristers. So downtrodden and yet somehow still surviving. Some call it hardheaded, but I think it's more inbred—something deep inside their character. The Cristic people have a role to fill in mankind's future, I'm sure of it."

"Yeah, thanks, I guess," said Paul, becoming confused, wanting to stay on track to push home his point. "But, Dr. Richter, I'm just wondering what you meant when you said that he was a credit to his 'race'. What race did you mean?"

"Why, the Cristic race of course," said Dr. Richter, looking back at Paul with an equally bemused expression. "Is there a problem with that?"

Paul took a swallow, trying to gauge his response. "Yes, I think there is. You must know that Cristicism isn't a race, Dr. Richter. It's a religion, just like... well, just like Rhettianity."

Dr. Richter leaned back in his chair, studying Paul. He started to rub his chin, the way he did in class when he was trying to explain a particularly difficult period in history. He sat this way long enough to make Paul self-conscious—he could feel his ears starting to burn. Finally, the teacher sat forward, placing his elbows on his desk and clasping his hands.

"Yes, of course, Paul. It's a religion, just as Rhettianity is a religion. I didn't say that Cristicism *wasn't* a religion. What I said was that the Cristic *people* can, in some sense, be considered as a race."

He thrust up his palm toward Paul, who had begun to open his mouth. It struck Paul as curiously resembling a Nazi salute. "Now, before you say anything, let me explain. I know what you're thinking—you're thinking that Cristers aren't a race the way that, say, black people are a race, or Orientals are a race, or white people are a race. And you're not entirely wrong in thinking that way. But the fact is that most Cristers trace their heritage to the Mediterranean and Southern Europe—a specific region of the world. And, for several hundred years, the Cristic people lived in what amounted to closed communities, and they married each other so that, over time, they have adopted characteristics that make them distinct from other peoples, and in that sense they can be considered a race of people."

"But, Dr. Richter,..."

"No, let me finish," Dr. Richter interrupted. "I think that you are having trouble understanding that the term 'race' doesn't always have to mean specific physical traits, Paul. It can be as general as being able to trace one's ancestry to a common source, or having adopted certain mannerisms or characteristics. Isn't it true that Cristers refer to themselves as *The Cristic People*? They consider themselves to have a special bond, something that ties them all together and makes them different than all other people. Isn't this true?"

"Well, yes, it is," Paul conceded, and then hastily added, "but it's not because we see ourselves as being a separate race. We just consider ourselves different because of what we believe in."

"If religion were the only difference," Dr. Richter retorted, "then there wouldn't be such a schism between the Rhettian and Cristic cultures, or the differences in customs and behavior, or any other determinant of differences between populations. No, I'm sorry, Paul. Unless you can provide me with sufficient evidence to the contrary, I frankly see no reason to dwell on this. Now if you'll excuse me, the next session is about to start and I need to be prepared."

And with that, Dr. Richter looked back down at his desk, put his reading glasses back on and began to shuffle papers about. It was clear that he considered their talk finished... end of discussion.

Paul slowly turned and left the classroom as students trickled in for the next period. His mind was racing with thoughts of what he had meant to say—what he should have said: that the cultural differences were largely the result of centuries of isolation imposed on the Cristic people by Rhettians. That marriage within the group was true for any religion—Rhettians married Rhettians, but that didn't make them a race. And he thought about how the Nazis had categorized the Cristic people as a different, inferior race, and how they used that justification to slaughter Cristers, the same way they had annihilated the Jews. But the Nazis had lied: the Cristic people weren't a different race. They were exactly the same as other people—unlike the Jews, who *were* different...

Paul caught himself, stopped up short, standing still in the hallway as students raced by him to their classes.

Not like the Jews, who are different.

They are different, aren't they? That's what I've been taught, ever since I can remember: the Jews are not just Jewish—they're the Hebrews—a race unto themselves, the tribes of Abraham. Maybe it isn't Abraham, maybe it's somebody else... Moses? But, the point is that the Jews are different. Isn't that right?

Isn't it?

Dave. I have to find Dave. Now. His mind raced... *Fourth Period—where would Dave be? It's a Red Day, so... lunch.*

Paul turned and headed down the corridor toward the cafeteria.

What will I miss? Biology, which is fine—no test today, just lab, and I can make that up next week. Besides, it doesn't matter—I need to find Dave.

He entered the cafeteria as the Fourth Period bell sounded. An odd feeling gripped him, seeing the familiar hustle and bustle of the lunchroom activity, but with entirely new faces. The same, yet at the same time slightly skewed—strange. He looked around for his friend, scanning the rows of tables, trying to check each face without making eye contact. Not here... not there... not there... or there... where the heck was Dave? *Do I have it right: Fourth Period lunch? Yes, had to be.* He checked again, back along a row. Some of the students noticed him looking at them and met his gaze. Paul turned and walked toward another table. *Where?*

Of course—the lunch line! Paul glanced over to the far wall where the line was slowly feeding through the service entrance. Now that he knew where to look, he quickly spied the big fellow shuffling along, almost inside the entrance doorway.

Paul found a seat at the end of an empty table and sat down, waiting for Dave to re-emerge through the service door at the cashier station. As his friend brought his tray to the cashier, Paul stood and crossed over to him. Dave saw him approaching.

"Hey, man, what're you doing here? Don't you have Bio or something? It's a Red Day. We have lunch together on *Blue* Days, remember?"

"Yeah, but I need to talk to you," Paul whispered. "Let's find a place to sit where we can talk in private."

"Sure, whatever—but I gotta tell you, you're weirding me out."

Wait until you hear what I want to ask you, Paul thought to himself.

They walked over to an empty table at the far corner of the lunchroom and sat across from each other. Dave immediately dug into his lunch—with a mouthful of pressed chicken, he looked over at his friend.

"Okay, lay it on me, what is it? What could be so friggin' important that Mr. Four-Oh is skipping classes?"

Paul took a slow breath. "Look, I'm not sure how to ask you this, and I'm pretty sure that no matter how I say it, it's going to come out wrong... but I need to know something."

"Man, you are *really* weirding me out now. No, I'm not a homo. Does that answer your question?"

"Shut up, asshole! Let me ask this." Paul took a measured breath, then started again: "What I need to know is.... what race are you? What I mean is, what race do you consider yourself, or do you think you belong to?"

"Now it's official. I'm definitely weirded. Are you being serious?"

"Yeah, I'm being serious. I told you it wasn't going to sound right. But I just need to know, from you."

"Well, Dr. Fairchild, that's a sticky question," Dave began, "because I don't agree with the common definition of 'race'. To my way of thinking, there's really only one 'race' of people—the human race. If you ask me, this whole separating people into so-called racial groups is dumb, because it's based on physical characteristics and there are way too many exceptions to the rules, especially in this day and age."

Dave paused and looked at Paul, seeing that he was not satisfied with the answer.

"Okay, if you had to pigeon-hole me—and I swear I hope that this isn't leading up to some kind of accusation or inquisition, because like I said, I don't agree with it—I'd have to say that I'm Caucasian—what we fondly refer to as 'white folks'. Does that answer your extremely personal and entirely bogus question?"

"So, you consider yourself white."

"Duh! I mean, what else am I? African-American? Asian? Native American? Pacific Islander? What else *could* I be?"

"Jewish."

Dave stopped chewing, looking quizzically across the table at his friend. "Excuse me? 'Jewish'? Did you just say *'Jewish'*?"

Paul nodded.

Dave tossed down his fork in exasperation. "Oh, man, don't tell me that you're one of them, Paul. Damn, I really, really thought that you were a bit more enlightened than that, a wee bit smarter than the average bigot. I mean, for crying out loud, you're Cristic. Do you think that *Cristers* are a race?"

"No, of course I don't..."

"So why the hell do you think that Jews are? You know, there was a time not too long ago when a lot of people thought that crap. They were called Nazis and Fascists. Unfortunately, there are still quite a few Nazis around—a lot of them here in America. I thought they were all Rhettian... guess I was wrong."

Paul shook his head. "I *don't* believe it, Dave. I mean, I don't *really* believe it. I admit that I've been told that Jews are a race, but it doesn't make sense to me and I really, honestly, don't believe it."

Dave picked up his fork again and stabbed another piece of processed chicken. "So who's been telling you that crud?"

Paul shrugged. He knew who had been telling him "that crud"—his folks, for one. And there were allusions to it in almost every church sermon that dealt with the Jews: about their being singled out by God to bear the sins of man, to wander the Earth without a haven or home until Armageddon. They were a separate people, different from others. "Well, for example, isn't it true that Jews call themselves the Chosen People? What does that mean? Don't you consider yourselves to be different, special?"

Dave looked down at his tray and smiled to himself, then looked up intently at his friend. "Yeah, Paul, we refer to ourselves the Chosen People. But that has nothing to do with being a different race. It means... it means that the ancient Hebrews entered into a covenant, an agreement with God, to live by His Commandments, and to honor the tenets of our faith. That's all it means." He put his fork back down, gesturing with his hands. "Judaism is about carrying on these teachings and traditions from one generation to the next. It's the same way that Cristic people teach *their* children about their faith, or Rhettians, or Hindus, or Muslims, or Buddhists, or whoever. Y'know, the fact of the matter is that *each* religion considers itself to be special and to be the right religion—it wouldn't be much of a religion if it didn't. Does that make them a different race?"

"Okay... okay, I get that," Paul said, "but how about the ethnic part? Jews do tend to look the same, with dark hair and dark eyes and big noses—okay, your nose isn't big—but you're the exception. Isn't there a physical similarity between Jews that makes them different?"

Dave let out a sarcastic chuckle, "I can tell you don't believe that crap even as you're saying it. What color are my eyes, genius?"

Paul leaned over the table, peering closely at Dave. "Light brown, with a bit of green and gray... sort of hazel."

"Uh-huh. And you've already given me a back-handed compliment on my 'not-so-big' nose. So, by your 'logic', I guess I'm not completely Jewish, then. Hey, how about Arabs? They have dark eyes and dark hair and even bigger noses—ergo, they must be more Jewish than me! So do Italians, and Greeks, and a lot of other Rhettians. So there goes your race rationale. Here's another question for you... how about Marilyn Monroe? And do you remember a guy named Sammy Davis Jr.? Are they part of this Jewish 'race'?"

"They're different. They converted."

"Oh, I see... they *converted* to the Jewish Race. Neat trick. Or, on the other hand, if Jews *are* a race, then maybe you *can't* convert to Judaism. So, if Marilyn or Sammy had kids, and these kids grew up Jewish... what? Are they still not *really* Jewish? Maybe they're only *part* Jewish. The Nazis lost a lot of sleep over this. As I seem to recall, after they finished deciding who had 'Jewish blood', they started figuring out who had 'Cristic blood'."

"Yeah," sighed Paul. "That's right. They did."

"So, what do you think now, Einstein? Are Jews a different race? Here's a thought for you, and it's a radical one, so hold tight to your BVDs: maybe... just *maybe*... Judaism has nothing to do with race. Maybe it's a religion, plain and simple. At my synagogue, we have a family who look like they're from China. You know why? Because they *are* from China. They're as devout as I am—no, correction—much more devout. I haven't gone to services in a long time. And we have some other families who are dark-skinned. Not all African-Americans are Rhettian, you know."

"I know that," Paul replied. "We have a couple of black families at our church."

"There you go! Now, how is this possible if Jews—or for that matter, Cristers—are a race?" Dave pushed his chair away from the table, stood and picked up his lunch tray. "I rest my case before the court of prejudicial public opinion... Q.E.D."

"Q.E.D.?"

"Yeah, Q.E.D. *Quod erat demonstrandum*—'Thus has it been demonstrated'. Don't they teach you anything in Latin class?"

"I'm not the one taking Latin," Paul reminded him. "You are."

"Oh, yeah... that's right. Anyhow, you get the point."

"Yeah, I do," nodded Paul. "To be honest, I don't even know why I thought that way. I guess I just accepted it, and I never really thought it through until now."

"That describes a lot of prejudice in this world, my friend. People just accepting the bigotry without thinking about it. Hey, do me one favor. You *owe* me a favor for making me sit in the corner for lunch. The next time someone tells you that Jews are a race, set them straight. What this world needs are a few less ignorant people."

Paul smiled, "You got it, Professor. I will dispense the truth to all who care to listen."

Dave leaned over the table. "It will be a mitzvah—a good deed."

"Maybe I'll avoid going to Hell yet."

"Hey, that's your religion, not mine," Dave winked at him,

"but if it works for you, who am I to pass judgment?"

Their discussion reminded Paul of a friend back in middle school named Pete Merrill, who used to try to ingratiate himself to Paul by mentioning that he was "one-quarter Cristic", since one of his grandfathers was a Crister. Paul had wondered what quarter portion of Pete was in fact Cristic. *What the heck does that mean: "one-quarter Cristic"? Does it mean that only a quarter of Pete believes that Jesus is the Messiah, while three-quarters of him considers Goseth to be the true Son of God?*

The notion of being part-Cristic was racist, Paul now realized. It presumed that there was something in a Crister's heredity that made him, or her, a Crister—that Cristicism wasn't a religion or a set of beliefs, but rather a racial characteristic. The Nazis believed that about both the Cristers and the Jews, and it was sadly apparent that many Rhettians still felt that way. This allowed Rhettians to assume that a person's being "born Cristic" was an innate condition rather than a personal conviction—that they only worshipped Jesus because of some predisposition, some DNA marker, some God-ordained genetic *defect.*

Pete Merrill wasn't "one-quarter Cristic": he wasn't Cristic at all. Pete never had been, and considering his concept of Cristicism, he never would be, either.

That evening after dinner, Paul went up to his bedroom and sat down at his computer to check his e-mail. There was a letter from Dave waiting for him:

Pauley —

Had fun at our little tête-à-tête over lunch, if only to bear witness to Mr. Four-Oh skipping class. Hope this major dent in the Fairchild Medallion of Academic Perfection doesn't cost you that Dittisham Scarf you've been sweating bricks over these four years.

In the spirit of our discussion, I decided to put together a little game for you to play. I call it: Who's The Jew?

I surfed around and found some publicity pics of four lovely contestants from last year's Miss Universe pageant. One of them is Miss Norway, one is Miss Sweden, one is Miss Germany, and one is Miss Israel. I'm guessing you didn't watch the competition, so you don't know who is who. As you probably figured out, only one of these fair ladies is Jewish. However, you will notice that none of the contestants are identified as to which country they represent.

The rules of this game are simple: take a gander at all four pics and figure out Who's The Jew. Since we all know that Jews are a different race, this game shouldn't be too difficult ;-)

P.S: Almost forgot: there's a bonus round. It just so happens that one of these ladies is Cristic. An extra fifty points if you can figure out which one she is. All you have to do is look for those telltale Cristic racial traits, too...

Good luck!

-- Dave

Paul scrolled down to the attached photos. All four women were extremely attractive, and all of them were dressed in bikinis. Although they were wearing the sashes that identified the country they represented, Dave had carefully blotted out the names, leaving a blank white banner draping each contestant. Three of the women were brunettes and one was blonde. Two had blue eyes, one had brown eyes, and one had green. Two of the brunettes and the blonde had fair skin, while the third brunette had darker skin—or was it just tanned? One of the brunettes had curly hair, one had straight hair, and both the tanned brunette and the blonde had wavy hair—but were they naturally curly or straight?

He wondered whether the blue-eyed blonde was the Israeli, since this would be the most obvious way to refute the Jews-are-a-race claim. Then again, why was he assuming that the Israeli was the Jew? Dave hadn't said that she was, and Paul remembered reading that, a few years back, Miss Israel was Muslim. The tanned brunette looked a little Arabic, but so did the one with the curly hair. Maybe Miss Norway was Jewish... there had to be at least a few Jews in Norway. But which one *was* she? Miss Sweden had to be the blonde... all Swedes were blonde, right? And Miss Germany... who the heck was Miss Germany? And which one was Cristic? He scrutinized the four photos for a necklace with a gabel, a crux, a Star of David. No necklaces on anyone. This was absurd... how in hell was he supposed to figure out who was Jewish or who was Cristic?

He suddenly sat back in his chair and laughed out loud.

Dave! Damn you, Dave! Game, set, match!

The soft, satisfied glow of accomplishment filled him from deep within, as he realized that he had just completed the challenge.

Chapter Seventeen

Rhettag

*S*uch wondrous joy!

The entire place was aglow with blinking lights and glittery balls, with sweet music and happy faces. It was a fantasy world of wonder—a child's dream come alive. Store upon store brimming with goodies and candies and toys for all ages.

It was Rhettag at Clifton Mall, and no other experience compared. Bedecked end-to-end in garish ornaments and canopied in fake evergreens fashioned from gold and violet streamers, with jingling bells and good tidings to all. In the central plaza where the two concourses converged stood a two-story flower-draped castle adorned with golden-colored tinsel. And seated at the end of the long winding ramp leading up to the parapets sat the Three Selgas in their bright violet finery, each in turn taking an eager child on their lap, patiently listening to their carefully-rehearsed soliloquies of what they wanted for Rhettag.

They were there together: Peggy to do her Rhettag shopping, and Paul just to be with her. Walking along the concourse, holding her hand as she skipped with unbounded glee at the merriment surrounding them, Paul couldn't help but feel a surge of elation.

"Isn't it just lovely?" she exclaimed, doing a spin to take it all in.

You are just lovely, thought Paul. In truth, her happiness delighted him to no end.

"It's just beautiful, just perfect!" Peggy said, squeezing his hand. "The whole Rhettag season fills me with a sense of joy! Doesn't it make you feel that way, too?"

It was hard not to feel good in this place: the manufactured joyfulness was so pervasive that any feelings to the contrary were like swimming against the tide. And yet even amid the splendor, Paul couldn't help thinking about the dark past of Rhettag—just two generations ago across the Atlantic, when the holiday was used as an excuse to attack Cristic villages—and how the holiday taught the imperfection of Jesus and his failures as the Messiah. Plus, there was something disconcerting mixed in with all the joy: a sense of artificiality and insincerity, so divorced from the pious origins of the holy day. This complete and total pervasiveness practically *demanded* everyone's participation—it was impossible to go to the mall or to any other public place during the months of Ilsembre and Gosiery without being inundated with Rhettag Cheer.

"It's... nice," agreed Paul. "But it does seem like overkill to me."

"Oh, don't be a Grinch!" laughed Peggy, squeezing his hand again. "It's just a celebration! People are having fun!"

"Well, some people never stop celebrating it. Like those Rhettag-Year-Round stores. I saw an ad for one last summer that sold Rhettag Trees for people to have in their homes the entire year. You never take it down!"

"So, what's wrong with that?" She smiled at Paul. "I think that's sweet... people wanting to keep the joy of the season in their homes all year round!"

As they walked through the mall, one of the kiosks in the middle of the concourse caught Peggy's eye. It was the size of a large handcart and every square inch was covered with glinting gold and silver chains and bracelets bearing charms and pendants of every imaginable knick-knack: pandas and eagles; monuments and race cars; fruits and vegetables; flowers and flags; and of course, gabels.

Peggy gravitated toward the display, gazing over the glittering gabels dangling on their delicate chains. She lifted her hand, palm up, and lightly couched one after another of the golden Y's, her eyes wide with fascination.

It reminded Paul of the time, a few years ago, when he had decided to wear a small crux. It seemed like all of the kids in middle school wore gabels around their necks. Even Dave had started wearing a mezuzah on a thin chain, and Paul felt the need to do the same with a symbol of his faith. The next time his mom went to the mall, he tagged along, cash in his pocket, ready to select the perfect silver crux.

What he got instead was an acerbic lesson in supply and demand.

Including the jewelry kiosks in the center aisle, there must have been two dozen stores in the mall selling necklaces and charms, and Paul visited every one. They ranged from low-budget stands hawking imported silver jewelry of dubious quality, to the high-end retailers with price tags that made Paul gasp. But as he went from one store to the next, he discovered that they all had one thing in common: no cruxes.

They had gabels. Boy, did they have gabels! Great big gabels and tiny little gabels; bright gold gabels and burnished silver gabels. Traditional gabels; modern gabels; art deco gabels; and abstract gabels. Gabels adorned with jewels; gabels embedded in polished shells; etched gabels; stretched gabels; ceramic gabels; wooden gabels; wrought iron gabels; even plastic gabels. Gabels to fit every need, every occasion, every fad and whim.

But no cruxes. At least, not until he came to the novelty shop with its walls lined in black lights and iridescent posters of the latest teen idols and pop culture icons. In the store's jewelry display case, stuck in the corner almost as an afterthought, was one little silver crux. It looked so sad, sitting there alone. It wasn't what Paul had wanted: he was looking for a well-crafted crux, small and silver, but with clean, sharp lines and a sophisticated, high-quality shine. The crux in this display case looked like it had been crudely pounded into shape in a matter of seconds, and the dented metal looked more like tin than silver.

Still, it exuded sincerity to Paul. A tiny oasis of Cristicism at the edge of the Rhettian desert.

"How much for that crux?" he asked the sales clerk with the nose ring behind the counter.

The clerk looked quizzically at Paul. "Huh? The what?"

"The crux. There, near the corner," Paul said, pointing into the case.

"Y'mean a gabel?" asked the sales clerk, pulling on the ring that was lodged in his left nostril.

"No, not a gabel," said Paul, still pointing, "the crux—the one that looks like a plus sign."

"Oh, that thing?" asked the clerk, peering into the case. "Y'mean the little tee-shaped thing? Hold on, let me get the key."

He returned a moment later and unlocked the display case, carefully removing the thin little pendant. "Y'know this kinda looks like that Four Criminals symbol," the clerk said. "What do they call that? Oh yeah—The Crux! Hey—that's what you called it, too!"

He screwed up his eyes and gave Paul a look. "You into that kinda stuff, man?"

Paul struggled to control himself. "Yeah, I'm into that kinda stuff, man."

"Whatever," the clerk shrugged. He looked at the price tag. "It's twenty-four ninety-five." He handed it to Paul to hold.

Twenty-four ninety-five! Paul had twenty dollars and change with him, but that was just in case he had found the perfect pure-silver crux, or perhaps even one made out of gold. Not for this tiny, bent, pitted thing!

The kid behind the counter was playing with his nose ring again, watching him. "Why you want a crux, man?"

Paul eyed the sad-looking pendant in his hand. "It's the symbol for Cristicism, just like the gabel is for Rhettianity."

"Cristicism, huh? So, you a Crister?"

Paul sighed. "Yes. I can't find cruxes anywhere. This is the only one I've found. And I need a chain, too, and I've only got twenty dollars."

The sales clerk leaned on the counter. "Look, tell you what. I'm not supposed to do this, but if you want that crux thing, I'll throw in a nice silver chain for free. I got some in the back room that I just fixed, and I'll let you have one."

"Really?" asked Paul. He looked at the crux in his hand, hating to let it go. "But I still only have twenty dollars," he said, handing it back to the clerk.

"Well," said the sales clerk, returning the crux to the display case, "If you get the rest of the money, come on back. I'm sure it'll still be here."

Heading home from the mall, Paul wanted a crux more than ever—one that he could proudly wear to school. But the mall catered exclusively to Rhettians. No cruxes, no Jewish Stars of David, either—and certainly no mezuzahs. Dave must have gotten his from somewhere else.

Paul asked him at lunch the next day.

"The synagogue," said Dave, stabbing at the salad in his Tupperware container.

"You mean, your synagogue has a store that sells those?"

"Well, it's not really a bona-fide store. It's just a little shop that sells religious things for the congregation—like yarmulkes and tallit, and menorahs and candles around Chanukah time, and Seder plates for Passover—stuff like that. My mom volunteers there sometimes. And they also have a little display case with some jewelry—like mezuzahs and a few Stars of David. I saw this mezuzah and I liked it, so I bought it." He took a bite of salad.

"I don't suppose they sell cruxes, too?" Paul enquired.

They both laughed.

"Doesn't your church sell things like that?"

Paul shrugged. "I don't know. I never looked."

"It's worth checking out," offered his friend.

When Paul suggested to his parents that they all go to services on Sunday, they almost fainted. The family hadn't attended regular Sunday services since Easter, almost half a year ago.

"I'm not going to ask what brought this on," said his dad, "but the answer is yes. I think that's an excellent idea."

Come Sunday morning, the family was on the road to church. The closest Methodist church was a half-hour drive away in Sg. Clifton. With only eight million Cristers in a country of three hundred million, there weren't that many Methodists. One-third of Cristic Americans were Catholic, and they were mostly cloistered around Boston. The Orthodox accounted for another million, and they were concentrated in the Pittsburgh—Detroit—Chicago corridor The remaining four million or so were splintered into about a dozen Protestant denominations scattered around the country, and Paul guessed that there were perhaps a half-million Methodists, total. In all of Clifton County, there was only one Methodist church, and it wasn't very large. In fact, until a few years ago there wasn't any church at all, and the fledgling

Methodist congregation had held services in a local Paxist Rhettian shrin. Since Rhettians held their services on Mondays, there wasn't a scheduling conflict, but his congregation had to make certain that everything was spic and span by Sunday evening. It was also a bit disturbing to hold services in a sanctuary surrounded by gabels adorning the walls, including the giant one suspended over the pulpit—as well as stained glass windows depicting the life and conflagration of Goseth. This was not their house, and they felt like intruders. It was a welcomed change when they were finally able to attend their own church, even if it meant having to drive some distance to get there.

They arrived half an hour before services. While his parents chatted with a few friends, Paul went into the church office off the main lobby to enquire about purchasing a crux necklace. He discovered that the church did, in fact, have a small gift shop downstairs.

The basement of the church was austere, with whitewashed, undecorated drywall and concrete flooring, lit by a row of fluorescent fixtures running down the middle of the main hallway ceiling. Several dozen collapsible chairs and folding tables were stacked along the corridor. Near the end of the hallway, there was a small room not much larger than a walk-in closet. A few desk-height cabinets lined the walls and one of the folding tables was set up in the middle of the room. Paul saw several items on display on the table: matching pairs of silver candlesticks, several packs of Cristmas cards, a display that said *Cristic Holiday Calendars*, storybooks and coloring books for children, a cardboard case with CDs of Cristic folk songs and hymns, and a small stack of Cristic Bibles.

A tiny elderly woman was seated on a folding chair in the room, reading a magazine. As Paul entered, she put the magazine down and gave him a warm smile, her eyes magnified behind thick lenses set in a wide pink frame.

"Why, hello there," she said, slowly standing and walking the few steps over to Paul. "I don't think I've ever seen you in here before. What's your name, dear?"

"Paul, ma'am. No, I've never been down here before. I didn't know this even existed."

"Oh, it exists," the elderly woman said, laughing. "It's very nice to meet you, Paul. I'm Beverly. How may I help you?"

"I'm looking for a small silver crux—you know, the kind you wear on a chain around your neck. I went to the mall and there wasn't anything there."

"Yes," sighed Beverly, "it's difficult to find any Cristic items at the mall. That's one reason we decided to open this little gift shop. We don't have a big selection, I'm afraid, but with any luck we might have what you're looking for."

"What's this?" asked Paul, walking over to the Cristic holiday calendar display.

"The calendars? Well, Paul, you know that the Cristic holidays are not based on the secular calendar, don't you? Unfortunately, most of the calendars you see in the stores don't list our holidays—except perhaps Cristmas, and maybe Easter Sunday. But these calendars here show all of the holidays. It's a useful calendar to have, since the secular dates for the holidays change from year to year."

Paul paged through one of the calendars, noticing that it was arranged the same as a regular calendar, with thirteen months and twenty-eight squares in each month, starting with the Rhettian New Year on Gosiery 1st and ending with Ilsembre 28th. But in small print at the bottom of each square was the name of the Cristic month and date. The Cristic days went up to thirty-one, while some had thirty. Only one month had twenty-eight days like the Rhettian months—February. His thoughts flashed back to a rhyme he'd been taught in Sunday School about the Cristic months, designed to help the class learn about the discrepancy in the number of days in each month:

> *Thirty days has [something]*
> *[Something, something, and something]*
> *All the rest have thirty-one,*
> *Excepting February, alone...*

He was surprised he could remember that much of the verse— and he could only remember February because he'd just read the name in the calendar. What was the use? It was confusing as all get-out.

Paul flipped through the calendar to Franzen 17th, his birthday, and saw that it was July 27th in the Cristic date. He pointed to the date and turned to Beverly. "It says that my birthday, Franzen 17th, is actually July 27th. I never knew that!"

"Well, dear," said Beverly, smiling sweetly, "it's pronounced 'Joo-LYE', like, um... like shoo-fly, with the accent on the fly... not 'Julie' like the girl's name."

"*Joo-LYE*," repeated Paul. "Sorry about that. I don't know the names of the Cristic months. I guess I really should, though."

"Don't fret about it, dear," said Beverly, patting his hand, "not many Cristic people do. Also, keep in mind that you might *not* have been born on July 27th."

"But it says right here..." said Paul, pointing to the calendar.

"Yes it does, but you need to remember that the secular and Cristic calendars don't stay the same from year to year. In the year you were born, Franzen 17th might not have been on July 27th. I know it gets very confusing, dear. You'd have to look at a calendar for that year to find out."

"Well, I was born in 666."

"I'm afraid I don't have any calendars that old around here," laughed Beverly, "but perhaps you can find one somewhere and look it up."

"Anyway," said Paul, handing the calendar back to Beverly, "what I really came down here for was the crux."

"Ah, yes, the crux. You said a little silver crux to wear on a necklace, is that right?"

"Yes, ma'am."

"Is it for yourself, or for a relative? A girlfriend, perhaps?" she asked, giving him a smile and a wink.

"No, just for me."

"Some of the young men who ask for them want a large crux, but most of ours are fairly small…"

"No, that's fine. That's perfect. I'm really looking for a simple, little crux."

"I'll show you what we have." She walked over to a cabinet and pulled open a drawer, removing a wooden display case with black velvet lining that looked homemade. There were about twenty cruxes and chains of various sizes displayed on the velvet. They were all silver-colored and, as Beverly had said, most of them were small.

Paul scanned the arrangement in the box and saw it almost instantly: a small, beautifully crafted unadorned crux on a delicate-looking chain. He pointed to it.

"Is that pure silver?"

She carefully lifted it out of the case. "I think that all of our cruxes are sterling, but let me check." Turning it around, she raised her glasses, trying to focus on the back of the crux with her bare eyes. "Does it say '925' right there?" she asked Paul. "That would mean it's sterling."

Paul peered closely at the stem of the crux. "Yes, I think that's what it says. It's awfully small."

"I'm sure it's sterling. It's very pretty. Very simple and clean. It has a nice shine to it, even in this light."

"That's the one I want!"

Beverly looked at the tag attached to the chain, lifting her glasses again to read it. "The crux and chain together are sixteen dollars."

Hearing that, Paul realized how big a rip-off the mall had been. Of course, the church probably wasn't looking to make a profit, but even so—sixteen dollars for a sterling crux and chain, compared to twenty-five for a crappy piece of tin. He reached into his pocket for his folded-up twenty dollar bill, and handed it to Beverly.

"Excuse me," came a voice from behind them. "I don't mean to be spying, but I overheard you two."

Paul swiveled around to see his mom standing in the doorway.

"Why hello, Mary," said Beverly. "Come right on in. I'm going to take a big guess that this handsome young man is your son."

"Yes, he is," said Mrs. Fairchild. "We were looking for him upstairs. Services are about to start."

"We were just finishing up here," said Beverly. "Paul was doing a little shopping. He's a fine young man."

Mary Fairchild walked over to her son. "I heard something about a crux and chain. May I see it?"

Paul pointed to the crux that Beverly was holding in her palm. "It's that one."

"May I hold it?" asked his mom. Beverly handed it to her, and she held it up to the light. "It's lovely! Very, very beautiful."

She turned to her son. "Paul, you never mentioned to me that you wanted to wear a crux. You know, I never told you this, but when I was about your age, my father gave me a pair of little gold crux earrings. I loved those earrings. I still have them, in fact.

"What made them extra special," she continued, handing the crux back to Beverly, "was that they were given to me by my dad. Would you consider letting me do the same for you, and allow me to pay for this crux?"

"Um… yeah, sure. That'd be great!"

"Box it up, Beverly," said Mrs. Fairchild, "for my son. Then let's hurry up to the sanctuary."

On the way home from church, Paul pulled out the small cardboard box containing the crux and necklace, opened it and carefully inspected them in the sunlight streaming through the car window. The crux was beautiful, with the soft silver color of polished sterling and perfectly straight, clean lines. He grasped it in his hand, thinking about Beverly and the small shop and the fascinating items it held. He thought about the calendars, and the Cristic holidays he didn't even know about—and his Cristic birth date, which he still didn't know.

"Dad," he asked, "what day was I born?"

John Fairchild glanced back at his son through the rearview mirror, then looked over at his wife, who shrugged her shoulders. "What is this, a joke? Okay, I'll play along... what I am supposed to say?"

"No, it's no joke," said Paul. "I mean, what Cristic date was I born on?"

His father glanced back at him again. "You mean, based on the Cristic calendar? Whatever Franzen 17th is. I have absolutely no idea. Why do you want to know?"

"I dunno. Just curious."

"Well," said his father, "I know a few of the Cristic months. There's January... and March... and the one Cristmas is in... December. Oh, and June. June's in the summer, I think, so maybe your birthday's in June. Does that help?"

"Not really."

"Truthfully, I'm not even sure what Cristic year you were born in. It's 2001 now, because we just observed the millennium the winter before last. And you were born... how many years ago? How old are you now?"

"Fourteen, dear," said Mary Fairchild. "Your son is fourteen years old." Paul saw that she was giving his father a look. "You really ought to remember how old your only child is."

"I knew, I knew," protested his father. "I'm just busy driving. Okay, so that would mean you were born in... well, let's see... your birthday was a couple of months ago... 1987. There you go, you were born in 1987. But I have no idea what the day was."

"Do you, Mom?" asked Paul.

His mother turned around to look at him. "No, dear, I'm sorry, I don't. It was Franzen 17th, as far as I'm concerned. That's the date that I will always remember... six thirty-two in the evening on Franzen 17th, 666. It was very hot that day. Like a mid-Greten day. It must have been close to a hundred degrees, very humid. I thought I was going to faint walking into the hospital."

"The whole month of Franzen was hot that year," said his dad. "Remember? Janiery and Pendiery were nice and cool. I really thought your last trimester was going to be a cake walk. Then, *bam*, Franzen came roaring in like a lion. It was a scorcher for those last couple of weeks! You were pretty miserable."

Paul sat back in his seat. Janiery, Pendiery, Franzen... this wasn't helping him. What did it matter if he figured it out anyway? The Cristic calendar was dead. Dead and buried for six hundred years. Still, he just wanted to know...

After an early dinner that afternoon, Paul went to his room and logged onto the Internet to search for Cristic calendar references. After a little searching, he found a website that offered a

Cristic calendar spreadsheet and built-in Rhettian-Cristic date converter. He typed in Franzen 17, 666... up popped July 26th, 1987.

July 26th—so that's my birth date! July... that name sounds so weird—who would name a month Joo-LYE? He spent some time checking through the spreadsheet, looking at the other eleven months. All of the names except *January* were strange, like *August* and *October*. He had no idea how they were pronounced. Did they mean anything at all?

He did some more checking and found that the Cristic months were named after a mixture of Roman gods, Latin numbers and Caesars. He learned that the calendar was developed during the reign of Julius Caesar, before Cristendom even existed, and that July—his month—was named after Caesar himself.

Control of the days and months and years meant control of everything: of holidays and observations and celebrations. Of culture... of society. The Romans realized this, and so did the Rhettians. The Luxembourg Council of Cardinals didn't create the Erikan calendar because the Cristic calendar was less accurate: they changed it because it didn't conform to their new religion. By emphasizing the Cristic holidays, the Julian calendar ran counter to their beliefs.

The Rhettian calendar rectified that absolutely. So much so, that the Cristic people had abandoned their own calendar in their daily lives, and they now had to do mental somersaults to figure out when to observe their own holidays. Indeed, Rhettians had expanded their major holidays of Rhettag and Mithran far beyond mere calendar observances—turning them into a completely commercialized, inextricable, ever-present part of the culture, of everyday life.

The calculated demise of Cristicism—not through the spiritual, but rather the profane.

Such were Paul's thoughts as he watched Peggy looking through the myriad of gabel necklaces at the kiosk. She had been eyeing one in particular for some time and finally turned to Paul, holding it out from the stand for him to see better.

"Look how beautiful this gabel is, Paul! It's just heavenly, don't you think?'

Paul peered more closely at the charm. As far as he could tell, it looked just like the hundreds of others. "Yeah, it's nice enough, I guess."

Peggy turned to the salesgirl seated on a bar stool at the kiosk who was occupied with a teen fashion magazine. "Is it okay if I try this on?"

The salesgirl nodded without looking up.

Peggy gingerly lifted the necklace from the stand's wooden peg and undid the clasp, bringing it around behind her neck with her back to Paul. "Here, help me with this."

Paul obliged, grasping the ends of the necklace and struggling to lock the two pieces. As he worked with the clasp, he noticed how delicate and lovely Peggy's neck was: the tiny golden hairs in perfect symmetry; the soft, gentle mounds of her vertebrae; the subtle, enticing scent of her perfume. Finally managing to close the clasp, he reluctantly let go.

Peggy spun around to him, holding the golden gabel at the end of the necklace in her hand.

"Isn't it beautiful, Paul?" she smiled.

"Yeah, sure," he shrugged.

"What is *wrong* with you, Paul?" she asked, exasperated. "How can you not like this? It's so lovely!"

"I said it was beautiful. I agreed with you, didn't I?"

"I can tell you didn't mean it." She frowned at him.

"Look, it's very pretty. It's just that it doesn't mean the same thing to me that it does to you. To me, it's just a piece of jewelry."

"Well, not to me! It has a lot more meaning than that—it symbolizes pure love and goodness and devotion. How can you say it doesn't affect you like that? Look at how beautiful it is!"

Beautiful.

He wanted to tell her what it meant to him: that it was the transcendent symbol of oppression and hate and intolerance—a miniature replica of an instrument of torture against a hundred thousand Cristers at the hands of the Rhettians. The totem of the Nazis, whose legions goose-stepped behind the Hakengabel's bent branches, idolizing insidious bigotry. The representation of centuries of forced conversions and mass killings, and of continued prejudice and brutality even to this day.

But he held his tongue. For five seconds.

"I'm sorry, Peg," he began, trying to carefully select his words, "but the gabel just doesn't mean the same thing to the Cristic people that it does to Rhettians."

"Well, it *should*," Peggy glared at him. "There's no reason for you to criticize something that's so important to me! I think it shows that you really don't care about my feelings."

"Your feelings have nothing to do with it," he protested, and quickly bit his tongue, wishing he'd thought before answering. "I mean, of course your feelings matter, a lot, but I can't help feeling the way *I* do about that thing."

"About that *thing*," Peggy repeated. "Are you listening to yourself? About that *thing*. That *thing* just happens to be the most sacred *thing* in my life. Goseth Rhetter *died* on that *thing* for our sins. That *thing* is the symbol of His undying love for you, too, Paul, whether you want to believe it or not."

Paul could feel himself becoming frustrated and angry with the one person in the world he didn't want to argue with—not now, not ever. But he couldn't just let it pass by… to let her go on thinking that he was uncaring and being callous for no reason. Surrounded by the mall's incessant holiday music and glitz and jolly Selgas, prancing ponies and dangling gabels, the whole commercialized sham of Rhettag—this forced joy at the expense of history and memory and human decency bore down upon him.

This needs to be resolved.

"His 'undying love'? How about the quarter million Cristers who were tortured and burned to death on the gabel? How about *their* undying love? How can you tell me that their suffering means nothing? What were they guilty of? That they didn't accept Goseth as their god? That they were responsible for his death? How can you ignore the horror that that thing represents? The centuries of pain it has produced, the lies that it spreads, the hatred and bigotry that it still teaches? How can you ignore this and chastise *me* for not embracing his 'undying love'?"

That was what Paul was thinking of saying.

And in the instant that he opened his mouth to say it, he realized how pointless it was to argue with this delicate person with the sweet-scented neck, this beautiful and kind soul who wanted this gabel, not because it represented hate to her, but rather love... who would never in a million years understand its meaning to those who didn't worship Goseth as their True Savior.

He shut his mouth and sighed.

"Let me buy it for you. It can be my Rhettag gift to you."

"Really?" she asked, searching his eyes. "Do you really want to? But you just said that you didn't..."

"Forget what I said. What's important is what it means to you. I'd love to get it for you. Really."

And with that, he walked over to the salesgirl with the teen magazine and paid for the gabel—something he could never have imagined doing in his life.

Peggy proudly wore it for the rest of the shopping trip, occasionally lifting it up to admire it and each time turning to Paul and smiling, grasping his hand and hugging it to her chest in thanks.

Paul thought back to when he was a freshman in high school, when he still wore the silver crux—about how the other students would stare at it with curiosity and some would ask what it was, while others who were more knowledgeable would say "Oh, I didn't know you were Cristic!" and then treated him differently than they had before—like he was an anthropological curiosity, a walking museum piece. A few would say that they were interested in Cristicism and had learned about the Cristers in Monday School, but he knew that they viewed it as an "ancient" religion, relevant only for having presaged Rhettianity.

Then, in his sophomore year, the Clifton County School Board passed a new regulation that prohibited students from wearing "gang symbols" on their clothing or on jewelry. One local gang had apparently used a crux as one of its symbols, so wearing cruxes was banned. Paul wrote an article in the school paper, arguing that the crux was an established, universally recognized religious symbol, and that this took precedence over any gang adopting the symbol as their own. He also mentioned that some gangs were known to use variations of the gabel, but there had been no attempt by the school board to ban students from wearing these.

There was ultimately enough of a general outcry that the ban was revoked, but Paul never went back to wearing his crux: it was no longer perceived by the other students—and faculty—as simply a statement of faith, but rather as a political statement, and it ostracized him too much.

And now Peggy was wearing the gabel. She was wearing it whenever Paul saw her during Spring Break, which was practically every day. And when the break ended, she wore it to school every day.

He felt good about getting something for her that she so clearly loved, and he was relieved that their quarrel at the mall hadn't escalated into something hurtful. But he also felt the unease of serious issues unresolved… of problems glossed over for the sake of convenience.

The tensions that existed between people and within oneself— was it like currency in a bank, adding up incrementally, deposited into some vault? Or was it transient, able to disappear on its own into the ether, leaving no lasting scar or pain? Couldn't a person take a deep breath, decide to shake off doubts and anger like so much bad baggage and banish it, never to return? Couldn't people resolve to shake hands, let bygones be bygones and start anew, disposing of past disagreements?

Bury the hatchet, in other words.

But the hatchet, though buried, rests just beneath the surface. Never completely gone, and never completely forgotten.

Chapter Eighteen

Ardour of the Rhetter

There was a light breeze on the last day of Spring Break, just enough to keep the swarms of recently-hatched gnats from forming bothersome biting clouds that would chase people indoors during the hot and humid days to follow. This early Edel day was anything but humid: a crisp, bright day of newness—of blossoms blossoming and wispy clouds gliding giddily across an azure sky. A perfect day for two teenaged boys to be outside, having a leisurely baseball catch and soaking up the sun.

Inside, a pair of headphones wrapped snuggly over his head, Paul feverishly pounded buttons on the controller, desperately trying to retake his home base from a thousand heavily-armed, power-boosted, force field-shielded mutants.

Stretched out on the sofa a short distance behind him, a second, much larger teenager wasn't engaged in cybernetic combat. Instead, Dave's face was planted in his world history textbook, boning up for the first test of the last quarter of senior year. Perusing the pages, he frowned and looked over at Paul: "Hey, can you hold up for a minute? I need to know something."

Paul continued his suicide mission, oblivious.

"Hey, Pauly," Dave yelled, "*put the friggin' thing in pause for a second. I need to ask you something.*"

Paul hit the Pause button, yanked off his headphones and

spun around. "What, *what?* What the hell's the matter with you?"

Dave flashed him a disarming grin. "Gosh, you're beautiful when you're angry, dear. I just need to know how Cristers feel about something, is all."

Paul rolled his eyes heavenward. "Oh, sweet Goseth, not again." He gave a long sigh of resignation. "Okay, Professor... what is it this time?"

Dave pointed to the textbook. "It says here that, back in the First Century JH, thousands of Rhettians were martyred by the Cristers, and they even show a picture—some sort of woodcut or engraving of a group getting massacred. I thought you told me it was the *Cristers* who got massacred, not the other way around."

"Huh? Wait, let me see that," Paul said, standing and crossing over to where his friend was reclining, twisting his body to look down where Dave was pointing. "We *did* get slaughtered by the Rhettians."

"Well, that's not what it says here. It says that the Cristic kings were threatened by the rapid rise of Rhettianity, and they started to kill the Rhettians... see? Right here." Dave began reciting:

> **...in gruesome spectacles staged for the entertainment of their subjects, the kingdoms staged public hangings and forced imprisoned followers of the new faith to fight to the death.**

Paul scratched his mop of hair. "That's not the way I learned it. I mean, sure, maybe early on some of the kings tried to stop the spread of Rhettianity, and maybe they did kill a few Rhettians—but even if they did, it wasn't nearly as bad as what the Rhettians did to the Cristers after they took control."

Dave's recumbent body took up the entire couch, so Paul sat down on the far armrest to continue his explanation.

"After the Rhettians came to power in... let me think—it was either late in the First Century or early in the Second Century—they started a whole series of attacks against Cristers all over Europe. They'd erect hundreds of gabels in a field and they'd nail Cristers to them and then set them on fire. Just brutal. You probably don't know this, but even today a lot of Cristers have a really deep loathing for the gabel symbol because of that. And it wasn't just the burning at the stake—it was the whole persecution of Cristers by the Rhettians. It went on for centuries. It's true, I swear it."

Dave pointed at himself with a look of innocence. "Hey, no argument from me. I was just reading from the book..."

"Well, it figures that it wouldn't be in the textbooks... not when ninety percent of the school's Rhettian."

Dave gave a chuckle. "You got *that* right, Four-Oh. What was it that Churchill said about writing history..."

"*History will be kind to me, for I intend to write it,*" Paul recited.

"Right, that's the one! I *knew* I could count on you to remember it."

Paul tapped his head with his index finger. "Like a steel trap. It all goes in, nothing comes out."

"You got that one right, too," Dave smirked, "especially when you're up on stage!"

On stage. Memories of his panic attack during the sophomore class performance in *Twelve Angry Jurors* came tumbling back to Paul.

It felt like it had happened yesterday... not two years ago. He could remember sitting in the drama department dressing room, painstakingly applying the grease paint and streaking his hair with white and gray tints to become the grizzled old man, and practicing for the last time his walk and his talk: the mannerisms that had earned him accolades from Ms. Kincaid, the director.

Then the flurry of activity before show time, and the moment when the curtains parted—the other actors going through their well-rehearsed paces, performing their lines on cue. He could even recall the sporadic coughs and clicks and murmurs in the darkened auditorium just beyond the harsh halo of the klieg lights.

Mindful that this was his first theatrical performance, Ms. Kincaid had made it as easy as possible for Paul. In the play, his character—Juror Number Nine—was supposed to make an entrance onto the stage at the start of the first act, but she chose to eliminate that action and instead seated Paul at the jury table from the outset. He didn't speak until ten minutes into the play.

In retrospect, this may have been a mistake. If he'd had some activity at the start of the scene—even something as simple as walking onstage and crossing over to a chair to sit down—he'd have been in character, inured in his role rather than thinking about it.

As he sat onstage in the chair and the minutes ticked down to the moment when all eyes would be on him, a bizarre and terrifying sensation began to overwhelm him: a feeling of total dislocation and disorientation. He felt as though he was outside his body, watching himself trying to stay in character. And when the moment finally/suddenly arrived for him to stand and deliver his lines, a canopy of snow seemed to suddenly descend, causing a chill to enfold his petrified mind, turning everything pure white, and within this impenetrable shroud his mind went completely, utterly blank. The only thing he could feel was his rapidly pounding heart: it felt as though it would burst through his chest.

How long he stood there with the audience silently watching him in anticipation, he had no idea. It seemed like an eternity. Somewhere beyond the whiteness he could faintly hear Juror Number Ten whispering him lines, but he couldn't understand her. It was like she was speaking in another tongue. If someone had asked him what his name was, he couldn't have told them. He couldn't have told them anything.

He was lost. Someone's hand finally grasped his and he was helped off the stage.

And that was the end of his acting career.

Paul snapped out of his reverie and looked over at Dave.

"Yeah… well, screw you! I haven't seen *you* in any plays."

"And you won't," Dave assured him. He looked back at the textbook. *"History will be kind to me, for I intend to write it."* He snorted and tossed the heavy textbook onto the coffee table, sat up and rubbed his eyes. "It's all a bunch of crap. It's all picked over and processed and neatly packaged in Rhettian flavors to satisfy their own screwed-up taste buds."

He looked over at Paul. "Like calling us 'Jews' and calling you 'Cristers'."

Paul stared at his friend, the revelation striking him like a hammer blow:

They feel the same way!

"You, too?" he asked. "But you call yourselves Jews…"

"And you call yourselves Cristers, so what's your point?"

"No… what's *your* point?"

"I think you know what my point is, Einstein. They made up slang terms for us in order to make themselves feel superior. 'Jew' is demeaning. It's borderline insulting. So is 'Crister'. You've told me that yourself several times."

"So, what should Jews be called?"

"Good question, grasshopper," Dave said. He thought for a moment. "The proper term for members of the faith is 'Yehudim' in Hebrew. It means 'people of Judah', since Judaea was a large part of ancient Israel. It's what 'Jew' was taken from. So…" he thought for a moment, "the appropriate Anglicized term would be 'Judaean', I would think. That has a nice sound to it—and like 'Rhettian', it can be used as both the adjective and the noun, like: 'I met a Judaean fellow the other day', or 'Those Judaeans sure are smart!'"

Paul mulled this over as Dave spoke. It made sense. "So, why don't Jews... I mean, Judaeans... use that?"

"Another good question," Dave said. "My guess is that it comes down to sheer numbers. When you're only a tiny minority in society, you have to accept what the vast majority call you—it just becomes a given, and it's too hard to fight it. Whether you agree with it or not, you're forced to deal on their terms. Just like when African-Americans were called 'Negroes' or even 'Niggers' in the South. I'm sure that black people considered it offensive as hell, but even *they* used that term wherever white people had forced it on them." He looked at Paul. "Your turn."

"Huh? My turn for what?"

"You don't like 'Crister'—so why do you use it?"

Paul shrugged. "Well, like you just said... you can't fight City Hall. Too many people making it stick. I suppose it's because, like you said, it makes them feel superior by putting us down."

"So what should it be instead?"

Paul thought a bit. "You have a good point about that adjective-noun thing, like Rhettian. So maybe it should be 'Cristian'. Yeah... 'Cristian'... I like it already! 'He's a good Cristian fellow.' 'I met a Cristian the other day.'"

"Cristian... like Cristen—good luck getting that to stick," Dave said.

Paul didn't say anything for a while. He looked down at Dave, who had retrieved the textbook from the coffee table and was turning the pages.

Dave gave another snort. "Do you know that there's nothing

in this whole goddamn book about the history of the Jewish people? Absolutely nothing! Except for Moses and the Ten Commandments—like that's the only thing Jews ever did! Oh... and a section on ancient Jewish sacrificial rites. I mean, give me a break—that was *two thousand years ago*! Do you know that idiot Sean Reynolds actually asked me if Jews still make animal sacrifices?"

He angrily gestured toward the textbook again. "They get all that crap from here! The only other place it talks about Judaism is some incredibly stupid paragraph about ancient Hebrews naming God 'Yahweh'. *Yahweh*! What a load of crap! Jews don't name God—in fact, that's the whole friggin' point! There are names we use to *refer* to God... like *Hashem*, which just means 'the name', or *Elohim*, which basically says that God is divine—and in our prayers we say *Adonai* or The Lord. But we don't *name* God—God is unknowable... it's foolhardy to personify God!"

Dave paused a moment, trying to calm himself. "In the Bible, in Exodus, when Moses asks God what name he should call Him, do you know what God replies?"

Paul shrugged and shook his head no.

"God's answer is simply: 'I am that is'. 'Nuff said. Perfect in its simplicity. Now, did Moses actually converse with God? It's an allegory, a parable—whether it happened or not doesn't matter. What does matter is the lesson it imparts about God. Except that Rhettians can't handle it: 'Sorry, God,'" Dave continued sardonically, "'but we Rhettians can't wrap our primitive minds around the idea that You are beyond our comprehension—we figure you must be just like us, except maybe bigger and stronger and a whole lot smarter, and you look like some wise old guy in a white robe with a big white beard... oh, and you can fly, too. So we're gonna give you a name we can pronounce... how about *Baal*? That's pretty cool sounding! Oh, right... the Babylonians already took that one. How about *Ra*? Oh, yeah… the Egyptians beat us to that. Is *Zeus* taken?'"

Still in character, Dave looked down at the textbook, pretending to carefully scrutinize it. "'Gee—what do those four letters in these ancient Jew scrolls stand for? They refer to you—could they be symbolic letters that are used to refer to you? No—that's too hard a concept for us to grasp: they must be *your real name*. Let's see now… there's a yud… and a hey… and a vov… and another hey… but how the heck do those Jews pronounce it? Yehvah? Yeeveh? Oh, screw it—we'll make it up: It's *Yahweh*, got it? *Yahweh*. That's better—it'll be a lot easier for us to picture and idolize you and your offspring, now that we're on a first-name basis.'"

He sat back up and spat toward the book with disgust. "Idolize—that about sums it up. It's just like those Rhettian paintings of the Almighty, like the one Michelangelo did on that ceiling in Sg. Pender's Konigslich. It's the whole personifying God thing. They read in the Torah that God made man in God's image, but they completely perverted that and made God in *their* image. Rhettians can't cope with abstract concepts—they've got to be able to *picture* God, and they need to *name* God, too."

He turned to Paul. "For cryin' out loud, there isn't even any 'w' in Hebrew, so where the hell did they get 'Yahweh' from? Apparently these 'biblical scholars' don't know Hebrew from the holes in their asses!"

Paul eyed his friend. "Wow, somebody's really teed-off. Forget to take your Midol again?"

"Laugh all you want," Dave muttered sullenly. "This is serious. They cram all these lies in our friggin' textbook!"

"Maybe they believe that God *does* have a name." volunteered Paul.

"Hey—I don't have any problem with that. For all I know, God might have a name. What I have a problem with is these so-called 'scholars' making bogus claims about what that name *is*. Rhettianity traces itself back to Judaism, so they've concocted some story about ancient Hebrews naming God *Yahweh*. It's their way of dissing Jews, just like they harp on those ancient sacrifices! They're trying to make Judaism look primitive compared to Rhettianity—but *they're* the ones who drool over this fake name, like it's some sort of secret code word to join the Monotheist Club."

He mimicked again: "Hello? Jews? May we come in? The password is 'Yahweh'!"

"I don't think they asked permission to join the club."

"Damn right, they didn't. They just barged right in and made themselves at home. Stuck their flag in the middle of the religious muck they piled up in the middle of the floor and laid claim to it in the name of 'Yahweh'... and Goseth... and Jesus... and the fourth one—I forget what they call it—the Sacred Specter or something."

Paul studied his friend for a moment. "You know, Dave, we've celebrated holidays together, and we've been to each other's churches... I mean, church and synagogue... and I think I understand the basics about Judaism, but there's one thing I'm still not too clear about."

The big guy reclined his large frame back down on the sofa. "Ah, so... yet another question for the honorable master! Well then, young grasshopper, by all means inquire of Rabbi Dave," he said, back to his good-natured self, pretending to pull at his chin. "I'll tug on my sage-like beard and give it my best Talmudic interpretation."

"I think you're mixing your cultural metaphors, Honorable Master Rabbi."

"Whatever. Anyway, ask away."

Paul thought for another moment, carefully choosing his

words. "What I want to know is—how do Jewish people feel about Jesus? I mean, I know that you don't accept Him as the Messiah, but who do you think He is, if He isn't the Messiah?"

"No idea."

Paul was taken aback. "No idea? You must have *some* idea. You've got an opinion about *everything*..."

"It's a gift," Dave nodded.

"Some people might call it something else," Paul riposted. "But seriously... you've got to have *some* notion of who Jesus is."

"Tell you what," Dave said, propping his feet on the coffee table. "I'm going to do the stereotypical Jewish thing here and answer your question with a question: How do Cristic people feel about Goseth? Who do you think *he* is if he isn't the Messiah returned?"

Paul thought for a moment, then smiled. "No idea. The whole Lorswers thing is probably made up... but even if Goseth did exist, he was just some guy. Some guy who, whether he meant to or not, corrupted Cristicism."

Dave cocked his finger at Paul and clicked his tongue. "Ditto."

"So then... Jewish people don't accept either Jesus or Goseth as their Messiah, but Jews *do* believe in a messiah, right?"

"Well, yes and no," Dave answered, clasping his hands behind his head. "Some Jews—excuse me, Judaeans—still expect the Messiah to arrive to usher in peace to the world, but others think it'll be more like an evolutionary process by all of mankind—not necessarily through a single anointed person. At any rate, the whole concept is completely different from the Cristic and the Rhettian ones, because in Judaism the Messiah will be chosen by God, but he won't be a part of God—like in the Trinity or the Quadriny, or whatever. In other words, he'll work through the divine, but he won't *be* divine himself. He won't be The Savior—at least, not in the Cristic or Rhettian sense."

"Then how do Jews achieve salvation?"

"We leave that up to God, but the road there is through performing *mitzvot*—following the commandments and doing selfless acts of goodness and kindness."

"Mitzvot," repeated Paul.

"It's Hebrew."

"Yeah, I figured that one out, Professor—excuse me—Rabbi Dave. But, how about original sin—and the Fall from Grace—and Satan—and achieving personal salvation through the Crucifixion and Resurrection of Jesus?"

"That's all fascinating, in a way, but it isn't part of Judaism," Dave said. "There's nothing in Judaism that says the Messiah has to die to fulfill his mission, and it definitely doesn't say that he'll be tortured and crucified. If that was what it took to be the Messiah, there were a quarter-million Jews during the Roman Conquest who were crucified solely because of their faith—all of them suffered greatly for their love of God and could have qualified for messiah-hood. That thing about Jesus' martyrdom and the miracle where he's resurrected makes a great story—it's very passionate and sentimental and it's even kind of inspiring—but it doesn't have anything to do with the path to salvation, at least not in Jewish thought. Unfortunately, like most myths, the whole crucifixion story needs a villain, and the villain was the Judas character and the nation of Judah, and millions of Jews were butchered because of it."

Paul's ears were starting to burn. "What the hell are you talking about? Jesus' Crucifixion and His Resurrection isn't a 'myth' and it doesn't have anything to do with villains and with blaming Jews—it's exactly the opposite! It's all about love and redemption..."

"... like the Conflagration story," Dave finished.

"No, it's not like that stupid Conflagration story at all!" Paul was beside himself. "You want a myth—*that's* a myth! And a God-awful one! You want to talk about villains—*that* one blamed the whole thing on the Cristic People! I mean, c'mon, like you just said: Cristen and Cristic—how much more obvious can you get?"

"Hmm… let's see… how about Judas and Judah."

"What about Judas? That was his name. It's historical fact!"

"Uh-huh. Just like Cristen is historical fact. Very odd coincidence that the villain happened to be named Judas—considering that Judaism is named after the tribe of Judah. Judah—Judas. Very, very convenient. Both of those stories were written and codified generations after those events supposedly happened and those people supposedly existed. Plenty of time for choosing a villain's name that—gosh, will you look at that—just happens to match the previous religion."

"So you think that was a calculated move, too?" Paul asked. "Oh, get real—that's pretty paranoid, Dave, even for you! It's the Bible, for Gozesakes!"

"I think you mean the *Old Teachings*," corrected Dave. "Not the New, Improved Teachings. Your liturgy is outmoded, Bro'."

"Crap on that! They renamed the Gospels the 'Old Teachings' just to make them obsolete!"

"Exactly. Just like the 'Old Testament'."

Paul stared at his friend. "No, not like the Old Testament. That was… that was…"

"I'll tell you what it *is*—It's the Torah and the rest of the Tanakh. And I'll tell you what it *isn't*—it isn't a *testament*. The Gospels are a testament—at least according to Cristers—because they're a bunch of supposedly eyewitness stories. The Torah and the rest of the Hebrew Bible are the *Holy Scriptures*. You want to talk about renaming something to satisfy new dogma—I can't think of a better way than renaming the Holy Scriptures as the

'Old Testament'. And I can't think of a more devious way than repackaging that faith as a warm-up act to your new, 'improved' religion. And not only that—you hammer it home by concocting a new plot twist, so that the people who follow the 'old' religion now become the bad guys who kill your Savior, led by some devious money-grubbing character who just happens to be named after the religion you're defaming."

Paul's ears were on fire. "It's not a 'new twist'! It's the... it's the goddamn foundation of our faith! If The Crist hadn't been martyred, there would be no salvation! He *had* to be sacrificed! Why can't you accept that? And it's not about blame—it's about love and... passion... and... and... forgiveness!"

Dave put up his hands in defense. "Whoa there, cowboy! Chill, pardner! Pull back on those reins! Look—I can see where this is going and I'm gonna head it off at the pass. All I'm saying is that ultimate sacrifice requires ultimate blame, and Jews have been blamed enough over the past two thousand years—first for the Crucifixion, and then for the Conflagration..."

"Chill yourself! It's the Cristers who were blamed for the Conflagration, not the Jews."

"Both Jews and Cristers, then. Maybe millions of Cristers were burned on gabels as payback for the Conflagration, but so were millions of Jews. The Cristic and Jewish people have been the Rhettians' scapegoats for centuries."

Both teenagers fell silent. Paul's thoughts turned to the recent film that was still stirring so much controversy—*L'Ardeur de L'Rhetter*—the self-financed "historical account" of the last days of Goseth by action movie star Len Lemieur. Lemieur, an ultra-orthodox Rhettian from Quebec, based his epic movie on his own interpretation of the Lorswers from the New Teachings—an interpretation in line with the *Ardour Acts* staged by the Shrin in the Third Century to justify atrocities against the Cristic people.

In these plays, responsibility for the death of Goseth was placed squarely on the Cristers—not with the papal garrison at Avignon, nor with the Nordic invaders who had arrested and burned Goseth at the gabel.

A veteran actor of ultra-violent movies, Lemieur devoted most of his film to a horrendously graphic portrayal of Goseth's pain and humiliation leading up to the Conflagration at the hands of the jeering Cristers. He embellished the most gruesome Lorswers accounts of Goseth's torture with a grotesque brutality—devoting the final half-hour of the film to slow-motion close-ups of Goseth's searing, flaying flesh on the gabel, as the mob of Cristers taunted him and Satan skulked among them, celebrating Goseth's torturous death.

That the film capitalized on the Rhettian obsession with the graphic death of their Lord in order to enhance its box-office appeal was monstrous enough, but for it to exploit the deeply entrenched emotions of Rhettians blaming the Cristic people for his demise—accusations that had led to the persecution of millions of innocent Cristers over the centuries—was obscene.

Lemieur had scripted the film in Old German and Old French with subtitles, to give it the veneer of authenticity. The Cristic plotters depicted in the movie even spoke in Kristisch—and although historians who had seen the film noted that the version of Kristisch used in the movie didn't exist until 400 years after the depicted events, that hardly mattered to filmgoers. Rhettians who had seen the film said that they found the use of old dialects very convincing—reinforcing the myth's veracity. Even the ailing Heiliger Väter Franz VI, having been given a private screening in Luxembourg, gave the film the official ecumenical stamp of approval, issuing a press release that said, simply, "It is as it was."

Rhettians were flocking to the movie by the millions, many of them encouraged by their shrins, which had organized pilgrimages to their local theaters, booking large blocks of seats.

There had been other major theatrical events based on the life of Goseth that had sparked interest among shringoers, most notably the 50's blockbuster musical *Goseth Rhetter Superstar*, followed some years later by the off-Broadway *Lordswords*—a wordplay on the Lorswers—but the level of attention paid to these by fundamentalist shrins paled to the missionary zeal that greeted the release of *L'Ardeur*. The differences between the messages of the two musical productions and *L'Ardeur* was like day and night: while the musicals emphasized the story of Goseth's life and his teachings of love, humanity and peace, Lemieur's film fixated on the pain and horror of Rhetter's violent death—and ultimately, its blame. Interviews with many of the younger Rhettians who saw Lemieur's film illustrated how profoundly it affected them: some were so overcome with emotion that they had to leave the theater during the more brutal scenes. One tearful teenage girl implored after seeing the film: "How could they have done such a terrible thing to our Lord?"

Paul knew who *they* were. *They* were the Cristers—and not just the mob of Cristers depicted in the film, but *all* Cristers: the killers of God, in league with the Devil, forever condemned. They were accused of using the gabel to sacrifice God—the same instrument of torture used to sacrifice countless innocent Cristers in retribution for this... this myth. This sick and damning play on people's mindless, violent passions.

The Greatest Story Ever Told—that was the subtitle of *L'Ardeur*.

Crap on that, thought Paul—*more like The Vilest Lie Ever Told*.

For his part, Lemieur relished the additional fame—and considerable wealth—that *L'Ardeur* brought him. A consummate actor, he skillfully deflected the muted outcry from Cristic groups with patronizing platitudes. In one interview with a Rhettian television network, when asked about allegations that the film was anti-Cristic, Lemieur gave a surprised, wounded look and touched his chest as if stabbed by an unseen foe.

"The truth is that I *love* the Cristers," he protested. "I pray for their salvation all the time!"

Paul hadn't seen the film: he had no desire to contribute money to such exploitative, bigoted propaganda. He did go to see a different movie about a week after *L'Ardeur de L'Rhetter* opened and had difficulty finding a place to park. Cruising around the lot in search of an empty space, he had noticed several rows of cars all sporting an identical metallic symbol of a bird in flight representing Goseth—with two golden curves joined together:

He had read that some scholars felt the symbol dated from several passages in the New Teachings referring to Goseth's spirit taking flight during the Conflagration, and from Goseth having said of himself: "I am the wings of mankind." Others claimed it was a reference to the mythological Phoenix rising from the ashes, just as Goseth had. Still others asserted that it was an acronym of the German word "vogel" meaning "bird", with the letters standing for "*Völker* (the people) *Opfer* (had sacrificed) *GEben sie* (the one who was giving them) *Licht* (light)" Again, Paul knew who the *Völker* were: the Cristers.

The symbol seemed so simple and pure: two curves joined together to create a universal symbol of a graceful flying bird. So superficially innocent, yet its underpinning was that of blame— of casting an entire people as eternally culpable, of justification for six centuries of persecution and slaughter.

Years ago, in response to the popularity of the *vogel*, some Cristic group had fashioned an abstract fish from the same two curves by simply overlaying one atop the other, to recall the ancient symbol of *ichthys* that had been used by pre-Rhettian Cristers. But considering how the *ichthys* had become an execration—particularly its use as a wreath of fish heads mockingly placed by the Wayward Crister around the neck of the doomed Rhetter—few Cristers were about to attach any fish symbols to the backs of their cars, no matter how innocuous and cute.

Even among the nation's policymakers, the ugly mask of bigotry parading as righteousness was constantly on display. On Tuesday, the newspapers had carried a story on the senate bid by a congresswoman from Florida who, in her campaign address before a large Rhettian congregation, warned against electing Cristers and other non-Rettians to Congress. She claimed that casting such a vote was "a sin against God, because those who do not have faith in Goseth legislate sin."

The week before, Paul had read the transcript of a speech by one of the senators from South Carolina, railing about "the monopoly that Cristers in this administration have on American international policy", and how "the Cristers have always wielded a disproportionate amount of political power and influence in this country". The senator went on to assert that "the Cristic lobbying group, UCPAC, has many congressmen neatly folded into its thick wallet, but I'm proud to say that, as a God-fearing Rhettian, I'm not one of them".

Reading this had angered Paul to the point that he had started to write a rebuttal to the paper, but after a few sentences he tore it up.

What's the use… bigots are bigots, and a letter to the editor isn't going to change their minds.

But this sordid, entrenched bigotry wasn't limited to southern politicians. The previous month, The Washington Post had carried an article on a former mayor of D.C., a renowned African-

American leader in the civil rights movement, who was spreading centuries-old conspiracy theories about "World-Destroying Cristers." His rants were directed at something he termed "The Five Fiscal Families of Cristendom", whom he claimed had secretly funneled tens of billions of dollars in cash, stocks, gold and uncut diamonds to every American president since Jefferson in order to control the White House. He called these mysterious, faceless families "The Rulers of Darkness", accusing them of being part of an ancient world-wide Cristic Cabal that ran the international banking system—manipulating global affairs and responsible for every major political assassination from Abraham Lincoln to the black civil rights icon, Marion Verner King, Jr. He went on to claim that seven Cristic companies owned and controlled the world's media, ensuring "a Crister Stranglehold on American Thought."

And no one took him to task.

If there was ever anyone attuned to prejudice—sensitive to stereotyping and spreading sickening myths about a people—you'd think it would be a black person who'd experienced bigotry first-hand. Then again, the simplest way to consign blame is to fashion another scapegoat—especially a smaller minority than your own that's been targeted far longer than you, for far greater sins. It's such an easy, brainless way to neatly package society's evils and your own dark demons...

Paul's musings ended, and he noticed his friend studying him. "Look," he told Dave, "this is pointless, comparing suffering and blame. People have persecuted other people out of hatred and fear and conceit and God knows what else. The fact is that we've both endured bigotry, Cristers and Jews."

Dave let out a long sigh. "True enough. Just look at the Shoah."

The Shoah, thought Paul. *The Holocaust.* Hitler's minions in

Germany and most of the rest of Europe, fortified by centuries of social conditioning in bigotry: by their clergy, rulers, families, and peers. From the start, it was based on deep-rooted anti-Semitism—Jews as scapegoats, blamed for every possible ill. The insidious encroachment of Shrin-endorsed persecution by the Nazis and the Fascists: first taking over Jewish properties and businesses... then suspending their rights and their citizenship... then the outright attacks and organized riots... then murders in the streets... then forced deportations in cattle cars to concentration camps... then mass slaughters of villagers in the forests... culminating in mechanized extermination in the death camps. And through it all, the other minority—the Cristers—remained silent. No protest over what was happening to their Jewish neighbors... perhaps out of fear that the Nazis might turn on them.

Or maybe it was something far more appalling: a feeling that the Jews deserved their fate—that it was God's way of punishing them for... what? For killing the Crist? For not accepting Jesus as their Savior?

But the silence didn't help the Cristers, didn't protect them. If God was punishing the Jews, then He also punished the Cristers—if for nothing else, for their indifference. After the death camps had been emptied of Jews because there were no more Jews to kill, the Nazis and the Fascists found their next scapegoat in the Cristers. Entire communities were rounded up, destined for the firing squads and gas chambers. Five million Cristic people perished in the death camps, nearly as many as the six million Jews. If it hadn't been for the Allied invasion and victory, millions more would have followed the same torturous path as the Jews, who the Cristers had watched being marched off to their deaths, thankful that it wasn't them. In the end, almost one third of Europe's Cristers were lost in the death camps. The Jewish communities had fared far worse, completely annihilated by the Nazis and their Rhettian allies.

And now there were—what? Maybe twenty-five million Cristers remaining in the world, and half that many Jews. How many Rhettians were there? Well over a billion... probably closer to two billion.

"Dave, do you think... do you think that God was punishing us—the Jews and the Cristers—with the Holocaust? Had we committed some sin that made Him angry?"

"I think," said Dave, "that the Nazis were punishing us. This was man's inhumanity to man. God created all of us... gave us this Earth and the opportunity to make it perfect. Obviously, we still have a long way to go."

"Amen to that, Bro'," Paul nodded. He sat quiet for a moment. "A lot to think about."

"Yeah, a lot to think about. But right now, back to your game. You still have a screen full of frozen mutants to frag."

"Nah, I need to stretch. Grab your glove and let's throw a ball around."

"Now *that* sounds like a plan," Dave said, and they headed outside into the warm sunshine of a perfect spring day.

Chapter Nineteen

Principal Peters

Two weeks after spring break, as Paul stood at his locker collecting books for his first two classes, he felt a tap on his shoulder and turned to see Dorbensheyer.

"Morning, Paul. How are you doing today? Principal Peters and I need to talk with you. Can you stop by the main office during Resource?"

"Sure," Paul replied. His mind raced back to the laughing episode in Beckworth's class last semester. "Does this have to do with that thing in AP English...?"

"Nothing at all to do with that. See you during Resource, main office. Don't forget."

"Do I need to bring anything?"

"Nope, just yourself," said Dorbensheyer, and he turned and disappeared into the tide of students.

Resource was third period. After his second class ended, Paul headed over to the school's main office. One of the secretaries was tapping on her keyboard behind the counter, glancing up as Paul entered.

"May I help you?"

"I'm here to see Principal Peters and Mr. Dorbensheyer."

"Oh, you must be Paul. Congratulations!" smiled the secretary. "Quite an accomplishment... your parents must be very proud of you! Go on in," she said, pointing down the short hall-way leading to the principal's office. "They're expecting you."

As Paul approached Principal Peters' office, he could hear the low murmur of the principal and Dorbensheyer in conversation, punctuated by a shared laugh. He imagined that Dorbensheyer was regaling the principal with anecdotes about the imbecilic stunts of students sent to the Disciplinary Office over the years. When Paul knocked on the beaded glass door window, the discussion abruptly stopped, followed by Principal Peters shouting "Enter."

Principal Peters was middle-aged, with only a wisp of blond hair on an otherwise bald head that sported a perpetual shine. He was a large man, nearly as wide as he was tall, yet he moved with an almost graceful ease—negotiating doorways and tightly-packed classroom desks with the dexterity of a much smaller person. There was a joke that, unlike other high schools in the county, Forbach Valley didn't have two assistant principals because it didn't need the second one: Principal Peters was large enough to cover both jobs, and then some.

"Ah, yes, Paul," Principal Peters said, standing as Paul entered the office. He motioned to an empty chair. "Come on in and sit yourself down next to Assistant Principal Dorbensheyer. We won't keep you long, but we need to talk with you about graduation."

"Graduation?" asked Paul, still standing. Worries swirled around him—what had he done now? Or, what hadn't he done? His mind raced over the past few weeks: never tardy... all homework turned in on time... took every test and every quiz... quiet in Resource... did he miss something, do something wrong? Then like a hammer blow, he remembered the biology class he had skipped to talk with Dave about race, and raw fear gripped him.

Dorbensheyer read the trepidation in his face. "Stop sweating, Paul. You're not here to be grilled. In fact," he stood up and offered his hand, "you're to be congratulated. But I'll let Principal Peters have the honor of telling you."

"Telling me what?" asked Paul as he shook Dorbensheyer's hand.

Principal Peters walked over to him, extending a massive arm. "That you're our valedictorian, of course," he beamed, shaking Paul's hand, which was swallowed by the principal's fleshy fingers. "Congratulations. Very fine achievement. Straight-A's—we only had two perfect students this year." He turned to Dorbensheyer. "How many in this senior class, Ray?"

"Just over four hundred."

"Four hundred," repeated Principal Peters. "Not a small accomplishment, beating out four hundred of your classmen for top honors." He returned to his chair behind the desk and sat down as Paul sat next to Dorbensheyer.

"Now, as you know, there will be a commencement ceremony in about six weeks… on Tuesday, Pendiery 9th, and as valedictorian you will be given the opportunity to address your class. The schedule gives you ten minutes for your speech, and although that isn't a hard and fast rule, we strongly recommend that you keep it to between five and ten minutes. Do you foresee any problems with this?"

"Um, no, sir. I don't think so."

"As to the content of your speech," continued the principal, "we don't dictate what you should or should not say, but there are specific guidelines that we expect you to follow. For example, there will be no obscenities, no demeaning comments directed at teachers or staff, and no personal attacks on people. Also, you cannot use this opportunity to espouse political manifestos or any other types of declarations that might be considered inappropriate or offensive. Do you have any problem with this?"

Paul shook his head no.

"We require that you provide the school with a copy of your speech two weeks before graduation, which gives you the next four weeks to put it together. Mr. Dorbensheyer has a packet that contains all of this information. Give it to him, Ray."

Dorbensheyer handed Paul a thick 9x12 manila envelope. "It's all in here," he said. "The schedule, the rules, the do's and don'ts. And it also includes some copies of past valedictory speeches that you can look over for ideas."

"No plagiarism though," warned Principal Peters, "either from these speeches or from any other material. If you quote someone, make sure you give them credit. And if you use something from the Internet, I suggest you double-check your sources. Oh, and that reminds me—no off-color jokes. We had one speech several years ago that raised quite a few eyebrows. That's one reason we instituted the review requirement. We don't want any curves thrown at us."

Principal Peters motioned toward the envelope. "There's a parental form in there, also. You need to get your parent or your guardian to read it over and sign it. The sooner the better. Once it's been signed, bring it back to the main office and ask one of the secretaries to put it in my mailbox. There will be a commencement ceremony walk-through in about five weeks. The information about it is in the packet. Oh... and appropriate attire underneath the gown!"

He turned to Dorbensheyer. "Remember that girl from—which graduation was it—seventy-seven, Ray? I think her name was Ladimore."

Dorbensheyer shook his head and let out a low whistle. "It *was* unusually hot that year, but there was absolutely no excuse for that."

Principal Peters chuckled. "Remember the old saying, 'if you've got it, flaunt it'? My gracious... Miss Ladimore certainly took *that* to heart. She was an arresting young woman, that she was! Well, well, well... I suppose we'll just have to keep adding to our 'thou shalt not' list every year."

He gestured toward Paul. "That's about all I have for Mr. Fairchild, here... anything you need to add, Ray?"

Dorbensheyer shook his head. "Not at this time." He stood and once more extended his hand. "Congratulations again, Paul. The honor couldn't have gone to a more deserving student, and I mean that sincerely."

"Thanks, Mr. Dorbensheyer. And thank you, Principal Peters."

As Paul left the office and headed to Resource, he made a mental note to find a copy of the '77 Yearbook and look up Ladimore.

* * *

That night, after completing his homework, Paul turned on his PC and opened a new Word file. At the top of the white page that flashed onscreen, he typed:

Valedictory Address

He stared at the heading.

The reality of having to stand before the entire high school teaching staff, all four hundred of his classmates, plus hundreds—perhaps as many as a thousand—family members, was beginning to sink in. What was he going to *say*? Anything he said was going to sound lame. Better to keep it as short as possible. What did Principal Peters say? Five to ten minutes. Maybe he could shave it down to four and a half: just a simple thank-you to his parents and teachers.

Under the title, he typed:

> *I wish to thank my parents, my teachers, and all of the support staff at Forbach Valley High for this honor. I am proud of my academic record at this school, and I will always remember my four years here.*

What was that? Ten seconds? He started to feel sick.

Why didn't I think about this beforehand? Nothing's worth subjecting myself to this kind of punishment! If I had something to say, then this would be okay... but I've got nothing—zip. Maybe five minutes is just a suggestion. Everyone will probably be relieved if I give a really short speech. After all, they're there for the ceremony—they certainly aren't there to hear some long-winded lecture from a seventeen-year-old just because I got perfect grades.

He continued typing:

> *I learned a lot at Forbach Valley High. I learned about many of the sciences, such as biology and chemistry and physics. I also learned about English and about literature, and I learned about ancient history and American history. I took French as my foreign language, and I learned how to converse in basic French fairly well.*

He paused and read over what he had written.

Totally lame.

Disgusted, he closed out the document and leaned over the desk, his head in his hands.

This is useless. I'm going to die in six weeks, tossed to the wolves and eviscerated in front of everyone. Twelve Angry Jurors was a cake-

walk compared to this! Don't I have <u>anything</u> to say? Wasn't there some lesson learned, some message worth delivering? How about: "The only reason I spent four years busting my balls was to get that scholarship to Dittisham. Nothing else matters. Thank you."

Forget the message. All I need is a nice, simple and polite thank-you speech, maybe with a famous quote tossed in for good measure—some frivolous observation about realizing one's dreams, attaining one's goals—that sort of thing.

He opened up a search engine, typed "famous quotes", and hit Enter. Tens of thousands of hits came back within an instant, many to websites with compendiums of quotations searchable by keyword.

This is going to be easier than I thought!

He chose one of the more promising sites and typed in "dreams".

Dozens of quotes appeared. He found a good one by Thoreau:

> **Go confidently in the direction of your dreams. Live the life you have imagined.**

That's innocuous enough.
He typed in "achieve".
Dozens more popped up.

> **The positive thinker sees the invisible, feels the intangible, and achieves the impossible.**
>
> **– Sir Winston Churchill, My Early Life, 553-583**

Can't go wrong with Churchill, thought Paul. And it was a perfect quote: inoffensive, superficially profound, with nothing that could get him into trouble.

A few more of these and I'm home free!
He went back into Word and started again:

> *Thank you, Principal Peters, distinguished faculty,*
> *parents and students. I am honored to be given the op-*
> *portunity to address you today. The great poet and*
> *philosopher, Henry David Thoreau, once wrote, "Go*
> *confidently in the direction of your dreams. Live the*
> *life you have imagined." This inspirational quote tells*
> *us that we can achieve our dreams if we pursue them...*

He was finished within the hour. A half-dozen harmless quotes and filler to paste it all together, with an obsequious opening and an equally ingratiating closure. He read it aloud, timing himself.

Five minutes and change—piece of cake!

Chapter Twenty

Prom Night

*D*id *I ask her, or did she ask me?*

Perhaps it was mutual—a shared glance, a casual nod—he couldn't remember just how it came about. But they were going to the prom together, that much was certain. It was a nice feeling, being able to forgo all of the awkward formalities without fear of rejection.

They were an item—like Bogart and Bacall.

Or was it Bogart and Bergman? No… that was just in the movies. Bogie and Bacall was in the movies and it was in real life, too. He wondered how that would be: acting out the fantasy and living it, too.

No need to do or say anything—just whistle.

Hell—Peggy and I don't even have to do that! Just nod is more like it… no worries.

The worries started afterward: what to wear, how to get there, what to do. Paul hadn't given it any thought until three weeks after Rhettag, when the prom was only a couple of weeks away.

"You need to wear a tux," his mom reminded him.

Sure, no problem. Go to the store and rent a tux. What's the big deal?

Except that, when he finally got to the formal wear shop, there were a gazillion tuxes and most of them looked really gay.

No way I'm wearing frills... and who in his right mind wears baby blue, or lavender, or peach? But that standard black formal looks lame, too. And there are a million variations of even that: one-button; two-button; three-button... even <u>ten</u>-button; single or double breasted; shawl, peak or notch collars; tails; cutaways; black vests, gray vests, white or colored vests, striped vests or no vest at all. And what's with these cummerbunds?

Paul suddenly had a deep appreciation for the dilemma confronting girls choosing their prom gowns. Even with all their frivolous nuances, at least tuxedos followed a paradigm. But faced with an infinite variety of styles and accoutrements, how could a woman ever find the perfect dress? He wondered what Peggy would be wearing, then decided it didn't matter... she could wear a sack cloth and look fantastic.

He finally settled on an ivory-colored, one-button, single-breasted tux with shawl collar sans vest, with a white pleated shirt, black cummerbund and a black bow tie.

Very Bogeyesque, he decided. *Not as stiff or nerdy as a black tux — but definitely not gay, either.*

With the tux issue settled, it was on to the florist for the corsage.

Goseth Rhetter—how could such a simple thing as a prom be so complicated? Single flower or spray? Pin-on, wrist corsage, or nosegay? And what color scheme? What is Peggy wearing??? Will a purple dendrobium orchid clash with her gown? Is a yellow orchid the safer choice?

He finally chose a pin-on spray of mixed petite flowers with miniature pink roses, white alstroemeria, and light blue delphinium, and prayed that she wasn't allergic to any of them.

Transportation was the easiest part. He and Dave had decided to split the cost of a limousine, and the big guy had volunteered to make the arrangements. Dave was taking Iliana: a pretty, win-nowy blonde junior. They had first met on Ilsembre 28th at a New Year's party given by a mutual friend and immediately hit it off. In the several weeks since the party, the two had become very close. *Strange how the chemistry between people works*, thought Paul. He had known Peggy for years before they started going out. Dave and Iliana reached that point in a matter of days, or perhaps only a few hours—maybe just minutes.

Can you really know someone in the space of a single conversation? Or even less time: in a glance across a crowded room—like the Rodgers and Hammerstein song? Is that simply the stuff of fairy tales, or does it really happen?

He thought back to the day that Peggy's sister, Patty, had answered the door in her short cutoffs at the Forsythes a year and a half ago, and then last Vintner, reclining in her tight sweater and ski pants in the back seat of the Escalade on the way to Fox Hunt.

That wasn't chemistry. That was... what? A thunderbolt. A nuclear meltdown. Concupiscence. Raw, unadulterated lust. Or was it more than that? Didn't we click? Not in the same way as Peggy and I, but still... there was something there. Something magical. Wasn't there? The way we had touched, kissed, made love.

He still longed for her, ached for her... did she ever think about him?

Paul slowly shook his head.

Get a grip: Peggy is the one. Patty was an unintended side trip—a wild and crazy off-road thrill ride, but now completely over and done with. Finis. Prom's in two weeks and Peggy is your date.

Peggy—not Patty.

He sighed.

God, she was something!

The next two weeks flew by, which always seemed to be the case after the excruciatingly protracted, months-long buildup to

Rhettag. Before Paul knew it, it was Janiery 7th—Prom Night.

Time compressed as day turned toward dusk. *Dinner! Who made the dinner reservations? Oh, right... I did, weeks ago. Some snotty jerk on the phone took them... must have known that I was a kid on a prom date. This is all so weird—this whole stupid charade: fake fancy dinner, fake fancy clothes, fake fancy limo. Limo! Who got the... oh, yeah, Dave did. Relax.*

He wrapped the black bow tie around the stiff collar of the pleated shirt and tried to tie it the way he had practiced a week ago: *Make the right side longer... over the top... through the loop... straighten it out... fold the left... over the top...*

He stood there in front of the bathroom mirror holding the ends of the bow tie, hopelessly lost. *Now* what was he supposed to do?

He tried folding the right portion into a loop.

Where does it go? Nowhere.

He straightened it back out and tried wrapping it around the shorter loop.

No, that looks dumb.

Frustrated, he pulled off the tie and tried it again.

Still wrong.

Six tries later, his mother poked her head into the bathroom. "David should be here soon. Are you all ready?"

"All except for this stupid tie!"

"Here, let me try," she said, reaching up to grasp the now-wrinkled ribbons. "Maybe I should try to iron it..."

"No time. Look—it's fine! I think I can get it."

"Stop fidgeting, Paul! I can't tie it when you're squirming like that!"

After a few attempts, she was also getting flustered.

His father poked his head into the bathroom: "Problems?"

"It's this bow tie, John. Paul and I can't get it tied. Do you know how to do this?"

"Of course... it's really very simple."

Paul's mother left the bathroom as his father firmly wrapped the tie around Paul's collar and commenced to expertly tie the knot. "Nervous?" he asked as he formed the bow.

"Uh, a little I guess. I wasn't until a few days ago, but now it's like such a big thing."

"Well, it *is* a big thing, in a way," his dad said, pulling the flared ends of the tie to even the bow. "I was nervous, too. I wanted the evening to go perfectly for..." he paused in thought. "What was her name?" He chuckled. "Can you believe it? I can't even remember her name now. It wasn't your mother, of course—we didn't meet until after college. Damn, doesn't that beat all... for the life of me, I can't think of her name!"

He chuckled again and resumed straightening the bow. "She was beautiful, I remember that. I can even picture her face. I liked her a lot, maybe even considered marrying her at one point. And we..." John Fairchild stopped, looked at his son. "I should have discussed this with you before," he lowered his voice, put his hands on his son's shoulders, "but do you have... or do you need... protection? If you do, just tell me, because I have some that I can give you."

Paul turned red, looking down at the floor. "Dad!"

"I'm serious, Paul. Things can get... can go beyond a certain point, and you might find yourself... I mean, I'm sure you know what I'm talking about. And you need to be ready, be prepared... if you need something, please tell me..."

"I'm fine, Dad. Really. I'm fine. Okay?"

"Okay, fine," his dad nodded, "that's all I needed to know. You're a smart kid, Paul, and you can take care of yourself. I know that. I just had to ask to make sure." He patted his son's cheek. "Now go have a great time!"

From downstairs came his mother's voice: "Paul, David just pulled up! My God, what on earth is he driving?"

"It's a stretch limo, Mom," Paul shouted downstairs.

"Paul, darling, I think I know a stretch limo when I see one," his mother shouted back upstairs. "This is *not* a stretch limo."

She was right. It was a sunshine yellow Humvee with jet black trim. An extra row of spotlights graced the front roofline, making the vehicle seem even more massive, if that was possible.

Dave, smartly attired in a black tuxedo, bounded out of the front seat, hardly able to contain his excitement. "Paul, look at this thing! Isn't it wicked? Beats a limo hands down! Oh, hi, Mr. and Mrs. Fairchild," he said, giving a slight bow and wave. "How are you doing?"

"We're fine, David," said Paul's dad, stepping outside the front door to take a closer look at the huge SUV. "So, I'm guessing this is your transportation to the prom?"

"Yessir," Dave said proudly. "I figured everybody else is coming in some kind of limo. Not in a Hummer, anyway."

"You're probably right about that," Mr. Fairchild agreed, sizing up the vehicle. "How's it drive?"

"Really sweet! You wouldn't think it, being a truck and all, but it handles great. A lot better than Matilda... I mean, my wagon. Here," Dave extended the keys in his hand, "would you like to try it out?"

"Dave," Paul cut in, "we better get going. Peg and Iliana are waiting."

"Oh yeah, right," Dave nodded. He turned back to Paul's dad. "I've got it until five o'clock tomorrow. Maybe I can bring it by around noon or so."

"Sounds good," smiled Mr. Fairchild. "And thanks, Dave. I appreciate the offer. Now you two go have a ball."

Having anticipated a chauffeur-driven limousine, Paul was at first taken aback by the sight of the truck—but the more he thought about it, the more he liked the idea of showing up at the prom in a hot yellow Hummer. The whole thing reeked class, and the idea of two tuxedoed guys and their dates in formal gowns stepping out of this brute was just too cool. Climbing into the front seat, he also understood why Dave was so excited—a limo would have been more spacious than a regular car, but the Humvee was cavernous inside. Watching Dave easily swing his immense frame into the driver's seat, Paul realized that here, finally, was a vehicle that his friend felt comfortable in... even more so than driving Matilda.

Peggy was the first stop, and Dave idled in the circular driveway as Paul hopped out to fetch her. As he rang the bell, he wondered what her parents' reaction would be to the Hummer.

Will they be as confused as my mom, or as impressed as my dad? Probably not. Probably not impressed at all, possibly even...

As was the case the previous summer, Patty answered the door. But not in her baggy sweatshirt and those endless legs extending from tight cutoffs.

Not hardly. She was wearing a prom dress. The most beautiful dress Paul had ever seen. Elegant... enticing... spellbinding.

His head swam. *Peggy, not Patty! Peggy's my date! Why is Patty wearing the gown?*

"Well, look at *you!*" Patty said, giving him an appreciative once over. "You look like Double-O-Seven in that getup!"

She held her hand out to Paul, narrowing her eyes into a sultry gaze. "Take me to the Kasbah, James! Or the Riviera, or Monte Carlo, or wherever it is you want to take me. I'm yours all evening." She laughed disarmingly and did a pirouette for him as Peggy had done, ages ago, wearing her new winter outfit in the cafeteria. "At least we're both dressed for it. How do I look?"

"Stunning. I mean, *really* stunning. Amazing, Patty."

She gave him a fake pout. "You don't sound like you mean it, James."

But he *did* mean it. One hundred percent.

"I bet you say that to *all* the girls."

Not on your life.

Still pouting, she looked down at his hand. "I'll bet those love-ly flowers aren't for me, either."

"No, they're for Peggy, but...." Paul became flustered, searched for the right response. "But if I had known, if I knew you were... going..."

"Paul, you are *so* sweet!" she said, flashing him her gorgeous smile. "Well, maybe next time, hey?" She gave him a wink and licked her glossed lips, making them glisten... timed, he thought, to make his knees almost buckle with desire just as her parents reached the door.

"Why hello, Paul!" said Mrs. Forsythe, "We haven't seen you since Mithran. How have you been? You look so dashing! Patty is also going to a prom tonight. It has been *hectic* here all day." She stopped, peering around him into the street. "Why is there a yel-low truck parked in our drive? What on earth is that thing?"

Mr. Forsythe peered with her. "I believe that's a Humvee, Amanda." He peered harder. "There's someone sitting in it."

"That's Dave," Paul said. "Dave Gershwin. He's a friend of mine. We're going to the prom together. With him and his date, I mean. I mean, he needs to get his date. I mean, he *has* a date, but we still need to get her."

Mrs. Forsythe looked up and down the drive. "Where is your limousine, Paul?"

"There isn't any limousine, Mrs. Forsythe. Dave's driving the Hummer, I mean, the Humvee. That yellow thing."

She raised an eyebrow. "That yellow thing? You mean to say, that yellow thing is your limousine?"

"In a way, yeah. It's our limousine, I guess."

"My gracious," Mrs. Forsythe said, placing her hand on her chest in astonishment, "Things certainly have changed since *I* was a girl."

"What's everybody looking at?"

Paul turned to the voice coming from the long spiral staircase.

She descended the stairs as if in slow-motion: her slender white-gloved hand lightly caressing the banister; her auburn hair a bouquet of delicate curls tied in a cascading peach-colored bow; her gown a sequined satin wonder flowing with her flawless form; her visage... her visage...

While Patty was positively stunning, Peggy was absolute perfection.

As she reached the bottom of the stairs, Paul noticed how the sheer satin molded to the sensuous curve at the small of her back, tight enough to trace the soft arch of her spine into the smooth, taut curve of her posterior. She rounded the balustrade and walked toward him in impossibly thin heels with the grace of a beauty contestant: the silky split gown shimmering against her tanned legs, tracing the curvature of her hips and the contours of her slender midriff, then rising to cup her pert breasts.

He stood entranced, hoping the vision would never end, yet wishing that she would hurry to his side. All these years... first acquaintances... then schoolmates... then friends... never imaging it would lead to this moment, standing in an ivory tuxedo in her doorway, watching her draw near to him in her exquisite evening gown.

And finally she was standing next to him, and the Forsythes were taking pictures as they posed the couple in the foyer beneath the chandelier and ornate stairs, and she was wearing the spray of tiny roses, white alstroemeria and blue delphinium that he had given her.

And then, with farewells, they were out the door.

"What is *that*?" asked Peggy, pointing at the Humvee.

"That's our ride," said Paul.

"Sweet!" she said.

And he helped her into the back seat, climbed in beside her, and they were off.

Dinner was at Le Petit Chien, an ostentatious French restaurant nestled in a wooded area just outside Maynardsville. It was a favorite among prom dates simply for its pretentiousness—although in truth the food was excellent. Following the maitre d' to their table, Paul noticed several other young couples in tuxedos and gowns seated throughout the restaurant. He tried not to make eye contact—he didn't want to know who else was pretending to be sophisticated that night.

Once seated, the four were handed menus by the maitre d', who then marched back to the reception area.

Dave opened his and quickly scanned it. "Oh, crap!" he exclaimed in a voice loud enough to be heard by the next table. "I knew it! It's all in French... not a single normal word in this whole damn thing!" He looked up from his menu at the others. "Paul, you're taking French. You've got to help me out here."

"I'll try, buddy," Paul said. "I can figure out most of it, I think."

"And I can help, too, Dave," Peggy chimed in. "I've had most of these entrees, so I can tell you what's in them."

"Ne craignez pas, mon chéri. Je crois que nous pouvons tout être utiles." said Iliana.

Dave stared at her, duly impressed. "Dang, I *knew* I had the perfect prom date!"

Their waiter, a short man dressed in a white server's tuxedo with slicked-back hair and pencil-thin moustache, appeared at the table.

"Bonsoir, mademoiselles et messieurs," he said. "Are we ready to order?"

Dave handed the waiter his menu and pointed over to Iliana. "She's ordering for me. Incidentally," he whispered, leaning over toward the small man, "you don't serve Korean food here, do you?"

"No," said the waiter, "Why do you ask?"

"The name of your restaurant—I thought it might be your featured dish."

"Dave!" Paul hissed, "Don't."

"Hey," Dave said, turning his palms upward in mock innocence. "I was just asking."

After dinner selections were made and the waiter departed, Dave leaned across to Paul. "It was just a joke. Gopes, if they can't take a joke…"

"Yeah, right. Well, you'd better hope that their idea of a joke in the kitchen isn't spitting in your food."

Dave slowly leaned back in his chair, frowning. "Hmmm… I hadn't thought of that…"

The rest of the dinner went flawlessly, with animated conversation and delicious food—except that Dave suspiciously examined each bite.

As always, the prom was held at the Forbach Valley Marriott. Considering the modest size of the hotel, it boasted an exceptionally large ballroom: Paul surmised that it had been built specifically to accommodate high school proms and other local pageants.

By the time they left the restaurant, dusk had turned into nightfall. As the Humvee approached the Marriott, Dave flicked on the row of flood lamps along the roof edge, bathing the road with light. The arrival of the bright yellow Hummer produced the anticipated response from the small crowd of other prom-goers outside the hotel—staring and pointing and shouting with approval as the vehicle slowly pulled up under the columned portico. Applause spontaneously broke out among the gathering as the foursome disembarked, Dave handing the keys over to a very grateful valet, who clearly relished the opportunity to drive the behemoth. Paul felt like a movie star on premier night: dressed in a tuxedo, a beautiful young woman on his arm, walk-ing along the red carpet as onlookers clapped and cheered on each side.

It doesn't get any better than this, he decided.

As if to confirm his musings, the interior of the Marriott was a bit of a letdown: the lobby furnished with a few overstuffed faux-leather wingback chairs and two sofas; the hotel registration desk a bland row of fake wood paneling starkly lit by overhead fluo-rescent lights. Even though Rhettag had ended more than a month ago, there was still an artificial pine tree ornamented with gold and violet tinsel in the lobby, with the requisite fake gifts piled underneath. *Somebody needs to get on the stick and put that dust-caked thing away*, thought Paul. *Then again, perhaps it's a per-manent fixture...*

Even before he entered the lobby, Paul could feel the pulsing beat of the dance music emanating from the ballroom. Once in-side the hotel, the sound seemed to engulf him, coaxing his foot-steps to match its cadence. The two couples automatically fol-lowed the sound down the long hallway to the ballroom, whose entrance was gaily decorated in the theme of the prom: *Caribbean Cruise*. Two large cardboard cutouts of palm trees laden with co-coanuts framed the entrance, and several papier-mâché monkeys dangled from the trees, grasping nuts that had been halved into cups with cocktail umbrellas and straws protruding from them.

A wide beaded bamboo curtain stretched across the doorway.

Two fold-out prom registration tables were positioned in the hallway just before the entrance with signs posted above them: A-M and N-Z. Since both his and Peggy's last names began with an "F", Paul headed toward the table to the left. He wondered which table a couple with, say, "D" and "T" last names went to: the one for the guy, since it was technically his "date"—or to the girl's table, as that would seem the courteous thing to do. Or, did they have to split up to sign in, which would be even more awkward.

As he approached the left table, he regretted not having a "T" last name: Miss Snodderbee, Principal Peters' personal secretary, was handling the A-M registrations. A dour person even on her best day, Snodderbee looked especially rankled this evening. Paul wondered whether she was getting paid overtime to work the table... probably not, he decided, based on her demeanor. He had never had a pleasant encounter with her during his entire four years at Forbach Valley. Judging from her looks, she was well into her forties. As far as he knew, she never married: *Small wonder*, he thought. *Who could ever put up with such a grouse?*

His dad had once told him that there were two kinds of people in the world: energy-givers and energy-takers. Energy-givers were the ones who, after you spent time with them, left you feeling energized, satisfied and positive. Conversely, energy-takers robbed you of your mental and spiritual vigor, leaving you feeling spent and depressed.

Pessimists were a kind of energy-taker, and Snodderbee wrote the book on pessimism. Why does Principal Peters keep her as his secretary? Maybe he doesn't have a choice—maybe because of her seniority, she gets to choose the high school she wants to work at, and Principal Peters just has to bear it. Or maybe there's a sort of perverse chemistry at work—a sort of yin-yang, where his phony optimism is balanced by her incorrigible negativism...

Maybe it's her name—a font for endless derisive jokes. Who would ever go out someone named <u>Snodderbee</u>? I mean, if they looked like Peggy—well, yeah, sure—but like <u>her</u>? He wondered whether the woman had always been so unlikable, or whether she had slowly calcified as she went through life without a boyfriend, without a date. Maybe it was a combination of both: a vicious cycle exacerbated by her unfortunate name. He'd have thought her name would be sufficient incentive to *get* married, if only to change it.

Paul looked back for Dave and noticed that he was standing in the other line.

But Gershwin comes right after "F", so why is he over there? Ah! Iliana's last name is Norstrom, so that explains it—Dave decided to go there first. A true gentleman. Or is it because of Snodderbee?

When Paul got to the front of the line, Snodderbee didn't even look up.

"Name?" she asked, almost shouting to be heard above the music. Even that single innocuous word was laden with disgust, sloughing off her tongue with years of practiced animus.

"Fairchild," said Paul, quickly adding: "and Forsythe"

"One at a time," snapped Snodderbee, shooting him a scowl, then looking back down at her printout. "Fairchild first. Rhettian name?"

Rhettian name? Snodderbee has known me for four years. True, we've never exchanged more than a few words each time... but even so, over the past four years we must have talked at least once a month, maybe more. She knows I'm this year's valedictorian—she put together that packet of commencement materials for me just last week. She knows my name!

Indignation built inside him. He wanted to say it, thought the better of it, then said it anyway. "I don't have a *Rhettian* name."

Snodderbee slowly looked up at him, locking his gaze with

her sneer. "*Everybody* has a Rhettian name, Mr. Fairchild," she hissed, "even *you*."

Let it go, Paul, his little voice was pleading.

"Nope, you're mistaken. I have a *Cristic* name. I was baptized Cristic, not Rhettian."

"Babbized?" Snodderbee slurred. "What in heaven's name are you talking about, young man? I couldn't care less about your being babbized, or whatever you just said. I asked you for your *Rhettian name,* your *given* name."

"You're not listening. I was never given a *Rhettian* name. I'm not *Rhettian.*"

Peggy was squeezing his hand. Hard.

Snodderbee slowly put her pencil down and clasped her hands on the table. She had finally met her opponent for the evening, and she accepted the challenge with relish.

"Now, you have a choice, young man," she growled. "You can either do as I asked and give me your *Rhettian* name, and I can then check you off my list, or…" she waved toward the long line of students that had formed behind Paul, "you can continue to play games and make all of these nice young people stand in line and wait for you to act like an adult."

The nice young people in the line were beginning to grumble.

Another squeeze. Even harder.

As much as Paul ached to continue the fight, this wasn't the time. He sighed.

"Paul. It's Paul. Paul Fairchild."

Snodderbee checked his name off the list, the flourish of her hand signaling triumph.

"And you, Miss Forsythe? What is your *Rhettian* name, please?"

"It's Margaret," Peggy said.

Margaret! Did I know that? Paul wondered. *I suppose so—just never thought about it. Margaret... Margaret Fairchild. Sounds nice.*

"Thank you. You may both go in," Snodderbee said.

With any luck, thought Paul, *this is the last time that old bitch and I will ever exchange pleasantries.*

The party inside the ballroom was in full swing when they entered. Paul felt that the beaded curtain was a nice touch—it created a sort of transitional moment, as if they were entering another realm. And it really did feel like a different world... almost magical: the bright, colorful lights sparkling through the ballroom's impressive chandeliers and dancing off two giant suspended mirrored balls; the pulsing beat of the music by a local band named Crash that really rocked; and the mass of well-groomed students all dressed in their Monday best, as it were. Normally unkempt guys had transitioned into dapper gents in sartorial rentals; and the girls were also transformed—metamorphosed from their usual gum-snapping slouches, with their midriff-revealing tops and low-riding jeans, into perfectly-postured lovely ladies straight out of *Pygmalion.*

He noticed several violet-and-gold tinseled decorations from the school's Rhettag celebrations over a month ago that had been tossed into the mix.

It never, ever goes away, Paul decided. *It's like Rhettians need to have constant reminders of their holiday year-round in order to keep them in the right frame of mind: a spiritual fix to cope with the pressures of daily life. If so, then perhaps it's a good thing—helping to prevent them from backsliding into the savage hatred and intolerance that marked their first six hundred years. But it would be so much sweeter if Rhettians didn't need to tie their notion of goodwill, hope and joy to a single day, or even a certain season—if they understood that these were fundamental moral principles that should be observed every moment of every day, and not attributed to a certain celebration, or to a specific event...*

Paul caught himself.

What the heck am I doing? Enough of this! I'm here to have a good time—no... make that a wonderful time. A fantastic, memorable time with Peggy, finally liberated from my incessant ruminations over Rhettianity. I can do that, can't I? Just flush it all from my mind, free my head of all the clutter, the preoccupations. I know it's become an obsession. Well, no longer: starting tonight, my fixating on all this crap is banished—flushed down the toilet to disappear into the sewers and beyond. I have passed through the beaded curtain, crossed the Rubicon, burned that bridge. Tonight is the beginning of a new outlook, a new perspective, a new...

"Hey, girlfriend!" the shrill valleyspeak singsong of Heather Markose pierced the thumping music, as she ran up to Peggy, embracing her. "I haven't seen you since forever! We had, like, such a wonderful Rhettag! My family went on a cruise to the Bahamas, and, like, everything on the boat was decorated and all the crew guys were dressed up like elves which was kinda grody, but hey—the food was, like, totally awesome, and I got tons of stuff when we got home! What did the Selgas bring *you*?"

Scratch that.

And then he realized that he wasn't the one who was fixated—it was *them*. Them with their Selgas and golden carriage bells and bright-nosed prancing ponies and elves and violet-and-gold tinsel and violet-and-gold lights and violet-and-gold flowers and violet-and-gold everything and presents under the evergreen trees and Ho-ho-ho's and incessant caroling and Rhettag in Greten and Hansen and Jurgen and every other month except Vintner, when it was *Mithran Mithran Mithran* with its brilliant bonfires and pastel-draped everything and acorn-hiding chipmunks and billions of chocolate treats to entice and tease even the most observant Cristic child.

Rhettianity was implacably woven into the fabric of American society. Increasingly vocal protestations by Rhettians that Rhettag and Mithran were being "spiritually diluted" by the observances of "competing" religious holidays—and by this Paul knew they meant Cristmas, Easter, Chanukah and Passover—were not only groundless, they were laughable. Instead, the exact opposite was true: during the past century, Cristic and Jewish holidays and festivals had become increasingly "Rhettianized", incorporating many of the outward symbols of the two Rhettian juggernauts. He knew of at least three families in his church who decorated evergreen trees in their homes during Easter—self-effacingly referred to as "Easter Bushes"—simply because they had given up and given in to the pressure. And more and more Cristic families held treasure hunts for treats, toys and other prizes at Cristmas to pacify their children's lamentations over the Mithran Acorn Hunts.

If there had been any adulteration of the "True Meaning of Rhettag and Mithran", it was from the overwhelming commercialization of these holidays and their secularization through political fiat, the mass media, and the machinations of Madison Avenue. And Rhettians had only themselves to blame for this. They had removed these holy days from their shrins and placed them in their front yards, in the public square, in the shopping malls and in the schools. By force of will, they had mandated that these holidays must be observed by all people regardless of faith, and stigmatized any who dared to demur as "Grinches" and "Scrooges". Rhettians themselves had taken the Rhettianity out of Rhettag by transforming what should have been a private, intimate religious observance into a universal, acculturated event.

"... and the usual mess of clothes, and I finally got that iVid Card I wanted for my iPod, um... let me think... and Dad upgraded the Entertainment Room to HD with a really awesome projector system, and..." With Peggy rattling off the season's spoils to Heather, Paul excused himself and walked over to the punch bowl table to collect drinks for the two of them.

When he returned with a drink in each hand, Heather had left and Peggy stood alone in the crowd, her gloved hands clutching her small peach purse. She looked fragile at that moment: a perfect porcelain doll that, mishandled, could shatter into a thousand pieces. That vision of delicate vulnerability made her even more beautiful... but it also scared Paul, reminding him of the secret he had kept from her and could never tell her, ever.

The evening flowed like a dream, each rock song an adrenaline rush, each slow dance a lyrical waltz, holding Peggy in his tuxedoed arms, her head nestled against his shoulder. He knew they were meant for each other, their disparate paths like the trunk of a myrtle tree... ultimately converging, entwining into an inseparable bond. They hardly talked that evening—didn't feel the need for polite conversation. When they weren't dancing, they shared a small table with Dave and Iliana, who made up for Paul and Peggy's silence with an animated exchange that roamed from the silly to the profound, filled with anecdotes about high school life and peppered with a healthy dose of Dave's biting wit.

Which is better? wondered Paul. *A life of silent contentedness—or one of lively, challenging conversation?* He decided that a combination of the two would be best.

When the hour passed midnight and the band began to wind down, the foursome piled back into the Humvee and set out for the sandy beach along the western shore of the Chesapeake just south of Calvert Cliffs. It was here that Paul appreciated Dave's choice of vehicle even more, as they drove where no limo would dare—onto the deserted public beach and up to the water's edge. Facing away from the District's yellow glow, the moon slowly rose and the stars shone in the blackness over the still bay waters.

Paul and Peggy excused themselves and stepped out of the truck, leaving their shoes and stockings behind to walk barefoot through the sand. The coolness of the granules on that Janiery evening felt luscious between his toes, and the soft periodic churning of the small waves along the shore was a mesmerizing song that seemed to say *"live life to its fullest… live life to its fullest…"*

She saw him looking out over the water. "Want to go for a dip?"

"No way," Paul laughed. "That water must be fifty degrees. Besides, this is a rental tux… I can't return it full of sand."

"I'm kidding, silly!" she smiled. "Let's just walk. It's lovely out here tonight."

They walked slowly, hand-in-hand along the narrow beach until they were out of sight of the Humvee, found a small rocky outcrop along the bottom of the eroded cliffs to sit upon, and gazed out over the moon-glinted waters. Paul turned to Peggy, holding in his hand some course sand he had scooped from around the ledge.

"This beach is filled with fossils, did you know that? Honestly, there are hundreds of different species of ancient shellfish buried here in the sand. They've been buried here for millions of years. I bet that…"

A slender finger touched his lips.

"Don't talk," she whispered.

And they kissed. As the moon slowly rose and the waves lapped at the shore, they kissed, and touched, and held each other. With each lingering kiss he desired more, to hold her closer and to make love to her. He could feel her nipples harden through the material of the gown… the taste of her kiss had a strangely sweet bouquet, and he knew that she wanted him as much as he wanted her. But not here, not now—soon, but not now...

They kissed and embraced for almost an hour, though it seemed like seconds, relishing the moment and the incessant, fervent waves of desire that young lovers feel. Finally, fatigued but content, they walked silently hand-in-hand along the enchanted beach, back toward the Humvee and their friends.

They could hear the rhythmic squeaking from some distance away, and the subtle shifting of moonlight reflecting off the chromed light fixtures gave evidence that the Humvee was alive, rocking to an ardent beat that could only be caused by one thing.

"Sweet Goseth!" whistled Paul. "I didn't know a Hummer could do that!"

"Only Dave could make a Hummer do that," snickered Peggy. "I hope Iliana's all right."

"How long you think they've been going at it?"

"Beats me. How long have we been out here?"

They sat down in the sand, watching the spectacle with fascination.

Paul thought he could see the silhouette of Iliana's head bobbing in the back seat. "I think she's on top."

"Thank God," Peggy sighed. "I'd hate to have three hundred pounds on top of me all night."

Paul burst out laughing, and his laugh must have been louder than he thought, because the squeaking and shaking suddenly stopped. There was dead silence for about a minute, then the rear passenger door opened and Iliana staggered out, her prom gown down at her waist. She quickly pulled up the straps and straightened her dress, tossing her long blond hair as she smoothed out the wrinkles. The Humvee shuddered once more as Dave, unseen, exited from the other side. Paul thought he heard the faint sound of a zipper being pulled up, but decided it was probably his imagination. After a moment, Dave came around the front of the vehicle—a bit disheveled, but at least fully dressed. He noticed Paul and Peggy and waved to them, then walked over to Iliana and embraced her.

"Maybe they're going back in for Round Two," Paul ventured.

"Maybe it's time to go home," Peggy countered, standing up. "I hate to spoil their fun, but it's way past midnight and we need to get back before that Humvee turns into a pumpkin."

Arms encircling each other's waist, they slowly walked back to the truck. Dave and Iliana had finally finished their kiss and re-entered the vehicle—but this time in the front. As he and Peggy climbed into the back, Paul warily glanced at the seat. No worries. Dave might be crude, but he was fastidious about cars. Even Matilda, ready for the scrap heap years ago, was clean as a whistle inside.

All too soon, they were entering the Forsythe's circular drive. Paul walked around to Peggy's side and helped her from the Humvee, and arm-in-arm they silently walked to the front door. Reaching the portico, she turned to him, holding him with her azure eyes. "This was the best senior prom date I have ever had," she said.

"Oh, got it..." Paul smiled. "Yeah, well, it was my best senior prom date, too."

"Okay," she said, looking down at the ground, trying to squelch her smile, "it was the best prom date, period."

"But not the best *date* ever... just the best *prom* date?"

"Goze, what do you want?" she asked, frowning up at him. "All right, it was the best *date* I ever had, satisfied?"

"But not the best *time* you ever had..."

"No, not the best time I ever had."

Even within the framework of their joke, Paul was crestfallen.

Peggy reached up, lifted his chin so that their eyes again met. "The best time I ever had... the best time I ever had in my *whole life...* was at Fox Hunt at Mithran with you."

"Really?"

"Really."

"Even with the broken leg?"

"Even with the broken leg. And besides, it wasn't broken."

"Even with my just sitting there at the pool?"

She looked at him quizzically. "Yeah, even with that."

"Even with..."

Stop.

Shut up.

What in hell are you doing, Fairchild? Are you really stupid enough to ruin the most perfect night in eternity?

Just stop.

She studied his gaze. "Even with what?"

Don't talk.

He pulled her to him and kissed her hard, harder than he had meant to at the end of the most perfect night in eternity. At first caught off guard, Peggy quickly recovered and surrendered to the kiss, and as it subsided she returned it in kind, pulling him tightly to her and frenching him deeply, as she had done when they shared the Dove chocolate acorn at Fox Hunt. He ached for her, wanted to ravish her right there on the portico if only he could. She wanted him, too—he could feel it, which was why she suddenly pushed him away.

"I was wrong," she breathed heavily.

"Wrong?" He was panting as well.

"*This* is the best time I've ever had."

And with that she grasped his face and kissed him hard on the lips once more, then disappeared into her home, quietly shutting the door behind her.

He asked Dave to drop him off at the corner. He wasn't quite ready to go home and face the inevitable "how did it go?" from his parents. They'd be up waiting for him... at least his mom would be. She was probably pacing the kitchen, fidgeting with things, keeping a wary eye on the clock.

What time is it? Two a.m.? Three? The moon's heading down toward the horizon, but what does that mean? You can't tell time by the moon.

The Hummer disappeared along the street into the darkness at the end of the neighborhood. Dave was driving Iliana to her house... or was he? Maybe they weren't ready to go home, either. Maybe they were heading back out to Calvert Cliffs, eager to go one more round until the sun rose over the bay...

Should I have done it with Peggy on the beach? She wanted to, just as much as I did. Why didn't we? Because of the sand—the mess to her gown and my rented suit? Are we waiting for a more appropriate venue? A bedroom... hotel room... swimming pool changing room...

He shook his head. *Stupid idiot. What was I going to tell her there at the door? "Oh, by the way, Peg, my most perfect time ever was with your sister at Fox Hunt, naked in the shower stall. She was wonderful!"*

Secrets. Sinful secrets, daring to leak out and ruin everything. God, what a jerk I am.

He found himself walking back down his street past the Smith's house, still covered in violet-and-gold wreaths and Rhettag lights.

Five weeks past Rhettag. Will they ever take the stuff down? At least the crèche scene with the motorized Virgin Ilsa and the two baby bundles is gone—stored away in the basement, I suppose, until the next "Rhettag Season" begins right after Mithran. What if my family put out "Cristmas Lights" or Easter decorations all over the front of our house and left them there for months? Not only would we be considered totally weird—we'd probably get a nasty letter from the Homeowners Association about it. But not so with Rhettag ornaments: these are offi-

cially approved. They symbolize Goseth and Peace and Love and Good-will Toward Men. They can stay up all year. After all, they're as much a part of America as apple pie and lemonade... as patriotic as flying the flag.

He reached his house and walked in the front door.

"Oh good, I'm so glad you're home! So... how did it go?"

Chapter Twenty-One

The Letter

The letter arrived on the Tuesday after the prom.

Anticipating its arrival for weeks, Paul had kept an eye out for the mail truck on Sundays, and he checked the mailbox on his way home from school every day. As the days dragged into weeks, he first became apprehensive, then anxious, and finally resigned to a long wait. After all, it was a small college with an inordinately high number of applicants. It must take time to carefully review each application: to give it proper consideration and weigh all variables equitably. That's what he admired so much about Dittisham: its unwavering commitment to intellectual integrity.

So when he retrieved the stack of letters and advertisements from the mailbox and automatically rifled through them on his way to the front door, he was half-surprised to find it buried midway in the pile. It was a thin white envelope—but even so, the high-quality linen weave of the paper stood out.

He gingerly extracted it from the stack, careful not to crease it. The envelope featured the now-familiar sepia logo of the college on the flap portion of the reverse side. Gorgeous, thought Paul... simply and elegantly beautiful. He hurried indoors out of the warm Janiery air and into the living room—the most tastefully appointed room in the house. There was an unspoken rule in the

Fairchild household that the living room was off-limits, intended only as a showpiece for visitors to admire from the foyer, but Paul decided that this occasion warranted trespassing. *Besides... what more appropriate place is there for reading mail from Dittisham College?*

And not just any mail: a letter of acceptance—and with any luck, a scholarship offer. The propitious beginnings of a new journey. Although his parents had urged him to consider additional Ivy League schools, Paul had ignored their advice. He couldn't conceive of going anywhere else.

Why had he singled out Dittisham over the other highly-respected, prestigious schools in the Ivy League? He couldn't say, exactly. Perhaps it was due to its small, almost intimate size, compared to the other schools. Perhaps it was the college's pastoral location, tucked away in the verdant hills of Vermont—a setting tailored for quiet study and academic enrichment. Perhaps it was because, unlike the other Ivy League schools, Dittisham still considered itself a college, not a university, dedicated exclusively to the liberal arts. Or perhaps it was Dittisham's reputation as the most elite of the elite: an institution of higher learning that had educated renowned artists and statesmen; philosophers and Nobel laureates; great orators and poets. If you told someone that you went to Harvard or Princeton or Yale, they might give you an appreciative nod—but if you told someone that you attended Dittisham, they would gaze at you with awe.

Collectively, these reasons had painted an idyllic portrait of Dittisham. Something deep inside told him that he was destined to attend the storied school: to study there, excel there, and with enough hard work, graduate summa cum laude. He had adopted sepia and white as his favorite colors, decorating the walls of his bedroom with a couple of Dittisham pennants and a college poster. His backpack was Dittisham Sepia with the college's logo—

the simple unadorned word "Dittisham" in serif lettering—emblazoned on its front. Any school with as much class as Dittisham, he would tell his classmates at Forbach Valley, didn't need some contrived coat-of-arms for its emblem. He had purchased the backpack in Southampton when he visited the school with his parents the summer before last. He made no secret of his plans: it was understood by friends, classmates and faculty alike that he was Dittisham-bound.

On his parents' insistence, he had submitted applications to two Maryland schools—the University of Maryland and tiny Bainbridge College in Annapolis. He had already been accepted at U of M, and Bainbridge was a shoo-in: the school had gone residential coed in 681 and was eager to admit male students.

But none of that mattered, since he was going to Dittisham.

This was what he had worked so hard for throughout high school: maintaining his perfect grade point average; taking every Honors and AP course he could; prepping for months for the SATs; lettering in varsity soccer; being active in student government and civic groups and countless academic clubs. This was what he had sacrificed for: forgoing parties with friends on Sunday nights in order to work on extra credit projects; cramming for tests until he knew the answers by heart; staying late at school to complete every lab assignment perfectly. But now it was finally reward time, and he wanted to relish it.

He sat down in the winged-back chair upholstered in a burgundy and green floral print, propped his sock-clad feet on the matching ottoman and carefully pried open the flap of the envelope so as not to damage it. He wanted to preserve both the letter and the envelope as a keepsake. He smiled, relishing the moment, knowing that it marked an important milestone in his life.

Inside the envelope was a single folded letter. *So characteristic of Dittisham,* thought Paul, *not mucking up a letter of acceptance with admission forms and pamphlets and other bric-a-brac. Much better to send these under separate cover.*

He delicately unfolded the letter, adorned with the same reddish-brown Dittisham logo as the envelope. The letter read:

> **Dear Mr. Fairchild,**
>
> **As Dean of Admissions at Dittisham College, I wish to thank you for your interest in attending our institution. Each year, Dittisham College receives many more applications from qualified students than can be accepted into our undergraduate program.**
>
> **It is with regret that I must inform you that we are unable to approve your application for admission at this time. On behalf of the college, I wish to thank you for your interest in Dittisham. We wish you the best of luck in your future endeavors.**
>
> **With kind regards,**
>
> **Harold P. Huntington, III**
> **Dean of Admissions**

Paul reread the letter, then a third time. He must have misread something. He looked in the envelope for additional papers—a pamphlet—a card—something to explain it better.

Wait... this must be one of Dave's pranks. The big guy knows that I'm waiting to hear from Dittisham. He knows what Dittisham's logo looks like from my backpack. Maybe he downloaded the logo from some website and printed it on the envelope and letter, to make it look official.

Paul checked the postmark:

Southampton, VT. Maybe he doctored that, too. It could have been doctored.

Tears started to well up in his eyes.

This isn't possible.

Two seniors from Forbach Valley had already been accepted into Dittisham: Timmy Brentman and Angela Hanson. Paul knew that Tim had, at best, a low-B average. Although he didn't know Angela as well, he figured that she was no better than a B student—*for crying out loud, she's taking remedial Algebra as a senior! Neither of them take any AP courses, and their SATs probably stink, too. They didn't letter in sports, didn't belong to any clubs—okay, Angela's in the chorus if you can count that—and they aren't involved in student government.*

They're average students. How in hell did they get into Dittisham?

Truth be told, he knew how.

He knew that Angela's dad was the Central East Coast Regional Coordinator for admissions at Dittisham. He knew this, because Mr. Hanson had interviewed him back in the fall. At the time, he had acted very impressed with Paul—especially the AP courses and his extensive list of extracurricular activities. The interview had gone so well, in fact, that it had dispelled any doubts Paul had harbored about the school or about his prospects for a scholarship, much less admission.

With her dad handling admissions, as long as Angela managed to get her diploma, she was on her way to Dittisham. It probably didn't hurt that she was African-American, too.

Tim didn't have a parent who worked for Dittisham, but he had something even better: a legacy of family ties to the college. Rumor had it that his great-grandfather was a major benefactor to the school, donating both money and land, and that one of Tim's uncles actually lived in a house right on campus.

B-minus Timmy: Dittisham scion. Ergo, Timmy's a shoo-in as well, and two admissions are probably the maximum number that Dittisham allows from a small public school like Forbach Valley. So... three applicants for two slots. If that's the case, which two will make it in?

Duh.

Crap. Crap on Dittisham. Crap on everything.

He gave his parents the distressing news as soon as they arrived home from work. His parents were conciliatory, but they reminded Paul that they had urged him to apply to at least one other Ivy League school as a contingency. That didn't help, now.

"It *is* very odd, though, John," his mom said to his father. "With Paul's grades and his test scores, I would have thought they'd place him on their waiting list, at the very least."

"Yes, very odd. Almost reminds me of the old quota systems these schools used years ago."

"Quota systems?" Paul asked his father.

"Yes... not too long ago, in fact. There used to be an unwritten practice among the Ivy League schools—and most other universities, for that matter—to limit the number of Cristic and Jewish students they'd admit. They were fearful of their schools becoming too 'ethnic', as they phrased it. So, even though many Cristic students qualified for admission, they were turned down."

"Really? I mean, they taught us in history class that a lot of school didn't accept blacks and other minorities, but nobody ever told us about that..."

"Very true—everyone knows about past racial discrimination, and about the affirmative action programs designed to rectify these, but the whole dirty practice of religious bias has been swept under the rug."

His dad sat down at the kitchen table with the letter, and Paul sat down next to him as he continued:

"This kind of discrimination was also supposed to have ended a generation ago... 'supposed to' being the key phrase, here. Dittisham turning you down flat, without even placing you on their waiting list, certainly raises some red flags—especially considering your academic achievements. Unfortunately, there really isn't much we can do about it, short of filing a lawsuit. Even if we pursued that, it would be very difficult to prove, and we simply don't have the resources to do that, Paul. I'm afraid you'll just have to chalk this one up to life's bitter lessons, and move on to Plan B."

Plan B? There isn't any Plan B.

If he had known about the anti-Cristic and anti-Semitic discriminatory history of the estimable, ivy-draped, blue-blood colleges, would that have altered his plans about Dittisham? *Probably not*, Paul decided. *Worrying about past prejudices amounts to paranoia... right? Valedictorian... straight-A's... ninety-seventh percentile on the SATs... National Merit Semifinalist... a plethora of extracurricular activities—how many other applicants have these stats? Even with Timmy and Angela guaranteed admission, my college boards alone should have at least placed me on their waiting list. Unless... unless... they had already reached their quota...*

But how could they even know I'm Cristic? Granted—Fairchild is a fairly common Cristic name, but there have to be almost as many Rhettians with that surname. So how...

Then he remembered the single-page U.S. Department of Education Equal Opportunity form that had been included in the application:

> *Applicants are requested to provide the following*
> *personal information:*
> *Gender*
> *Race / Ethnicity*
> *Religion*

And under Religion:

Rhettian / Cristic / Jewish / Muslim / Other

He had debated filling it out. After all, what business was it of theirs to know what religion he was? A student's religious beliefs weren't supposed to factor into the decision: in fact, the form specifically acknowledged this in its disclaimer, adding assurances that any information provided would not influence a candidate's consideration.

If that's the case, they can collect the data after selections are made. Why do they need to know it in advance? Granted, providing this information could help ensure compliance with non-discrimination statutes, but it could just as easily be a means to exercise discrimination, intentionally or not.

At the very bottom of the form, in extremely small print, was a terse assurance that providing the information was strictly voluntary.

Yeah, right—voluntary.

Deep down, Paul knew that refusing to provide the requested information was tantamount to crumpling up the entire application and tossing it in the trash... a tacit declaration by the applicant that he or she was refusing to follow federal affirmative action rules. It flagged the student as uncooperative—a giant warning hand-stamped across the entire 15-page application:

CAUTION: PROBLEM APPLICANT

So he had marked "Cristic", reassuring himself that there was nothing underhanded about it—that in keeping with the USDE's assurances, no one at Dittisham would even so much as glance at the form prior to the admissions committee making its selections.

Yeah, right.

Discrimination or not, the whole thing gave Paul a sickly, gnawing feeling in his gut. He was bitter not only with Ditti-sham, but also with himself for being so naïve, so trusting—for assuming that, by virtue of four years of hard work, discipline, dedication and effort, he would be welcomed at the influential school sequestered in Vermont's mountains.

Elitist. Pompous. Feckless.

Four years of scrupulously dotting every "i" and crossing eve-ry "t"—of slaving away on every assignment and studying for every quiz and meeting every challenge in order to nail that all-important A. In *every* class.

Every goddamn, shitty class.

For what? A polite two-paragraph rejection letter.

He let out an acerbic laugh.

Crap on all of it.

Chapter Twenty-Two

Final Bell

It was the last class of the last day of the last year of high school for Paul Fairchild, and the minute hand on the clock on the wall in Dr. Richter's history class had stopped moving.

Most teachers were having end-of-school parties, with pizza and cake and music—but not the good doctor Richter. In his universe, students could party to their hearts' content *after* school. School was for learning.

Having completed the coursework for the final quarter, Dr. Richter was revisiting his favorite subject: America at the end of the Industrial Revolution. He was rambling on about the immigration of the Cristic and Jewish people from Europe to the United States prior to the turn of the century, their processing at Ellis Island, and the changes to their family names.

"Many of these names were foreign to the processors at the registration desks," Dr. Richter was saying. "In fact, the processors couldn't even pronounce many of them, much less spell them correctly—considering that they were based on Greek, or Cyrillic, or even Arabic and Hebrew alphabets. As a result, in order to keep up with the deluge of these millions of immigrants, the processors would amend Jewish and Cristic names to something more American-sounding—so that, for example, Rosenzkowitz might be shortened to Rosen, or Archemeidius might become Armstrong."

Half-listening to Richter, Paul wondered what Fairchild had been. He shook his head... *no idea. I really ought to find out. There are tons of genealogy websites—when I get home, I'll try plugging Fairchild into some of them and see what comes up... it's worth a try.*

"Now," Richter continued, "as these immigrants came through Ellis or some of the other disembarkation points on the East Coast, they fanned out into the major urban centers. Some of them joined family who had preceded them here, while others without relatives set about trying to familiarize themselves to this new and exciting culture that held so much promise. Many of these Cristers had never experienced such freedom before. Back in Europe, they had often been treated as a lower class, without the same opportunities as their Rhettian countrymen. This was attributable to the stigma the Cristers carried as a people, since it was they who had plotted and killed Rhetter. This one fateful act had destined the Cristic People to become drifters, without a country, and without a home. That is why so many of them viewed America as their salvation."

Paul blinked, shaking his head to make sure the cobwebs were gone. Did he hear that right? His hand instinctively shot up, catching Richter's eye.

"Yes, Paul, you have a question?"

"Yes, sir." Paul stammered. "I'm not sure I heard what you just said, about the Cristic people and Rhetter, I mean, Goseth."

Richter cleared his throat. "What I said was that the killing of Goseth by the Cristers was a major contributing factor to the Second Diaspora that left them without a homeland."

"Excuse me, Dr. Richter, but that just isn't true." Paul could feel his heart starting to race, his head becoming flushed as the rest of the students trained their eyes on him. He hated calling attention to himself, becoming the focus of their annoyance. It was the second time that he had confronted Richter over Cristic matters, but this was different—the first time was just the two of them talking after class had ended. He wished that he had kept his hand down and dealt with this a different way, yet he also knew that he had no other choice. This had to play out, even if it meant confronting Dr. Richter in front of the whole class. It was time to flush this demon out from the subconscious recesses where it had festered for countless generations.

"The Cristers didn't kill Goseth," Paul continued. "That's a myth." He wanted to go on and say that Goseth himself was a myth—that there was no historical proof that he had even existed. But surrounded by a room full of Rhettians, he thought the better of it. He lowered his arm, feeling faint.

Richter cleared his throat again. There was a moment of silence as he prepared to speak. "I think that it is important for me to explain here that I am *not* saying that the Cristers as a *people* killed Goseth. In other words, a million Cristers didn't march en masse up to Aachen and burn Goseth at the gabel."

There was a murmur of laughter among the students.

"But there is a *wealth* of evidence, from both eyewitness accounts in the New Teachings as well as secondary sources, that the Cristers did indeed plot to conflagrate Rhetter. Now, I'm also not saying that the Cristic people should have been persecuted for this. We all know that Rhettianity is a religion of tolerance and of love, and that it teaches us to forgive the sins of others. That is, after all, why Rhetter died on the gabel. But the fact is that the Cristers were held accountable for this terrible act, and they suffered as a result of their role in the Conflagration."

Paul felt sick. It was like talking to a brick wall, explaining that the world is round to a people who, from time immemorial, were taught that it is as flat as a pancake. How many shrins each week instructed their flocks that the Cristic People had killed their

Lord? How many families raised their children believing that the Cristic People were being punished by God, destined to wander the world as sacrificial sheep until Saarsenke? It was futile trying to argue the matter. Futile and hopeless, like fighting City Hall. An ugly, damning universal myth that was embraced as fact, now and forever more.

The final bell of the final class of the final day of high school rang out, and the students stampeded to the door.

Chapter Twenty-Three

Goodbyes

As he prepared to leave Dr. Richter's class, Paul anticipated being overwhelmed by a torrent of emotions: relief that the Herculean task of maintaining a straight-A average was finally over; sadness about leaving what had amounted to his home of four years; apprehension over what lay ahead. Instead, when the final bell sounded and Principal Peters came on the intercom to congratulate the seniors and wish everyone an enjoyable summer, and after Paul had collected his books from his desk and walked out the door of his final class of high school, he felt oddly serene. Maybe it would hit him later, he decided. Students all around him were laughing, joking, getting their yearbooks signed and talking excitedly about their summer vacation plans, but he was removed from all of it.

He walked out into the bright early-Pendiery sunlight, looking for his bus. Over in the student parking lot, he heard a familiar voice cry out:

"DAMMIT! DAMMIT! DAMMIT!"

Dave was standing by his car, kicking at the asphalt with disgust. It was easy to see why—Matilda was covered with toilet paper and shaving cream, and it appeared that a couple of buckets of blue and yellow paint had been poured over the roof. As Paul approached the mammoth aging Buick, he could see that the paint had cascaded down the sides of the car, covering large swaths of the windshield and the other windows. As he got nearer, he began to see the full extent of the mischief.

There was toilet paper everywhere—lots of it—several rolls at least, wetted down by shaving cream and pelted eggs, all of it stuck in the paint. On each door panel, scrawled in fat letters with what appeared to be black magic marker, were sarcastic stabs: OFFICIAL STINK CAR and AIN'T I PRETTY? adorned the driver's side, while DON'T CLEAN ME—JUNK ME was written across the two passenger-side doors. On the back bumper of the wagon, someone had strung a few strands of twine with tin cans attached, and a hastily-drawn sign was stuck on the rear door panel that said: JUST GOT LAID.

"Look at this crap!" the usually gentle giant yelled when Paul was within easy earshot. "They goddamn trashed her! And I just got the damn thing out of the shop today!"

Vandalizing seniors' cars on the last day of school was an honored tradition at Forbach Valley High, and there were perhaps a dozen other casualties in the student parking lot suffering some form of indignity, but Dave's was by far the worst. It was probably no coincidence that his '66 Buick was also the biggest junker in the lot—with its worn paint, patches of rust, and an engine that was perpetually on its last legs. Whoever was responsible must have figured that this gave them fair license to do their worst: after all, who wanted to risk ruining the paint job on a brand-new Beemer or Lexus?

The pranksters' handiwork on Matilda drew an appreciative crowd that had gathered at a safe distance. It was obvious that Dave was steamed, and no one wanted to risk being within punching length.

Paul looked at the car as Dave paced around it, disgustedly pointing at each indignity, running his massive hands through his hair in exasperation. Whoever the culprits were, they had done a real number on the car—but the damage was all superficial. Paul figured that, with a couple of hours effort, it could all be removed. In a queer sort of way, the vandalism gave the Buick a bit of character it had lacked before—like those quirky cars covered with thousands of bottle caps, or hundreds of bumper stickers, or painted in wild splashes of color.

Dave finished pacing around the wagon, looked at Paul and pointed to the passenger door. "Get in. We're leaving."

Paul dutifully walked over to the passenger side and was about to open the door when Dave cried out again.

"DAMMIT!"

He was holding his right hand in the air, shaking it as if trying to fling something off. "Shit! They stuck something under the handle!"

Paul backed away from the passenger door. "What do you mean, 'stuck something'? Stuck what?"

"I don't know," Dave said in complete disgust, wiping his right hand on his pants leg. "Something greasy. It's just gross." He cautiously sniffed his fingers. "Peanut butter."

"You sure?" Paul asked, still wary.

Dave nodded, wiping some more.

Paul gingerly touched the passenger door handle. It appeared to be dry. "Mine's fine," he said.

"Well, thank goodness for small favors," sneered Dave. "Get in."

They both entered the car and Dave looked around, expecting to find additional vandalism inside, but it appeared untouched. He reached into his backpack and pulled out a half-full bottle of spring water. "Hand me that rag," he said, pointing to an old t-shirt on the floor behind the passenger seat. Paul reached behind his seat and gave it to Dave, who exited the car and poured some water on the windshield, wiping the paint and shaving cream and egg and toilet paper off as best he could. Thankfully, the vandals had had the sense to use water-soluble paint, and it wiped off the glass fairly easily. After several dousings and wipes, Paul could see through the windshield.

"Good enough?" Dave shouted from outside the car.

"Yeah… enough to drive to the nearest car wash."

Dave got back in and started the old wagon, backing out of the space and slowly proceeding up the hill that led out of the parking lot, the cans clanking behind. Dozens of students were laughing and pointing at the car as they crawled by, and Paul feared that it might set Dave off in a tirade. But then he noticed that the big guy was actually smiling, enjoying the attention and appreciating the humor of it all.

That is, until Matilda died.

It happened as they were about to exit the parking lot, preceded by the pungent odor of car exhaust and acrid smoke that seemed to enter the car from underneath.

Dave tried restarting the car, without success. "DAMMIT!" he swore, banging the dashboard with his fist hard enough to make the whole car rattle. "They better not have screwed with the engine! I just got it fixed!"

"Looks like there's smoke under the hood," Paul observed, pointing through the windshield.

Dave popped the hood release and exited the car, walked to the front, unlatched the hood and set the support rod. With the hood open, the smoke quickly dissipated, indicating that the engine wasn't on fire. As the fumes cleared, Paul also got out of the car, and the two young men looked around at the myriad of wires and fluid reservoirs, Dave gingerly touching this and tweaking that. "Nothing's disconnected," he said, checking another wire. "Damn. Everything looks okay."

"What about gas? Maybe they drained your tank."

"Nah, I checked that. Tank's got plenty of gas. Besides, that wouldn't make it smoke up like it did." He reached under the hood, undid a few latches and popped a round cup-like piece of plastic off the top of the engine.

"What the hell is that thing?" asked Paul.

"It's the distributor cap. This car was made before they went to EFI engines." Dave turned it upside down and felt around the contacts with his finger. "But it looks okay, too" He realigned the cap on its posts and snapped it back into place.

The two stared at the engine a bit longer.

"Potato in the tailpipe!" Paul suddenly blurted out.

Dave looked at him. "What the hell are you talking about?"

"A potato in the tailpipe," Paul repeated. "You cram a raw potato up into the tailpipe, and it cuts off the exhaust and chokes the engine. It would explain all the smoke."

"Yeah, right. Who told you that? Homey?"

"No, it's true, I swear."

Dave unhooked the support post and lowered the hood, then walked around to the back of the car. He knelt down and peered into the exhaust pipe, then slowly stood up. "How do I get it out?" he asked.

Paul laughed, incredulous. "You mean, there really *is* one in there?" He ran to the back of the car, got down on his knees and looked at the exhaust pipe. Sure enough, a large russet was tightly lodged several inches inside the pipe. He stood back up, scratched his head. "If we could find something long enough, maybe you can try to chop it out of there," he said.

"Hold on," Dave said. He opened the passenger door and reached behind the seat, retrieving a thin metal coat hanger. With several bends, he managed to break off the hook portion, and then straightened the remaining part into a long rod. He brought it to the back of the car.

"Maybe I can carve it out with this."

Lying down on the asphalt under the back of the wagon, he started poking at the lodged potato with the rod. After a couple of minutes he stood back up, frustration on his face.

"I put a couple of holes in it, but it's still sealed tight in there."

"Well, maybe you put enough holes in it to let the exhaust escape," suggested Paul. "Maybe you can make it home now."

Dave shook his head. "I don't think I poked the holes all the way through. The hanger kept bending on me."

The two were silent for a moment. Paul thought about the old car's propensity to backfire, and an idea suddenly came to mind. "Hey, I remember reading something else about this! The way the potato works is it cuts off the exhaust from escaping, so the gases can't go anywhere and they back up into the carburetor, and so the air mixture gets screwed up and the engine can't run."

"Yeah, I got that, Einstein. So what's your point?"

"Well, if you can get it started and rev it to build up enough pressure in the exhaust, the potato might pop out on its own!"

"Yeah, and probably trash my catalytic converter, my carburetor, my muffler *and* my engine in the process." Dave knelt down and inspected the crammed potato again. "Man, oh man," he mumbled. "It's really stuck way in there. They must've shoved it in with a crowbar."

He stood back up. "Oh, what the heck," he shrugged. "No car lives forever. Let's give it a go."

With that, they climbed back into the car. Dave put the key in the ignition and looked over at Paul. "Ready?"

"Let 'er rip!" Paul said.

Dave started up the Buick, leaving it in park, and immediately pushed down hard on the accelerator. With a startling VRRRRRROOOOOOOOOMMM, the old car shuddered under the power of all eight cylinders cranking at maximum capacity.

"WELL," yelled Paul over the roar, "IT'LL EITHER CRAP OUT AGAIN OR THE ENGINE'LL ..."

He was cut off by a thunderous KABOOM—the loudest back-fire he had ever heard. This report was immediately followed by a high whistling sound, quickly dropping in pitch and fading in-to the distance, then by the distant sound of shattering glass that, after a short pause, was followed by thunderous applause and hoots of joy throughout the parking lot.

Dave shut off the engine, and the two friends slowly emerged from the car to be greeted by the adulation of a hundred students standing around the lot.

"I guess it came out," said Dave.

Homey came puffing up the hill, beside himself with excite-ment. "Holy Rhetter! That was fantastic! What'd you guys do? That looked like a potato! What you got—a potato cannon? That must've been going over a hundred miles an hour! They find out about that gun, you're in deep shit! You better get out of here! Hey, Dave," Homey suddenly stopped, staring at the decorated Buick, "what happened to your car?"

"What did it hit?" asked Paul.

"Huh?" asked Homey, still mesmerized by the trash job done on the old wagon. He looked up at Paul. "The potato? That win-dow, over there. Looks like the Science Quad, maybe Pressler's classroom. I can't tell for sure."

"Wow!" whistled Dave. "That must be a couple hundred yards, easy."

"You better get!" Homey said again. "Hey, give me a ride home, will ya? I gotta hear how you did it!"

The trio piled into the car and headed down the main road leading away from the school. On the way home, Paul began re-counting events to Homey, who rolled around in the back seat in hysterics over the whole mess, especially the peanut buttered handle. Paul had only gotten as far as the car conking out when they arrived at Homey's house.

"Damn, you gotta tell me the rest," pleaded Homey, "especially about your potato gun! Where is it, anyway?"

"It's under the car," said Dave.

"*Under* the car? Ef'n-A!" exclaimed Homey. "I mean, how cool is *that*? Hey, you guys have to clean out your lockers? I'm heading back to school later... I'll pick you up and you can tell me the rest of what happened."

"Count me out," said Dave. "My locker's already empty. I'm through with that place... you couldn't drag me back in there for anything."

"I need to do mine," said Paul. "I'll ride with you, Home."

"Great!" said Homey, climbing out of the paint-smeared wagon. "Ugh! I think I just got egg in my hair! Get this mess cleaned up, Dave!"

"I intend to," answered Dave, as he and Paul drove off to their neighborhood.

They set about cleaning off Dave's car in the Gershwin driveway. It was hot for Pendiery 6th—close to ninety degrees, which made spraying the car—and each other—a welcome relief from the heat. After working on the side doors, Dave took the front of the car and Paul tackled the back. The first thing he did was to peel the JUST GOT LAID poster from the rear door panel of the wagon. He wasn't prepared for what was hidden underneath the sign.

Someone had painted a crude Star of David in blue. Underneath it, scrawled in the same black marker used on the side doors was a single word:

KIKE

It was no secret around school that Dave was a Jew—one of only a handful of Jewish students at Forbach Valley. But Paul had never seen such a blatant example of anti-Semitism as this before. It reminded him of when he was a child, visiting relatives in Baltimore and seeing a dumpster covered with graffiti, including a bright red crux that seemed to be dripping blood, with GODDAMN CRISTERS and JEEZ BOY scribbled next to it. He hadn't heard the term "Jeez Boy" before that.

Now he was looking at similar bigotry, done by someone at his high school.

He didn't want Dave to see it, and he successfully wiped off the star with his detergent-soaked rag, but the permanent marker refused to budge. The best thing, he decided, was to not draw attention to it.

The toilet paper, eggs, shaving cream and remaining paint all washed off easily—the paper leaving soggy wads of pulp scattered around the wagon, the paint blending into puddles of army green. As the car rapidly dried in the mid-afternoon sun, Paul ran up to the front of the wagon and the two boys debated how to remove the black lettering on the doors.

"Turpentine?" suggested Paul. Dave looked at him.

"Spoken like someone who's never owned a car. You really think it'd be a good idea to rub turpentine on the finish?"

"*What* finish?" Paul grinned. "There hasn't been any finish on this thing for a decade!"

"Nix on the turpentine, Einstein. Any other brilliant ideas?"

Paul's brow furrowed as he listed possible solutions: "Mineral spirits... kerosene... fingernail polish remover... what else takes off permanent marker?"

"Wait a minute!" Dave snapped his fingers. "Permanent markers are alcohol-based, right? Water cleans up water-based markers, so alcohol should remove this stuff!" He flicked his head with his forefinger. "Am I brilliant or what?"

"What are you gonna do? Raid your folks' liquor cabinet?"

"No, genius... rubbing alcohol. Hold on."

He raced into the house. Paul ran to the back of the wagon and feverishly tried to buff the offensive graffiti off the rear door panel, to no avail. He raced to the front of the car just before Dave came out of the house carrying a plastic bottle of isopropyl alcohol. He poured a little alcohol on the corner of a dry rag, and lightly rubbed at some of the black marker on the front passenger door. It worked like a charm.

"Here, let me have some," said Paul, grabbing another dry rag and holding it out to Dave.

"Slow down, son. It isn't *that* much fun. Hey," he said, eyeing Paul, "this is *rubbing* alcohol. You can't drink this stuff, you know."

"Duh. Thanx fer tellin' me, Paw."

"Well, it's just that you're so eager," Dave said, pouring some of the cool liquid onto the rag.

Paul quickly walked to the back of the wagon and rubbed the graffiti off the panel. He breathed a sigh of relief. *Thank God it's gone—no telling how Dave would have reacted!*

After several more minutes of scrubbing and rinsing, they were done. Dave untied the twine with the tin cans from the bumper and stepped back to examine his car. Matilda was back to her old self—worn down, rusty... bland.

"That's my baby," he grinned.

* * *

Paul walked up the street to his house and let himself in. He went into the kitchen, poured a glass of tropical punch juice and grabbed a box of chocolate grahams from the pantry, then sat down at the kitchen table to have his snack.

The newspaper was sitting on the table, still folded. He opened it up and scanned the front page, looking for something of interest. *Middle East... the economy... civil war in Africa... another sports figure charged with assault... same old, same old.*

He turned the page, and a photo on the top half of the sheet caught his eye. It looked like an abstract painting: several blobs of black and gray on a canvas divided into quadrants. Looking closer, he realized that the quadrants were window panes, and that the picture was a photo of a window covered with what looked to be either stains or shadows. The caption underneath the photo read:

> **An image in this dry-cleaning window is claimed by many to be that of the Virgin Ilsa.**

Paul looked at the photo again and studied the oddly-shaped splotches on the panes. *Virgin Ilsa, my ass.* He scrutinized the photo once more. *Maybe part of the gray area looks a little like a head, and I guess that black area around it could be a hood or a cape... but what's that other gray area above it? A cloud? A bird?* He read the story accompanying the photo:

> **Akron, Ohio —A mysterious image that has appeared in a window of a dry-cleaning establish-**

ment in downtown Akron has begun attracting massive crowds, causing traffic tie-ups and creating a logistical headache for city officials here. People from as far away as Colorado Springs have made a pilgrimage to the city to look at the window, which many claim portrays the Virgin Ilsa under a glowing gabel.

Paul inspected the photo a fourth time. *Glowing gabel? Maybe that gray thing I thought was a bird over the head-like blob?* He rubbed his eyes. *Either this photo doesn't do it justice, or some folks have really sick imaginations!* He read on:

Onlookers ranged from the simply curious to the devout, with many pious Rhettians falling to their knees in prayer at the sight. Tears flowed freely, as many of those praying were overcome with emotion. One young woman became hysterical, rending her blouse and eventually having to be escorted from the area by police.

"It's there plain as day. Can't you see it?" asked Ilsa Marner, 22, from Pittsburgh. "I feel goose bumps just looking at it, it's so beautiful."

"I kind of see it," said Jerry Frommich, age 15, who came with his parents from Fairfax County, Virginia to view the window. "You have to stand back from it. It looks better from across the street."

There were also skeptics among the crowd, but they were clearly in the minority. One dubious specta-

tor voiced his opinion that the image was just a big stain, an analysis that was immediately booed down by the crowd.

According to at least one expert who has inspected the window, the markings appear to be the result of several layers of mildew that have accumulated over time from the interaction of dry cleaning chemicals and water vapor on the window, which has a broken seal. This has not dissuaded the faithful, however.

"It doesn't matter how it got there," said Katolish Pastor Kirk Jolenshire of The Shrin of Rhetter Our Lord and Savior, located in Flint, Michigan. "Whether or not they try to give it a scientific explanation, it's still a sign from God and a message for us all."

As for cleaning the window or replacing it, that is out of the question. The huge crowds have almost tripled business at the dry cleaning establishment, and the owners clearly want it to remain as it is.

City officials are not as pleased.

"Miracle or not, it's created a real mess in this section of downtown," said one official, who requested anonymity. "We're privately hoping that the image morphs soon into something a bit less sacred."

Paul muttered to himself in disbelief. He didn't have a problem with miracles—Cristicism had its fair share of miracles, as recounted in the Gospels.

But get real—in a dry cleaning store window in Akron, Ohio? This isn't the first time that Rhettians claimed to see their Virgin Ilsa in windows—there was that large plate glass window at that bank in Corpus Rhetti—it received international acclaim! And several years ago, there was that image of Goseth in a skylight at some office building in Knoxville. Plus there were all of those "weeping" Goseths on Conflagration statues—and countless reports by the Shrin of spontaneous combustion of Conflagration tapestries during worship ceremonies.

It occurred to Paul that there were no modern reports of Cristic miracles—certainly not such mundane wonders as images in moldy window panes. Perhaps this was because there were so few Cristic people: based on percentages alone, it would stand to reason that only one miracle in thirty would be Cristic. But ever since the rise of Rhettianity, there weren't any weeping crucifixion statues or apparitions of the Virgin Mary that he knew about.

Maybe they did exist, but weren't publicized like Rhettian miracles. Any claim of a Cristic miracle would undoubtedly invite ridicule—and they were such a small minority, there was the real possibly that it could lead to ridicule or even harassment. He imagined what would happen if someone made the audacious claim that the Akron image was actually the Virgin Mary and not Ilsa. Witnessing miracles, he decided, was clearly a luxury reserved for those who controlled society—especially when it came to holy virgins in dry cleaning windows in Ohio.

Virgins in mildew... Rhetter on a piece of toast... wasn't that auctioned on eBay recently? The gullibility of people is limitless.

Then Paul remembered his encounter with the succubus over two years ago. It had seemed so terrifyingly real... he could still feel it, could still recall every excruciating detail: the paralysis;

the sense of powerlessness; the dread; the gripping fear of impending death. He remembered how she had looked—and felt—poised over him: her sensuous, gyrating form with those ardent emerald eyes… a personification of his most elemental desires and fears.

He had done some research on the Internet after the episode, learning that his experience was a classic panic attack where the mind plays tricks on itself. These were often caused by some underlying phobia or anxiety—perhaps triggered by his own subconscious fear of the unknown, and exacerbated by Homey's convincing claims of demons and spells. Paul had been on the verge of sleep, in the twilight of consciousness. He remembered the breeze through the open window animating the curtains, the shadows…

But it didn't matter. He could read a thousand journals on panic syndromes, examine every scientific study on physical and mental reasons for the phenomenon, learn the Latin names for each nuance of the disorder—but it wouldn't change his conviction that it had happened, and that she had visited him that night and held him prisoner to her whims. Compared to that, claiming to see holy personages in cracked window panes seemed pretty tame.

As Paul scanned the Metro section, the name Goseth in one of the stories caught his eye. The article was about a man who had been convicted of a rape-murder back in 665 and was exculpated by DNA evidence last month. The bulk of the story was about the falsely-accused man's struggle to cope during his eighteen years in prison, unable to convince anyone that he was innocent. For years his bitterness had consumed him, and he was constantly fighting with the guards and the other inmates, ending up in solitary confinement for longer and longer periods.

The story continued:

Then in 674, almost a decade into his incarceration, Carter was able to liberate himself from the grip of his anger by joining an inmate shrin prayer group and accepting Goseth.

"Goseth was there with me," said Carter. "He came to me like a bird through the prison bars and took me under His wing."

After accepting Goseth, the ice within Carter's heart began to melt away.

"I felt Goseth's love and I didn't feel any more anger, or any hate," he said.

Since his release, Carter has become active in his neighborhood shrin, counseling troubled youths. He continues to credit Goseth for his spiritual salvation and for his eventual release from prison.

What if this guy had found Jesus instead of Goseth, Paul wondered... *would the paper print a similar story? The way it reads, Goseth isn't some spiritual figment of this guy's imagination, but rather a real being—a historical, factual, savior of souls. If he had embraced Cristicism instead, would the reporter have written:*

> *After accepting Jesus, the ice within Carter's heart began to melt away.*

Yeah, right.

He turned the page to see yet another Rhettianity-related article. *Goseth Rhetter! Is the paper always this filled with Rhettian stories? Maybe I just haven't noticed it before—Rhettianity's so ingrained in our culture that it's imperceptible.*

The article was about a judge in Mississippi who had commissioned a sculpture of the Ten Commandments to occupy the center of the rotunda floor in the state courthouse. The story was a follow-up to a previous article about civil rights groups filing suit in federal court against the unauthorized sculpture. They had argued that it violated the separation of the shrin and state clause of the First Amendment, and a federal appeals court had sided with them. The Mississippi judge, though, had remained defiant: he refused to accede to the higher court's ruling, claiming that the state constitution invoked God and thereby authorized the placement of the Commandments in the courthouse.

Since Rhettianity, Cristicism and Judaism all venerate the Ten Commandments, its placement in the courthouse doesn't seem all that contentious... then again—what about other religions observed by people in Mississippi? Their religions have moral codes just as applicable and inspiring as the Ten Commandments—so why aren't these also carved in stone in the center of the courthouse? Displaying a sculpture of the Ten Commandments in their rotunda clearly promotes western religion over others.

And in truth, it isn't all three western religions, since it's the Rhettian version of the Ten Commandments. That one differs in several ways from the Cristic version.

Paul shook his head in disgust.

The Rhettians manage to corrupt everything—even something as inviolate as the Ten Commandments! Most Rhettians don't even know about the changes that the Shrin made to the Commandments—they just assume that their version is the same one given to the Hebrews by God.

The one given to the Hebrews...

Paul recalled Dave explaining over lunch one day that the Cristic version of the Commandments also differed from the Hebrew original. According to Dave, the Commandments given to Moses by God emphasized the oneness of God, and it forbade using graven images for worship. These had been modified by the Catholic Church to accommodate the tri-theism of the Father, Son and Holy Spirit, and to permit the creation of mosaics, paintings and sculptures of the Trinity for veneration.

If the Church could alter the Commandments to suit its needs, then why couldn't the Shrin? And if Cristers consider the Rhettian version corrupted... then what do Jews think of the Cristic version?

Why did the Rhettians change the Commandments? Was it, like the Cristic alterations, done to accommodate changes in practices and rituals? Was it to remedy what they perceived as flaws in the Cristic and Jewish interpretations of the tablets? Or was it simply to claim them as their own?

He thought about the graffiti on Dave's car.

Is contempt for Cristers and Jews germane to Rhettianity? After all these centuries, is it still an integral part of their tenets, their dogma?

A photo accompanying another article next to the Commandments story caught his eye. It was about the month-long commemoration of the sixtieth anniversary of D-Day on Janiery 22nd.

The Nazis and Fascists—they were all Rhettians. All of anti-Cristic and anti-Semitic Europe was Rhettian. Then again, so was America—and we fought the Nazis and the Fascists. Rhettians fighting Rhettians... maybe we didn't specifically fight the Nazis for the welfare of Cristers and Jews, but it still proves that Rhettians can surmount the bigotry—doesn't it?

The photo showed the U.S. Servicemen Gravesite at Normandy, France, where more than nine thousand American soldiers were interred. In the picture, thousands of white marble gabels stood all in neat rows marking the graves, their Y-shaped arms seeming to reach towards the heavens. Looking closely, Paul could make out a few little cruxes and stars of David sprinkled among them. Just a handful—maybe one out of fifty. He did a quick calculation in his head figuring that, sixty years ago, Cristers and Jews together comprised about nine percent of the population in the United States. *So why aren't there more cruxes and stars in that cemetery?*

He remembered his dad telling him that many Cristers and Jews who had fought in World War II chose not to have their religion printed on their dog tags—because if they were captured by the Nazis, announcing that they were Cristic or Jewish meant transport not to a POW camp, but rather to a concentration or death camp—or even being executed on the spot. Perhaps that explained the scarcity of cruxes and stars in the cemetery.

Paul grew somber at the idea of dying in a foreign land, his religion unknown, buried under a gabel marking his grave. He thought about the hundreds of unknown soldiers in that cemetery—the remains of servicemen found without their dog tags.

Were they automatically buried under gabels? To a Rhettian, placing a gabel over the grave would seem innocent enough—after all, it's the standard grave marker. To them, there's nothing overtly religious about it. But what if the unknown soldier wasn't Rhettian: what if he was Cristic, or Jewish?

Since there were nine times as many Rhettian American servicemen as all other religions combined, the chances for guessing right with the gabel were pretty good—but do you play the odds with someone's gravestone? Would Rhettians be so accommodating if their loved ones were buried with a Cristic crux or a Jewish star marking their grave?

Maybe the Army didn't use any religious symbols for the grave markers of unknown soldiers… maybe it's just a tablet-shaped stone.

Paul shook his head.

Not likely—since both Europeans and American consider white gabel markers synonymous with graves. For centuries, millions of graves have been marked with gabels, regardless of the religion of the dead. Why should the Armed Forces of the United States, or the French government, or whoever set up and maintained the Normandy cemetery, be any more sensitive to the religious beliefs of the minority?

Plus, there's that activity sponsored by several Rhettian groups, where they place garlands made out of purple and yellow plastic poppies on every grave at Arlington Cemetery at Rhettagtime. They claim that they avoid placing these Rhettag garlands on graves that are clearly marked Cristic and Jewish—but they go ahead and place them on every grave anyway. When anyone points this out, their pat response is always: "We don't refer to them as Rhettag garlands... they're simply commemorative garlands."

"Commemorative" garlands—which by incredible coincidence are identical to Rhettag wreaths and are placed on the graves as part of Rhettag celebrations. Bullshit.

This insistence on pushing Rhettianity on everyone was offensive enough, but it was the patronizing lies to justify this insensitivity that irked Paul the most.

Later that afternoon, Homey drove over to Paul's house, and they traveled to the school to clean out their lockers. Unlike Homey, who would be returning to Forbach Valley as a senior in the fall, this end-of-school ritual held special significance for Paul. It was the last time he'd be visiting a locker at his alma mater—perhaps the last time he'd ever walk these hallways. Memories rushed at him as he placed the last few remaining items in his backpack: the countless times he had stood at the locker joking with Dave and Homey after school... the chats with Peggy between classes... all the stupid locker pranks—like the stink bomb somebody had squeezed through the vent slats on Ergenne

Fools Day, and the entire can of liquid string someone sprayed inside the slats and outside the locker. He realized that his locker was the nexus of his high school experiences: congregating there several times each day; the storehouse for his jackets, sweats, hats, umbrellas, books, papers, combs, lunches and snacks; the only area in the entire school that had been his own personal space. He shut the flimsy metal door for the last time, listening to the conclusive click of the handle falling in place and the hollow reverberation of the now-empty enclosure, trying to commit that sound to memory.

As the two boys walked back through the vacant hallways, Homey suddenly pulled up short, raising his hand in front of Paul to stop him.

"What is it, Home?"

Without a word, Homey loped across the hallway in two bounds and stooped to pick something off the floor. As he stood back up, he carefully checked the object he had collected. Turning toward Paul, his downcast expression revealed that he was clearly disappointed with his find. "Aw, heck," he said, walking back to his friend, "it's just a penny!"

"Well, a penny saved, Home... could be good luck."

"It's just a friggin' penny, Paul!"

Suddenly, a wide grin filled Homey's face. "Hey, I got an idea!" He turned to face down the long corridor, then snapped his arm back and flung the penny so that its edge hit the polished floor with a sharp "ting", rolling down the length of the hall.

"Let's see if there's any Jeez hiding around here!" he said.

The word hit Paul like a hammer... he had never heard Homey use that term before.

"What did you say, Home?"

"I said we'll see if there's any Jeez around here. You know... roll a penny and a Jeez will dive for it!"

"You mean, someone who's Cristic?"

"Yeah, a Crister, you know... you roll a penny or a nickel and a Crister will hear it a mile away and come runnin' for it, they're so goddamn cheap!" Homey laughed and smiled. Then he noticed that Paul wasn't smiling back. "What? What's wrong with you, man? All I said was... oh, wait, you got friends who are Cristers, right? Look, it's just a joke, Paul. It doesn't mean anything. It's just a little joke about them. I bet they say it about themselves, too."

"No, we don't say it about ourselves, Homey. We never say that about ourselves."

"What do you mean, 'we'? Oh, Goseth..." Homey's mouth hung open in disbelief. "You don't mean you're a... shit, Paul, you never told me. You really are a... damn, I mean... I mean, shit, man. I mean, you don't *look* like a Crister. How was I supposed to know?" He paused, then gave a short disarming laugh. "Hey, it's just a saying. Just a stupid saying. It doesn't mean anything, really. C'mon, everybody says it... it's just a stupid joke."

Just a stupid joke.

A stupid joke—based on centuries of demeaning slurs against a people, stereotyped as cheap, miserly, dishonest, conniving, wicked. An innocent little joke that the Nazis repeated to themselves as they justified stealing Cristic property and possessions—after all, The Cristers must have stolen it all to begin with—they were born that way, damned by God for killing Goseth Rhetter and destined to skulk like rats in the shadows of alleyways—or in the locker-lined hallways of Forbach Valley High School, always listening for the telltale clink of falling coins.

How long have I known Homey? Since fifth grade—beginning with the cooties. Seven years. And in these seven years, no mention of "The Jeez"—no anti-Cristic jokes or slurs. Yet clearly they're there, second-nature to him. Did I just slough off the bigotry during these seven years—deaf to the jibes in order to maintain our friendship?

Is that why Dave doesn't like Homey? I always assumed that was be-cause of the cooties episode—but the cooties weren't Homey's fault to begin with. Dave's smart enough to realize that. Besides, it's not like him to carry a grudge for a week, much less several years. Maybe Homey made some sort of anti-Semitic slur early-on and it stuck in Dave's craw, just like his Cheap Crister comment.

"Listen, Homey," Paul said, looking intently at the slight boy he had considered a friend for so many years, "maybe you think it's just a stupid joke—that it doesn't mean anything. But it does mean something. It means that the same sick stereotypes, the same goddamn crap used by Rhettians to justify persecuting and killing Cristic people for hundreds of years still exists, here in your screwed-up head."

"What the hell are you talking about?" protested Homey. "Nobody's talking about killing anybody! For cryin' out loud, it was a joke, get it? It wasn't for real. Heck, I should know it wasn't for real… I'm part Crister, too! One of my grandmothers was a Crister!"

Paul walked up to Homey so that his face was just inches away. "Then you should know better."

He turned and walked down the hall.

"Hey, where you going?" asked Homey.

"Home," Paul replied, still walking.

"You're forgetting that I'm the one who drove us here—how you plan on getting home?"

"Walking."

"Suit yourself," shouted Homey. "If you're gonna let one joke ruin our friendship, that's fine with me… one little joke. What's wrong, can't take one little joke? One little goddamn joke—that's all it was! You're so full of yourself, Paul… you think that you're always right and everyone else is wrong. One little joke… and you act like it's the end of the world. Oh, God forbid that I made some little joke about Cristers! You act like the whole world is out to get you. Well, with that attitude maybe they are! Screw *you*, Fairchild!"

But by then Paul had left the school.

* * *

When he arrived home an hour later, Paul went up to his room and lay down on his bed. He picked up a copy of the commencement program from his nightstand. The cover featured a drawing of the school's mascot, the Forbach Valley Falcon, wearing a mortarboard and grasping a rolled-up diploma in its talons.

Below the cartoon of the falcon were the words "Forbach Valley Commencement, 683"

The Class of '83, thought Paul. *My class. The end of my long journey through public education. The end of countless hours of researching, reading, studying, prepping for an "A" on every homework, every report, every project, every quiz, every test, every exam. All for what? I'm not going to Dittisham. They didn't give a crap about all of my hard work—that obsessive pressure to achieve, the knots in my stomach before every exam at the end of every semester. What did four years of hell get me?*

He turned the page. Under the heading VALEDICTORIANS were two names:

Cynthia Davenport
Paul Fairchild

Valedictorian! Big goddamn shit. What does that mean: "valedictorian"? College of my choice? Only in my asinine fantasy. Scholarship? Yeah, right. Admiration of my peers? Give me a break.

"So, Fairchild," he said to himself, "what did it get you? What's your reward?"

My reward is that I get to speak. I, Paul Fairchild, miserable victim of severe stage fright since before I can remember, deathly afraid of appearing before an audience of even a handful of strangers, will now be rewarded by having to deliver a valedictory address to over a thousand people.

Well then—I'd better do it right.

He thought about Homey. About the slander on Dave's car. About Rhettian attitudes toward Cristic and Jewish people. About the numbing of conscience and blind acceptance of bigoted stereotypes. About how teaching children that other people are inferior, stained and cursed by God, is routinely accepted and nurtured in their homes, and loudly proclaimed in their places of worship.

He thought about how easily Nazism and Fascism had spread throughout Europe, readily embraced by reputedly civilized people because they had been conditioned by centuries of state-sanctioned bigotry, spoon-fed to them by their parents and their clergy until it became integral to their perception of the world: as instinctive and rudimentary as breathing.

Intolerance. The many forcing their beliefs upon the few. The State turning a blind eye, even giving a nod and a wink to the imposition of Rhettian prayer, holidays, observances and beliefs on everyone. Prayers to Rhetter at football games... songs praising Goseth as the Messiah in school functions... Rhettag "Universal Peace" Trees... Mithran "All-Faith" Acorns... Rhettian "Holiday Concerts"... prohibitions on students wearing cruxes and stars of David, while encouraging—even rewarding—the display of gabels...

Paul again scanned the commencement program:

Schedule of Events

Processional of Graduating Students
music: "Pomp and Circumstance" by Sir Edward Elgar

Convocation
The Right Reverend Frank Groman
Pastor, First Light Shrin of Our Savior Goseth Rhetter

Welcome
Principal Jorgen Peters

Valedictory Addresses

Awarding of Diplomas

Parting Remarks
Principal Jorgen Peters and Faculty

Recessional of Graduated Students
music: Canon and Gigue in D by Johann Pachelbel

My speech is preceded by the Convocation: a Rhettian adoration cloaked as a call to assemble. A prayer of worship to Our Lord Goseth, the True Messiah, beseeching Him to bless this public school event.

He got up from his bed, sat down at the PC and started typing.

Chapter Twenty-Four

Commencement

The early morning sunlight welcomed him, pouring through billowing lacy curtains and bathing his face. Tuesday, Pendiery 9th, the Summer solstice. Commencement Day.

A cold front had blown through Clifton County overnight, temporarily replacing the humid heat with a welcoming breeze and milder temperature.

A good sign, Paul thought. *Standing up there is going to be hard enough—it'd be brutal in hot weather.*

He rose and showered, going over his speech in his mind as he lathered, rinsed, and toweled. He stood at the sink looking in the mirror, deciding he'd better shave and being especially careful not to nick himself. The last thing he needed was to be bleeding in front of the crowd.

Walking back into his room, he crossed over to his desk and picked up the copy of the speech he had printed out last night, folding it and placing it in an envelope that he carried downstairs.

His parents were seated at the kitchen table: his dad sipping coffee and reading the paper; his mom spreading preserves on a toasted English muffin. They both turned and smiled as he entered the room.

"Good morning, darling," his mother greeted him, getting up

from her chair. "What would you like for breakfast?"

"Well, well," said his father, lowering the newspaper, "if it isn't the valedictory boy—all fresh and clean and ready to face the lions. Butterflies in your gut?"

"They're fluttering around in there a little bit."

"Stop it, John!" scolded Mary Fairchild. "He'll be just fine. He just needs a good breakfast, something to settle his stomach. What would you like, dear? Some cereal? Toast? An English muffin? I can make you that fried egg and bacon sandwich you like."

"Just some toast, I guess... and a glass of juice—that orange juice blend if we still have some."

Paul sat across from his dad, who was paging through the paper. Flipping to the end of the section, he placed it on the table and took a sip of coffee.

"So, really, are you ready, Paul? I know I've told you a hundred times that I was valedictorian at my high school, too. I remember how nervous I was! There were only a couple hundred seniors in my graduating class—I'm guessing you must have twice that many, at least—but I was still nervous. Of course, it all worked out... I received a long round of applause when I finished. So I know you can't help feeling a little scared, but it'll be fine."

"We're very proud of you, Paul," his mother said as she poured his juice. "And I know that your classmates are proud of you, too. Mrs. Henderson was telling me yesterday about how much her son Arnold admires you."

"Arnold? I don't know any Arnold."

"He's a sophomore, dear," his mother said, walking back to the kitchen. "I'm not surprised that you don't know who he is. But he knows *you*. He saw your picture in the yearbook—the one for valedictorian."

"It's a gross picture, Mom. If this Arnold kid really liked it, he needs serious help."

Mary Fairchild brought the toast to the table and sat back down. "Now, now—that's not a nice thing to say, Paul. And I like the picture. I think it makes you look very dignified."

"Whatever," Paul muttered, buttering his toast. He really didn't want to discuss Arnold or his picture. He was thinking about his speech.

One hour to go.

* * *

Even with cooler winds arriving from the northwest, the early-Pendiery sun had risen strong. By mid-morning, it had cleared the top of the grandstand, its golden rays streaming onto the playing field—bathing the entire stadium in a vibrant light as though bestowing its blessings on the commencement.

As *Pomp and Circumstance* filled the air, the graduating seniors entered the stadium single file: the boys with their navy blue robes in one line; the girls wearing their golden-yellow gowns in the other. As they reached the rows of folding chairs that covered the playing field, the lines diverged at right angles, with blue costumes filling the seats on one side, yellow the other. From Paul's vantage point on the stage, the flow of four hundred gowns gave the impression of rivulets of brightly-colored water filling irrigation troughs on two squared fields.

The processional music ended as the last students reached their seats. Pastor Frank Groman, of the First Light Shrin of Our Savior Goseth Rhetter, walked over to the lectern to deliver the convocation.

"Let us all bow our heads," Pastor Groman said, first raising and then slowly bringing down his hands. As he lowered his hands, the heads of the students on the playing field, the relatives in the stadium bleachers and the faculty seated onstage all bowed in unison. All except Paul's.

"Dear Lord," continued the pastor, "We are gathered here today for a most holy and revered event—the event of passage: of moving from learning to achieving; from preparation to fulfillment. As Goseth taught us in the hour of his greatest peril and his greatest glory at the hands of those who would destroy Him, we are but ashes and dust, and our toiling here is preparation to a far greater end. That it is through our actions on this earth that we shall earn His Love and His Grace. In Edel 12:33 we are taught that You are a loving God, a God of mercy and compassion, and that all who accept You through Goseth Rhetter shall be welcomed into Your House. May we all strive hard in this life as we leave our school and journey forth, to fulfill Your teachings and accept You as Our Light and our Salvation, in the name of Goseth Rhetter, our Lord and Savior. And may we all say, Amen."

A collective *amen* from a thousand voices answered in response. Principal Peters walked up to the lectern and shook Pastor Groman's hand, and the clergyman returned to his seat on the stage.

"Thank you very much, Pastor Groman," said Principal Peters. "Your words are always an inspiration to all of us. I hope that our graduating students take them to heart and learn from them.

"Today," he continued, "Is Pendiery 9th—the Summer Solstice. It is the day when the sun reaches its highest point in the heavens, as many of you who are not in cap and gown and who are not wearing sunblock will no doubt discover."

This was met with laughter from the crowd.

"The sun, having reached its zenith before beginning its journey onward, is an appropriate symbol for our graduating students who have reached the zenith of public education, and who are now set to continue their journey in life.

"As is our custom, we are proud to honor two graduates who have reached their own impressive zenith, having excelled at their studies during their four years here at Forbach Valley. These two scholars—for indeed they are scholars in every sense of the word—have accomplished what few students are able to achieve even in their dreams: they have earned an "A" in every single one of their courses over all four years."

He paused as applause and hollers of approval filled the stadium.

"As freshmen—straight A's. As sophomores—straight A's. As juniors and as seniors—straight A's. A perfect four-point-oh, not even counting advanced placement and honors points. And because of this praiseworthy feat, the faculty at Forbach Valley has bestowed upon them the well-deserved title of valedictorian. I would like for these two students to stand as we show them our appreciation. Please join me in a round of applause for Cynthia Davenport and Paul Fairchild."

On that cue, Paul and Cynthia stood as the football field erupted into applause, punctuated by shouts of: "Way to go, Cynthia!", and: "Atta boy, Paul!", as well as the requisite: "You geeks!" As the applause slowly subsided, the two valedictorians sat back down and Principal Peters turned back to the lectern.

"It goes without saying that both of these students are blessed by our Creator with intelligence. But they are also blessed with something just as important: the desire to excel, and the discipline to turn that desire into achievement. No matter how smart a young person is, no matter how easy it is for them to learn even the most challenging lessons—in order for a student to earn straight A's, they must work at it, and work hard. The homework. The classroom participation. The written and oral reports. The quizzes and tests. The extra-credit projects. And of course, the final exams. Devoting the necessary time each night and weekend to ensure that every assignment is complete and turned in on time. This is what determines whether a student earns the right to be called valedictorian."

He turned and once again gestured toward Cynthia and Paul.

"And with this hard work comes something that, as Rhetter has taught us, is more precious than silver, more precious than gold. With this devotion to learning comes the most valuable gift that we as human beings can acquire, and that gift is knowledge. These two students have gained a great deal of knowledge during their matriculation here at Forbach Valley. I think that it is only fitting that we ask them to share some of this knowledge with us today. From what they have learned, we can also surely learn. From what they tell us today, we can all surely benefit. In this spirit, I humbly offer the podium to our honored scholars, beginning with Miss Davenport. Miss Davenport, if you would be so kind."

As Cynthia rose to approach the lectern, Paul began to feel squeamish, his head filling with second thoughts. His fingers tightly grasped the two speeches he held. Which one? Which one was the right one? His mind was arguing for the safe speech, the pre-approved, plain-vanilla, insipid thank-you-all-I-am-so-very-honored-get-it-over-with-and-sit-back-down address.

But his heart... his heart was pushing for the other. *This is the time and the moment,* it was saying. *This is the good fight: the reason for all of the years of dotting i's and crossing t's and cramming to ace every test—for earning this right to talk to my classmates and their parents and the faculty of my school. Isn't that what Principal Peters had just said?*

Cynthia was talking, but he couldn't make out what she was saying. That was partly due to his sitting behind her: the echo from the loudspeakers was interfering with her words. But it was more because he couldn't concentrate on her speech... she seemed to be talking in slow motion to a field full of bluebells and buttercups—a surreal scene, like something out of an avant-garde film. Paul looked down at his speech and saw that the ink was slightly smearing. He realized that his palms were sweating. He rubbed them on his gown, but the satiny cloth didn't help dry them.

"...and so, I go off into this world a better person, thanks to Forbach Valley. Thank you," concluded Cynthia. The crowd of students, the parents in the bleachers and the faculty erupted in applause and stood in appreciation as she collected her papers. Principal Peters crossed over to the lectern and shook Cynthia's hand, and she half-skipped back to her seat on the stage.

As the applause ended and people returned to their seats, Principal Peters spoke again.

"Thank you very much, Cynthia. That was truly an inspiration. You know, I was remiss to not mention this before: Cynthia not only received straight A's for her final grades, she is the first student in the *history* of Forbach Valley to have received an A in *every* class in *every quarter* during her four years, for a total of one hundred and twelve straight A's! Let's give her a special round of applause for that truly outstanding accomplishment!"

Once again, everyone stood and delivered a resounding clap for Cynthia, who stood and took a gracious bow of acceptance. As the applause faded, Cynthia sat back down.

"Now," Principal Peters continued, "our next valedictorian did *not* get one hundred and twelve straight A's..."

Laughter from the crowd.

"... but he did get straight A's for his final grades in every class. For anyone who does not think that this is an admirable feat, I offer to have them come back to Forbach Valley and repeat their four years here, to see if they can match it. Anybody?

What... no takers?"

More laughter.

"I didn't think so. Anyway, without further ado, I am pleased to call Paul Fairchild to the podium. Mr. Fairchild, the podium is yours."

Paul's head was swimming: *a thousand people. I have difficulty giving a book report to my English class. How am I going to do this? I'm a fool, an idiot. Querk em kapf—cork for brains. I could have told my parents that I was sick this morning—just not showed up. What right do I have to lecture to these people, to tell them what I think?* He felt as if he had a lump in his throat the size of a walnut.

You can do this, Fairchild, he thought to himself. *Straight and steady. Piece of cake.*

He reached the lectern and set his speech down, reached over and adjusted the microphone, which answered with a shrill whine of complaint. He tried clearing his throat.

"Good morning."

As he began to speak, the same strange feeling came over him that he had experienced during the first act of *Twelve Angry Jurors*. It felt as if he was watching himself as he spoke—watching Paul Fairchild mouth the words that he was giving him: an otherworldly sense of being disembodied and disengaged.

His ears were burning. He could feel them, glowing red.

"I... uh... would like to begin with a prayer, if I may. Please, let us all bow our heads."

And in unison, just as with Pastor Groman, just as with all the student-led prayers at the football games and basketball games, everyone bowed their heads. *Just like in their shrins*, thought Paul, *except that this isn't a shrin.*

"Dear Lord, please bless all who are in attendance here today: our faculty, our parents, and our students. Please have mercy on this assembly and show us your love and your grace."

He took a deep breath, and then continued.

"With this prayer, we beseech You to protect us, and to herald in the time when all mankind shall accept Jesus as our Lord, and when the spirit of Goseth and of all other mortal men shall accept that there is only one true Savior, and that is Jesus the Crist. And may we all say, Amen."

There was no *Amen*. Just dead silence, slowly followed by a deep stir throughout the crowd.

Paul paused. The lump in his throat had swelled, threatening to choke him. He didn't dare look out over the crowd. *Straight and steady*. He looked down at his speech and continued, a bit louder to be heard over the rising murmur.

"Now, some of you... many of you... might have found the prayer that I just recited not only peculiar, but also improper and perhaps even offensive. And to be honest, that was not a standard prayer recited by the Cristic people. We never mention Goseth in our prayers, for the simple reason that, in our religion, Goseth is not significant. He is not the True Messiah—he is not the messiah at all, nor is he a prophet. If he existed, he was at most a learned man, nothing more. And there are good and sound reasons to question whether he ever even existed at all."

Out of the corner of his eye, Paul could see Principle Peters gesturing wildly, talking to Dorbensheyer who was seated next to him. Dorbensheyer was shrugging his shoulders, clearly protesting ignorance. Paul continued:

"But the prayer that I just said, from the standpoint of a Cristic person, is not meant to be insulting or demeaning to Rhettians. It is simply a statement of fact—just as, to a Rhettian, praising Goseth as the Messiah is considered a statement of fact. In my religion, however, Jesus is the Son of God, not Goseth, and public prayers that declare Goseth to be the True Messiah are therefore inappropriate."

He noticed Principal Peters stand up and quickly cross over to the lectern. *The guy moves surprisingly fast for someone his size,* thought Paul. When the principal got to the lectern, he placed a fleshy hand over the microphone, covering it completely. He hissed at Paul:

"What in hell do you think you're doing, young man?"

"I'm... giving my valedictory address, sir."

"This is *not* the speech you submitted, and you know it," snapped Principal Peters in a harsh whisper. "Step away from the microphone, *now*."

"But, I'm not finished," protested Paul. He was suddenly no longer scared. Now he was feeling anger, resentment.

"Yes, you *are* finished," hissed Principal Peters. "You are good and finished! Now go sit down!"

Principal Peters uncovered the microphone. In his most polite tone, he told the audience: "Um, unfortunately, because of the demanding schedule for confirmation ceremonies, we have had to limit the valedictorian addresses to five minutes. Our valedictorians were aware of this, and we do need to move on, now..."

"But I'm not finished," repeated Paul, loud enough to be picked up by the microphone.

"I'm afraid that, due to time constraints, you *are* finished, Mr. Fairchild, thank you. Now, if we..."

"LET HIM FINISH."

The voice was loud, booming, coming from the sea of deep blue gowns. Paul looked out over the audience to see where it had come from. It wasn't difficult to tell. It was from the only standing student, a giant of a man.

"LET HIM FINISH," boomed the giant, again.

Principal Peters' face turned a bright crimson. He stammered, "I'm... I'm afraid that just isn't possible..."

"Yes it is!" Another voice, this time from the yellow side. A young woman, now standing—a very beautiful young woman with auburn hair. Her voice was strong, resolute, and it carried over the entire crowd. "Let Paul finish. You said we can all learn something from our valedictorians. Let's hear what he has to say."

"Let him finish!" rang out another voice. Paul peered out into the crowd.

"Let him finish!" from yet another: one of the parents sitting in the stands.

"Let him finish!" This one came from behind Paul.

He glanced back at the black gowns of the faculty on stage. One member was now standing. Paul immediately recognized the grizzled old visage of Dr. Richter. He seemed to be shaking, his expression more severe than Paul could ever remember. "Let him finish!" Dr. Richter repeated.

Paul turned back around. Several more people were standing—both students and parents.

"Let him finish!" It had turned into a chant. The majority of attendees remained seated, looking around at the scattering of standing people in silent bewilderment.

"Let him finish!" Close to a tenth of the people were standing, chanting, loud enough now to fill the stadium and echo back from the opposite stands.

Principal Peters slowly removed his hand from the microphone and, without a word, quickly walked off the stage. The chanting faded away, and the people who had been standing sat back down.

Paul cleared his throat. No longer able to focus on his printed speech, he improvised.

"What I was going to say was that... although my prayer was, from my perspective as a Cristic person, a proper prayer... it was wrong. It was wrong because most of you do *not* believe it to be a proper prayer, and you probably find that it's contrary to your deeply-held beliefs. So, it was wrong for me to use this public ceremony... this school event... to pray in this way.

"But it would have been wrong even if most of you *had* agreed with my prayer. And it would have been wrong if even only *one* of you had found my prayer offensive. In fact, it would have been *more* wrong. Why would that be? Why, if only a handful of you, or just one of you had been offended, would it have been wrong?"

He paused. There was absolute silence. No babies crying. No coughing. No clearing throats.

"It would have been wrong because prayer in a public gathering—a gathering that has nothing to do with religion—is a form of coercion. When a speaker such as I uses a secular forum such as this to compel others to pray the way *I* think they should pray, that is wrong. And when the majority of people attempt to impose their religious beliefs on a minority *in any way*, it is *very* wrong. Our Founding Fathers recognized this, and they began the very first sentence of the very first amendment of our Bill of Rights with a guarantee that this should not happen. Ever.

"Freedom of religion means two things: first, it means that we are free to exercise our beliefs freely—and, thank God, here in America we are free to do just that. We worship freely in our shrins, in our churches, in our synagogues, in our mosques, in our temples, and in our homes. We as individuals are even free to worship in our cars, in a bus, on a train or a plane, on a bench in the park and in the bleachers at a ball game. We can even pray at our schools.

"But here is the other side of this freedom—and as our Founders so clearly understood, it is just as important: that freedom of religion means freedom *from* the religious beliefs of others. Whenever we exercise our religious beliefs in a way that imposes these beliefs on others, it is no longer protected. It is no longer free. When we choose to pray outside of our shrins, our churches and our homes—when we pray in a bus, on a train or a plane, on a bench in the park, or at our desks in our schools, we should do it privately. Religious belief is a deeply private thing. And as much as we value our own privacy, we should value the privacy of our neighbors. We should respect their beliefs and their right to be free of *our* beliefs.

"My fellow students, all of the parents and siblings in attendance and our honored faculty, I thank you for allowing me this opportunity to address you. I hope that Principal Peters was right, and that my words were worth listening to."

Paul turned from the lectern and sat down.

There was silence. No talking. No applause. No one went to the lectern.

Then a low murmur began in the back of the crowd. Paul peered from his seat on the stage, trying to follow the sounds. From the rear of the audience, proceeding down the main aisle, he could discern a large figure leading two others wearing brown shirts and hats. As they came nearer, Paul realized that it was Principal Peters, followed by two deputies from the Clifton County Sheriff's Department. The murmur followed them, and the students and parents rose like a wave as the trio passed by them, the wave reaching the front as they approached the stage.

The three men climbed the steps and walked directly over to Paul, Principal Peters pointing a pudgy finger at him.

"Mr. Paul Fairchild?" asked one of the deputies.

"Yes sir."

"Stand up, please, and turn around," said the deputy.

Paul stood, and as he turned around, the other deputy pulled Paul's arms behind his back and slapped a pair of handcuffs on his wrists.

"You are under arrest, Mr. Fairchild," said the first deputy. "You are under arrest for creating a public disturbance. We are escorting you from the stadium. Please come with us."

The deputies led Paul off the stage. He turned to see the entire faculty rise from their chairs as he left, talking among themselves. As he was hurried down the steps at the end of the stage, he glanced out over at the sea of blue and yellow gowns. He saw Dave standing, his fists shaking in the air and shouting something, but he couldn't make it out over the noise.

Chapter Twenty-Five

Denouement

They walked from the stadium, the agitated murmur of the crowd fading into the distance. Paul was led to a sheriff's cruiser at the edge of the parking lot. Arriving at the car, one of the deputies walked behind Paul and removed the cuffs.

"You're not arresting me?" Paul asked, rubbing his wrists.

The other deputy nodded toward Principal Peters, who had accompanied them to the lot. "Your principal isn't pressing charges. He requested that we peacefully remove you from the grounds. However," he looked at Paul through aviator sunglasses, "you are not permitted to re-enter the stadium until after the graduation ceremony has ended. Is that understood?"

"Yes, sir," Paul nodded, "I understand."

"Paul," said Principal Peters, "I am extremely disappointed in you. I am disappointed because you deceived us by submitting a fake copy of your valedictorian address, and because you exploited this solemn and dignified occasion to deliver a personal manifesto that had nothing to do with this ceremony and the honor that we had bestowed on you."

"What manifesto did I deliver, Principal Peters?"

"You know full well what manifesto! Your attacks against Goseth Rhetter. Your bashing Rhettianity. Your personal, skewed religious beliefs have nothing to do with graduating from this high school!"

"What about the pastor's speech? What did that have to do with graduation?"

"That was not a speech!" Principal Peters declared, his face reddening, his fleshy finger slicing the air. "That was a convocation, a call to assembly. That was part of the tradition of our school, of this ceremony. *Your* speech, young man, was *not* a convocation. It was... it was an *instigation*—an intentional incitement, and an affront to those in attendance. It was a slap in the face to both your fellow students and to their parents! You owe everyone in that stadium an apology!"

"What's going on here?"

Paul turned around to see his dad and mom walking briskly across the parking lot toward them. John Fairchild strode up to Principal Peters. "Why is my son under arrest?"

"He's not under arrest, Mr. Fairchild," said Principal Peters. "We just thought it best that Paul be escorted from the stadium, due to the commotion that his speech had elicited. It was for his own safety as much as anything."

John Fairchild turned to his son. "Are you all right, Paul?"

"Yeah, dad. Let's just go home, okay?"

"Not just yet," said his dad. John Fairchild turned to the two deputies. "Which one of you was the arresting officer?"

"I was, sir," said the deputy on the left.

"Why did you handcuff my son? Was he resisting arrest?"

"No, sir. We just felt that..."

"Is he under arrest, now?"

"No, sir."

"Why did you place him under arrest? What was he charged with?"

"Creating a public disturbance, sir."

"He was giving his valedictory address. In what way was he

creating a public disturbance?"

The deputy nodded toward Principal Peters. "We were notified that your son had created a disturbance by Mr. Peters."

"I see," said Paul's dad. "And did either of you officers witness my son causing a public disturbance?"

"No, sir, but Mr. Peters, here…"

"I understand what Mr. Peters told you. But you placed my son under arrest without having seen him cause any disturbance yourselves, is that correct?"

"Yes, sir, I mean, no, sir," said the deputy, becoming flustered.

"Let me rephrase my question," said Mr. Fairchild, speaking slower. "Did either of you two officers see my son create a public disturbance before you placed him under arrest?"

"No, sir," both deputies answered in unison.

"Alright," said Paul's dad. "Before we leave here, I want both of your names and badge numbers. I plan to file a complaint with the sheriff's department regarding this matter."

He turned to Principal Peters. "On what grounds did you notify these deputies that my son had caused a public disturbance?"

"Well," sputtered the principal, "his speech had created a ruckus. That was not the same speech that he submitted in advance to the school. It was inflammatory, demeaning, in many ways offensive. It was…"

"It was a valedictory address," interjected Paul's dad, "nothing else. You took exception to it because it was not what you expected, and it wasn't the polite 'thank you' speech that most valedictorians deliver. You turned a perceived slight into a personal vendetta, Mr. Peters, and you used—correction, *abused*—the arresting authority of these two deputies as the means to exact your revenge. You can be assured that the School Board will be hearing from me regarding this matter as well."

Mr. Fairchild turned to Paul. "You and your mother get in the car. I want to finish my business with these three gentlemen, and I'll join you shortly."

Paul walked quietly with his mother through the parking lot to the car. He had never been more fearful and more proud of his dad. Halfway across the lot, he turned back to look at his father and the other men. John Fairchild was writing something down on a small piece of paper… Paul guessed it was the name and badge number of the two deputies, judging from the uncomfortable way they stood with their hands on their hips, shifting their weight from one foot to the other. Principal Peters was mopping his brow with a handkerchief. It was starting to get warm under the late morning sun, but the principal wasn't sweating from the heat.

The trip home in the car was very quiet. A couple of times, Paul's mom tried to break the silence with upbeat comments, but it was clear that his dad was not in a talking mood. Paul's own thoughts were in a jumble, desperately trying to sort out what had just transpired. Although it had happened only moments ago, the entire chain of events seemed like a dream: the streams of blue and yellow gowns filling the stadium field… the sonorous reverberations of the PA system as Pastor Groman… then Principal Peters… then Cynthia Davenport spoke at the lectern… his own remarks echoing around the stadium… Principal Peters interrupting him… the slow-motion return to his seat, soon followed by the deputies entering the stadium and his arrest… and finally the confrontation in the parking lot.

And now, home.

Paul's dad parked in the garage and, for a moment, all three of them sat silently in the car.

"Go upstairs and change out of your gown," his mother instructed, and Paul dutifully went into the house to change.

Undressing upstairs, he realized that he had been perspiring heavily under his gown. His shirt and trousers felt clammy from the sweat. He collected together a change of clothing, then went into the bathroom and started the shower.

The lukewarm water refreshed him, helping his mind cut through the haze of immediacy. He saw Principal Peters' angry face as he cupped the microphone with his beefy hand, his livid complexion a reddish purple. In all four years Paul had never seen him turn that color. *He must have been really pissed off, especially to go summon the deputies. Was what I did really that bad? What had I done? Changed my valedictory address—recited a prayer—expressed my beliefs about the separation of church and state, about religion and coercion...*

There was a knock. "Paul," his father shouted through the door to be heard over the water, "I'd like to talk with you when you get out of the shower."

"Sure," Paul shouted back. He finished lathering and rinsed, then stepped out of the shower stall and patted dry. He stood for a moment looking in the mirror, his reflection gazing back giving him a strange feeling, as if he was looking at someone else. "Paul," he said, staring himself in the eyes, "you're such a stupid ass. Deadly handsome, no question... but utterly, totally stupid."

He found his dad seated at the kitchen table, perusing the newspaper as he had been that morning. Mr. Fairchild looked up at his son, folded the paper and motioned toward the seat next to him.

"Sit down, Paul. We need to talk about what happened."

Paul sat down, feeling an odd mix of emotions: nervousness, worry, curiosity. He knew what his dad was going to say... yet, he didn't know for certain... and he didn't really want to know... but needed to just the same. Deep down, he knew that this moment would come the instant he had decided to rewrite his speech. Now, he would discover what it was he had done.

His dad looked at him without a smile and without a frown, pensive.

"That was quite a valedictory address you gave up there to-day. It took me, and I imagine your mother, too, by surprise."

Paul nodded. "I guess it did."

"Your principal said that it wasn't the same speech you had given him in advance."

"No, he's right—it wasn't."

"So, do you mind explaining to me why you did that?"

Paul shrugged. "It wasn't intentional or anything, Dad. I mean, I didn't do it to trick him or anybody. Principal Peters said that all valedictory speeches had to be submitted a couple weeks in advance, so I did that. But I didn't decide to change my speech until Saturday night."

"Alright—we'll get to why you did that in a moment. But after you changed it, why didn't you give a copy to the principal?"

"Because like I said, it was just this weekend. He wanted it two weeks ago. I just figured there wasn't enough time."

John Fairchild studied his son. "There wasn't enough time? Let me ask you something, Paul—why do you think the school requires students to submit speeches in advance?"

"Principal Peters said that they needed to check them for ob-scenities, personal attacks on teachers, stuff like that. But I didn't use any obscenities and I didn't attack anybody in my speech, so I didn't think it would be a problem."

"But clearly there *was* a problem. Did your original speech have anything to do with the Bill of Rights and with freedom of religion? Did it include that prayer you delivered?"

Paul shook his head. "No, it was pretty much a standard vale-dictory address. You know—'thanks to my parents, my friends, the faculty, Principal Peters...'—that kind of stuff."

"So," his dad was looking at him intently, "what made you decide to change it?"

Paul's thoughts were a jumble: *Why __did__ I change it? Why did I have to go broadcasting my personal beliefs to everyone? What made me think that commencement was the appropriate place to lecture a thousand people about the proper time and place to pray? Maybe Pastor Groman's prayer to Goseth Rhetter was wrong, but do two wrongs make a right? What the hell was I thinking?*

He looked down at the table, shrugging again. "I don't know... lots of things, I guess. But now I think that it was stupid of me to do it. I should have stuck with my original speech."

Mr. Fairchild still studied his son. "Sometimes it's not easy being Cristic in a Rhettian society."

Paul let out a sarcastic laugh. "Tell me about it."

His dad nodded. "You run up against injustices, double standards, maybe even an occasional slur against the Cristic people. You want things to be equal, for people to be righteous and fair, but that isn't the way things are. And you get frustrated. You want to change the world, to make everyone understand. From that perspective, I can understand why you did what you did. You saw an opportunity to remedy injustice, to expose some of the hypocrisy and bring about change. Those are lofty goals."

John Fairchild paused.

"However, regardless of how lofty you consider your goal, no matter how virtuous your intent, there is a time and a place for everything. Forbach Valley High School is part of our community. We know quite a few of the families who were in attendance. We consider them friends, and we want to keep them as friends. Looking at some of their expressions during your address, I think that they were baffled and, quite frankly, they were a bit put-off by the tone of your speech.

"Look," he said, leaning over to his son, "I know that the convocation delivered by that Rhettian preacher... what was his name—Pastor Groman? I know that it's not right for the school to sponsor prayers like that during commencement ceremonies, or any other school event for that matter. And I admire you for speaking up about it. No, let me amend that... I'm damn proud of you for wanting to change it. But there are better ways to influence people and bring about change."

"Like how?"

"Well, such as through petitions to the School Board. Or letter-writing campaigns to the state legislature. Or perhaps articles in the local newspapers, or even setting up a social action group to deal with the issue. The thing is, the way to influence people is through persuasion, not through reprimand. People don't like to be put on the spot, to be told how to behave. As you get older, you'll find that the way you communicate something is often just as important as the message itself."

"You mean, like the way you spoke to the deputies and Principal Peters?"

His dad was taken aback. "Well, that was different," he said. "I was telling them that they..." His voice trailed off, then he laughed. "Yeah, just like that." He tussled Paul's hair. "Alright, smart guy. I think you know what I'm talking about. Do you understand what I'm getting at?"

"Yeah, Dad," Paul nodded. And he did, really. But the more he thought about Pastor Groman's prayer and the Rhettian prayers at football games—about the school-sponsored Mithran and Rhettag festivities—about Homey's comments yesterday and Principal Peters' today—he wouldn't have changed what he did for the world.

Chapter Twenty-Six

The Lake

T ime to let loose.

In keeping with Forbach Valley tradition, the party for graduating seniors was held at Fairmount Regional Park on the western edge of Clifton County, the only place in the county where the land climbed into wooded hills overlooking a natural lake. It was a favorite picnic spot for residents from early spring through late fall, but it was especially popular during the summer months, with its towering oaks forming a welcomed canopy from the midday sun, and the lake providing a refreshing respite from the oppressively humid heat that plagued southern Maryland from Pendiery through Greten. On the sixty-acre lake's northern shore, a swath roughly the length of a football field had been converted into an artificial beach with truckloads of coarse sand from the Chesapeake Bay. The portion around the man-made beach had been cleared of sharp rocks, submerged beer cans and broken bottles, and then given a sandy bottom, with the perimeter delineated by a yellow rope. There was even a lifeguard on duty during the day whose main chore was to blow his (or her) shrill whistle at bathers venturing beyond the rope into deeper water.

The picnic area was a large clearing halfway up the hillside overlooking the lake. On a mid-winter day it was possible to see the glinting azure water below, but in the full foliage of Pendiery, the lake was completely hidden from view. The leaves, however, did not muffle the piquant shrieks of laughter from teenagers enjoying the beach and water: a siren song of summer freedom and relief from the heat, beckoning those who still lounged on the hillside.

As Paul wandered through the picnic area, one sharp shriek of laughter caught his ear—an inimitable laugh filled with surprise and joy that made him instinctively turn to look toward the obscured lake. He wanted to head down the pathway to be with her, but decided to wait. There was plenty of time. After all, it was only three o'clock, and the party would last well past sunset—most probably beyond midnight, if stories from past senior parties were to be believed.

He made his way over to the refreshment table sporting two large glass tureens of punch in the school's colors: one bright yellow, the other a deep blue. As he approached the colorful bowls, he spied Vince talking with several other seniors from the football team. Paul slowed his walk and started to turn around—he could get something to drink later—but he was too late. Vince caught his eye and immediately started toward him with the other jocks in his wake.

"Hey, Fairchild," Vince said in his Texas drawl, walking up to Paul. He reached out a hand and placed it on Paul's chest to halt his progress. "Where you runnin' off to so fast?"

"Just wanted to get a drink, Vince."

"Really—'zat so?" Vince said, turning and looking back at the rest of the jocks, who all snickered. "I thought you were in jail."

"Well, as you can see, I'm not, so if you'll excuse me..."

"Hey," Vince said, pushing harder on Paul's chest. "Don't you wanna to talk to me?"

"Sure, Vince," Paul sighed, wishing he had followed his first impulse and headed down to the lake. "What do you want to talk about?"

"That was some speech you gave up there today, Fairchild. About Jesus bein' the lord and all." He looked back at his entourage to more snickers, then turned back to Paul.

"Y'know, Cindy got a lot of applause for her speech. S'matter of fact, I think she got a standin' ovation." Vince stuck his face close to Paul's, so that their noses were almost touching. "You didn't get much applause for your speech, did you, Fairchild? I don't think you got any applause at all."

Paul could smell Vince's beer-tinged breath. He wondered if Vince was already drunk, and whether his reflexes were slowed by the beer—if he ran, would Vince and the other jocks chase him? If they caught him, could he land a few punches before he got pummeled?

"Well, *did* you, Fairchild?" demanded Vince. "Did you get any applause for that?"

"No, no applause," Paul admitted. "Look, Vince, I really don't want to talk about it, okay?"

"Well, *I* do," said Vince. "You stand up there an' tell everybody about your Cristic beliefs an' end up getting yourself arrested. That was *wrong*, Fairchild."

"Well," whispered Paul, "You're entitled to your opinion."

"Damn right I am! This is *America*, not some Third World Commie country!" He pushed Paul's chest again, causing him to take a half-step back. Paul clenched his fists, steeling himself.

Vince was practically shouting, now. "That was damn wrong, you hear me?"

He extended his hand to Paul.

"I respect you, Fairchild. That took guts. There ain't too many people who got what it takes to confess their beliefs in public like you did. They were wrong to take you off that stage. You had every right to be up there an' pray the way you did. This is *America*, an' in America we're free to worship the way we see fit—Rhettian, Crister, Jew, whatever."

Perplexed, Paul shook Vince's hand.

"Y'know," Vince continued, "Goseth Rhetter teaches us that we must each seek our own love of God, an' that the truly blessed are those who profess their beliefs openly. You're a true patriot in my book, Fairchild. I admire what you did up there."

Then, another equally remarkable thing happened: in turn, each jock walked up to Paul and shook his hand, patting him on the shoulder, telling him "Way to go," and "Attaboy, Fairchild."

Vince flashed Paul a final thumbs up, gave him a wink, and led his retinue down toward the lake.

As Paul watched the group of jocks saunter away, he shook his head in disbelief.

That's one for the books, being congratulated by Golden Boy himself... Vince admiring me! The whole message of my valedictory address seems to have been totally lost on the poor guy—but still, if a born-again Rhettian can admire me for at least speaking up, maybe there's hope for the world.

He smiled.

Perhaps I've pegged Vince and the other jocks wrong all along. Maybe they approach life from the opposite side of the field—but in the end they judged me by my actions, not by my religion.

Walking over to the refreshments, he began to ladle a cupful of the yellow-tinted punch when a cool, slightly damp hand grabbed his arm. He twisted around, his gaze locking onto cerulean eyes.

"Hey."

"Hey."

"C'mon," she said, pulling him away from the punch, "I've got something better than that."

He followed Peggy through the picnic area and into the surrounding thicket of oak and maples, along a lightly-trod path. Her svelte, glistening body seemed molded into the one-piece high school swim team suit, the spandex tight and smooth around the taut curves of her posterior. She was wearing cork-soled high-heeled sandals that made her calves arch catlike with each stride. Watching her lissome body being caressed by the sunlight glinting through the canopy of leaves, Paul felt like a cameraman shooting a segment for the Sports Illustrated *Swimsuit Edition*. He wished the scene could last forever— but the hope was quickly dashed when the woods suddenly opened up into a small clearing: a campfire circle with felled split logs serving as crude benches. Seated around the dormant fire ring were about a dozen seniors—a few of them leisurely passing a joint— everyone holding plastic cups filled with beer from three kegs propped against a nearby tree. Recalling Vince's beer-tinged breath, Paul figured that the kegs were courtesy of the jocks.

As they entered the clearing, all eyes turned to them, and a few hands were raised in greeting. But then the teenagers all quickly turned away, resuming their conversations.

Too quick? Were they talking about me—about my speech and the arrest? Were they even thinking about it at all? Which was worse— their thinking about it, or not thinking about it?

He decided he needed a beer.

Although the legal age for consuming alcohol was twenty-one, this was rarely enforced, even at state parks such as Fairmount. Several of the students, including Paul, weren't quite eighteen, but that didn't seem to matter. Even so, he was surprised that there were tapped kegs freely available without any adult supervision. It was possible that the party organizers and adult chaperones hadn't known about these kegs, although that seemed unlikely.

Perhaps, Paul surmised, *this is considered a sort of post-graduation initiation—a rite of passage into adulthood.*

Paul had only consumed spirits a couple of times before, including the spiked Mithran Nog at Fox Hunt, and he had only been drunk once. The drunk had occurred at a cousin's wedding when Paul was fifteen. One of the bride's brothers, also fifteen, had stolen a magnum bottle of champagne at the reception, and they sequestered themselves in the boy's bedroom, taking swigs from the bottle as they played video games. Over time, the game lost focus and the screen started to spin around, but Paul and his cousin hardly cared at that point, laughing and spinning themselves, rolling around the floor and acting totally strange and stupid—until someone came into the room and announced that the reception had ended, the party was over, and Paul didn't feel so great on the long drive home, with his head pounding like a hammered anvil.

He didn't get sick, though—didn't have to heave his guts the way he'd heard kids did when they got soused. But it took a full day for the dizziness and the headaches to wane, and when he finally felt halfway normal, he made a vow never to get so drunk again.

He was thinking about that as he drew a draft from one of the kegs. He handed the foam-topped cup to Peggy, then primed the keg with the plunger—the way he'd seen other guys do it—and poured a second cup for himself.

They walked together back into the woods along one of the lesser-trod paths, hand in hand, sipping their beers. After a while, they came to another small clearing and sat down on a mossy area. The filtered fading sunlight and the soft warmth of the breeze caressing the hillside was refreshing; the cool, mildly acrid taste of the beer a pleasure to Paul's senses. It was, simply put, perfect. He turned to the exquisite young woman reclining next to him.

"Thanks."

"For what?" she smiled, her eyes inquiring his.

"For everything," he said, quaffing down the rest of the amber brew. "For being such a good friend. For speaking up for me at the commencement. For showing me where the beer was."

She poked him playfully in the ribs. "You!"

"No, I mean it. Seriously. We've been friends a long time. Since seventh grade. And it's always been—you've always been there for me... well, except for Vince... and those other jocks... and just about every other guy at the school..."

She poked him again, harder. "Stop it!"

"Okay... I admit it's my fault. I should have asked you out earlier."

Peggy propped her head on her arm and looked up at Paul, her brow furrowed. "Why didn't you?"

"I dunno." He casually picked up an old hickory shell and tossed it into the woods, "I just wasn't ready, I guess."

"But you went out with other girls. You saw Linda for a while. And you asked Sheryl out. And Valerie..."

"Yeah, I know. And I wanted to ask you out. I really did. Honest. It was like, I dunno..." Paul shook his head. "Never mind. It's just dumb."

Peggy lifted herself to a sitting position and gazed at him, grasping his hand. "It's not dumb. What were you going to say? Tell me."

He shook his head again. "Nothing. It's just dumb. It's just that... it's just that, I guess I just didn't feel... like I was ready for you... like I was ready to go out with you."

"Not ready for me? Oh, Paul, that's so sweet! That makes me feel special! So, the other girls were like... practice?"

"Yeah, exactly," Paul nodded. "I mean, I liked them and all, but they weren't... you."

Peggy settled back down on the bed of moss, her arms behind her head, smiling up into the trees. "They weren't *me*."

Paul now reclined next to her, propping himself on his arm. On his empty stomach he was feeling the beer, getting a pleasant high. "Hey, don't get too smug on yourself. Okay, forget that, get smug. You deserve it." He sighed, playing with the silken auburn locks on her forehead. "Damn you're beautiful, Peg. I've always thought so, ever since middle school, ever since I met you."

"Really?" Her deep blue eyes entreated him, touched his soul. "You've always felt that way? About me?"

Paul smiled down at her. "Always."

Peggy rose slightly, her rose-colored lips a divine bow, her sweet breath caressing his lips. "Show me," she whispered.

As their lips slowly met, it was the most natural thing on earth, and the world closed around them, enveloping them in its blanket and making them one in heart and in soul, joined in a passion beyond words, beyond cares.

He could barely stand the almost excruciating tingle of her warm, moist lips pressed against his, the aching sensation of shared desire building upon itself, making each kiss more plaintive, more insistent, more demanding. His arm instinctively encircled her waist, pulling her close. And unexpectedly, she rolled on top of him, her hips pressing against his, and he wanted nothing more in the world than this, nothing at all, but it wasn't right, not here, not now, and he suddenly thought about Patty and the ski lodge and felt embarrassed that she could feel him responding and he gently turned to the side, pushing her away, gasping for breath, trying to collect himself.

"What's wrong?" Peggy asked, brushing the hair from her face. "Did I do something...?"

"No, no, it's fine. You're fine." He looked at her inquiring eyes. "You're wonderful. God, you're absolutely perfect."

He took her cheek in his hand, caressing it. "It's me. Not you. It's me. I want you so bad, Peg. I'm hurting for you, I want you so much. But I can't here. I'll lose control and, I can't do it, not here."

"Silly!" Peggy laughed. "We don't need to *do* it. So what if you lose control? There's the lake down there... just take a quick dip."

Paul stopped caressing her and sat up. "I need to tell you about something."

She also sat up, not sensing the anguish in his voice. "What? Oh, God—let me guess... you're gay."

He couldn't help but laugh. "Stop it!"

Peggy tickled his sides. "I've heard gay guys are ticklish. Let's find out!"

Paul squirmed, grabbing her hands and holding them down.

"Oh, you're a tough gay guy, huh?" she teased. "I like my gay men to play rough with me."

"Peggy, stop it! I really need to tell you something."

What in God's name am I doing? First the graduation outburst and now this. What is this—True Confessions Day? Change the subject! Don't get into this... don't do it. Just shut the hell up!

"When we were at Fox Hunt over Winter Break," he began, "when I went with your family on that ski trip..." He trailed off, realizing how senseless this was but unable to stop himself, unable to dam it up.

"Yes?" She was quieter now. "What about it, Paul?"

Why in God's name do I need to tell her this? What good will it do?

"I, uh... I don't know. This is stupid. Really stupid. Forget it."

Peggy rolled her eyes, smirking. "Here we go again. You're going to make me beg, aren't you?"

"No, really, this was stupid," Paul shook his head, looking away. "I shouldn't have said anything. In fact, I don't know why

I did. Please, just forget it."

"You know I can't do that," she insisted, laughing. "You've got to tell me, Paul! Come on, just say it. Tell me what you were going to say just now. What about the trip?"

Shut the hell up, Fairchild.

He couldn't let it rest, had to get it out. He turned back to her.

"Remember that last night, after dinner—your dad had us go to the pool, and later you left to go to your room?"

"Yes, of course I remember. You had that cast and couldn't play in the pool with us, poor baby! Stuck in that chair. You looked really miserable. You said you left soon after I did."

"Well, the thing of it is, I *was* going to leave, in fact I got up to go and Patty... she had to shower and she asked me to... to hang around so that she wouldn't be in there alone... and while I was waiting, I heard her shout and I asked her if she was okay, and she said that she had hurt herself, and she asked me to help her, and so I... I mean, Patty and I... we..."

"You what?" She was still smiling, her lovely eyes bright with curiosity. "Patty and you what?"

Paul let out a long sigh, again looking away. "It was my fault. I should have said no. I shouldn't have..." His voice trailed off.

"You shouldn't have what? What happened? What did you do?" She stopped, a cloud of awareness slowly shrouding her features. Her smile vanished. "You didn't, you don't mean... Patty and you didn't..."

Paul glanced at her, wishing he hadn't. She saw it in his eyes in an instant.

"God, Paul, that's my little sister! You and her... you two... oh, God! Oh, *God! My sister?*"

She jumped up, stood over him.

"At that lodge, while I was... I invited you... I thought we... *goddamn* you, Paul! *Goddamn you!*"

"Peggy, it wasn't like that. I didn't know she was going to, I mean, it wasn't planned or anything, it just happened..."

"Right, it just *happened*. Don't give me that, you... you *bastard*. I saw how you looked at her. In the car, at dinner, on the slopes. I saw it. I *knew*..." Her hand flew to her mouth with the sudden realization. "Oh, God. I *did* know! And I just ignored it, pretended like I didn't. And it was true. It was true all along."

Paul stood up, grabbing Peggy's arm.

"No, listen, it wasn't like that! I didn't..."

"Let *go* of me!" Peggy screamed, violently twisting her arm out of his grasp. "*Don't touch me!* Stay away!" She began running along one of the narrow trails. "Stay *away* from me! You *bastard!* You *goddamn bastard!* Stay *away* from me!"

He stood still, watching her vanish into the trees, listening to the footsteps as they slowly receded, listening to the fading sobs which lingered a bit longer until they, too, were consumed by the woods.

After what seemed like an eternity, he slowly bent over, picked up the empty plastic cups, and went down another pathway, back toward the picnic and the lake, swearing at himself for being himself.

* * *

The sun was setting as the graduation party got into full swing. Nearly four hundred seniors filled the park; some sitting in close-knit circles around the blazing fire pits to reminisce about the past four years, while others ventured off into the woods to partake of bootlegged booze and stashed hash. Several pairings disappeared into the thicket for amorous adventures—and still others reveled on the sandy shore by the lake, dancing to pulsating rhythms blaring from giant speakers stacked in the bed of one of the pickups parked nearby. All of it had the unmistaka-ble aura of ritual: of choreographed passage from one age to the next; of inevitable change.

Paul wandered alone, past the cliques of students embellish-ing tales of past triumphs and tragedies, past the unseen clink of bottles, and sweetly acrid scents, and coughs and murmurs and rustling leaves and muffled moans, his mind a jumble of disjoint-ed memories. Big and small events he hadn't thought about in ages suddenly resurfaced: making out with Brenda Profette on the bus on the way home from the seventh grade field trip to Philadelphia—her cute button nose and freckles beneath wide emerald eyes with a bit too much mascara, the tart-sweet taste of her cherry lip gloss, her perfect teeth and warm smile, her sighs and giggles as they explored and learned together... playing hardball catch with Dave in the backyard on a sterling spring day when they were twelve, each throw a little harder than the last until they were daring to see who would flinch first, his palm stinging and burning whenever he caught Dave's zingers in the thin part of the glove, then launching a fastball back at him that left his fingers wrong and watching it arc in slow-motion into the neighbor's yard, missing their large maple tree but not their kitchen window, then warily walking over to their house to con-fess, hoping that they might forgive the damage but instead hav-ing to pay for the repair and being stunned by how much it cost... watching his mother mop the linoleum floor when he was thirteen, her sudden slip and fall through the large plate glass window pane, the jarring crash and desperate calls for him to come help, carefully removing her torn and bloody clothes, cleaning out the glass from the gaping gash in her hip and band-aging it as best he could, insisting that she needed stitches, then driving her eight miles to the emergency room, glad that he had watched his parents drive the car so that he knew what to do...

visiting the Vietnam War memorial, finding the statue of the three war-scarred men more interesting than the wall itself, counting the names on one line and the number of rows, multiplying and then counting the number of panels, taking into account the twin tapering wedges to see if it really added up to fifty thousand... watching Cal Ripkin smash a bases-loaded homer from the nosebleed seats between third and home at Camden Yards, the hotdog and popcorn and peanuts and soda and soft pretzel slathered in mustard sitting heavy, but it didn't matter because the Iron Man had just hit a grand slam and everybody knew the legend would be retiring soon and maybe this was the last one Cal would ever hit, and he had witnessed it at the ballpark.

Random memories, each an episode in his short life: sensuous, bittersweet, tragic, ebullient. Scores of them, stitched together like a patchwork quilt—*do they tell a bigger story? Or are they nothing more than disjointed vignettes... quaint recollections for me to treasure, or regret, and eventually forget? Things that had seemed so trivial at the time are now saturated with meaning. Things that seem so significant to me today—will they be important tomorrow? Will I even remember them a few years from now?*

Each step is like a fork in the journey—for every choice I make, a different road isn't taken. What if I hadn't kissed Brenda on that bus? Would I have been so interested in exploring further? Would I have had the confidence to start dating other girls—to pursue Peggy?

What if I'd been more adventurous with Brenda? What if I'd asked her out after that Philadelphia trip and we'd become close? What if, at some point, we'd slept together and she'd gotten pregnant? Would I have married her? Dropped out of school? That's what had happened to Brenda—she slept with a guy and got pregnant and left school. What if it'd been me instead? Or what if we'd sex and taken precautions— would we still be together? Then, maybe she never would've met the guy who knocked her up, who she ended up marrying. Do they love each other? And the baby—boy or girl? No idea. Is she happy? At eighteen, she has a kid... Brenda Profette, the first girl I ever kissed—a mother now! Our paths are so completely different, forever split... yet at one point, on a bus heading south from Philly, we'd shared an intimate moment in space and time, and our lives and memories are forever intertwined.

* * *

He found himself down at the lake, walking along the man-made beach toward a large group of revelers gathered around a small bonfire. It was almost pitch dark, the moon a thin crescent on the horizon. The only light was from the fire and the headlights of several cars parked nearby. The pickup with the tower of speakers was still cranking music, and most of the teenagers were dancing barefoot in the sand to its throbbing beat. Paul stood and watched the gyrating silhouettes in the distance, their wild abandon as much a declaration of freedom from school as it was a celebration of youth.

Most of them are going on to college... will that be any different than high school? The same tedious classroom lectures, and boring homework assignments, and cramming for tests, and anxiety over finals. But it's different—for one thing, having their own place away from home, and hanging out without parental curfews, and being treated more like an adult and less like a child. At Dittisham, they consider every student an adult... at Dittisham...

"Hey, Four-Oh, you just gonna watch?"

Paul spun around to see the big fellow approaching, his beaming face lit yellow-orange by the nearby fire.

"Hey, Dave. I guess I was daydreaming."

"Daydreaming? Hmm, is that possible at night? Maybe you

were just plain dreaming standing up. Hey..." Dave peered around, "something's missing. Where's ol' what's-her-face?"

Paul shrugged, "Dunno. Around here somewhere."

Dave gave him a look. "Sorry, but something's not computing—end of school, big party, great music, free food and drinks... and you're standing here by your lonesome. I saw the two of you heading up into the woods earlier," he gave Paul an elbow and a wink. "Pretty titillating stuff, if you catch my drift. So, where is she really?"

"No idea. We had sort of an argument, and she took off."

"Uh-huh... and what exactly *did* she take off? Wait, don't tell me—it's best left to the imagination."

"I'm not kidding, Dave. We fought about something and she left. I guess she's still around here, I just don't know where."

"Man, how many times do I have to tell you... never, *never* argue with a beautiful young woman in a swimsuit who goes off into the woods with you. Never! I don't care if you have to admit that romantic movies are better than action flicks, or that you'd look good in lavender underwear with a Cupid heart. For the love of Mike, just agree with her!"

"By the way," Paul said, changing the subject, "thanks for standing up for me at the graduation."

"Hey, no problemo. What are friends for? Besides, it was more out of curiosity than anything. I wanted to see how you were going to dig yourself out of that hole you dug. And I always wanted to yell at PDB."

That was Dave's name for Principal Peters: PDB—The Pillsbury Dough Boy.

"Well, I think you saved my ass up there. I was just about to cave and sit down."

"I'm glad you didn't. You were great up there. Really. Maybe even borderline eloquent. That took chutzpah, buddy. I'm proud of you."

Odd, thought Paul, *that's almost exactly what Vince had said.*

"And I wasn't the only one rooting for you in the peanut gallery," Dave continued. "Miss Peggy got her two cents in, too. She told me afterward how much she admired you."

Peggy.

"It was my fault. The argument," Paul said. "I did something really, really stupid. She has every right to be angry with me. She probably doesn't want to ever see me again."

"Wow, that's like serious, even. Want to talk about it?"

"Not really. What I really want to do is party."

"Well, that's easily remedied," Dave said, pointing down the beach. "Take about thirty steps that way. In fact, I think I'll join you."

The two friends took off their shoes and walked along the coarse sand into the thick of the celebrants. Within minutes, Paul was lost in the music, dancing and laughing and forgetting for a time about what had been and what might be.

* * *

The party started to wind down after midnight; the music emanating from the pickup changing over the hours from hip hop, to rock, to retro disco, to country pop, and now, much quieter, the introspective tempo of ballads. The few remaining couples moved slowly in the sand to the plaintive rhythms, and the bonfire had exhausted itself into small bluish flames dancing on glowing embers.

Paul once again sat alone with his thoughts—Dave had gone to relieve himself in the woods. He decided that, when Dave returned, he'd ask him for a ride home. It had been a long day, like a roller coaster ride—the fearful ascent to the waiting abyss, the frightening plunge and jarring turns, then more twisting and climbing and plummeting until it all finally coasted to a stand-still: the anticlimactic finish to a frenetic journey. Maybe that was for the best... now it was time to step back and take stock of everything, and decide tomorrow the next path to take with eyes wide open.

He half-heard it as he waited on the beach. A sort of plaintive call, like a loon. Somewhere out on the lake. A bird? No... more like words. Singing? No... pleading. Others heard it, too. Some-one was pointing out into the water. It was hard to see, almost completely dark.

Paul strained to hear, but the cry was distant and the water swallowed the sound. Unintelligible words. Sobbing. A call for help. He jumped up, running toward the pointing figure on the beach. It was Troy, one of the jocks.

"I think I see her," he was shouting, pointing out into the blackness. "She's way out there."

"Where?" Paul asked. "Who?"

"I dunno. Some girl. I think she's crying."

Paul turned back toward the pickup truck. "Turn off the mu-sic! Somebody turn off the music! Do it *now!*" Within seconds, the music was off. In the new silence, the calls from the lake were clearer, but the words were still muted. Whoever it was, it sounded like they were tiring, giving up.

He cupped his hands to his mouth, shouting out toward the sounds. "Are you okay? Do you need help?"

This time the words came back, faint but clear:

"Yes... help me... please! I'm scared!"

"Can you swim toward my voice?" he shouted.

"No... where are you? I can't... see. I'm tired. I'm really... tired."

"Hold on! Save your energy! We're coming to you!"

Paul tore off his shirt, quickly undid his belt, unzipped his pants and stepped out of them. He heard a loud splash off to his right followed by the sound of churning water. Someone else had dived in, was heading out. In only his underwear, Paul waded into the water, old senior lifesaving lessons suddenly flashing to the forefront: *don't dive in, keep my head above the water so as not to lose orientation. Swim toward the sound using a strong, steady stroke—speed is important, but accuracy more so. The important thing is to locate the victim.*

He swam using the crawl, but not dipping his head, then switching to the breast stroke to shout. "Can you hear me?"

No response.

He went back to the crawl and quickened his pace, thinking that all the accuracy in the world wouldn't help if she'd gone under.

He swam for what seemed like hours, not because he was tiring—in fact, he was feeling exceptionally strong—but because he knew that every second mattered. *How long has she been out here? She's pretty far out... could have been a long time. Is she drunk? Stoned? She's disoriented, clearly panicking. Panic steals the body of strength, exhausts you mentally and physically.*

He switched to the breaststroke again, shouted "Can you hear me?"

This time a response: "Got her! Hurry!"

A man's voice... Dave! He's the one who dove in!

"I'm coming, Dave! Swim toward my voice!"

"Hurry!" came the reply.

Something in Dave's voice isn't right. Is she unconscious? Not breathing?

"Keep talking, Dave, so I can find you!"

"Okay! Hurry!" Almost a plea.

A couple of minutes later he was able to make them out in the darkness. Dave wasn't swimming toward him, just treading water. He was holding the girl with one arm.

"Paul. It's Peggy!"

It hit him like a brick.

"Is she... is she breathing?" Paul asked.

"Yeah, here. Take her. Quick. Can't hold her." Dave sounded like he was swallowing water with each word.

Paul swam up next to him. "You okay, man?"

"Yeah, yeah, take her, here. Got her?"

Paul grabbed her. She was surprisingly light. He thrust his hip under her to provide support, threw his left arm over her chest and tucked his hand under her right underarm in the fireman's carry he had been taught. He was expecting a fight, some resistance like they did in lifesaving practice, but fortunately there was none. She was limp, but she was breathing... he could feel it.

"Got her," Paul said. "You okay?"

"Yeah. Yeah. Go."

Something made him hesitate. "You sure?"

Dave managed a smile. "I'll be fine. Piece of cake. Go!"

"Okay, Professor, see you on shore."

Paul turned back toward land. Some of the students had the presence of mind to turn their car headlights on. He swam toward them. *Now that I have her, the key is to save energy. Slow and steady. The side stroke... strong and even strokes... time the pull of the arm with the scissors kick, one stroke.... recover... another... recover... keep my lungs full for buoyancy... keep her head above water, no talking, just one thing to concentrate on — the stroke... staying strong... I can do this, no sweat... take my time... piece of cake...*

Long minutes, but it didn't matter. He had made up his mind that he could do this, no matter how long it took. It could be the Chesapeake Bay. It could be the Atlantic Ocean. He could do it.

A brief lapse of concentration caused him to swallow some

water. *No problem. It was bound to happen. Just don't drink the whole lake! She's feeling a little heavier... is she conscious?* He decided to check.

"Not much farther, Peggy. Almost there."

No response.

That's okay, he said to himself. *Better even. No crying, no panic — less problems to deal with.*

He glanced up toward the car lights. *Definitely larger. Getting there.* He was glad she was in her swimsuit, not a dress. A dress would be bad... lots of drag. *She's feeling heavier, though. Would be nice if she could help a little.*

"Peg, can you hear me?"

"Yeah..."

She's conscious!

"We're really close now. Can you swim?"

"Yeah, I think so."

"I'm going to let you go, but I'll still hold onto your suit. Can you do the backstroke?"

"Yeah, I think so."

"Okay, on three... one... two... three."

He let his arm slide off her chest and grabbed the back of her swimsuit at the neck. Peggy started doing the backstroke, feebly, but enough to stay afloat.

"Good, we're almost there. Just keep going."

A minute later they were there, close enough that other students ran into the water to help. He passed Peggy to them and made the last few strokes to shore, suddenly aware of how tired he was, every muscle in his body spent. He rested his hands on the sandy lake bottom and just floated for a moment, then forced himself to crawl the last few feet to shore and collapsed, breathing heavily. After a few more moments recuperating, he slowly rose to his feet and trudged up the beach.

His clothes were right where he had tossed them. Picking them up, it seemed as if he'd disrobed just an instant ago. Had this really happened? He looked over toward Peggy, who was sitting on the beach, her head buried between her knees.

He put his pants and shirt back on and walked over to her.

"You okay?"

"Yeah, I guess," she said. "I was scared."

"What were you doing out there?" he asked, sitting down next to her.

"I dunno. I just felt like going for a swim."

Paul was about to say "Well, you almost got yourself killed," but decided against it. The last thing she needed right then was a lecture.

Instead, he patted her knee reassuringly.

"Well, you're safe now. That's all that matters."

Suddenly, Peggy reached over and hugged him, holding him tightly, sobbing.

"Hey, hey… it's alright," Paul said, hugging her. "You're okay now."

After a few moments, her crying ebbed and she broke the embrace, wiping her eyes, sniffling. "I was really scared. I couldn't see anything. It was like black everywhere. I was getting really tired. I really thought I was going to die."

"Yeah, well, if Dave hadn't found you…" Paul said, then stopped abruptly. *Dave!*

He jumped up, peered around in the darkness, then ran over to a small knot of students conversing on the beach.

"Has anybody seen Dave? Dave Gershwin?"

The students looked at each other, shrugging.

"You know, big guy. Dave."

They shrugged again.

He ran down to the water's edge, trying to hear the steady

splash of someone swimming, the sound of someone talking, anything.

"Dave!" he shouted into the blackness.

Other than the background chirps of frogs and crickets, nothing.

"*Dave!*" he shouted again, louder. Waited for a reply.

Nothing.

Then a sound. What was it? A far-off cry, sort of a wail.

He strained to hear it more clearly.

The distant howl grew louder. Several high-pitched strains. Followed by staccato scarlet flashes piercing the trees as police and emergency vehicles rounded the main road in the distance, speeding toward the lake.

Within moments the cacophony of blaring sirens drowned out everything. Paul grew more desperate, pacing the shoreline, peering into the ink of the lake, now speckled with glinting red reflections from the rapidly approaching vehicles. The screaming horns and alarms turned everything chaotic—he held his hands over his ears, trying to get his bearings, wondering what to do next.

A minute later the first sheriff's car pulled up to the lake. Paul ran up to the deputy as he exited the car and was immediately struck in the face by the intense white beam of the deputy's Maglite, blinding him. He shielded his eyes from the glare, trying to see the man's face behind the harsh light, to talk to him.

"Sir, I think he's still out there. We've got to help him!"

"Slow down, boy," answered the unseen voice. "Now… who's out where?"

Paul frantically gestured back toward the lake. "Dave. A student. I think he's in trouble. He's in the lake."

"What in heck is he doing out there?"

"Helping someone."

The deputy took the light off Paul, reaching up to press a button on the small walkie-talkie hooked onto his left shoulder strap.

"Headquarters, this is one-one-three."

A short delay, then a crackle and: "Go ahead one-one-three."

"Confirm two persons in the lake. Emergency vehicles on site. Will advise."

"Roger, one-one-three."

By this time the fire trucks and the EMT vehicle had also arrived, and the sheriff's deputy walked back to meet them. Framed by the large Red Gabel insignia emblazoned on the side of the ambulance, he shouted something to the fire marshal while pointing toward the lake. The fire trucks trained their spotlights out onto the water as other members of the emergency response team trotted down to the shoreline with an inflatable raft.

Paul felt completely helpless, watching the well-rehearsed, mechanized activity around him. Things were moving beyond his control. An admixture of conflicting emotions flooded him — fear, gratitude, desperation, hope. *What took them so long? No matter, they're here now. Dave's in good hands. They'll find him.*

They have to.

Chapter Twenty-Seven

Revelations

They found him.

In the virgin light of the new dawn, they found him.

Paul had stayed by the lake watching the blur of activity: the police communicating by radio; the rescuers in their scuba gear and inflatable boats; concerned county officials; inquisitive news crews; and worried parents. His own parents arrived during the night, holding vigil with him and with the Gershwins. As the teams spread out along the perimeter of the lake, as their flashlights and floodlights searched among the weeds and rocks and underbrush without success, the thread of hope they had clung to for hours slowly unravelled.

Peggy had been taken to the hospital for observation soon after the emergency teams arrived, so she was not there to share in the wait, to learn the fate of her rescuer.

The coroner's report attributed the drowning to severe involuntary muscular contractions caused by hypokalemia, overexertion and fatigue. The strongest person Paul had ever known had died from muscle cramps.

He thought back to the bench pressing episode in Dave's basement, and Dave's admonition to know one's limits—but were there any limits when saving the life of a friend? He could just as easily have fallen victim to cramping as Dave had. It wasn't some foolhardy decision, to swim out into that lake to rescue a drowning person. It wasn't even a choice.

He played their encounter in the middle of the lake over and over in his head: Dave's brief pleas masking what must have been agonizing pain—the strained desperation and resignation in each word. Treading water instead of swimming toward shore. Imploring Paul to take Peggy. Gulping water between his words—*why didn't I see that he was in trouble? Even if I had realized it, what could I have done?*

I could have gone back into the lake, found Dave, brought him back to shore.

I should have tried.

God, how I miss him.

* * *

The postmortem was finished that evening, and Dave's body was released to the Gershwins early the next morning. In keeping with Jewish custom, the funeral was the following day—Friday, Pendiery 12th.

In the small remembrance booklet given to mourners during the memorial service, it listed Dave's death on the Hebrew date: Tammuz 3, 5764.

Five thousand, seven hundred sixty-four! Quite a bit more than the Rhettians' six hundred eighty-three years. Paul wondered what month it was on the Cristic calendar. *What year, even? Two thousand something. Two thousand and...* he tried counting from the Cristic millennium TV specials... *how long ago was that? Four years? So, two thousand and four.* He hoped that when he died, his gravestone listed the Cristic date instead of the secular one.

More than a hundred students from Forbach Valley attended the service. Looking over the faces, Paul wondered how many of them really regarded Dave as a friend, how many simply came out of respect for a classmate, and how many were forced by their parents to attend. He wondered whether the student who had written KIKE on Dave's car was among the mourners. It was quite possible that this student, whoever he—or she—was, might actually have regarded Dave as a friend, and considered the graffiti to have been nothing more than a playful joke. Or perhaps the student considered it to be a derogation of Dave the Jew, but not Dave the classmate... that in a bigot's perverse perspective, an individual Jew or Crister might be considered acceptable, perhaps even praiseworthy—but as a people, Jews and Cristers were sinners and heathens: tightwads, cheaters and scoundrels... killers of the Crist and murderers of Rhetter, forever deserving of contempt.

Peggy was conspicuous in her absence from the service. Her parents explained that she was still too exhausted, both physically and emotionally, to attend.

Whether or not that's true, it seems like a slap at Dave. But realistically, how could she be here, with everyone knowing that her stupid midnight swim in the middle of that goddamn lake caused his death?

The gravesite was about twenty miles west of home, in a memorial park situated on a bluff overlooking the Potomac. The site made a good place to reflect, Paul felt: modest and tranquil. Even though there wasn't a fence or railing segregating areas of the cemetery, it was evident from the names and symbols on the grave markers that one small section was devoted to Jewish internments, and another narrow area was reserved for Cristers. It was telling, he decided, that despite intermingling with people of other faiths during our short stay on this earth—when it came to the finality of eternal rest, we were most comfortable among our own.

Much of the service was in Hebrew, including a long prayer for the dead called the Mourner's Kaddish. Paul had no idea what the words meant, but the prayer was recited in a singsong cadence by the rabbi and several of the mourners, which made it lyrical sounding and poetic—both mournful and uplifting at the same time. He guessed that it was an ancient prayer, recited for countless generations.

After the funeral service had ended, his family walked over to the Gershwins to pay their respects. Fighting back tears, Paul hugged Dave's parents. Mr. Gershwin handed him a small wooden box.

"Paul, I know that Dave would have wanted you to have this," Mr. Gershwin quietly said, his voice breaking.

Paul opened the box. Inside was Dave's mezuzah pendant—the one he had worn since middle school, that had inspired Paul to wear a crux to school.

"I... I can't take this," Paul stammered. "It belongs to you."

"Now it belongs to you," Mr. Gershwin said. "We have many things to remember Dave by. We wanted to give you something, too. Dave told us about how, when the two of you first met, you had asked him about the mezuzah on our doorpost, and about his pendant. It gave us *nachas*—great joy—to know that you were interested enough to ask. We're sure that Dave would want you to have this, as a gift."

Paul thanked Dave's parents and left the gravesite tightly clutching the little box with the mezuzah inside. On the ride home, he thought about the need to display the symbols of one's faith, whether it was a tiny mezuzah, or a small silver crux, or a giant golden gabel. Or three fat plastic waving Selgas on prancing ponies, for that matter. The symbols served not only as expressions of faith, but also as constant reminders and a means to focus on the spiritual—in a sense, a pathway to God.

Arriving back home, he went up to his room and carefully removed the sterling pendant from the box, holding it up by its chain, examining the mezuzah as it slowly rotated in the sunlight. It was beautifully simple—a thin silver case not much more than an inch tall, with a tiny Star of David welded to the top portion and a couple of odd symbols beneath. Paul guessed that they were Hebrew letters—though not the W-like shin he had seen on the mezuzah on the doorpost of Dave's house. The larger character on the pendant reminded him of the archway made by the Stonehenge boulders, and the short symbol to the left of it looked a bit like an apostrophe.

A check on the Internet under "Hebrew alphabet" revealed that the Stonehenge shape was the Hebrew letter "Chet", and the apostrophe was a "Yod". Together, they made the Hebrew word "Chai", which meant "life".

He turned the mezuzah over and noticed a thin strip of metal that was slotted into grooves, forming a backing to the case. Using his thumbnail, Paul carefully slid the strip from the back, discovering that the case held a tiny rolled-up piece of parchment. He remembered Dave explaining to him that the mezuzah on the door contained a written prayer, and he guessed that this was the same prayer. As delicately as he could, Paul extracted and unrolled the miniature paper, and saw that it was written in Hebrew in extremely neat, tiny characters. It was clear that the text was handwritten—he marvelled that some scribe would have the patience and talent to write such small, intricate characters so perfectly.

He had no idea what it said, or why. Typing "mezuzah" into his search engine, he soon learned that the prayer was comprised of passages from the Jewish Bible—Deuteronomy 6:4-9, and Deuteronomy 11:13-21. These passages, which were pronouncements of absolute love for God and commitments to observe God's Commandments, were part of the Cristic Bible and Rhettian Bible as well. As far as Paul could determine, they weren't at odds with Cristic or Rhettian teachings at all.

So why don't we also post mezuzahs on our doorposts? Why don't Rhettians? Perhaps not in the original Hebrew... but in Latin, or German, or English for that matter? Why is it that Jews follow these commandments, while the other faiths spawned from these same teachings don't?

He carefully folded the mezuzah parchment back into a tight pleat and placed it into its case, sliding the protective metal strip snugly shut, then placed the mezuzah case into the small wooden box, and the box into the top drawer of his dresser. Almost every day, he would open the drawer to fetch his wallet, or his watch, or sunglasses or a pair of socks, and he would see the box and think of Dave and recite a silent prayer for his friend.

But he didn't need to see the box to remember Dave. Everything reminded him of their discussions, and the insights into life that they provided. At each juncture, he asked himself what Dave would have done, and he thought back to their conversations and more often than not found guidance in them.

Chapter Twenty-Eight

The Road No Longer Traveled

Guilt is a terrible thing.

It is visceral, gnawing at you, corralling you into a dark corner where you never wanted to go, trapping you in a web of self-loathing from which there is no release.

In early Franzen, a few weeks after graduation, he had tried calling her, to see how she was doing. She didn't answer the phone and he didn't leave a message, in a way relieved that she hadn't picked up. What would he have said? He'd rehearsed a multitude of options, thought through a thousand scenarios, none of them satisfactory—nothing that would have made things right.

Still, he wanted to know how she was faring. Did her conscience bother her half as much as his bothered him? Did she blame herself... or did she blame him? Perhaps she didn't dwell on it every minute of every hour of every day like he did. Perhaps she had dispensed with it like a bitter seed in a slice of tangerine, spitting into a napkin and depositing it neatly in the trash, and then continued on with her life.

He hated her for what had happened to Dave—almost as much as he hated himself. The entire chain could be traced back to the moment he had entered their Escalade that winter morning and saw Patty spread out in the back in her tight turtleneck and

fur-lined boots. Peggy was right—the entire trip had been nothing more than an intricate overture to their tryst in the changing
room. Had Patty orchestrated the whole thing? It didn't matter: it
took two to tango. He could have said no, walking away at any
point. But he didn't.

Maybe this was just foolishness... assigning blame where
there was none. But the inescapable truth of the matter was that
if he hadn't climbed into that SUV, hadn't gone to Fox Hunt,
hadn't hobbled into that steaming shower, Dave would still be
alive.

He decided to put off college in the fall, wondering whether
he was the first valedictorian in Forbach Valley's thirty-year history not to continue on to higher education, or at least not right
away. It was his mistake, of course, applying only to Dittisham.
True—he could have attended U of M or Bainbridge for a year
and then transferred to another school—but what was the sense
of that? A year away from academics would probably do him
good, forcing him to focus on real world matters and perhaps
helping him gain a bit more maturity. And the money he earned,
although not substantial, would help to defray some of the costs
when he did enter college.

After a few weeks scanning employment ads, he landed a job
at a local county newspaper office as an assistant copy editor,
layout and paste-up artist, and occasional gofer. The newspaper
offices were eight miles from his house—a doable commute by
bike if the weather permitted—but now he had a car: a '66 Buick
LeSabre Estate Wagon named Matilda—another gift from the
Gershwins. Dave's father had given him the keys and the title a
week after the funeral. At first Paul demurred, feeling awkward
about receiving gifts on the event of his friend's death. But Mr.
Gershwin had insisted, pointing out that if Paul didn't take it, it

would end up scavenged for parts and sold as scrap.

Within a month, Paul appreciated both the joy and frustration of owning a used car. The freedom to come and go, to have wheels to travel wherever and whenever, was a blessing, but the voracious appetite, constant maintenance, and costly repairs of the seventeen-year-old behemoth were more like a curse. Still, he loved the wagon—both because of the memories she cradled in her worn vinyl seats—and because, as it had been with Dave, Matilda was his very first car.

He visited the grave every weekend. If it wasn't too hot or too humid, he left Matilda at home and rode his bicycle to the cemetery. Although State Highway 226 ran east-west most of the way and was easily the most direct route, Paul avoided the major thoroughfares, preferring instead the quieter country roads. The forty-two mile round trip was a challenge by bike, but the tobacco-growing farmland that comprised much of southern Maryland was flat the entire way, and the blacktop was well-maintained and lightly-travelled. Ninety minutes there and ninety back: a good workout.

On the third Sunday in Greten, as his friends made final preparations for college, the weather turned cooler and Paul set out on his bike to the memorial park. A couple of hours spent pedalling on the level ribbon of asphalt gave him plenty of time to think about his peers heading off to school, and his own decision to delay matriculating. It felt wrong, listening to them talk with a mixture of excitement and apprehension about heading off to some distant university while he remained at home in a low-level job. But was it wrong? Would he regret it later, or would he be thankful he'd made that choice?

Worries, doubts and second-guessing. Years ago, his dad had told him that life became more complicated with age. The added freedom that came with adulthood meant more responsibility, and the greater likelihood of major missteps and wrong decisions. Well, wrong or not, it was done. In a few weeks he'd complete his applications to colleges for next year. The University of Pennsylvania and Princeton were now on his list, as were the University of Virginia and William and Mary. There were eight schools, total: a lot of money spent on application fees, and a lot of time spent filling out forms, arranging for transcripts and SAT scores, and writing entrance essays—but he wanted to cover all of the bases this time around.

In the distance to the right across a fallow field, the Big Chief Barn came into view and slowly grew in size as Paul rhythmically pedaled along the vacant road. Now abandoned, the tobacco curing barn was the largest in Southern Maryland, covering a full acre: its rafters stood forty feet tall. "BIG CHIEF" in giant red and white letters could still be discerned across the expansive side of the barn, but each year they faded away a bit more, never to be repainted.

Big Chief had been the largest tobacco company in Maryland—not on par with the neighboring Virginia giants, but still an institution in Clifton and the surrounding counties. As a child, Paul could remember seeing bags of Big Chief roll-your-own cigarette tobacco and chewing plugs tucked into the back trouser pockets or poking out of the denim shirts of construction workers, game hunters, mechanics and other blue collars throughout the region. But as tobacco consumption declined—first among cigarette smokers and then among the smokeless crowd—so did Big Chief. The last time a tobacco auction had been held in the Big Chief Barn was years ago... an oddly nostalgic event, since the participants knew that it was a final farewell—the last hurrah of a dying industry.

Paul turned off the main road and bicycled along the choppy

gravel lane that traversed the field, propping his bike against the mammoth side of the barn. He gazed straight up at the pale thirty-foot-tall "B", draped in a headdress of feathers like those worn by Indian chiefs. Even worn and faded, it was an impressive sight.

He walked around to the end of the barn: the main doors were still chained shut but, being a tobacco barn, there were plenty of openings to allow air to circulate freely throughout the structure, and Paul stepped through one of the gaps into the expanse.

The acrid-sweet, pungent aroma of cured tobacco immediately greeted him, filling his nostrils and reaching deep into the back of his mouth. He knew, of course, about the evils of tobacco smoking and chewing—realizing how carcinogenic it was, and the host of diseases it could cause—but Paul still loved the smell. He wondered whether just carrying a pouch around to take an occasional whiff could possibly be bad for someone: *could particles in the air just from smelling the stuff also cause cancer?*

It was dark in the barn, but the sunlight streaming through the ventilation holes throughout the building and the raised roof provided sufficient illumination. In fact, the deep earth tones of the wood highlighted by streaming shafts of light had an especially sensuous feel; a very pleasing aesthetic, like some ocher-hued classical painting. He slowly walked along the rows of empty scaffolding still divided into neat partitions called... *what are they called?* He searched the recesses of his mind, trying to remember the Wikipedia articles he had read about tobacco curing. *Bents! They're called bents.* He tried to imagine each alcove filled with bundles of hanging tobacco leaf—and on auction day, the men with wide-brimmed hats and clipboards inspecting each bent, quickly jotting figures on their ledgers. *This barn had experienced periods of absolute calm and frenetic activity over the decades: lots of stories, lots of memories...*

He stepped back out into the open field and walked some distance away, then turned back to study the barn from afar.

Worn but still standing... but for how long? Inevitably, the paint will fade completely away. In another generation, kids will have no inkling what the letters used to say, what the barn housed, or what had transpired inside. Eventually, the structure itself will start to crumble—the walls slowly buckling as the rafters weigh down on weakened beams, until it finally collapses upon itself. The last thing to fade will be that pervasive, intoxicating scent of millions of cured tobacco leaves— the lingering memory of times gone by, never to return.

An hour later, he arrived at the memorial park. The cemetery used plaques set in the ground as grave markers instead of headstones. The recessed markers gave the park an uncluttered look, and its location on the cliff overlooking the Potomac was, Paul felt, actually quite beautiful: quiet and serene, a nice place for sharing personal thoughts with the departed.

The echoing syncopated honks of a large group of Canada geese approaching from the north made Paul brake to a stop and look skyward. They were heading south along the river and making good time, it seemed. Several geese led the rest in a thin line, creating a gable shape. As he watched them fly overhead, the formation shifted, and before it had disappeared from sight the leaders had melded back into the group, so that it formed an almost perfect "V". He breathed a sigh of satisfaction: *perhaps that was a harbinger of good fortune... why not?*

Slowly bicycling through the cemetery, he caught sight of a solitary figure sitting on the stone bench in the shade of an oak tree not far from Dave's grave. It was the bench where he usually had his lunch... to reflect on things, to talk to him. As he approached, he saw that it was a young woman.

He parked his bike nearby, walked over and sat down on the

bench beside her, quietly unpacking his lunch. He took a bite of his sandwich and a sip from his water bottle. She was looking at the grave, pensive. Then she looked down at the ground.

"Do Jews believe in heaven?"

"I don't know," he said pensively. "I guess so. I don't think we ever talked about it."

She looked at him for the first time, brushing her auburn hair from her eyes.

"Do Cristers?"

"Yes, of course we do. Maybe not the same way you do."

"What I mean is," she said, slowly choosing her words, "do you believe in life after death, in a place of reward for having lived a good life—never mind about accepting Goseth as your Savior, since I know you don't believe in Him."

"Well, that's the difference," said Paul, quietly. "In Cristicism, only those who accept Jesus as their Savior can enter heaven."

She was silent for a moment, and then turned back to the grave.

"But Dave... he didn't believe in either one, did he? He didn't accept Goseth or Jesus. But he was a good person and he died doing a very brave thing. He *deserves* to be in heaven!"

Between her long strands of hair, he could see the glisten of a teardrop slowly working its way down her cheek.

"Maybe..." Paul said, tenderly wiping away the tear, "maybe that's the way Jewish people think of heaven."

She stared at him through reddened eyes.

"I hope so. I hope they do, because God needs to reward him."

They sat together in silence a long time, looking at the grave. Not an awkward silence—a comforting silence of prayer for a friend. Paul tried to remember the Mourner's Kaddish he had heard at the funeral. He didn't know any of the Hebrew, but the poetic recitation played itself out in his mind, and when it finished he whispered, "Amen."

He took her hand in his.

"He'll be fine."

As they sat there in the quiet shade of the oak tree, he realized that life was what you made of it. For every road not taken, another presented itself, with new opportunities and lessons.

He felt as though a chapter in his life was drawing to a close. It was time to turn the page and start a new one, wherever it might lead.

And he looked forward to writing it, every word.

Addendum

Dictionary

avie (ăv'-ē or äv'-ē) *n*. Kristisch for grandmother

Crister (krīs'-tər) a person who worships Jesus of Nazareth (the Crist) as their messiah and savior

Cristic (krĭs'-tĭk) *adj*. of or representing Cristers and Cristicism

Devotee (dĕv'-ə-tā') an original disciple of Goseth Rhetter

Feier (fā'-ər) *n*. the central divine act of worship in the Shrin

gabel (gā'-bəl) *n*. the "Y" shaped tree trunk upon which Rhetter was conflagrated, and the central symbol of Rhettianity

Goseth Rhetter (gō'-zĕth or gō'-sĕth rĕt'-ər) the True Messiah, whose reappearance is prophesied in the Cristic Old Teachings

Cristen (krĭs'-tĭn or derogatorily krīs'-tĭn) the brother of Goseth, whose betrayal led to Goseth's conflagration *n*. a traitor

Katolish (kə-tō'-lĭsh) an orthodox Rhettian shrin headed by the Heiliger Väter

Kristisch (krĭs'-tĭsh) a phonetic language derived from High German, Latin, and the Slavic languages

Lorswers (lôrs'-wərs) the teachings of Goseth and the Devotees; the Rhettian doctrine of man's redemption through Rhetter

Mithran (mĭth'-rän) an annual Rhettian festival held on Vintner 23rd celebrating the resurrection of Goseth as Rhetter

Paxist (păx'-ĭst) a denomination of Rhettianity

Rhettian (rĕt'-ē-ĭn) *adj*. 1. a person professing belief in Goseth of Trier as the Rhetter 2. a kind, humane and decent person

Rhettianity (rĕt'-ē-ăn'-ĭ-tē) the Rhettian religion, based on the Old and New Teachings

Rhettag (rĕt'-ăg) an annual Rhettian festival held on Edel 1st celebrating the birth of Goseth Rhetter

shrin (shrin) *n.* 1. a building consecrated for public worship, esp. Rhettian 2. *Cap.* all Rhettians regarded as a single entity

selge (sĕlj) *n.* 1. a holy person 2. *Cap. Sg:* a deceased person who has been canonized by the Shrin as able to intercede for sinners

Selga (sĕl'-gə) one of the three holy characters of Rhettian folklore who deliver gifts to children at Rhettagtime

wamme (wäm'-ā) *n.* literally: womb; the consecrated bread used in the Rhettian Eucharist

zeichism (zī'-kĭz'm) *n.* the sacrament of admitting someone into the Rhettian shrin 2. any ordeal that serves to initiate or purify

Months of the Year:

> **Gosiery**—gōz'-ē-ĕr'-ē
> **Edel**—ād'-əl
> **Janiery**—jăn'-ē-ĕr'-ē
> **Pendiery**—pĕn'-dē-ĕr'-ē
> **Franzen**—frăn'-zĭn
> **Greten**—gret'-ĭn
> **Hansen**—hăn'-zĭn
> **Jurgen**—jûr'-gĭn
> **Konradin**—kŏn'-ră'-dĭn
> **Vintner**—vĭnt'-nər
> **Brie**—brē
> **Ergenne**—ûr'-gĕn
> **Ilsembre**—ĭl'-sĕm'-brā

Addendum

Erikan / Julian Calendar Comparison

Erikan (Rhettian) Calendar Year 683

Gosiery	Edel	Janiery	Pendiery	Franzen	Greten	Hansen

Spring Break

New Year — Rhettag — Prom — Commencement

Easter

March	April	May	June	July	August	September

Julian (Cristic) Calendar Year 2004

Jurgen	Konradin	Vintner	Brie	Ergenne	Ilsembre
		Mithran			

| October | November | December | January | February | March |

Cristmas⌐   ⌐New Year

Julian Year 2005

Cover illustration by A. Roth

About the Author

B. G. Holmsted

B. G. Holmsted resides on a hilltop overlooking the capital of the most powerful nation in the world. The author enjoys canoeing, taking long walks and the occasional nature hike, and has a knack for getting along with people—especially friends.

Also by B. G. Holmsted:

Serendipity (2015) — Sarah Prendergast, a teenager living on the outskirts of Cincinnati, remembers her involvement with a psychochromatic chemical accidentally created by her father. The substance reveals a person's most intimate feelings through a series of vibrant color shifts, like a mood ring on steroids. Though initially treated as both a scientific curiosity and chic fashion statement, the discovery leads to widespread social turmoil, ending with the government imposing dystopian controls. Realizing that he's inadvertently opened Pandora's Box, her dad sets out to destroy his creation, and Sarah finds herself in the middle of it all.

www.ingramcontent.com/pod-product-compliance
Lightning Source LLC
Chambersburg PA
CBHW031413240626
47154CB00001B/10